SAGITTA

StarFighter Book One

C.M. Benamati

Acknowledgements

This wouldn't have been possible without lots of help. This book is dedicated to my wife Kirsten, who is always up for a fantastic story no matter how silly, and to Will and Sam (my little space cadets).

Thanks mom and dad, for introducing me to the genres of science fiction and fantasy, and for reading and rereading the countless drafts of this book over 10 years. Your support is invaluable.

Thank you also to those who watched endless Star Trek episodes with me all through college, and to those who provided insight, editing, criticism, and support of my writing.

Alpha
Chris Guillory
Nate Benamati
Allen Daley
Kirsten Benamati
Jeff Turgeon
Noelle Todd
Critique Circle
Misty
Omega

Finally, I'd like to thank my first readers for plowing through the draft, no matter how painfully bad some parts of it were.

Prelude

The wind whistled through the forest, rustling leaves and carrying the crisp scent of the Ganjon Mountains down into the lowlands. Mog lay just inside the tree line. It was the perfect temperature here in the shade. A hundred marks away, the short sand beach transitioned into an endless expanse of sparkling blue and green.

He laid his head down against the cool earth. *Tired. So tired.* Waves pounded against sheer cliffs farther up the beach, just out of sight. Their fury shook the ground as they carried out their relentless onslaught. *Thum-thum. Thum-thum.*

A familiar voice wafted on the wind from some great distance. "Brace for impact."

Who was that?

"Someone get to the commander."

"Mog, are you alright?"

Forget about them. They're ghosts now, ghosts from the past. It's all over.

"The hull is buckling, we're venting atmosphere."

"Commander Mog!"

"Leave me alone," he growled. *May I never leave this cool forest floor.* He stretched his aching body, extended a claw, and dragged it through the dirt. He paused, ears twitching, staring at the line. *What was that sound?* He dragged his claw some more, wincing as it screeched like a knife across a sharpening stone. He tapped the earth. Sharp reverberation shot through his hand. *What's going on?*

He tried to push himself up, but his hands slipped in something wet. *Blood?* The sticky, glistening trail led towards the beach. He looked up. Someone was sprawled out not even ten marks away, just at the edge of the sand. How had he not seen him? Mog crawled over and put a hand on the youth's shoulder, rolling the body over.

His little brother's fur was cold and matted with blood. Gray sightless eyes stared up at Mog.

Nam? Nam!

Strong arms slid under him, lifting him. "Sir, you have to get up."

He growled. Pain flared across his back and neck. His head swam with familiar voices.

"They're almost on top of us."

"Hold one more second!"

"Sir, your orders?"

Mog opened his eyes and the forest of his childhood disappeared. The bridge lurched and he stumbled forward, catching the railing with his left hand. Kremp was supporting his right side. Vrail, the ship's astrogator, lay dead at their feet.

He jerked himself upright as the battle-scarred enemy cruiser bore down upon them. Green fire flashed across the viewscreen.

"Return fire!" said Mog.

Blue energy flashed from the forward batteries as Mog's ship sprang her trap. There was no way to miss at this range. The enemy's belly tore open, venting atmosphere into space.

With a roar, Mog stood to his full height and pushed the engineer away. "Thrusters, hard about."

The *Narma Kull* groaned in protest. Mog slipped, his clawed feet coming to a screeching stop against a fallen structural support. *Did that thing hit me?* He ran a hand over the back of his head and winced. When he pulled his hand away, his fingers were dripping with blood.

He eased himself back into his command chair and regarded the viewscreen. Mauria was still there: a small blueberry, ripe and ready to be squashed. All that stood between his homeworld and the destroyers was a motley assemblage of half-functional ships. *If we fail...*

"Helm, make us a target. Do whatever it takes to draw their fire away from the evacuation transports. Tactical, disable the charge limiters and fire at will. Watch the gun temps, don't let them melt."

As his officers made their acknowledgements, a small civilian transport burst onto the screen followed by a pair of enemy fighters, which were firing madly. The transport danced this way and that, desperately trying to evade.

It collided with a plasma bolt and went into a spin, its thin unarmored skin burning away. When the fuel tanks blew, the explosion bathed the bridge of the *Narma Kull* in golden light.

So much death. Had this been an earlier battle, maybe he would have felt something. Now he suffered no emotions. His soul was darker and colder than space itself. He had seen entire cities—entire worlds—sent into the black. Mauria, the seat of the Empire, stood on the brink. *Surely I must feel something. Surely I should weep?*

The deck fell out from under them as the ship reeled from a torpedo.

"Dorsal shields collapsing," said Nali. The tactical officer was hunched over her console, ignoring the stream of freezing coolant running down her back from a fractured conduit.

"Fleet status?" said Mog.

"Twelve percent." Laleg's face was impassive as he studied the communications display, but his quivering voice betrayed his fear. "The sub-admiral's ship has been destroyed and the Ta'Krell have broken through the planetary defenses. There are reports of heavy casualties in the cities. Arkara, Baraque, and Tenabria are gone. The Naval Command office has been obliterated."

The Supreme Commander is dead. We're on our own up here.

"Another report just in," said Laleg. He hesitated.

"Spit it out."

"I'm sorry Mog, but the Ganjon coast and much of the southern forest has taken fire from orbit. Casualties are estimated at sixty percent."

Mog stiffened. *Nam. Mom. Dad. My home, destroyed? It cannot be.*

"Ramas help us," whispered a crewman.

Around the bridge people muttered similar prayers. Mog bared his teeth; this wasn't the time for foolishness. "Ramas be damned! If he were real this wouldn't be happening. We must do this ourselves."

The praying stopped.

Mog pushed aside thoughts of burning jungles and screaming children. "Helm, bring us about. Engage those command ships and take the pressure off the transports. Nali, divert power from the aft shields to the weapons. We won't be running."

There was a pause as that sank in before the officers carried out their orders. *This is it, one way or another.*

His ship was turning. Stars trails and plasma bolts streaked across the viewscreen until an immense object blotted out the view: a Ta'Krell dreadnaught. The recessed weapons ports in its hull belched green fire. Two Maurian frigates exploded. A third went into a slow spiral as its port engine was shredded.

"Fire all banks!"

Five deadly streams lanced out, striking the target in a fraction of a second. Each bolt sent blue-white ripples coursing through the dreadnaught's shields. *Come on, come on!* It was like the soap bubbles that children used to blow in the streets before the war. *Only this bubble won't break.*

"Nazpah," he spat. "Keep firing on that forward shield face. Standby torpedoes. As soon as—"

The massive ship retaliated, shaking the *Narma Kull* so violently that Vrail's body tipped over the edge of the command platform. It landed face-down on the lower level with a wet thump.

"Evasive maneuvers, pull the bow up!"

The viewscreen went black as the burning transplasma melted the sensor array. Thunderous rumblings coursed through the hull. The bridge pitched downward, sending officers tumbling from the upper deck.

"Helm not responding," said Meela.

"Shield burn-through confirmed," said Kremp. "Hull breech, deck two, section four on the starboard dorsal wing. Commander, we're in trouble. That blast took out the PCMs and fried the vital bus. Engines are cold, we're not going anywhere."

The ship rocked again. "Casualties on all decks," said Laleg. "Gravity's out on the lower levels. Med teams report all access routes to sickbay are blocked. Mog, there's a new report from Mauria. The capital city is on fire."

Cold hands seemed to squeeze his hearts as Mog pivoted to view the tactical station. Nali was still standing. One of her triangular ears was torn, and dark blood stained her tawny fur.

"Do we have weapons?" he said.

Her ears drooped as she met his gaze. Her wide yellow eyes betrayed her terror.

"Nazpah," said Mog. He turned to the engineer. "Kremp, how long to connect the guns to the non-vital bus?"

"There's no way to do it before that beast blasts us to atoms. Decks two and three in the starboard dorsal are a disaster, and my teams can't get to the damage."

"Can you give me anything?"

"I've got the screen back. That's about it."

Mog gripped his chair. Sickbay was on deck two. His first officer was there, barely clinging to life. Or, was he dead? *Doesn't matter. We'll all be dead soon.*

The enemy ship filled the screen. It was an ungainly brute with a rectangular hull and wedge-shaped nose. Its only outstanding feature was an annular engine assembly that encircled its hull. Mog counted the glowing weapons ports. There were sixteen cannons on the bow, each emitting a dull emerald light.

He surveyed his bridge. Data cables dangled from the ceiling, and heavy smoke from burned-out consoles blanketed the deck. Air hissed from a slow leak. His crew gazed at him with the sunken eyes of corpses. Somebody was praying again.

Curse you Ramas, you make-believe bastard. There must be another way! We're out of fighter craft. Perhaps the shuttles? No, they'd be swatted like flies. Collision course? No, the engines are out. Manually launch torpedoes? No, they'd shoot them down before they got halfway there.

All was lost.

He turned back to face the screen, expecting to be blasted into dust.

It didn't happen. Thrusters fired, and the prodigious vessel pitched upwards, the plasma trail from its engine ring intensifying. Mog stared, stupefied, as it passed overhead. It was so close that the alien glyphs on its airlock doors were visible.

The screen switched to aft cameras. The enemy flagship was heading towards Mauria. The planet was encircled by a broad band that had never been there before—a slowly spiraling debris field of twisted metal and broken hulls.

A small missile launched from the dreadnaught's nose and sped towards the planet. Then another, and another. They began to glow as they traced their way through the atmosphere.

A flash. Two flashes. Three flashes.

Make it stop!

Flash, flash, flash.

The continents were on fire, but the Ta'Krell didn't stop.

Flash, flash, flash.

The oceans boiled. White steam mixed with black soot and fire as the planet died.

Mog sat back and watched it burn. He closed his eyes, but the crimson brightness of the fireball burned through his eyelids. The crew wailed.

"Ramas, how could you let this happen?" sobbed Meela.

"Azhra has won!" wailed Nali. "Ramas, why have you forsaken us?"

The target lock warning sounded as multiple enemy ships set their sights on the *Narma Kull*.

"There are no gods," said Mog, his voice barely a whisper. "And if there ever were, they are long dead."

* * *

Someone pulled something sticky from the back of his head.

I still exist.

What a cruel thought. He pushed it away, as the drowning man with lungs full of water pushes away the buoy. It was easier to simply die.

"Open your eyes."

No.

Someone grasped the fur of his chest and shook him. "Open!"

He was in a chair. In front of him was that accursed doctor, holding that damned scanner. He snarled. "Why do you deny me death?"

"I am helping you remember," said the doctor.

"Remember what?"

"You tell me. You were there."

"Where? When, when was this? How long ago?"

"Nearly two months."

Months! How could that be? He started to rise, but something cold pressed against the back of his neck.

"So you can rest for a little while," said the doctor. "One more treatment and I think things will be clearer."

"My crew," he said. "Where are they? My ship. I need to get back." Dimly, he became aware of the slurred sound of his own voice. He took a breath to steady himself. "Where are my…"

It was no use. The lights blended into a blazing ball of fire that would haunt his dreams for the rest of his life.

Chapter 1: Scorpion Driver

Early morning sunlight brushed over the peaks of the Rincon Mountains, revealing the desert's harsh beauty. Hardy mesquite and paloverde glistened from last night's unexpected rain. A red-tailed hawk circled above, far out of reach of the uplifted arms of the saguaro cacti that dotted the landscape.

A cactus' shadow stretched across the sand, ending just shy of a strange looking car. The doors, hinged at the roof like wings on a bird, were both up. A pair of boots stuck out from the open passenger side.

Morgan lay on his back, his lanky form contorted under the Scorpion's dashboard. The seat position lever was stabbing into his ribs, and his neck burned from holding his head in the one position from where he could just see the access terminal, tucked away as it was above the steering column.

"This sucks," he grumbled to himself, as he wiped the sweat from his eyes. "All-time, major-league suckage." He resumed tapping commands into the computer interface that some brain-dead engineer had brilliantly put in the most inaccessible place. The fuel controller couldn't have picked a worse time to go on the fritz.

"Good luck, Morgan," said a familiar voice from outside.

Morgan nodded without looking up. "You too, Ralph." *It's weird. They never talk to me at school, but out here things are different.*

His watch beeped—the race would start in ten minutes. *Must work faster.*

The stylus slipped, and his metal watch struck an exposed power relay. He yelped as a spark shot up his arm. The fuel controller beeped and rebooted. He threw the stylus against the floorboard.

"Why does the universe hate me?" he cried.

He checked his watch to make sure it still worked, then picked the stylus back up. *This is taking way too long.*

After two agonizing minutes, the injector pulse table finally made sense. He tossed the stylus under the driver's seat, not caring if it got lost in the nest of tools that resided there. Then, after a few seconds of awkward wiggling, he stuck his head out of the driver-side door.

About a hundred local bumpkins were roaming the makeshift bleachers, juggling plates of hot dogs and fries. Along with the snacks, several people held palm-sized display screens, each one linked to one of the camera copters that were buzzing around in the air above the starting line. He recognized a few classmates from Blairsford's tiny high school. He knew one or two of them, but most of their names escaped him. They knew who he was of course. Everyone did.

He scowled, then tilted his head to the side. The starting spot next to him was still empty. According to the roster, there were two new racers competing today. The one staged next to Morgan, some L. Fowler, still hadn't shown up. *He'd better hurry up or he'll miss the race.*

"So, how do you expect to beat anyone in that…thing?"

Morgan jerked upright, only to slam his head against the underside of the steering wheel. He clenched his teeth together, stifling a curse. He forced himself up into an awkward sitting position between the steering wheel and the driver's seat. The sunlight streaming in from the passenger-side was blinding. He squinted at a young man's smirking face.

The stranger was tall and bony, with sharp eyebrows and a protruding chin. He had a scraggly beard, and his shoulder-length black hair begged for a good wash. He looked a little older, probably around eighteen, and had extensive bioware implants – retinal projectors, a subvocalizer pickup, and holographic transceivers at the temples. He was wearing a black leather jacket, black jeans, and black gloves.

"This area's for drivers only," said Morgan. "You're gonna get in trouble."

The guy laughed, and pulled something from his pocket. It was a driver's pass. *V. Marris. So this is the other newbie. Someone call Darwin, we've got a winner.*

9

Desert racing wasn't something you did wearing clothes like that. Even with air conditioning, this guy was begging for heat stroke. Morgan's racing suit might not be fashionable, but the thin outer shell was fireproof and the refrigerated inner layer kept him at a manageable temperature. Since he'd taken up the sport last year, the suit had been his best investment, despite the 20k price tag.

The guy's eyes scanned the Scorpion with contempt. When he spoke, his voice was just as pinched as his face. "Do you actually think you've got a chance with a car like that?"

"Why else would I be here?" muttered Morgan, sliding back under the dash. He didn't have time to chat with this scumbag.

"You'd have better luck racing against lawnmowers," said the stranger. "They're your car's next of kin." He poked his greasy head under the dash. "I suppose you can't afford a real car. Too bad. Just don't expect any help when your relic gets a flat."

Can't afford? Morgan laughed. "Since you're obviously new here, let me give you a bit of free advice. Don't blab about what you don't know. It just makes you look stupid."

"You're the one that looks stupid. What is that anyway, a space suit? This isn't the moon, kid. You and the lunar lander must have taken a wrong turn."

Morgan snapped the access panel closed. *Cool out, this greaser's not worth it.* Yet, he couldn't help but notice how close the guy's face was. He tensed his leg. *A boot to the head will shut you up.*

"What's the matter?" said the stranger. "Cactus got your tongue?"

Morgan glowered at him. *What kind of stupid line was that?* "Just because my car uses wheels doesn't mean it can't dust you out here."

"Why's that?"

"Traction. You know, grip! Floaters don't track through sandy corners, because sand isn't engineered to provide stability with repulsor fields. There isn't enough shear stability. You probably think your advanced off-road emitter controllers make up the difference, but it's just not the same.

My tires dig in and bite the earth. It's basic physics, and I'm going to trounce you with it." He waved his hand, indicating the double-wide line of cars in front of them. "Just ask any of them, they can tell you."

It was true. Thanks to the Scorpion and his physics extension courses, Morgan could finally show everyone he didn't need the latest technology to do something well. *My car doesn't need a handicap to win this race, and neither do I.*

"Whatever kid," said the stranger, slapping the Scorpion's hood. "After I've whooped you, I'll beam you the number of my uncle's bank. You'll be wanting a new ride when you finish last, and Uncle Tony will lend money to anyone." He paused, looking up. "Ahh, so she shows up after all."

"Don't let him get to you," said a woman's voice from outside. "Victor does that to everyone."

Morgan sighed and slid out from under the dash, being careful not to bump his head on the bottom of the gull-wing door as he stood. Didn't people realize the race was about to start? He spun around, intent on telling everyone to get lost, but the words never made it to his mouth.

A girl was regarding him with an amused grin. She was wearing a carbon gray racing jumpsuit, the name 'L. Fowler' embroidered on the front. It fit her loosely, but not too loosely. Her sleeves were scuffed and darkened by grease. Her blond hair was tied back in a neat ponytail.

"I'm Liz," she said, extending a slender hand.

"Ma—Morgan," he stammered.

She cocked her head, her hand still extended.

I am an idiot. He jerked his hand out and shook hers.

Her skin was soft, but her grip confident. *Unlike you,* sneered the voice in his head. The last time he'd touched a girl had been in sixth grade, at his friend Greg's birthday party. He remembered it vividly. *You pretended to hug Jessica Brown, but then put a worm down her shirt. You had guts as a kid at least. WTF happened?*

Liz cleared her throat. Something tugged at his hand and he looked down. *Let go, you idiot! Let go!* He relaxed his grip and did his best to look casual.

"It's a cool car," said Liz. She turned to Victor, who had been watching them. "Just what the hell are you doing here?"

Victor shrugged. "Came to see you."

"Well, I don't want to see you."

They glared at each other for a moment. Victor opened his mouth, but then an announcement rang over the loudspeaker. "All spectators please clear the staging area. All drivers report to your cars."

Victor frowned. "After, then." He turned and walked between the row of race cars towards the starting line. Liz watched him go, looking miffed.

Morgan studied Liz. *She doesn't have any tech!* But then he noticed it. It was fine workmanship, subtly done. Her green eyes sparkled as they flicked from Victor back to Morgan, then to the Scorpion. Tiny implants around the insides of her irises projected a photonic overlay of information directly into her eyes. *She's looking something up.*

"A Saturn Scorpion," she said. "Cool, I didn't know these were a thing. Does it really handle better on dirt?"

"What? Uh, yeah," he said, as she turned her eyes back to him. His heart was trying to blast out of his chest.

"Cool. How's it work?"

"Um…the tires dig in, keeps it from sliding. The problem with floaters is their repulsion fields. They don't work as well with loose sand. They get off track in the corners."

Liz regarded the Scorpion skeptically. "Well, it is different." Her eyes flicked over Morgan's face. He started to blush, and fought the urge to look away. *Here it comes.*

But then she said, "You're different too. I like that."

"Thanks," he muttered. Was she being serious? *Maybe she's not like the others.* His brow furrowed as he remembered the taunts and insults that had plagued him growing up. *Vanilla! Freak! What's wrong with you?* Worse was the look on people's faces when they met him for the first time: the way their eyes played over his features, searching and not finding. *Vanilla. Bible thumper. Loser.* He could see their thoughts plain as day.

But Liz said she likes different.

His watch beeped out a warning, carrying with it an air of finality. He glanced down. "Race starts in five minutes."

Liz blinked. "Wow, an actual watch. You are full of surprises."

Morgan looked at his wrist watch. It was a big ugly thing, but it covered the scar well enough. "Yeah," he said. "I guess."

"Well, good luck then," she said. She flashed him a smile, turned, and walked off.

Morgan watched her go. *She has a nice walk.* It took a strong effort of will to look away. *Breathe man, just breathe. There you go.*

He regarded his car. The Scorpion mocked him silently. He kicked a tire. "Shut up." He stooped to get in, but stopped partway. He hadn't even seen what Liz drove.

She was standing next to a coral-blue POD 1000. A small crowd of teenaged guys surrounded her. Morgan wiped sweat from his brow, glaring at a kid who was quite obviously not looking at Liz's face as she chatted with the group.

Resting on an antigravity cushion of only two inches, her car was a greyhound amongst wolves. Its teardrop doors melted seamlessly into the flowing body, which, as its name implied, resembled a pod. Small hydraulic stabilizer fins extended from the car's sides, each widening just enough to contain a narrow strip of laser signals at the rear. The car's control thrusters were hidden beneath variable-geometry flaps, and a low-profile spoiler arced around an almost nonexistent trunk.

Liz opened a small hatch and began tinkering with something inside. The POD lifted slightly higher off the ground.

Alright, enough of the spectacle. Morgan turned back to his own car and grinned.

He had ordered the Scorpion from an obscure company from Tennessee that specialized in antique internal combustion vehicles. He'd spent two years converting it into a formidable desert race car. It had been a long process, with a good deal of the work taking place before he even had his driver's license. But the results had been worth it.

Where Liz's POD had grace, the Scorpion had determination. It was an all-wheel-drive two-seater with an elongated nose and short rear hatch. Morgan had cut away the fenders to provide clearance for the enormous knobby tires, which extended about a foot away from the rest of the vehicle and were mounted on black rims. Oversized suspension arms sprung by progressive coils and damped by dual-reservoir shocks provided eight inches of ground clearance.

The body was made of dark carbon fiber composite, pitted from countless hours of racing. Red electric bolts coursed along under the dusty clear coat. There were no windows. Two recessed slits in the hood marked the air intakes, and the two doors folded up like bird wings to grant entrance into the compact interior. An array of minuscule laser headlights ran under the curved front grill. Twin half-moon signal arrays accented the rear bumper, just above the dusty chrome exhaust tips.

His mom's father called these things dune buggies.

Morgan knelt and scooped up some sand. He ground it between his fingers. The Sonoran desert was no stranger. The other drivers didn't know it like he did. They floated over it without a second thought.

Beep Beep Beep.

He clicked his watch, silencing the two minute warning. An announcement over the track PA system sent Liz's admirers running back towards the stands.

He drew a breath, held it, and exhaled. He was second in this season's rankings next to Craig Marston. If he won today, he'd be at the top of the leader board.

His eyes lingered on Liz as she slipped into her POD. *I need to win this race.*

14

Chapter 2: Wrecked

Morgan slipped into the Scorpion and pulled the doors down. They locked shut with a solid click. He flipped a toggle, and the gray carbon interior melted away. He looked around, then dimmed the projectors by ten percent to compensate for the sun's glare. He grabbed the holographic rearview mirror and adjusted it.

"Welcome to the Blairsford Speedbowl!" crackled a deep voice through the ancient bullhorn speakers. The crowd cheered and whistled. Marc Lutstone, the track's owner, gave them a few seconds before continuing. "The first event today is the Division-A Youth Thunder Series: a single lap on the full course. In order of starting position…" Mr. Lutstone began rattling off the names of the drivers and their positions. It was the standard group of local teenagers. Until today, Morgan had been the newest racer on the track.

"And now we have Victor Marris, a visitor from Tucson joining us for the first time. Victor is seventeen years old. Welcome Victor."

There was a spattering of applause and shouts. Morgan grimaced.

"Also joining us for the first time is Elizabeth Fowler. Liz is sixteen, and she's just moved here with her father from Tucson. She competed for the first time this year in SCCA Solo and took third place in the Tucson club, C-Stock class. She's raced karts with her dad since she was six years old. Don't let the fact that she only just got her driver's license fool you: this young lady can drive. How about a welcome?"

The audience roared. Some idiots whistled cat-calls.

So she's my age, and she just moved here. Is this for real? Is she going to be in my grade when school starts back up? Morgan's pulse quickened. Maybe the universe didn't hate him. *Don't kid yourself. She's way too hot for you, and you're a chicken.* His face flushed, and he pushed the thoughts aside.

Mr. Lutstone cleared his throat. "I have one more announcement. Today, our young racers are being joined by a special guest. If I can direct your attention to the pit lane, you will see a gorgeous blue Porsche 927. The driver will be revealed after the race. For now, suffice it to say that he is a generous sponsor of our youth racing event, and he'll be racing alongside."

What the shit? They hadn't been told about this. He craned his neck, but he couldn't see around the cars in front of him. A 927 would be unstoppable if they were racing on gravpack pavement. In the desert he wasn't so sure. He frowned. The three new drivers in one day. There were too many variables, too many unknowns.

"Alright, you all know what time it is," said Mr. Lutstone. "Competitors, start your engines!"

Morgan tapped the ignition. The starter cranked twice and the Scorpion roared to life. *I'd like to hear a floater make this much noise.*

His holographic display showed the track layout. The cars were represented as sixteen colored dots, arranged in groups of four. The starting position was random, but nobody ever argued with Morgan when he offered to trade. His car was the black dot in the rear of the pack, situated between Liz's blue dot and Ralph Lawson's yellow one.

He energized his restraining field. In front, the rows of floaters wobbled on their repulsion fields, the humming of their force emitters barely audible over the Scorpion's throbbing exhaust. Morgan revved the engine, eyeing the two identical Kingston Mark IV's that would be his first victims.

A timer icon appeared above the steering wheel. He tapped it. Once everyone acknowledged the signal, the countdown would start.

The clock beeped. *Nine...Eight...Seven.*

His boot caressed the accelerator.

Six...five...four.

He gripped the wheel tighter.

Three...two...ONE!

He clicked the trigger shifter into first gear and hit the gas. The rotary engine roared, and the steering wheel danced as the tires fought for grip. The other cars surged ahead. Liz's car was a blue flash in his peripheral vision—her acceleration aided by thrust boosters.

The Scorpion slid sideways, all four tires spewing sand. Traction warnings flashed. His arms shuddered as he controlled the slide. *Got to give em a show!* After a few seconds of fun, he let off the gas just enough for the tires to get a grip.

The other cars were way ahead, but their booster rockets would soon be depleted. He'd catch them in the first turn, as always.

Brake lights flashed up ahead. He aimed right at them and buried the gas pedal into the floor. The speedometer flashed 120 in glowing crimson numerals.

The collision alarm blared. He locked his eyes on the tail lights of the nearest car. It was the Porsche. He grit his teeth as the RPMs on the tachometer flashed red. The engine bellowed

"Yee-hah!"

As the pack of cars entered the turn, their repulsion fields began kicking the loose sand out to the side. Their RCS thrusters fired, but it wasn't enough, and the pack slid to the outside.

Morgan tapped the brakes and cranked the wheel to the left. The Scorpion slid into the corner, but not as wide as the pack. He feathered the throttle, controlling the oversteer.

"Eat some of this," he whooped as he slipped around the Porsche on the inside. He passed the Frampton brothers' Kingston Mark IVs, and then shot past Ralph Lawson's Honda CZX.

Craig Marston was in front of him as he exited the turn, driving his usual Proton ZS-2 hatchback. Morgan risked a quick glance at the track model. Gauntlet Stretch was approaching.

The Stretch was a narrow section of track littered with rocks. Craig's car surged upward as its repulsors extended their field for extra ground clearance. Since the Stretch had been designed to give floaters a rough ride, its rocks were more like small boulders. Morgan bit his lip. Gauntlet Stretch was a place where his car's intimate contact with the ground was not so pleasant.

Sparks flew as Craig's car crashed down on a knife-edged boulder. Morgan cut the wheel to the right, and the rock narrowly missed his tires. His body pressed against the restraining field as an even larger rock lifted his passenger side wheels off the ground. When the car stabilized, the track's force wall was terribly close. He clenched his jaw and adjusted his course.

The Scorpion shuddered over the gravel and pot-holes, the shocks emitting tortured hydraulic shrieks. Ahead, Craig swerved to the left so violently that his car nicked the force wall. Why had he done that?

"Ah crap!" said Morgan. A car up ahead had spun out, and it was heading straight at him! He jerked the wheel, following Craig, then swore as the rear end broke loose. He fought the slide, feathering the throttle, and whipped the back end in line just in time to clear the stricken car. *That was close!*

A horn sounded, followed by a whip-crack as something made contact, jostling him into the restraining field. He looked at the rearview mirror. The once-beautiful Porsche was sporting a crumpled bumper and a broken headlight. Morgan grimaced. *That's at least forty grand of damage.*

The racers in front were bunching up at the turn at the end of Gauntlet Stretch. Morgan didn't slow; he had to catch them here! He risked a look at the rearview mirror. The Porsche was only inches away. Who was the driver? Mr. Lutstone had said he was a track sponsor. It must be some rich kid. *Someone like me.* The thought made him uncomfortable.

Craig entered the turn too tightly. His fender grazed the force wall and tore off. Morgan downshifted, slowing to dodge the debris and get in position for the turn. He was entering it too wide. He eased into the throttle, but the loose terrain refused to cooperate. He flipped a switch.

The roof flaps deployed with a pneumatic hiss, increasing the downforce. Morgan slid sideways into the restraining field as the tires dug in. "Take that," he yelled, as the g-forces squashed him. The passenger side tires lifted off the ground, and he carved into the corner on two wheels with the translucent blue force wall only inches from his face.

He held on, balancing long enough to exit the corner. *Yes, I'm through!* The Scorpion slammed back down with a thump.

Craig had passed two racers and was tearing off down the straightaway. The car in front of the Scorpion was a blue POD. His pulse quickened as Liz's brake lights flashed twice. Was it a greeting? He flashed the high-beams.

She was accelerating hard. Morgan put the pedal to the floor and grinned as the engine roared, devouring raw hydrogen. He caressed the trigger shifters, the tachometer in his peripheral vision, his eyes locked on Liz's car.

The turbo hissed as he executed a perfect upshift at nine thousand RPMs. Liz was still pulling away. He shifted again. *Come on, come on!* At one hundred and fifty miles per hour, he was nearing his car's maximum speed. *I'm not going to catch that thing on the straight.*

The seconds grew longer as Liz's lead expanded. Morgan glanced at the holographic track model. Craig was already through the next turn. The blue Porsche was still behind, but gaining. There was nothing else he could do but wait for the turn.

Liz was nearing the end of the straightaway just as the Dodge driven by Ralph Lawson spun out. Ralph had been passing a beat-up orange car, but the driver of the Whitney wasn't having it, and had executed a violent pit maneuver that sent Ralph spinning.

Liz dodged to the right, but not fast enough. Her car's left stabilizer snagged the Dodge and tore off. Her POD spun, its nose digging into the ground. It flipped and came crashing down on its roof, punching straight through the force wall with an electric flash. Even after being slowed by the semi-flexible barrier, Liz's car slid thirty feet before flattening a cactus and coming to a stop.

Morgan hit the brakes, slipped past the Dodge, and pushed through the weakened force wall. He forgot to downshift as he stopped, and the engine stalled.

"Field off!"

The restraining field fizzled out. He shoved his door up and ran to the smoking POD. At the edge of his vision, the Dodge turned around and resumed the race. "Could have stopped, asshole!"

He looked around. The orange Whitney that had caused the wreck was nowhere in sight.

Chapter 3: The Right Thing

Morgan wrenched open the POD's mangled door, releasing a plume of smoke and the stench of burning electronics. Static danced across the dash. Liz was upside-down, glued to the seat by a shimmering restraining field.

"Are you alright?" His voice was shaking. He tried again, louder. "Liz, are you alright!"

She didn't answer. Something dribbled down Morgan's chin. He wiped his mouth. *Blood.* He'd bitten his lip. *Get yourself together, she's only unconscious.*

Why hadn't anyone else stopped? Stooping, he placed a trembling hand on the edge of the door and stuck his head inside. It was hard to see in the haze, but he found the switch to the restraining field. He flicked it.

The field winked out, and Liz dropped from her seat to the roof of the car. Morgan recoiled. As if the crash wasn't enough, he had to go and drop her on her face. "Sorry," he stammered. He got an arm under her and half dragged, half scooped her out.

He laid her on the ground. *Thank God, she's breathing.* She had a nasty cut on her forehead. Her hair was matted with blood. A few drops dribbled down her cheek. Morgan pulled his phone from his pocket.

"Lutstone," he yelled.

A moment later, Marc Lutstone's chubby face filled the phone's display. His brown forehead glistened with sweat. "How bad is it?" he said.

"Bad," said Morgan. "Liz is hurt." He flipped the phone around to point the camera at Liz. The phone automatically translated Mr. Lutstone's image to the rear panel.

The track owner's face was grim. His eyes flashed with faint colors as he manipulated some control screen that only he could see. "Don't move her. Help is coming." His image blinked out.

Morgan scanned the sky, but all he saw was a tiny camera drone. Its ocular lens was darting between Liz and her wrecked car.

"Stupid thing," he grumbled, turning so the camera couldn't see his face. He sucked on his bleeding lip. Who was driving that Whitney? Was it Victor? He'd never seen the car before. If only he'd been able to pay more attention at the start of the race, instead of fixing his own car. *I bet it was Victor. I'm going to kill him!*

Liz whimpered. He spun around. "Hey there." He knelt beside her, trembling. She smelled like flowers and sweat. "Liz? Can you hear me?"

Her eyelids fluttered, then flew open.

"What?" she stuttered, jerking upright. "Ow!" She fell back, her palms pressed against her temples.

Morgan hesitantly put a hand on her shoulder. "You probably shouldn't move."

"Good idea," she mumbled, wiping blood out of her eyes. "Feels like a troop transport landed on my head. What the hell happened?"

He pulled his hand back. "Some guys up front got a little rough. One of them crashed and took you out."

Liz focused her eyes on him. "Morgan, right? Why?"

"Why what?"

She groaned. "Why'd you stop? You could have won."

He looked back at his car and shrugged. "I just, you know, thought it was the right thing to do." *Wasn't it?*

She rolled her eyes. "But now Victor's going to win."

Morgan couldn't believe what he was hearing. "Who cares! You could have been dying or something."

"I would have been fine. The track computer is bonded to all the cars, and my car is bonded to me." She rolled up her left sleeve and tapped the inside of her wrist, where a thin blue-green interface shifted out of screensaver mode. The artistic bracelet dissolved, replaced by a display of her pulse and body temperature.

"Ah, right," said Morgan. "Of course you'd have one. It's linked to your car?"

Liz eyed him strangely. "Obviously. They know I'm not dead." She pointed at something behind him. "Plus, there are those things. Don't you know you're not supposed to move someone after a car crash unless the car is on fire?"

Morgan looked over his shoulder at the camera drone bobbing above his head. He didn't know what to say.

"It's in case of a spinal injury," continued Liz. "You could have paralyzed me!"

"I know that," said Morgan. "I mean, I remember hearing that, but I forgot. I didn't mean to—sorry." He stopped talking. *Arg, the universe does hate me after all.*

"You could have won," said Liz. "I saw how you drive."

He looked down. *It doesn't matter. Stopping was the right thing to do.*

There was a rushing noise like the roar of a distant waterfall. A small craft was descending from one of the flight lanes, its silver hull sparkling. As the ambulance neared them, its stabilizer wings folded into its hull and its thrusters switched off, replaced by a shimmering repulsor field. Three landing struts unfolded from the ship's belly. The ambulance bounced slightly on the struts as it landed, its repulsion field kicking out a ring of sand.

The ship had barely stabilized when the aft doors burst open. A man and a woman jumped out with a floating stretcher. Morgan ran to meet them.

"Is she conscious?" said the female paramedic.

"Yeah," said Morgan. "Although something hit her on the head. There's lots of blood."

Morgan sucked nervously at his lip as they helped Liz sit up. The man waved a scanner over her and asked her questions. The woman pressed her own scanner against Liz's bio implant. There was a beep as something synced, and the woman nodded, apparently satisfied.

23

"Looks like you've been through quite the ride," said the man, pocketing his scanner. "But it's just a minor concussion and some contusions, nothing broken."

"Does she need to go to the hospital?" said Morgan.

The man shook his head. "We can treat her in the shuttle. She'll be fine, assuming she takes a few days off from this, uh, sport." He paused, considering Liz. "What's a girl like you doing out here anyway?"

Liz rolled her eyes but said nothing. Morgan grimaced. *Even I know not to say that.*

"Clamp it Jim," said the female paramedic, bringing the stretcher closer. "Sorry," she said to Liz. "He's an idiot. Here, I'll help you get on."

Liz shook her head. "I think I can walk, if you wouldn't mind lending a hand."

The woman took Liz's left hand. Morgan, not wanting the other medic anywhere near Liz, jumped forward and took her right.

"Up you go," said the woman.

They started towards the shuttle. *Well, at least if I have a heart attack, I'm in an ambulance,* thought Morgan, as Liz leaned against him. She seemed to regain some of her strength when they reached the shuttle. She let go of his hand and allowed the paramedics to help her up onto one of the beds, which they locked in a semi-upright position.

"We'll take you back to the parking lot," said the woman. "Can you get a ride home from someone there?"

Liz glanced at Morgan. "Could you?"

"Yes!" he said, perhaps a touch over-eagerly. "I mean, if you need one. I don't mind." He shut his mouth before he made it worse.

"You riding with us?" asked the male paramedic.

Morgan looked around and realized the man was addressing him. "Uh, I guess," he said. He looked out the shuttle's side window at his car. It should be safe where it was. Besides, the last thing he wanted to do was leave Liz. "Yeah, I'll ride with you guys."

"Cool," said the man. "Just sit anywhere you like." He ducked through a small arch that led to the cockpit while the woman strapped Liz in. Morgan sat down on a narrow metal bench protruding from the hull.

"We'll win next time," he whispered, looking out at his car.

The compartment doors folded inward and locked shut. The woman was waving a sterilizer over Liz's forehead. Most of the blood was already gone.

There was a surge of power and a plume of sand as the shuttle lifted. Below, a few cars were rounding the final corner. Morgan pressed his cheek against the glass. The beat-up orange Whitney in front was the car that had caused the crash.

"Liz, do you know what Victor drives?"

She nodded. "It's a Whitney MC2."

Morgan remembered Liz's first words to him, when she had told him Victor was mean to everybody. *I wonder how she knows him.*

Craig Marston was on Victor's tail. *Come on Craig, get him!* But Craig wasn't good enough. Victor kept darting left and right, making it impossible to pass.

"Well, that happened," said Morgan flatly, as Victor crossed the finish line.

"He won?" said Liz.

"Yep."

Liz groaned. "Figures. He just had to beat me again. My life sucks."

She pulled her knees up to her chin and was staring blankly into the space between her feet. There was definitely something going on between her and Victor, some sort of rivalry. Morgan wanted to know more, but wasn't sure how to ask.

They touched down in the parking area by the stands. People were rushing down to swarm around the winner. Nobody took notice of the shuttle. Morgan turned his head away from the window. Liz looked much better. They'd given her water, and the medic had used an autosuture on her forehead. There was no blood to be seen, only a thin glistening red line.

"There you go," said the female paramedic, removing the lap belt. "You can get up."

"That's it?" said Liz.

"Yep," said the woman. "Shouldn't even leave a scar. Just give it a week to heal. Oh, we will of course need a beam of your ID and insurance."

"Right," said Liz. Liz looked at the woman and tapped something on her temple. The next instant, a flash of light lanced between Liz's left eye and the woman's. Even though he'd never experienced such a thing himself, Morgan knew a line of sight hololink when he saw one.

"Everything checks out," said the woman. "You're good to go."

Liz got up off the bed as the paramedic tapped the door controls, releasing the shuttle's internal pressure seal. The doors folded outward, and the warm Arizona air rushed in to meet them.

"Take it easy," said the woman.

"I will," she said. "Thanks for your help."

Morgan followed Liz out into the hot desert. The ambulance lifted off behind them, its silver hull shimmering in the warm light. Liz found a spot on the wooden fence next to the parking lot to lean against.

"Feeling better?" he said.

She nodded. "A little." Her eyes were dark—she had activated her implants to screen out the excess sunlight. She kicked at the ground. "Look, I didn't mean to sound ungrateful. It's just that Victor always gets me so pissed off. He's such an arrogant pig! When he followed me out here, I was so angry, but I figured I might as well go along with the race and beat him. But now he's won, and he's gonna rub it in my face."

"You know him?" said Morgan.

She nodded. "Yeah, but I don't want to talk about it. Look, thank you for stopping."

He shrugged. "Don't worry about it."

"No really, I mean it." She looked towards the finish line. "You stopped, and you don't even know me."

Morgan followed her gaze. Victor was holding the first-place medal over his head. It was just a lame 3D-printed piece of plastic with the Blairsford town logo on it, but still. *That should be mine.* A couple other guys, probably Victor's buddies, were throwing fists in the air and shouting. Victor looked over and caught Liz's eye. He waved at her.

She gave him the finger. "I can't believe Mr. Lutstone let him get away with that. He should be banned."

Morgan agreed whole-heartedly. "There's Mr. Lutstone now," he said, pointing. "He's seen us."

"Good," said Liz. She straightened up and pushed off from the fence. "Let's go get this sorted out."

Mr. Lutstone was running out to meet them with a small group of followers. He was out of breath when he reached them, his brow beaded with sweat. "Are you alright Elizabeth?"

"Yeah, just a little sore." She pointed at her forehead. "The medics did a good job."

Mr. Lutstone looked relieved. He tapped his ear. "I just got off the phone with the medevac AI. Bloody thing is less than useless, but at least it confirmed you weren't dead. Your heart rate had us all a bit worried."

She chuckled. "Yeah, I was pretty pissed off when I woke up."

"I'm just glad you're all right," said Mr. Lutstone. "When I saw the wreck, it reminded me of, well…" He fell silent, but the lines on his face deepened as he looked off into the distance. A few of the people behind Mr. Lutstone shifted uneasily. Morgan recognized most of them as regulars at the track. Like him, they were probably all thinking of what had happened to Danny, Mr. Lutstone's son.

"None of this would have happened, except for that new guy Victor," said Morgan. "He's the one who caused this whole mess."

"He could have killed someone," said Liz. "He spun that guy out on purpose."

"We all saw," said Mr. Lutstone. "Ralph's alright, but he's pissed."

"I'll second that," said Liz.

"Me three," said Morgan. "That guy has no place here. He should be booted from the track for life."

There were grumblings of agreement from the crowd behind Mr. Lutstone, who held up his hands. "Yes, yes, we will take care of all of it. That kind of aggression doesn't belong on our track."

"You should take away his win," said Morgan.

"We'll see," said Mr. Lutstone, running a hand through his thinning hair.

Morgan glared at the track owner. *We'll see? What kind of answer is that?*

Mr. Lutstone coughed. "How bad is your car, Liz?"

She scowled. "It's toast. It'll need a flatbed to get home."

"Elizabeth," said Mr. Lutstone carefully. "The car was one of your father's, wasn't it?"

"Yeah, he's going to go ballistic on me. But screw him, I don't care."

Morgan didn't know what to say. Liz's eyes met his, and the intensity of her stare was too much. He looked away.

"But, I'm sure your dad will understand," stammered Mr. Lutstone. "He loves you."

Liz scoffed.

Mr. Lutstone shrank back. "Well, then I…I guess I should go talk to Victor. Elizabeth, don't worry about the POD. I'll call for a tow."

"Thanks," said Liz. "But I don't have any money to pay."

"I'll cover it," said Morgan.

Liz frowned. "Morgan, thanks, but you've already helped me enough. I don't need charity."

Mr. Lutstone cut in. "Don't worry, I'll cover it. I promised your father I would never let you race on this track, and I broke that promise today. So, it's the least I can do."

"You promised him that?"

Mr. Lutstone fidgeted with his hands. "Yeah. Long story, but suffice it to say that Ed Fowler's daughter would find a way to race whether or not it was on a track. Am I right?"

Liz said nothing. She glanced over at the finish line where Victor was still celebrating.

"I didn't think anything like this would happen," said Mr. Lutstone. "So please, Elizabeth, at least let me take care of the car."

"Ok," she said. "Just tow it to our house. I'll call my dad and explain so he doesn't freak out. But, I'll need a minute." She turned to Morgan. "Ok with you if I take a walk? I just need to cool down. I won't be long."

"Sure, take all the time you need."

"Thanks."

She smiled gratefully, then walked off, following the edge of the track away from the action. Morgan stared after her. *Of course I'll wait.*

"So I see you've met Elizabeth," said Mr. Lutstone.

Morgan nodded. "You know her dad?"

"Ed and I go way back, but their family moved away before Elizabeth was born. He bought a POD dealership in Tucson twenty years ago and did pretty well for himself. His wife was some sort of brilliant engineer."

Mr. Lutstone paused, looking like he wanted to say more. He shook his head. "Some bad stuff happened with his wife. I don't know the details. A few months ago, Ed wrote to me and said he was moving his business to Blairsford. I guess you'll probably see Elizabeth at the high school next year. She'll be a junior, just like you."

"Ah," said Morgan. *A POD dealership, here? Well, at least that explains how she got her car.*

"The Fowlers have racing in their blood, although Ed's given it up I think. He must have known his daughter would show up looking to race with her birthday present. He called me out of the blue when they moved back to town, told me I wasn't to let her anywhere near the track. He said something about it being too dangerous."

"Does she race a lot?"

29

"For a sixteen year old she's pretty good."

"What's that supposed to mean?"

"Well, you kids have only been driving legally for what, a year on a learner permit?" He patted Morgan on the back. "She doesn't race on dirt like you guys, at least not until today. She does autocross and go-karts, just like her dad and I used to. But I looked her up. She's really good. I was surprised when Ed told me not to let her race."

Morgan was silent for a minute. Both he and Mr. Lutstone gazed over at the commotion around Victor, which was finally starting to die down. Morgan kicked at the dirt. "Mr. Lutstone, would the medics have come if I hadn't called you?"

"Of course. I got the alert from her car before you called. Help was already on the way."

Morgan looked at the finish line and scowled. *You still did the right thing.*

"I've seen that face in the mirror a few times," said Mr. Lutstone. "Let it go. You can't win every race."

Geez, he's just a fountain of wisdom. "I know."

Mr. Lutstone prodded Morgan's shoulder. "Besides, it seems you've gotten a new friend."

"Do you really think she likes me?"

Mr. Lutstone laughed. "Yeah, I think she just might. Don't screw it up."

Chapter 4: Animus Redux

The communications console was beeping. Mog looked up from the viewscreen where Mauria smoldered, knowing no one would answer the hail. Grasping the railing surrounding the command platform, he hauled himself up.

He shuffled to the back of the bridge and climbed the steps to the upper deck. There, Laleg's body was strewn across the communications station, pinned against the controls by an I-beam that had fallen from the ceiling. Mog gently removed Laleg's hand from the control board. His arm fell to his side where it hung limply.

"Go in peace, friend," Mog whispered.

The bloody radio board was alive with flashing lights. The murderers wanted to talk. Mog wasn't sure if he was up to it. He looked at the tactical station. Nali wasn't there. He lowered his gaze. There was a pool of blood on the deck where she lay. Hearts pounding, he looked for the rest of his officers.

The two science stations next to tactical were buried beneath a pile of radiation shielding and fallen ductwork. The officers that had been manning them were nowhere to be seen. Kremp, however, appeared unharmed. He was strapped into his seat, staring off into space. Mog peered over the railing. The lower level of the bridge was partially hidden by a dense layer of smoke. Debris were scattered all around. Three lifeless men lay on the deck, their limbs extended at odd angles. At the helm, Meela stared up at him with a blank expression. He looked back down at the comm console. Accepting the hail couldn't possibly cause any more damage.

He tapped the blinking button. It would take a few seconds for the translator to relay the Ta'Krell's message. No living Maurian had ever seen a Ta'Krell or heard one speak; the mysterious aliens seemed content to let

31

the computers do the talking. Thus, Mog was shaken when he heard not the computer's artificial voice but the soft vocalizations of a living being.

"Maurian vessel," it said with perfect pronunciation. "We know you have a hidden base in one of the adjacent sectors. Prepare to be boarded. We will be removing your vessel's computer core. If you cooperate, you will be put to death quickly and without pain. If you resist, you will be tortured until we acquire all information we desire, and then you shall be ejected into space."

Mog blinked, astonished by the speaker's perfect Maurian. "We'll die before we give you so much as a crumb. Come, board my ship if you dare. End what you've started."

Although his voice was calm, his black fur bristled and his hands trembled. Let the swine board! He'd tear out their throats, if they had throats, until he no longer drew breath.

"Strong words," said the Ta'Krell. "But they are the words of a fool. You must understand; we will find Sledgim. If we do not learn its location from your computer, then we will rip the coordinates from your mind. And when we find this hidden world, we will do to it the same that we have done to Mauria. Such is the fate of the race of Ramas."

Mog couldn't believe what he was hearing. "Is that why you did this?" he gasped. "You butchered us because of some story? What do you know of Ramas?"

"Ramas sinned when he defied Tha'Hak. Ramas's creation was not blessed by the All-Father. By Tha'Hak's command, the galaxy will be purged of the unclean. This is the task of the Ta'Krell."

Mog ran a hand over his ears. He had just heard the answer to the question that every Maurian had been asking since the Ta'Krell had appeared at the edge of Maurian space four months ago. *And I'm not sure I understand it at all.* It was clear that they knew of the holy books. *But can they actually be those Ta'Krell? I don't believe it. They're using the story, but why? To what end?*

"How can you justify what you have done?" he said.

32

"Divine right."

The enemy severed the connection. Mog slumped against the console. On the screen, the cruiser circled around to face the *Narma Kull*. A group of small boarding craft detached from the underside of its hull and came towards his ship. *I can't believe it has come to this.* He keyed a command into the comm console.

"Attention all decks," he said. "We're being boarded by enemy troops. It seems we'll finally get to meet our demons in the flesh. My crew, I thank you for your service in the name of Mauria. Despite the outcome, we...." He felt tears threatening his eyes. From the front of the bridge, he could hear Meela sobbing. "Despite the outcome, we have earned more honor than any Maurian in the history of our race. Our people are not dead! Our efforts here have allowed thousands to escape. Although we face our end, they will live on."

He ended the transmission and surveyed his bridge. If it were possible, he would destroy the *Narma Kull* as soon as the Ta'Krell boarded. Without a functional power grid, there was no way to cause an overload.

The boarding party was nearing. Across from Mog, Kremp was reciting a prayer while scraping the tip of his service pistol against the charred bulkhead. Meela's sobbing intensified. Mog sat down in Laleg's empty chair. At least this hell would soon be over.

The engineering station chirped. He looked over at Kremp. The engineer's eyes widened as he observed an energy status monitor, and the pistol fell from his hand.

"Commander," said Kremp, his voice incredulous. "Main power just came back."

Meela stopped crying. Mog dragged a claw across the comm board, his engineer's words echoing around in his head. And then the meaning struck home. He was on his feet in an instant.

"Get us clear of that cruiser," he barked. "Maximum sublight, any heading."

Meela didn't move. She just sat there, a statue adorning the front of the bridge.

Mog growled and flung himself over the railing, landing hard on the lower level next to the command platform. He grabbed Meela and shook her. "Now, Meela, now!"

Her head jerked up, and her eyes locked focus on his. "By Ramas' grace, we live," she said.

She looked down at her controls. A second later, her nimble fingers danced over the navigational panel, bringing the vessel back to life. Mog's breath caught in his throat as he felt the ship shudder. Would the *Narma Kull* hold together for the jump into hyperspace?

The coils within the *Narma Kull's* sublight engines energized just as the first boarding craft was about to dock. The craft fired its port thrusters in an attempt to evade, but it wasn't enough. There was a slight tremor as the tiny ship smashed into the *Narma Kull's* curved bow. Mog envisioned shredded fragments of the vessel's hull bouncing off the curved contours of his ship as it advanced.

The *Narma Kull* barreled towards the remaining boarding craft, which were desperately veering out of the way, opening up a clearer view of the enemy command ship. Mog grimaced as the cruiser's bulk filled the screen. At nearly three times the size of the Maurian vessel, the Ta'Krell starship wasn't about to be swept out of the way.

"Turn, Meela," he muttered, as his ship plowed through two more boarding craft. "Turn."

"I'm trying!" she snapped. "Something's wrong with the exhaust nozzles. Switching to thrusters."

A tremble in the deck announced the firing of the RCS thrusters. Mog tensed. The Ta'Krell cruiser was filling the viewscreen, and his ship's turn rate was much too slow. They weren't going to clear it!

A gray beam of shimmering particles lanced out from the underside of the enemy ship. Mog stumbled. The bulkheads screamed in agony.

"Graviton beam," said Meela. "They're pushing us away."

The Narma Kull was coming apart at the seams. Part of the bridge's support structure fell from the ceiling, smashing a row of consoles only two feet behind Mog. The deck throbbed beneath his footpads. Through it all, he remained focused on the viewscreen. The underside of the Ta'Krell vessel was sliding off screen. *We might just make it!*

Just when he was sure his ship would disintegrate, the shuddering subsided. A status display on the port bulkhead indicated zero velocity. Mog wasn't sure if he should be relieved or angry. They hadn't died, but they were helpless once again. There was no way the *Narma Kull* could jump to light speed while trapped in a graviton beam. If only his ship still had its shields, then maybe they would be able to disrupt the Ta'Krell's lock. There had to be another option.

"They're hailing us again," said a voice from the upper deck. "Should I accept?"

Mog turned to see Kremp leaning against the comm console. "No. The last thing I want to hear is those bastards gloating over their catch."

"They probably want us to shut our engines down so they can reel us in," said Kremp. "I say we…."

"Wait a minute," said Mog. "That's it!"

He had been in a similar situation ten years ago, although then the roles had been reversed.

"Sir," said Meela, "There's no way the engines can break us free; their graviton beam is too strong."

"I don't plan to fight the beam." He rounded the command platform, brushed off his chair, and sat down. "I plan to drive us straight into it. If we shut down the engines, they'll be able to pull us in. When we're close enough to their belly, we fire the ventral thrusters at maximum power. The thrust, combined with the pull of their beam, should give us enough momentum to overload their shields and crash into their beam emitter."

"A collision with that vessel could destroy us," said Kremp.

"We're dead if we don't try it." When the engineer didn't respond, Mog knew the man wasn't convinced. "Look, I know it seems we don't have a reason to keep fighting. Mauria is gone. Most of our people are dead. But what about those who survived? It's our duty to protect them. That means we have to live, if we can."

Meela bowed her head. "Mauria is gone, but Sledgim still lives. A good cause."

"Save Sledgim, save our race", said Mog. He swiveled around to stare at Kremp.

The engineer bowed his head. "Switching to dorsal cameras."

"Meela, kill the engines," said Mog. "Ventral thrusters on my command."

The bridge stopped shaking. Mog watched quietly as the underside of the Ta'Krell vessel grew larger on the viewscreen. It was strange; he had welcomed death ten minutes ago, but now he wanted to live. Part of his determination was born of the desire to protect the remaining Maurians, but there was also something more. His tugged at his uniform, straightening it. If he survived, he wouldn't rest until every Ta'Krell that had ever raised a finger against Mauria lay bleeding at his feet.

"Two hundred marks," said Meela.

"Not yet," said Mog. "We can't give them any time to compensate."

"One hundred-fifty marks," said Meela. "One hundred. Seventy-five."

"Sir," said Kremp. "Sensors show four secondary graviton beams powering up. If they get those beams on us, we won't be going anywhere, and we'll be swarmed by their boarding craft."

"Five more seconds," said Mog.

Kremp's face contorted. "Sir."

Mog held up a hand. "Quiet. One more second. Yes, that's it. Now, Meela."

He grasped his armrests as the *Narma Kull* began to shake. He vaguely heard Kremp say something about the hull stress exceeding tolerances, but he couldn't make out the entire message over the sound of the ship's protests. The whole bridge angled downward, and a proximity alarm screamed from the helm console.

36

A tremendous clang reverberated through the hull. The lights died, and all the display screens flickered out. The ship gave one final shake, and then everything was still. Both Meela and Kremp were praying. Mog glanced about, not sure if it was safe to let go of his chair.

As if to answer his question, the power came back on with a reassuring hum. Peering through the smoke, he saw Meela working her console.

"Report." he said.

"Sensors down," said Kremp. "We obviously hit them, but I can't tell if we hit the graviton emitter or not."

Mog ran to the helm. "Dorsal thrusters, give us some room."

"Already done," said Meela. "We'll know soon enough if we took out their graviton beam."

A second went by, and then another. There was no lurch, no slowing down. They were free, and the starfield on the screen was clear of all obstacles.

"Get us out of here," said Mog. "Full hyperdrive, any heading."

"Aye sir, full—"

Meela couldn't finish her sentence, because the *Narma Kull* was hit by an enemy barrage, and everything started spinning.

"Stabilizers gone," said Meela. "RCS not responding."

"Inertial suppressors are overloading," said Kremp. "Hold on, they're firing again."

Mog ducked as more wires fell from the ceiling. "Meela, hyperdrive now."

"Sir we can't," she pleaded. "Not until I get this spin under control. We could phase right through a star or a black hole or—"

"Do it or we're dead."

An aura of energy enveloped the *Narma Kull*, distorting the image on the viewscreen. Plasma bolts burst into thousands of colors as they streaked past, and the stars melded together into dazzling streaks. Then, with a brilliant flash, space seemed to fold in on itself, pulling the ship into a colorful abyss.

37

Mog slumped against the railing. *Alive…somehow. But for what? Even if I could tear all their throats out with one single grasp, what difference would it make? Mauria lies in the grave.*

* * *

Mog stepped away from the painting of General Thelius and wondered why he had been admiring it, and why there was a painting at all. He looked around. The room was luxuriously furnished, and it had tapestries, paintings, and photographs on the walls. *What is this?*

He took a step towards the center of the room. The floor was soft, covered by some sort of artificial forest floor. He extended the claws between his toes and dug in. *It feels good.*

This wasn't right. He wasn't supposed to feel good. Rooms weren't supposed to be comfortable.

He found his green officer's uniform on a hook next to the door. He donned it without hesitation. Was he on a ship? It didn't feel like one. He went to the windows and parted the curtains to reveal the dim glow of a planetary atmosphere. There were small buildings with flat roofs, covered in snow. *This isn't Mauria.* There were no trees. Two ice-capped mountains rose above the desolate tundra in the distance, their white cloaks broken occasionally by gray cliff faces. He yanked at the curtain, pulling the entire rod off its mounts, and tossed the stupid thing on the floor.

There was a pad on the windowsill. He picked it up. It displayed a medical discharge form. His ears twitched as he read the first line: Sledgim Trauma Center, Memory Restoration Division.

He dropped the form as a wave of recollection rushed over him. Mauria was a smoldering ruin. The *Narma Kull* was plowing through boarding craft. They were in hyperspace, flying a disjointed course and masking their engine signatures. He'd entered his command codes and keyed in the coordinates that he alone knew. He'd been to Sledgim once before, long ago, and now he was going back. For all he knew, the hidden mining world was the last military installation in the entire Empire.

He backpedaled, crashing into the bed frame and falling onto the mattress. The rush of memories continued, becoming more fragmented. He was arriving at Sledgim, but for some reason it looked like Mauria. The doctors said there was something wrong with him, some sort of syndrome. They had taken him forcefully from this ship.

He blinked. He remembered it all; the brain scans, the terrible food, and finally this recovery room. They wanted him to stay here for another month. They never answered any of his questions.

That was going to change. He would make them take him to his ship. He would find his crew, make repairs, and then—

He tried standing, but his legs wouldn't support him. He fell back into the bed, completely exhausted. His head swam as he recalled the doctor's words. *Your memories will be out of sync for awhile. Just go with it. You will be with us in the present soon enough.*

* * *

Mog's dreams of revenge were interrupted by a chime. Rubbing his eyes, he sat up. He was in a dimly lit gray room. To his left, the small alarm clock continued to sound. He silenced it with a gesture and stood.

The room felt strange and familiar at the same time. There was a sound—a humming, almost sub-audible, and the slightest vibration coming up through the floor. With a jolt, he realized he was in his quarters on the *Narma Kull*. There was his desk in the corner, and the old wooden lamp his grandfather had fashioned from the planks of a long forgotten sailing ship. Pictures of his family adorned the walls. He paused, looking at the one where his father and mother cradled the bundle that was his younger brother.

Dead. All dead.

He crossed to the windows and looked out, confirming his suspicions. He remembered it all now. The treatments had worked. The doctors had said it would take some time every day for him to return to the present. They had warned him to expect frantic moments of forgetfulness, rushes of memory, and delusions, especially in the early hours of wakefulness. The trauma of Mauria's fall would always be with him, although in time the episodes should decrease in severity.

"Lights," he said.

Soft warm light filled the room, but it was no comfort. Mog stared at his faint reflection in the glass of the window and shivered at that phantom's bloody uniform and dead black eyes.

Chapter 5: Human Nature

The upper bleachers were nearly deserted, and the aluminum bench seat was nice and warm against Morgan's back. He hadn't realized he'd been so stiff. He stretched out, sighing as the tension between his shoulder blades finally eased.

A falcon circled overhead, riding the thermals. How would that be? Flying high above, taking simple pleasure from the winds, concerned only about what critter was for dinner. Did birds worry about their futures? Did they get nervous about what to say, or how they came across, when they met a beautiful lady-bird?

Probably not.

He checked his watch. It was eleven o'clock. The ten-o'clock demolition derby and the 10:30 dirt jump competition had come and gone. The food vendors were setting up, and the track was being re-groomed for the afternoon races. He sat up and looked towards the parking lot, then scanned the track and the grounds for what felt like the hundredth time.

Where is she? Did she get a ride from someone else?

He was about to call Mr. Lutstone to see if he had Liz's number when he spotted an orange car with a crumpled fender parked next to the track's garage. *Ugh.* Victor was leaning against the garage wall, his arms crossed. Mr. Lutstone was standing in front of him, waving his hands vehemently. *Good. I hope Mr. Lutstone bans that punk.*

Victor didn't seem to care. He leaned against the wall, staring nonchalantly at Mr. Lutstone.

An engine roared. It was a strange sound, in a world where most cars used fluoridic battery packs and electro-force propulsion. Morgan turned. The hovering robots that were grading the track scattered as a car rounded the final turn and charged down the straightaway. A few people on the

41

bleachers below put down their hot dogs and onion rings to clap and cheer.

Morgan nearly fell off the bench. "Hey, that's mine!"

He had forgotten all about his car. *And now, someone's stealing it!*

Engine roaring, the Scorpion barreled down the home stretch. Morgan dashed down the bleachers, stumbling over discarded soda cartridges and foil wrappers.

"Hey, watch it!" said a woman as he rushed past.

The Scorpion broke through the holographic finish line and slid towards the bleachers. Morgan jumped the last three rows, vaulted over the barrier wall's force emitters, and reached the car just as it came to rest. He grabbed for the door, but it flew open on its own, knocking his hand away.

He gaped as she killed the engine.

"You?" he stammered.

Liz flashed him a grin as she climbed out. "That was whippin! I brought it back, hope you don't mind."

Morgan stared at her, his mind piecing it all together. Finally, he managed to sputter a single phrase. "You've got to be kidding me."

Her smile faded. "Hey, I was careful with it."

He eyed the gouges in the sand. "Locking up the brakes is not being careful. Bouncing it off the rev limiter is not being careful." He spat the words, as if he'd sucked venom from a wound.

She held up her hands. "Hey, lay off, I was just doing you a favor."

"A favor?" He laughed bitterly. "I offer you a ride home, and you repay me by making me wait for over an hour. Then, you go for a joy ride in my car. How'd you get in? Break the door?"

Liz's eyes narrowed. "No." She pulled something from her jumpsuit pocket. "It was unlocked. This was in the ignition. Took me a minute to figure out what it was. Turns out, you just turn it…"

"Give that here," he said, snatching the key from her hand.

She glared at him. "If you don't like what happened, then don't make a habit of leaving your car unlocked."

Morgan squeezed the key so hard his knuckles popped. "Maybe you shouldn't make a habit of stealing cars. Now get lost."

Her lip was trembling. Morgan took a breath. *I can't believe this. Is she going to cry? What have I done?*

"I didn't steal it!" she screamed. She turned and stormed off towards the parking lot.

Morgan watched her go for a long time. He looked at the key. It was legit, cut out of metal and meant for a mechanical ignition cylinder. Most people had no idea what to do with such a thing. He put the key back in his pocket. *Way to go, man. That was real smooth.*

"Just in case you haven't noticed, Liz just isn't into losers."

Morgan recognized the nasal voice immediately. "Get lost Victor."

"And you are a loser," continued Victor. "Just like I said. The guys here say you've got no goods either. I should have known. What are you, Amish? I'm surprised you don't drive a horse and buggy."

"Shut up," said Morgan, without turning. He could feel Victor's eyes boring into him.

"You've got no goods and no game. Vanilla!"

Morgan spun, his fist arcing upward. It found only air as Victor jumped backwards. Before Morgan could recover, Victor lunged, crashing into Morgan's stomach and sending him to the ground. Victor landed on top of him.

"Think you're gonna hit me?" said Victor, straddling Morgan's chest. He pulled the glove off his right hand and made a fist. *A metal fist?* Gasping, Morgan tried to wiggle free. He raised his left arm just in time to save his face. He yelped, feeling as if his arm had been shattered.

Victor's mechanical hand grabbed Morgan's wrist and squeezed so hard that Morgan felt his bones grind together. Frantically, Morgan reached into his pocket with his free hand and felt for the Scorpion's key.

Victor wrenched Morgan's arm out of the way and punched him square on the cheek with his normal hand. Morgan's head snapped back against the ground, and he saw stars.

"Ahh!" screamed Morgan, pulling the key out of his pocket and slamming it into the meaty part of Victor's right leg. Victor screamed and pulled back. Morgan kicked out with both feet. He missed Victor's groin but connected with his kneecap. Victor fell backwards.

Morgan jumped up and tried to kick Victor, but someone grabbed him from behind and pulled him backwards. He lurched forward, but a pair of strong dark-skinned arms looped around him in a bear hug.

"Knock it off," said Mr. Lutstone. "Before I call the police."

Morgan squirmed, but the old man's wiry strength held him fast. "Morgan, please stop."

He stopped.

"Are you done?" said Mr. Lutstone.

He nodded.

Mr. Lutstone released him.

Victor had regained his feet and was staring at Morgan, his eyes full of cold hatred. "I'm going to kill you, kid. I'm going to cut your head off and mount it on the hood of my car." His lips turned up in a sideways smirk, as if he relished the thought.

"That's enough," said Mr. Lutstone, stepping between them. "You're banned from this track for life."

Victor's smirk vanished. "What?"

"You heard me. Now leave before I call the police."

Victor looked as if he would strike Mr. Lutstone. Then, he seemed to think better of it and spat at the ground. "Nobody here's a challenge anyway." He turned and started walking gingerly towards his car. After a few steps he looked back and shouted over his shoulder, "And stay away from Liz!"

"What's it to you?" said Morgan.

Victor continued without answering.

44

Mr. Lutstone turned to Morgan. "Are you ok?"

Morgan felt his forearm. There was a deeply tender spot where Victor's metal knuckles had smashed into it, but it wasn't broken. He flexed his aching fingers. *Shit, that hurts.* He bent and picked the ignition key off the ground with his uninjured hand. It wasn't bloody. *Too bad. I'll just have to stab him harder next time.*

"I'll be fine," he said.

"I thought you were giving her a ride."

He looked over at the Scorpion, then at Liz. She was already a good way through the parking lot and had almost reached the main road that would lead back to Blairsford.

"I was, until she decided to give herself one."

Mr. Lutstone was quiet. Morgan looked away, unable to meet Mr. Lutstone's eyes. He kicked at the dirt. He couldn't give her a ride, not after what she had done, and certainly not after what he had said to her.

"It's a long walk to town," said Mr. Lutstone.

"Too bad," said Morgan. The voice in his head wasn't letting him off that easily. *You're being a fool. Come on, admit it.*

"Morgan, I don't think she meant to anger you."

He bit his lip. The scab from earlier had barely formed, and he tasted blood. "It doesn't matter what she meant to do." *Why can't I let it go?*

Mr. Lutstone sighed. "I can't tell you what to do. But think about it from her side. She's new here, and she just wrecked her car. I know Ed Fowler, and he's going to be furious when he finds out."

Morgan shook his head. "There's nothing I can do about that. It's not like my giving her a ride home will solve all her problems." He winced as he spoke. *That's too harsh, and you know it.*

Mr. Lutstone turned to look down the track's driveway. Liz was out of sight. "No, but being her friend couldn't hurt. An hour ago, I was pretty sure the idea appealed to you."

"It did."

Mr. Lutstone smiled. "And it still does?"

45

Morgan looked away. There was no point in lying. But he had treated her like shit. How could he take it back? "I'm an idiot, aren't I?"

Mr. Lutstone shrugged. "Probably. Now, are you going to let her walk out of your life, or are you going to man up and apologize, and give her a ride home?"

Morgan gulped. "I'll try."

"Ok then."

Morgan trudged back to the Scorpion, got inside, and closed the door. Victor was driving towards the exit. Pulse quickening, Morgan started the car and took off.

He caught up just after the bend in the road. Liz was walking along the shoulder. Victor pulled alongside and rolled down his window.

She shouted something at him and started walking faster, looking straight ahead. Victor kept pace for a few seconds, then accelerated away. Morgan let his breath go—he hadn't realized he'd been holding it.

He swallowed, tasting bile. *Now it's your turn.* If there was one thing he hated, it was apologizing.

The Scorpion's tires crunched over the gravel as he approached. Liz made no acknowledgement, but kept walking as if the rumbling dune buggy didn't exist. Morgan leaned over and pushed up the passenger door.

"Get in," he said, a little too gruffly. He scowled, then added, "Please."

"Go to hell," she said, her gaze unwavering from the road.

For a second, Morgan thought about hitting the gas. *Don't be a child. Talk to her.*

"Liz, I'm sorry." It sounded mechanical and insincere. *You can do better. Don't be afraid.* Liz walked even faster. He gave the Scorpion more gas, being careful to not run her off the road. "Look, I'm not going to let you walk all the way back. I said I'd give you a lift."

"You also told me to get lost, so that's what I'm doing."

"I didn't mean it." He grit his teeth and looked down the road. "I…I overreacted. I'm sorry, I know you were only trying to help."

She didn't answer. He looked back out and realized she had stopped walking. He put the car in reverse until he was next to her again. Liz was on the phone. Her face was grim as her eyes flashed.

"My dad's wondering where I am," she said finally. "More or less."

"You tell him what happened?"

"Yeah. He flipped out. Now he's even more pissed that I'm not back."

"Then get in. I'll take you home."

She hesitated, glancing down the driveway and then back at the Scorpion. Then, she set her jaw and she slipped into the passenger seat.

Morgan accelerated down the rest of the dirt road and turned onto the paved road that led to Blairsford. Shuttles and air cars bustled through the sky, but the local ground traffic was light. There wasn't anything for miles around except desert. He considered putting the Scorpion on automatic, but decided against it. If he wasn't driving, the silence would be even more awkward.

Liz was staring out her side of the car, and Morgan couldn't see her face. They continued on for some time, until Morgan couldn't stand it any longer. He had to try to make things better.

"So, how did you like driving my car?"

Liz started. "What?"

"Did you have fun?"

She eyed him suspiciously. "First you get pissed, then you want to know if I had fun?"

He nodded.

She was studying him as if she didn't know what to make of him. When she finally spoke, some of the tension had left her voice. "I didn't mean to go so fast. It was addictive. The sound it makes, the traction...I've never driven anything like it before."

Morgan grinned. "I'm glad you like it."

"So, you're not mad?"

Morgan thought for a moment. The only anger left was aimed at himself for being such a meat head. "No, not anymore. I am sorry about that. I just, well, this car is just about the best thing going on in my life at the moment."

"Wow," said Liz. "Your life must suck."

"Haha, yeah, a little."

Except for Liz's occasional directions, they drove the rest of the way in silence. Morgan thought of things to say for when she finally had to leave, but the prospect of actually saying them was scary. *Hey, want to grab dinner some time? No, well, how about coffee? No, ah, you're not interested. Well, that's ok. I guess I'll just be going…*

No, it was better to say nothing.

Modest two-story houses lined both sides of the street. "Which one's yours?"

"Blue one at the end," she said, pointing at a modern structure with a triple garage.

Morgan guided the Scorpion up the broad driveway, stopping behind a gloss-black POD 1200. A faint reflection of the Scorpion glistened in the hovercar's glossy paint. He looked over at Liz. *Come up with something, you idiot. This is your last chance!*

"Well, thanks for the ride," she said, opening her door. "Sorry about earlier."

He shrugged. "No worries. Do you think it's going to be bad? You know, with your dad?"

"It always is with my father." She paused, looking pensive. "Hey, do you think you could stick around for a minute? In case, you know, I need a wheelman?"

"A what?"

"An escape driver, silly, in case my dad loses it."

Morgan tried to keep the schoolboy grin off his face. "Uh, yeah, sure, I'll be your wheelman any time."

She beamed at him. "Great, thank you so much! I give it a fifty-fifty chance of needing your services within the next two minutes." Her face fell. "You know, depending on if he's been drinking."

No one had mentioned that Ed Fowler was a raging drunk. Morgan tried to look unconcerned. "What do I do?"

Liz got out of the car. "Just sit tight with this door open and be ready to floor it."

She walked towards the house. The entryway sensed her and opened automatically. Morgan started to sweat despite the air conditioning. *What am I getting myself into here?* The last thing he wanted was to get in the middle of a family fight. *Man up, you pansy!*

The Scorpion's computer beeped out a proximity alert. The navigational screen showed a blue dot turning onto Liz's street. He sighed. He had forgotten to turn the settings down after the race.

He looked in the rear-view display. It was a blue Porsche with a smashed-in front bumper. *Mr. Lutstone's mystery driver followed me!* He had completely missed the unveiling of the driver's identity in the commotion after the race.

The Porsche slowed as it reached the end of the street. It drove through the cul-de-sac and stopped, waiting.

Angry voices tore his attention away from the Porsche. Liz was running out, her face streaming with tears. A large red-faced man in a gray suit toddled out after her, bellowing. "You were told, and you didn't listen. That track is too dangerous, and now you've wrecked the car and proven my point."

Liz turned to face him. "I knew it! You're just mad because I smashed the car. You don't care about me at all. All you care about is your stupid cars and your stupid dealership! You suck, dad. I hate you."

Smack.

Liz's head snapped around. Her father raised his hand again.

Morgan gaped. *The drunk bastard. How dare he!* He reached for his door handle, but his hands were shaking and he couldn't get it open.

Ed Fowler stared at his open palm as if in disbelief. "Liz, I'm sorry," he stammered. He pointed at the POD in the driveway. "I don't care about the cars, they mean nothing. But you—hey, wait!"

Liz was striding down the driveway towards Morgan.

"Elizabeth," wailed her father. "I shouldn't have. I didn't want you to get hurt on that track. I couldn't lose you, not after what happened to your mom. Marc Lutstone's own son died on that track, did you know that? It's not safe."

"Screw you!" said Liz. She ducked under the Scorpion's open passenger door and slid in next to Morgan. Her dad, noticing the strange car in his driveway for the first time, began running towards them.

"This can't be happening," said Morgan. He jammed the car in reverse the second Liz energized her restraining field. Her dad dived for the Scorpion, but he was too late. He hit the pavement with a dull smack just as Liz got her door closed.

Morgan cut the wheel to the side—grimacing as pain shot through the hand Victor had squeezed—and jammed on the brakes. The Scorpion whipped around, tires squealing. He flipped it into first gear and mashed the accelerator, tearing out of the driveway and down the street. Neither one of them looked back.

"You alright?" he said, once they were safely out of the neighborhood.

She laughed. "Yeah, I'm fine."

Morgan looked over at her. A huge red welt was spreading over her cheek. She turned her face away to gaze out the virtual window.

"It's alright," he said. "You can be honest with me."

She sniffed. "Just shut up and drive."

Chapter 6: King and Commander

Mog paced the length of the rectangular table, observing Sledgim's desolate surface through the conference room's massive windows. Sledgim was no substitute for Mauria. The latter had appeared vibrant and lively from space; the former was a dreary rock. Its frozen surface was pierced by mountain ranges, and a great ocean of ice dominated the lower hemisphere. If he squinted, he could make out the ugly mining complexes that harvested anitheum, a material used in reactors and computer cores. When he'd been much younger, Mog had been stationed here for a time. He'd been one of the few subcommanders with clearance to access the top-secret shipyard beneath Nock. *I never thought I'd see this place again.*

As natural sources of anitheum were scarce on Mauria, Sledgim was an invaluable resource. Although inhospitable, the planet supported nearly three-hundred thousand people. The original colony, Silverpeak, had been home to miners and their families for generations dating back to the founding of the Maurian Empire.

"Now it has to be home for everyone," said Mog.

"It does indeed," said a voice from the other side of the room.

He spun around. Standing in the archway, partially supported by a pearl white cane, was quite possibly the oldest Maurian in the galaxy. His name was mar-Ruba, but most people simply addressed him as Your Majesty.

The King was adorned in a deep blue robe laced with gold. His fur was white, except for the coarse gray strands sticking out from his ears. His back was hunched, his nose dry and cracked, and his lips shriveled, but his blue eyes sparkled with inner fire. They radiated power and hinted at a wisdom that only comes with the passing of many years. The sovereign drew back his black lips in greeting.

I am a child compared to him, thought Mog.

51

"Your Majesty," he said with a bow. "I didn't realize you were yet aboard. Welcome to the *Narma Kull*."

"You may call me Ruba," said the King, hobbling into the room.

"I'm honored by your presence," said Mog, bending lower. He gestured at the conference table. "Please sit."

"If you don't mind, I prefer to stand. You should too."

Mog straightened up. "Of course, Your Majesty."

The King's ears flattened. "Dispense with the titles. Ruba will do."

"As you command," said Mog, holding himself at rigid attention.

He had never met the King, but everyone had seen mar-Ruba's famous addresses and knew of the man's achievements. The Maurian Empire had done away with the formal position of emperor a century ago, but as King of Mauria, Ruba had been the de facto supreme leader for nearly two hundred years. As a child, Mog's mother had told him of the man who had crushed the Talurians, unified the separatist factions, and brought wealth and prosperity to over fifty nation states across the seven Maurian worlds. Songs were sung about his conquests, both on the battlefield and at the negotiating table. Nine years ago, when Mog was a new starship commander, he had fought under Ruba's banner in the liberation of Lubeck IV from the hand of the usurper, King Bor.

Mog had expected a demigod to walk into his conference room. Ruba's humility was a pleasant surprise.

"I trust my aides sent word of my arrival," said Ruba.

"Yes, but they did not tell me why."

Since he had returned to his ship, he had left the bridge only for essential distractions. The communiqué from the planet announcing the King's arrival had been one of those.

"You should know the answer to that, Commander," said Ruba. "But maybe you do not completely understand. They tell me you have been on the surface, suffering from Isamal's Syndrome."

"I have been back aboard these last three weeks, overseeing final repairs."

"Do not be ashamed. It is a common enough affliction, especially among warriors. I have seen many good commanders succumb to their darkest memories and never return." He paused. "I am glad you have returned. Excluding transport vessels, your ship is the only survivor of the fleet assembled to defend Mauria. The fleet commander is dead, and we have lost contact with the Seven Worlds. Our deep space exploration craft will not return for many years, which means the Navy has only a few dozen functioning warships. Of their commanders, you are the most seasoned."

Mog considered this. It wasn't new information—he had learned as much from his surviving crew after he returned from Sledgim. He had suspected Ruba might be coming here to debrief him, or to discuss plans to muster the remains of the fleet into a retaliatory strike force. More probably, the King had come to strip him of his command. What use could a mentally unstable commander be, especially one who had suffered defeat at every battle with the Ta'Krell?

Ruba began hobbling across the length of the conference room. "I have reviewed your record and I believe you to be a capable leader. Now, we will see if your talent can extend beyond the confines of this ship's hull. Molamogra, of the Old Salt River clan, son of Nintal and Shabek, I promote you to Acting Supreme Fleet Commander. You will lead our people to battle in these last days."

Mog snorted involuntarily, then wiped his nose, horrified. "Sorry," he muttered. Him, the leader of the fleet? "I'm honored sir, but are you sure?"

"Commander," said Ruba, his face hardening, "the fleet has less than forty ships left. Forty ships, out of a force that once contained almost five hundred. Of these, half have never seen combat because their commanders are only in their first year of service. Do you find it so hard to believe you are the one for this job?"

Mog smoothed a hand over his twitching ears. Since he was a boy, his dream had been to command a great starship. Ruba was asking him to leave his ship and take a desk job at Naval Command. There had to be someone else, someone older with more experience.

"No, there's not," said Ruba.

"I'm sorry, what?" said Mog.

"There's no one else, from this planet or elsewhere. You are the only possible candidate."

Mog's ears twitched. *Did he just read my mind?*

Ruba emitted a series of rasping hacks that could possibly be laughter. Mog stiffened, and fought to control his expression. *I've got to get it together. It seems he can read me like a book.* He looked out a window at the black void surrounding Sledgim. There was no way he would leave the bridge of his ship to cower behind a desk.

Suddenly, the end of Ruba's pearly cane was prodding him in the chest. He stared down at the King. How had the old man managed to cross the room without him noticing?

"Do not worry," said the King. "Our fleet is small, and I cannot see any reason why you should not direct it on the front line, from the *Narma Kull.*"

Mog realized his mouth was open and snapped it shut. *He can read minds.*

"Will you accept?" said Ruba.

"Do I have a choice?"

Ruba produced another series of raspy chuckles. "There is always a choice." His twinkling blue eyes cut into Mog.

"You're serious then? I can stay on my ship?"

"Yes."

But to coordinate such a force…I'll need help. And I want to choose who.

"If I do this, can I have my same crew?"

The King's ears dipped in acknowledgement. "That is acceptable for the time being."

Some of the tension left Mog. Maybe this would work out after all. "I guess…I will try."

"Good," said the King, walking back towards the windows. He pointed a gnarled claw at the icy world below. "From now on, this world shall be known as Mauria Prime. It is the new seat of power for our people."

Mog's face hardened. "Your Majesty, this world is nothing like Mauria."

Ruba bobbed his head. "There is no world like Mauria." He paused to smooth his robes with his bony hands. "It is a sad time when the first order of business is to amass a fleet of war. I have ordered the construction of two more shipyards. They will augment Mauria Prime's existing facility. As we are no longer in a position to build explorers, these facilities will be manufacturing warships like the *Narma Kull*.

"In addition, all of our current ships, including cargo freighters and civilian transports, are to be refitted for battle. It will be your job to organize and deploy this fleet. You will have access to all of our resources to accomplish this task." Ruba tapped the window with his cane. "We will rebuild our great navy, sparing no expense, until our families need fear no attack."

Mog got to his feet and joined the King at the window. *And then, revenge, if we live long enough.*

"What if the Ta'Krell find us before we can establish defenses?"

The King stared out at the icy sphere below. Beyond, except for the dim sun, there were no stars. Sledgim's system was caught up in a hyperspace bubble, an extra-dimensional layer of normal space that resided within hyperspace. Its accidental discovery by ancient explorers had proven fortuitous over the last thousand years. Having a presence that wasn't on any star map had given them a tremendous advantage in the old wars with the Talurians.

Still, despite the Empire's best attempts to keep Sledgim hidden, it was not impervious to detection. Over the decades, a few outsiders had stumbled onto the system by following the hyperspace wakes of careless Maurian commanders. Of course, these commanders had been relieved of their warships, and the visitors had never been allowed to leave.

The problem now was that every orphaned Maurian ship from a dozen conquered sectors in all corners of the Empire might be headed here. The coordinates were top-secret, but so what? The Empire had been crushed. Those few that knew the path would share it with the other survivors. Were they all taking care to mask their transit vectors? *The Ta'Krell will sniff us out, and they will kill us all.*

When the King spoke, it was in a voice barely above a whisper. "If they come soon, then we will be forced to evacuate those we can to start a breeding colony somewhere the Ta'Krell can't reach us."

"But what place is safe?" said Mog. "If they can find Sledgim—"

Ruba didn't seem to hear. "The colony would need young leaders like yourself to help rebuild, and repopulate the race."

Mog's ears perked up. "Me? No, I can't leave. If the destroyers come, I will fight them till they are driven out, or I draw my last breath."

"I'm afraid that last bit is a dream, Commander," said Ruba. "If the Ta'Krell find us here, before we have rebuilt our forces, then the only way to save this planet would be if Ramas took up his great bow and joined us in battle."

"That would be unlikely."

Ruba's ears twitched. "One never knows."

Mog looked down at the floor. The arrival of the so-called Ta'Krell— the supposed demons from the holy books—had awakened a sort of religious fervor in the Empire. It was one thing for his crew to get all wrapped up in it. But for the King? Why couldn't everyone see that these aliens were using the Mauria's ancient mythos against them?

"You are not a believer, are you."

Mog looked up. The King's strange blue eyes seemed to make everything else in the room seem dim. Mog realized it was not a question. "No," he grunted, perhaps more sternly than he should have.

Ruba snorted. "Well, Supreme Commander Mog, when this is all over, maybe you will be."

Chapter 7: Rouge

Hrain rolled onto his side and buried his head beneath his pillow. This did nothing. It would take a mountain of pillows to keep the confounded beeping away from his ears. He growled into his sheets.

He was just about to give in to the idea of getting up when the alert stopped. He sighed and rolled over. *Ramas be praised.*

Then, with a dull clang, the bed flipped up on its side, dumping him onto the floor of his tiny quarters. But it wasn't just the bed that had moved. The entire room had inverted. Hrain found himself tumbling towards the port bulkhead, along with his blankets, pillows, and the carcass of last night's dinner.

The inertial compensators came out of standby just in time to stop him from ramming the metal wall with his head. Last night's dinner streaked by his face and splattered against the bulkhead. Cursing all things Talurian, he jumped to his feet and staggered to the cockpit of the *Angel's Fury*. One glance out the forward windows told him all he needed to know: the Talurians had used their station's docking clamps to flip his ship on its side. Since he had surrendered his ship to the station's artificial gravity generators, the results had been disastrous. It must have been Ezek's idea.

The beeping started again. Hrain pounded the comm console, and the scaly head of the station's commanding officer appeared on the screen.

"Hello, Ezek," said Hrain. "Can I ask why you felt it necessary to knock all my fine dinnerware off the shelves?"

"You don't have any dinnerware," hissed Ezek.

Hrain grimaced and turned down the volume. "That's beside the point. I was sleeping in."

The Intendant's tongue flicked out, sending a drop of spittle straight into the imager lens. "I have work for you."

Hrain's ears perked up. "Pirates again?" Pirates were his specialty, and those sorts of dangerous missions paid well.

Ezek's face tightened. "No. We've lost contact with Mauria."

Hrain straightened up. "What do you mean lost contact?"

"I mean something, or someone, has jammed or destroyed all hyperspace comm buoys from here to Maurian space without anyone noticing, or something has silenced the planet itself. We haven't received data from our spies for six days."

"That's impossible," said Hrain.

Ezek's reptilian gaze didn't waver. "Over the last two months, we intercepted encoded distress calls from the Seven Worlds, claiming attack from unknown entities. There has also been the disappearance of the Maurian trade envoys, and the subsequent disappearance of our fast frigates sent to investigate. You have heard the rumors of mysterious alien ships being detected at the fringes of Talurian space?"

Hrain bared his teeth in acknowledgement.

"Well," said Ezek, "The rumors are true. My government has suspected those few ships we have catalogued to be part of a much larger invasion force."

Hrain's insides grew cold as he remembered last night's dream. Huge black starships of an unknown configuration, surrounding a planet consumed in flames.

"Why didn't you tell me about these distress calls?"

"It was classified. The Maurians encoded their transmissions. They were asking for help from their own navy, not from outsiders and especially not us. If we made it known we could decode their military communications, then the Maurian Navy would change their encoders, and we would be at a severe disadvantage in the event of another war with Mauria. Yet, at this point I do not agree with the government's decision to keep this bottled up. So, I am telling you, because you are my friend, and because it's your homeworld."

"Thank you," said Hrain. He didn't bother to tell Ezek he had only been to Mauria twice, and those trips had been covert adventures. He'd grown up in a government-run orphanage on Sledgim. The less the Talurians knew about that secret the better. He was careful to keep no records of the base's location. *I'm no traitor.*

"Yesterday, one of our unmanned high speed probes made a close pass at one of the vessels, which we had detected in deep space. There isn't much to tell, since the probe's scanners couldn't penetrate the vessel's hull." Ezek tapped a few commands. "Here."

An image resolved above Angel's control console. It was a dark, wedge-shaped craft. Hrain's eyes narrowed, and he flicked the image away. "They are the destroyers," he growled.

Ezek flicked his tongue. "Meaning?"

Hrain leaned back in his chair. It was really happening, just as Drakmara had said it would all those years ago. He hadn't wanted to believe—he'd been ignoring the visions, writing them off as unwanted fragments, products of his twisted education. But now, the image that had been haunting his dreams for weeks was a dream no longer. He recalled an old paper book Drakmara had given him. The ship sketched in the margin hadn't made any sense then, but it did now.

"I have seen these ships before. In visions, and nightmares. A planet, surrounded by those ships, on fire."

"I'm going to need more than one of your silly visions. Your mission is to track down one of the alien ships and disable it. Send us the coordinates, and we'll come pick it up. We need to know what these aliens are up to and if they're a threat to Taluria. Since neither you nor your ship is Talurian, they won't think to come here looking for revenge if your attack is unsuccessful. Be careful. The probe we sent was destroyed by the vessel, and we have lost four warships already in pursuit of this enemy."

"I see."

"I'm willing to pay you twice your normal rate."

"Huh," said Hrain. *I'd do this for free, but no sense telling you that.* "Make it three times, and I'll leave as soon as I can."

Ezek wrinkled his forehead in acknowledgement, and the comm image winked out.

"He didn't even flinch," muttered Hrain. Perhaps Ezek thought he wouldn't make it back to collect his fee. Then again, the lizard hadn't said goodbye. Talurians only said that if they didn't expect to see you again.

Hrain screwed his eyes shut and focused, directing his mind across hundreds of light-years towards the place of his birth. Had his recent dreams been more than dreams? What had happened?

The familiar, haunting image of a planet on fire appeared in his mind, followed by a word.

Ta'Krell.

He was intimately familiar with that word. He'd first heard it in the stories his father had told him out of the Book of Ramas, then later in the orphanage, under the tutelage of that evil man named Drakmara. The children of Adula had thought the Ta'Krell were a myth. But thanks to mar-Drakmara, Hrain had learned better. He bent over, his temples throbbing, as the word boomed again and again. *Ta'Krell, Ta'Krell, Ta'Krell.*

And then, something else, a cry from that first terrible dream.

Azhra has won! Ramas, why have you forsaken us?

The voice was older, battle-hardened, but hauntingly familiar. "Nail," he gasped, remembering the girl he'd left on Sledgim all those years ago. *Nail, why would you cry out, unless the planet that burns is...could it be Sledgim?*

He withdrew his mind and the pain subsided. Outcast though he was, he wasn't about to stand by while somebody messed with his people. *But what if that someone is Azhra's demon army, the destroyers, the Ta'Krell? If Drakmara's prophecy comes true, what can we possibly do?*

"Did you catch what Ezek said, Angel?" he asked finally.

A yellow light flashed on the communications panel. "Of course," replied the ship through the cockpit speakers. "How could anyone sleep through that? I've been holding my tongue, lest I blurt something out and scare that lizard senseless."

Hrain knew she was referring to the Talurian's distrust of artificial intelligence. As far as Ezek knew, the *Angel's Fury* was only a ship. A top-of-the-line warship, certainly, but nothing more. *If Ezek only knew.*

"So, all this is bad, right?" said Angel.

"Yes," said Hrain. He thought of what his father would do. "It's extremely bad." He flashed his teeth in a warrior's snarl. "But, as my father would say, we've got to help."

"Good," said Angel, her voice oozing with bloodlust. "We haven't had a fight in ages. Let's go hunting."

Hrain patted the bulkhead. "I wasn't going to suggest anything else."

Chapter 8

Liz eyed the beige three-story complex. "So, your family owns Greenfield Grain?"

"Yeah," said Morgan. "That's the research building. A bunch of scientists work there, plus the facilities staff and the boring finance people. A lot of the space is automated labs and conference rooms. We contract with other labs and farms all over to develop the actual product."

Morgan turned left and drove around the side of the building.

"So, you live in there?"

"In the lab? No, the house is out back."

"Lame. You can't ever get away from work. Rice, you said?"

He nodded. "Yeah, that's one of the main products. Hearty varieties engineered for space travel and cultivation. We also design the hydroponics equipment."

"Well, I guess someone has to come up with that stuff," said Liz.

Morgan considered that for a moment. Usually when people found out that his family owned the biggest business in town, they put on an air of amazement, or at least seemed enthusiastic.

"Sorry," she said, noticing his puzzled look. "It's just not my thing."

"Mine neither, to tell you the truth. But, it'll be mine someday, whether I like it or not. I don't have any brothers or sisters, and Greenfield Grain has been the family business for three generations."

"I see," said Liz. "So, you guys are loaded?"

He grimaced. "We do alright."

"That's nice, having your future figured out. You should be happy."

Morgan pictured himself as a fat old business man, beaming at the holographic magnification of some new wheat germ. *Ick.* He turned into the driveway and drove up to the large two-story home. It was of conventional design, having been printed in modules at some distant facility and molecularly bonded together on site.

"Here's the house. We can raid the fridge." *And then maybe watch a holo or something. What do you think?* His heart pounded. If only he had the nerve to actually say something like that.

"Sounds good," she said.

They drove around the solar harvesters to the attached garage. Morgan guided the Scorpion to the door, which opened automatically. He parked inside and shut off the engine.

Liz whistled as she hopped out of the Scorpion. "You have your own lift!" Morgan followed her to the middle of the garage. "Wait a minute, where are the force pads? Is this thing hydraulic?" She placed her hand on the lift's operating cylinder.

"Yeah," said Morgan. "No repulsors, just oil. It's my grandfather's, on my mom's side. It's been here forever, since when gramp was a kid. My parents aren't into cars, but when I turned fourteen they said I could have all this."

"I officially hate you," said Liz.

He chuckled. "Yeah, I am a spoiled brat. Then again, you're the one who gets free sports cars from her dad's dealership." He knew from the look on her face that he'd made a mistake.

A chirp from the workbench saved him.

"Page from mom," said the computer.

"Er, sorry," he said to Liz. "Hold on." He went over to the bench and clicked on the intercom.

The image of a plump woman coalesced, seeming to stand on top of the cluttered bench. Helen Greenfield fixed her gaze on Morgan. She must have been working this morning, since her hair was still in a neat bun. Never one to have robots in the house, Morgan's mother had thrown an apron over her work attire to make lunch. She pointed the pair of salad tongs at Morgan.

"There you are, finally," she said. "I was about to call. Did you win?"

He glanced over at Liz, then back at his mother. "Not exactly, but it could have been worse."

His mom smiled. "I'm sorry bud. I made you a nice lunch though. Make sure you wash up before you come in, and leave those boots out there."

"I will."

Her image dissolved.

"Are you sure she won't mind my being here?" said Liz.

"Of course not," said Morgan. *Are you kidding? She'll be thrilled!* Apprehension gripped him. Maybe it hadn't been a good idea to take her home. He hadn't had a chance to give his parents a heads-up.

"This is gonna be awkward," he said.

"Why?" said Liz.

Morgan looked at her. "Well, you know, because."

She blinked. "Because of what?"

He blushed. "Well, you're the first, uh, the first—er, never mind. Let's just eat, I'm starving." He stumbled forward, opening the door that led to the interior of the house.

He kicked off his boots next to the bathroom, then made a half-hearted attempt to wash his hands and straighten out his hair. His cheek was darkening where Victor had struck him, but the bruise didn't stand out too badly yet. He decided not to wash his face, as that would only make the bruise stand out more.

His left forearm was another matter. It was a mess of blue and black, and just rolling up his sleeve to inspect the damage caused him to cringe. He'd probably have to explain that one to his parents later. For now, he'd just have to keep his race suit on.

He finished up, then traded with Liz. As he waited in the hallway, he wished he'd thought to call home and explain things. It had been ages since he'd had a friend to bring home, and never a girl. He felt a twinge of pride, and more than a healthy dose of apprehension. *Please God, don't let them embarrass me.*

Liz came out of the bathroom and fixed him with a curious stare. "Is everything alright?"

He assured her that it was. *Come on man, chill out!* He led her down the hall. The door at the end opened into the kitchen. His mom wasn't in sight, but she could be heard. He put on what he hoped was a casual, uninterested expression.

"Harold, put that tablet down and come to lunch."

"Hold on," said his dad. "I just need one more minute…hey, give that back!"

There was the sound of running feet, and a victorious Mrs. Greenfield came skidding into the kitchen. She waved a computer tablet in the air. She caught Morgan's eye. "Your father can't part with his work, as usual. I—oh!" She stopped dead as she noticed Liz. "Why, hello there."

Morgan's father bounded into the kitchen. He reached for the tablet, stopped at the sight of his wife's face, then followed her gaze.

"Wow," said Mr. Greenfield, looking from Morgan to Liz.

Morgan fought the urge to slap his face with the palm of his hand. *Geez, thanks dad.*

"Wow?" said Liz.

"I mean hi," said Mr. Greenfield. "Sorry, we just weren't expecting any visitors. Especially not someone like yourself. I mean, it's just that Morgan here…" Mr. Greenfield trailed off.

Morgan wished he could melt into the floor. He glared at his father.

"Quiet, you buffoon," hissed his mother out of the corner of her mouth.

Liz turned to Morgan, one eyebrow raised. "Aren't you going to introduce me?"

"Uh, yeah," he said. "Guys, this is Liz." His mom blinked at him. His dad made a small beckoning gesture, coaxing him on. Morgan grimaced. "She's a friend from the track."

"Nice to meet you, Liz," said Mrs. Greenfield. "I'm Helen, and this one is Harold." Behind her, Mr. Greenfield was a grinning bobble-head doll.

"It's nice to meet you too," said Liz, taking a cautious step forward into the kitchen. She shook hands with both of them. "Morgan was nice enough to give me a lift after the race."

"Oh," said Mrs. Greenfield. "Did you have a good view? How did Morgan place?"

Liz shook her head. "I wasn't in the stands."

Mrs. Greenfield's looked Liz up and down. "Oh, you're a racer? But you said Morgan gave you a ride?"

"I wrecked my car."

Mrs. Greenfield's eyes widened as she registered the dried blood on Liz's dusty jumpsuit. "Oh no!" She rushed over to Liz. "Did you get hurt, dear?"

"No, I'm fine," said Liz. "The paramedics fixed me up."

Mrs. Greenfield didn't look convinced. "Why didn't you go home? You should be resting."

"That was the original plan." Liz glanced at Morgan, who dropped his gaze to study his feet. "Let's just say my dad wasn't too happy to see me."

"Oh," said Mrs. Greenfield.

There was an awkward pause. Morgan cleared his throat. "I thought maybe we could have lunch here, until things cool down, if that's ok."

"Of course it's alright," said Mr. Greenfield. "I'm glad you're here. Morgan doesn't have many friends, you see. It's nice he's found someone besides that silly car of his to talk to."

"Yes!" said Mrs. Greenfield. "But all we have are deli meats and a bag salad. I wish I had something more well-suited to the occas—"

"That'll be fine, mom," cut in Morgan, his cheeks flushing.

"No worries, I'm not picky," said Liz. "And, thank you."

Mr. Greenfield nodded. "So, you race too?"

"All my life."

Morgan's father put his hands on his hips. "Funny, Morgan hasn't mentioned you before. How long have you two been friends?"

Mrs. Greenfield waved her hands for silence. "None of your business, Harold." She looked from Morgan to Liz, as if she thought it was very much her business. "Come on Liz, some food will help you feel better. Here, let me get you a glass of ice water. Or would you like a Coke?"

"Water's fine," said Liz.

"Coming right up," said Mrs. Greenfield.

To Morgan's relief, lunch went smoothly. He and Liz filled his parents in on the events of the race, although Liz didn't offer any more details about Victor. As curious as he was, Morgan was too afraid to ask about it. He also didn't mention his fight with Victor. Liz hadn't seen that, and he wasn't sure it would be in his best interest to bring it up, especially not with his parents around.

Eventually the thread of conversation turned to the family business. Liz listened attentively as Morgan's parents went on and on. Morgan found himself zoning out, until the conversation turned to Luna Seven. This was his mom's favorite topic as of late. L-7 was a sim-stim narcotic, and one of the most commonly smuggled contraband within the solar system. It had been developed in the underworld of New Chicago, then made its way up to the Moon's surface, and then from there to Earth's space ports and to everywhere else.

"It's a downright epidemic," said Mrs. Greenfield. "And the ISF is completely incompetent in stopping it. They can't catch the small drug runners, so they make a show of stopping the easy targets just to keep the UN happy."

"The freighters carrying our shipments to Mars have been searched dozens of times," added Mr. Greenfield. "Each delay adds weeks to the trip."

"Did they find anything?" said Liz.

Mrs. Greenfield laughed. "Never! We hire only the best traders; honest captains that wouldn't mess with running drugs. Still, the ISF stops everyone they can." She snorted. "All the delays are making the freight companies charge triple for what used to be milk runs. L-7 is killing our business."

"Drugs kill other things too," muttered Liz. "Like people. And relationships."

Mrs. Greenfield looked slightly taken aback. "Well, yes there is that too, of course."

Morgan watched Liz intently. She met his eyes for a moment, then looked away. *I wonder if Luna Seven killed her mom. Mr. Lutstone said something bad happened.*

A chime sounded.

"Morgan, could you get that?" said Mrs. Greenfield.

Morgan got up from the table and walked toward the front of the house, glad for the interruption. He opened the door without checking the holoscan. It was a bad habit, but the home's computer wouldn't unlock the door if it detected any weapons, or if the visitor's face matched anyone with a warrant or a criminal record.

On the front landing was a middle-aged man in a Hawaiian shirt and blue jeans. His finely-trimmed black hair was graying near the temples. The man pressed a finger to his temple and his holographic sunglasses winked out. His dark eyes flicked over Morgan's face.

"Can I help you?" said Morgan.

"I hope so," said the man. He looked Morgan over. "Morgan Greenfield?"

"Uh, yeah." This was weird. *How does he know my name, and why does he want to see me? No one ever asks for me.* The car in the driveway caught his attention. It was a blue Porsche with a crumpled bumper. *Oh shit.*

"Something wrong?" said the man.

Morgan stepped back. "Look, if this is about that fender bender, it wasn't my fault. The guy in front of me—"

The man held up a hand. "Don't worry about that. I'm not after your insurance policy."

"Oh, ok." said Morgan.

"Although I am after you."

Morgan took another step back. The man was short but muscular. He wondered if he could slam the door shut fast enough to keep the guy out.

"I'm just here to talk about the force," said the man.

Morgan stared. "The what?"

"You don't know who I am, do you?"

"No, except that Marc Lutstone said you were a track sponsor."

"Ah, I can see how this is confusing." He held out his hand. "I'm Captain Benjamin Batson, International Space Force. You can just call me Batson. I saw how you drive and I'm impressed. That car of yours is incredible. I've never seen anything like it."

After a second's hesitation, Morgan shook Captain Batson's hand. His grip was crushing. He had a shiny pin on his breast pocket. It was a rocket with four stars underneath.

"So, you didn't stick around at the end of the race?"

Morgan shook his head. He thought about explaining the whole thing, but it was too complicated and he doubted the Captain would be interested in all the details.

"Well you missed my spiel then, but no matter. Have you ever considered a career in the military?"

"No, not really." Morgan pointed down the road at the lab building. "I've got something here."

"But you know about the ISF?"

"Everyone knows about the ISF. We were just talking about you guys inside."

Batson's face lit up. "Really? Good things, I hope?"

"I guess," said Morgan. It was probably better to not bring up the finer points of that discussion.

Captain Batson looked at his car, and then back to Morgan. "Well, I'll keep it quick." He pulled a data drive out of his pocket and handed it to Morgan. "Here's all the standard promotional material. You can watch it whenever. As for me, I'm an old friend of Marc Lutstone. A while ago,

Marc and I realized the skills needed for fighter pilots are the same as for racecar drivers. The Starfighter Academy is short on new cadets. I figured some of the racers at Blairsford might be interested. So, here I am."

"You're a recruiter?"

Batson nodded. "I saw how you drive, and you'd make a great pilot if you could pass all the quals. It's like racing, just in space with lasers."

"Yeah," said Morgan. "I've played the video games."

"It's better than any game. You'd love it."

I probably would. But mom would kill me. And besides, I can't do it. He cleared his throat. "Sorry, you probably didn't notice. I'm a vanilla." He took off his watch and pointed at the scar underneath. "My body rejects all biosynchronous technology. I almost lost my hand when I was six when the school installed the student tracking and health interface."

Batson held up his hands. "I thought you might be a non-augment. Trust me it's not a problem. ISF pilots rarely rely on biotech to fly."

"They don't?"

"Hell no," said Batson. "Bio mods might make a person's day to day existence more interesting, but good old eyes, ears, hands, and feet are all we use to fly. There's less latency, less delay waiting for the implant processors to send data to the brain. Besides, the space craft's user interface can do a better job at sensory enhancements than anything you can build into your eyeballs. Most mods, like muscle cell augmentation or hearing range expansion, are useless in a fighter ship."

"I see." *I wonder if any of that is true, or if he's just trying to bait me.* Someone cleared their throat.

"Oh, hello ma'am," said Batson, looking past Morgan. "I'm Captain Benjamin Batson, ISF. I was just asking your son if he'd ever thought of a career in the force."

Morgan turned. His mom's face went from suspicious to downright accusatory. "Hello," she said, ignoring Batson's outstretched hand. "And no, he hasn't. My son doesn't need a career that involves getting shot at."

Morgan grimaced. "Mom, I can talk you know."

70

"Ok, then tell him," said Mrs. Greenfield.

Morgan opened his mouth, paused, and then said, "I think I have to go now." He patted the thumb drive, which he had pocketed. "I'll think about what you said."

"Good," said Batson. "Tell your girlfriend too. Something tells me she might be interested in getting off this rock. Oh, and I'm glad she's ok. I watched the race record. There was no dodging that car, no matter how good your reflexes are. Tell her I'm sorry about her POD."

Morgan looked over his shoulder and was relieved to see no one else was standing behind his mother. "She's just a friend," he said. "But I'll tell her." He shook Batson's hand.

Batson grinned. "Well, you and your *friend* have a good day." He nodded at Mrs. Greenfield. "You too, Ma'am." He turned, took a step down, and then exclaimed, "Oh, I almost forgot." He pulled two slips of red paper from his pocket and handed them to Morgan. "Here."

Morgan took them. "What are these?"

"Tickets to the ISF's annual space show, all airfare paid. It's next Saturday on Starlight. We're showcasing the new Firefly fighters, and we'll be giving a few rides." He winked. "You should take your friend and go check them out. They're the best fighters ever made."

With that, he left them.

Mrs. Greenfield waited to speak until the Porsche was well out of sight. "What a silly idea, you running off to be a glorified traffic cop in outer space."

"Yeah," said Morgan. He smiled at the thought of pulling over one of his family's freight shipments. *I should do it, if only to spite her!* Of course if he did something like that, he'd never hear the end of it.

"You've got a better future, thank the stars," continued his mother.

"Yeah," he said half-heartedly. *A future collecting samples from zero-g rice paddies.*

"Oh come now, it's true," she said, hugging him. "You're not seriously considering anything that man just told you, are you?"

71

"Not really," said Morgan. It wasn't quite a true statement, but it wasn't worth the debate.

His mother seemed satisfied. "Good. Now, come back inside."

Morgan looked down at the tickets. A trip to low earth orbit wasn't cheap. Could he pass up a free ride? A space show might be fun to go to, especially if he had someone to go with.

Chapter 9

Supreme Fleet Commander, thought Mog. He sagged against the handrail of the transpod as it rushed through the innards of the *Narma Kull*. As a young boy, he had always dreamed of space and of his own command. It was a dream that many boys had but few achieved. Now, at only thirty-nine years old, he had his own ship plus everything else the Navy could muster. Unfortunately that didn't amount to much.

Words from his childhood classes came to him, unbidden.

Ramas: 2:21

There we stood before the rising tide, staring across the abyss at the Destroyers. Azhra, on his dark horse, stared back at me, resolute in his mission. He raised the banner of our father, and as the Ta'Krell swelled around him, he bellowed out our sentence: Death!

He snorted. It was all rubbish. Azhra, Ramas, the whole lot of them. *Then why are the Ta'Krell real? The army of darkness is real! The holy book predicted they would come again.*

His hackles began to rise. "Foolishness," he muttered. "This is not prophecy. They are not the Ta'Krell of legend. They are just using that to scare us. They can be beaten. We just need some help."

The problem was he had no idea where the help was going to come from. He needed dedicated advisors, but his officers had enough work on their hands already. In the battles to come, he would need them focused solely on the operation of the ship.

There was always the chance the Ta'Krell wouldn't find the hyperspace pocket that hid Sledgim. He doubted this fantasy would bear out—maybe they had a few years, but more than likely it would be only a matter of months. Then, he would just have to make do with the wounded leftovers of the once great Maurian Navy. Even Tiarg Noma, the mastermind tactician from the first Talurian war, would dread such an encounter were he alive to command it.

Mog straightened his uniform, savoring the remaining seconds until the transpod reached the bridge. He tried to imagine Mauria as it once was, alive with green and blue. Sometimes, he could almost convince himself it hadn't happened, and that all those people were still alive.

Almost.

A chime indicated the lift had reached its destination. Mog stiffened, and pushed away from the handrail. The doors parted, admitting a melody of beeps and whirrs.

At first glance, the bridge looked like it had nine years ago when Mog had first taken command. A new chair had been bolted to the command platform, its untested leather glistening under the lights. Most of the workstations had been overhauled—he had helped with this himself over the last few weeks, glad to have something to do to keep his mind off other things. The deck plating and bulkhead sheathing had been repaired, and new lighting installed. Still, it wasn't hard to see past the shine. If he allowed his vision to linger, he could see the scorch marks where power had overloaded, and creases where underlying stiffeners had been damaged. He supposed that, like himself, his ship would always carry her scars.

Still, it wasn't a bad patch job for two months.

In front of the helm was a magnificent new viewscreen. The immense display was twice the size of its predecessor, and curved to fit the bridge's profile. It was so large that its edges almost met the glowing workstations that lined the perimeter of the lower level. The image on the screen confused him at first. Then, he realized that he was seeing the latticework of the orbital repair bay that enveloped them. Beyond, there were no stars.

"Are you planning to hold up the transpod all day?" said a gruff voice.

Mog looked to the command platform, where a brown-furred officer was leaning against the railing. It took him a moment to recognize the man, and when he finally did, he leapt out of the transpod.

"Ryal, you're back."

The last time he had seen his first officer, Ryal had been bedridden in sickbay, barely clinging to life.

"You sound surprised," said Ryal. He bowed. "Commander on the bridge!"

All around, officers and crewmen stood to attention.

"As you were," said Mog. He crossed the upper level and went down the short flight of steps to the command platform. "Ryal, I thought I'd never see you on your feet again."

"I could say the same of you."

Mog grasped his friend's shoulder. Ryal returned the embrace. A glimmer of reflected light caught Mog's eye, and he looked down. Ryal's hand was metallic and cold. Mog saw a faint outline of his own face looking back at him from the hand's polished surface.

"Not quite the same am I?" said Ryal, releasing Mog's shoulder.

Mog looked up. "What happened?"

"My arm got cooked during the battle. The doctors on Sledgim tried to save it when we got back, but in the end they gave up."

He rolled up the sleeve of his green officer's uniform. It wasn't just his hand that had been replaced. It was his entire right arm.

"They just cut it off?" said Mog.

"I thought that much was obvious. It's not bad though—this isn't your standard can opener."

Mog flinched as Ryal flexed his hand. Five metallic claws sprang from between his fingers, their edges as fine as any combat knife.

"It's also got a communicator, a scanner, and an illuminator built in. Do you want a demonstration?"

"Do I have a choice?"

Ryal wiggled his shiny fingers. "Not really."

Mog took a step back. The bridge crew had stopped what they were doing to watch.

A terrible screech tore through the air as Ryal slashed his claws through the command platform's handrail.

"Stop that," said Nali from the tactical station. "The work crews just replaced that this morning."

"And they can do it again," said Ryal. "So what?"

Nali hissed at him, but Ryal ignored her. Mog grinned. The war may have taken his first officer's arm, but it hadn't stolen his spirit. "It's nice to have you back, Ryal."

Ryal inclined his head. "You too. I hear your stay on the planet wasn't a vacation either."

"That's right," said Mog. He looked around and found many sets of eyes watching him. There were many new crewmembers whose names he didn't know yet. "Alright everyone, back to work."

The crew snapped back to their tasks. Mog watched them for a moment. Laleg and Vrail were gone, and so was Vrag, the ship's astrophysicist. The replacement officers, whose names he didn't know, had some big shoes to fill.

"When they told me you had Isamal's Syndrome, I thought it was some sort of prank," said Ryal. "You've never been sick a day since you became a commander."

"It's not a normal illness," said Mog.

"Still, I never thought—"

"Enough about me," said Mog, running a hand over his ears. "What about you? The first thing Kremp told me when I got back is that we have you to thank for getting the power fixed before those monsters could board us. How'd you do it? Weren't you in sickbay?"

"Yeah," said Ryal. "Chock full of painkillers from our last fight. I'd broken three ribs."

"I remember," said Mog. "Go on."

"It was pure chance. I was coming around, and the medics hadn't had time to sedate me again. I knew the ship was hurt, because the power cut out and the jolt threw me off my bed. The medic's computer told me what

I needed to know. So, I dragged myself out there and shunted the power to the secondary bus. That's where I cooked my arm and passed out. I didn't know the outcome until much later. I woke up on Sledgim with a surgery team standing over me."

Mog looked into his friend's face. "We'd all be dead if you hadn't reset that relay."

Ryal looked away. "Might have been better off if I hadn't, huh? Considering…the general state of all this." Ryal waved a claw in the air. "Enough of that though. I'm sick of thinking about Mauria. Nothing to do now but get ready for the next one."

"Agreed," said Mog.

"What's the word from the King?" said Ryal. "Are we to fight?"

"We're not going back out there yet. The King wants us to rebuild the fleet and defend Sledgim. We won't be leaving until we regain a modicum of strength."

Ryal flattened his ears. "I thought as much."

"You sound disappointed."

"Aren't you? After what the Ta'Krell did—my hearts burn for Mauria." Ryal took hold of the sundered railing, which squealed as he twisted it with his artificial hand. "I will spill their blood, if it's the last thing I do."

"On that point, I agree," said Mog. "We'll have our vengeance. But we need to rebuild. Without more ships, we'll be crushed. We can't avenge Mauria if we're dead."

"I know. Ruba doesn't sit on the throne because he's stupid. We will follow the King's plan. But, when we are ready, he had better not hold us back."

"He won't. I'll make sure of that."

"You'll make sure? How?"

"I'll explain to everyone at once. Assemble the crew."

Ryal lowered his voice. "You can tell me what's going on, right now."

Mog knew Ryal wouldn't budge until his question was answered. He flexed his claws. "Ruba put me in charge of the fleet. That makes the *Narma Kull* the flagship."

Ryal flashed his teeth. "Excellent. We will be the tip of the spear that skewers their hearts. I'll get the crew together."

Ryal ascended to the upper level, leaving Mog alone on the command platform. He put a hand on the new chair, its virgin leather smooth, lacking the frets of age and war. He closed his eyes, and distant sounds of battle returned, echoing dimly from afar. He would never forget the way the bridge had looked on the day they lost Mauria.

He opened his eyes and the sounds faded. "We'll fight again," he said under his breath. "But this time, things will be different."

Chapter 10

Hrain reclined in the pilot's chair, hoping Angel's ECM system was sufficiently masking their presence as they pursued their target through hyperspace. It hadn't taken them long to locate a Ta'Krell cruiser; one had been skirting the border of Talurian space, executing a jump-and-scan search pattern. He studied the ship, which was magnified on his tactical displays against a backdrop of swirling hyperspace colors.

"They don't get any points for style," he muttered. "Nothing at all like you, Angel."

"No," said Angel. "Then again, my design possesses that quintessential beauty against which all ships fall short. Even the majestic Vinitavi pales in comparison to me."

Hrain stifled his response. *I may agree with her, but there's no sense stoking her ego any further.*

Unlike the *Angel's Fury*, the alien ship was massive and rectangular. Passive scans showed it to be almost twelve hundred marks long and four hundred wide. The ring of engines at the vessel's stern was nearly six-hundred marks in diameter. The emissions from the engines dimly illuminated the ship's hull.

Normally he wouldn't be concerned. He had gone up against massive warships before. But this time was different. This was the ship from his nightmares.

Active scanners would give him away, so he had no topographical map of the target's hull. He had considered reaching out with his mind, but a terrible foreboding had come over him and he had abandoned the idea.

"Well girl," he said into the empty cabin, "Let's see what we're up against." His reflection stared nervously back at him from the cockpit's curving windows.

He straightened up and tapped one of the control consoles, readying the containment field around the reactor for battle. Next, he brought the targeting computer online and locked on to what he thought was the enemy ship's power core. He wasn't sure of the location, but the bulge on the dorsal surface, just forward of the engine ring, was a likely target.

"Ok Angel, get ready."

She chirped at him. "Since the day you stole me, have I ever not been ready?"

"Good point," said Hrain.

What a day that had been. Angel had made the perfect escape vehicle. After learning of her existence from the minds of the government scientists, he'd broken out of the orphanage, journeyed by darkness to the shipyard, and liberated her. The Navy hadn't been too happy. During their escape, Angel had outfought a Vinitavi Class cruiser. It had been the most vicious fight they'd ever been in. *Until today, perhaps.*

"They're scanning us," said Angel. "Broad-spectrum active sweeps."

"Have they raised shields?" said Hrain.

"No."

"Good."

They had closed to optimum firing range. The electronic countermeasure panel showed that Angel's emissions might be detectable. That didn't matter anymore. If the Ta'Krell didn't know they were here, they would in a few seconds.

"Ramas guide us," he whispered.

Angel snorted. "I don't know about your silly god, but don't worry. I won't let you miss."

Hrain ignored her. With a flick of his wrist, he diverted the power from the stealth system into the PPC capacitors. On the tactical display, the three status bars that represented the compression coils for each plasma bank filled with color.

The first shot would be critical. He gripped the flight stick and aligned the targeting reticle. Angel made a few adjustments, and then confirmed weapons lock.

Hrain held his breath and squeezed the trigger.

There was a throbbing whine, and three PPC beams lanced out. The impact, magnified by the shimmering hyperspace eddies, was blinding.

Hrain whooped as the blue beams burned a hole into the Ta'Krell's hull. "Take that!" The vessel's engines flickered out. Angel shot past the stricken ship, which disappeared as it fell out of hyperspace.

"Quack quack!" said Angel in a sing-song voice. "We got you good, you ugly brute."

"Easy there," said Hrain, patting the control panel. "Let's not gloat too early." Still, it had been good. *Thank Ramas.* He switched off the hyperdrive. Outside, the menagerie of distorted colors and looming shadows became the star field of normal space.

He jerked the flight stick to the left and looped back around, his lips parted in a warrior's snarl. Angel told him that the Ta'Krell ship was a few light-minutes away.

"Micro-jump?" she said.

"Do it."

Angel hummed a playful tune as they popped back into hyperspace for a fraction of a second. When they emerged in normal space again, the Ta'Krell ship was a pea-sized speck on the sensor plot. Angel aligned their course and Hrain accelerated. As they came closer, Hrain saw through the cockpit windows a black dearth of starlight where his sensors showed the ship would be. Angel lit her searchlights and played them over the ship's dark hull.

It's massive, thought Hrain. The big ship, tumbling lazily about its central axis, showed no signs of life. "Full scan."

Angel's scans didn't penetrate far into the Ta'Krell's hull, but the damage to the surface was severe. In addition to the hull breach, one of their engine ring support pylons had been shattered. Plasma gushed into space.

"I wish the Empire could see us now, Angel. Maybe then they'd call off their head hunters."

"Don't worry," she said. "I recorded everything."

He wondered if this would change anything. *Probably not.* The Navy wanted their ship back, and Ruba wanted him. The Hunters had been after them for almost a decade, ever since their escape from Sledgim. *We're doing this for our people, not for accursed Father,* he reminded himself. As he glared at the Ta'Krell vessel, he thought of the children he'd grown up with at the orphanage.

They were the closest thing he had had to family, after he'd been driven away from his home in Adula and his family murdered by Paryah's Guard. A pang of guilt struck him as he pictured Nail. He had wanted to rescue her, to rescue them all, but he'd been too afraid. He had run away, failing them utterly. *If the Maurian Navy has been overrun, maybe I can get to them, assuming the orphanage is still there.*

In his dreams, a planet had burned. Which one was it? Nail's voice echoed in his mind. *Azhra has won! Ramas, why have you forsaken us?*

He had left her, and now she might be dead. *I have to know.*

He'd been avoiding Sledgim and mar-Ruba for years. How could he obey the King's command, after what he had done to the children? Hrain could never forgive him. Yet, the King had been right. Hrain could hardly believe it, even with the Ta'Krell ship staring him in the face. *I have to go back.* After this encounter was over, he'd send Ezek the coordinates to the Ta'Krell ship and then set course for Sledgim.

"Angel, are the drones ready?"

"Drones loaded," she said.

They'd gone over this plan en route. One drone would lock onto the enemy's hull and transmit an encoded pulse, a homing beacon to help the Talurians claim their prize. The other drone would enter the enemy ship and scan everything it could, providing advanced intelligence to the Talurians prior to intercept.

They were almost on top of the cruiser. It loomed before the cockpit windows. It was so massive that Angel could fly through the gap between the cruiser's engine ring and hull. Hrain spotted dozens of gun ports, all of them dark.

"Program the scanner drone to enter that hull breach. Find the ship's computer. I want a full download of everything they've got, and if we can't interface with their technology, just cut it out."

"Gladly."

"Launch drones when ready."

Hrain sat back and waited for Angel to finish her computations. He realized he hadn't been masking his mind, so he hastily cleared his mind of surface thoughts. It had been a long time since he'd had to worry about such things. Thankfully, *Angel's* hull was lined with anitheum, which impeded telepathy. *Although it wouldn't stop Azhra, if he's on that ship.* He shook off the thought. If Azhra were on that ship, then Hrain would already be dead.

"Uh-oh," said Angel. "Aborting launch."

"What?" said Hrain.

"Aren't you watching the sensors? They just raised their shields."

He looked up. Outside, navigational lights illuminated the enemy's hull as power came back deck by deck. Gun ports began to glow with emerald energy.

"Nazpah," he spat.

"Watch your mouth," giggled Angel. "There's a lady present."

"Enough."

A shrill alarm sounded. "Missile launch detected," said Angel. "Adjusting shields and readying countermeasures. Quack!"

Hrain thought Angel sounded much too happy. She didn't know what the Ta'Krell were. She had no idea that her creator was one of them. Hrain had never told her. The past was so painful, and he had ignored it, trusting that whatever part he was meant to play could be played by someone else.

As he stared at the warship, he realized how wrong he had been. Drakmara's war had come just as Ruba had foreseen, and no one had been able to stop it. *Yet.*

He grabbed the flight stick and slammed the throttle forward. Angel's wild acceleration threw him back in the seat. A moment later, they were clear of the cruiser. He switched the tactical viewscreen to a rear view.

The warheads were invisible except for their engine exhaust. They only had a few seconds before they caught them. He tightened his grip on the flight stick.

There was a dull clang as Angel deployed two pulse beacons. The beacons drifted for a moment and then went active, spewing electromagnetic noise and chaff into the path of the missiles. The Ta'Krell weapons were not fooled.

Angel tried the anti-warhead lasers next. The missiles' nose cones began to glow, but still they came on.

"Brace for impact," she said. The playful note in her voice was gone.

Hrain waited until the last possible second, then jerked the flight stick back while cutting engine power to one-quarter. He fired thrusters to accelerate into a loop.

The torpedoes curved upwards, but were unable to match the curvature of his climb. They shot past as he completed his loop.

The missiles were arcing back around. He flipped the mode toggle on the PPC emitters and fired a conical burst. There were two flashes of white light, and the missiles were gone.

"Nice work," said Angel.

A second alarm sounded. Hrain pushed the throttle, but it was too late. He was slammed forward against the restraints as wave after wave of transplasma rained down. The Ta'Krell were firing at extreme range, but the onslaught was still enough to destroy most ships.

The *Angel's Fury* wasn't most ships. A guttural roar came from the cockpit speakers. *They've got her angry now,* thought Hrain. *Good.*

Angel swore in Talurian as another blast struck home. "I'm going to kill them!"

"Disable," said Hrain. "Disable them!" He pulled up hard, flying vertically for a few seconds to gain elevation above the enemy before adjusting pitch to face them as he rose. He stared down at the behemoth, and at a rising sea of green transplasma bolts.

He fired lateral thrusters, moving away from their turrets' firing lines. Many bolts still found their mark, splashing across Angel's forward shields and obscuring his vision. The gravimetric distortions, triggered as the hyperspace-jacketed plasma collapsed back into the subspace layer, wreaked havoc with Angel's sensors. Every time a bolt struck, Hrain lost his lock on the enemy ship. He switched the targeting mode to manual and reverted the PPCs back to full beam compression mode. If he could just hold her steady for one second!

"Here, let me do it," said Angel.

Before he could protest, Angel overrode the controls. The nose tipped down half a degree and three blue PPC lances shot out at the enemy.

"Oh," said Angel. "That's not good."

Hrain had never seen Angel's weapons be so ineffective. The Ta'Krell's shields absorbed the blast without as much as a ripple.

He pulled up and accelerated, passing over the Ta'Krell and taking a good hit in the process. Angel fired off a few bolts from the aft transplasma cannon. Hrain spun around on thrusters and fired PPCs and all forward plasma cannons. He held Angel's nose in line with the enemy until the PPC beams had dwindled to nothing, and still the Ta'Krell ship remained.

"Hrain!" cried Angel, her voiced laced with panic for the first time he could remember. "My shields are at fifty percent."

Hrain turned away from the enemy and executed a full burn. *By Ramas' claws, it's a monster!*

The thought of running crossed his mind, but he pushed it away. That wasn't an option. The Ta'Krell must have scanned Angel by now, and they might be able to track her hyperspace wake back to Taluria despite the wandering course he'd plotted. If that happened, Ezek would expel Hrain from the system, assuming the Talurians survived the encounter. He scraped his claws together, remembering what Ezek had said.

Either someone destroyed all hyperspace comm buoys between here and Mauria, or the planet itself has been silenced.

Hrain had checked on a bunch of the communications buoys. They were all transmitting just fine, carrying the usual chatter between the Screll, the Talurians, the Wetu, and the Mekmek. There were no incoming calls from any Maurian-controlled system, and the outgoing transmissions went unanswered. Of Sledgim he knew nothing, but no one sent transmissions to or from there on the standard comm buoys.

Angel was rocked by another plasma bolt. Hrain glanced at the display screen. A stream of blue exhaust trailed behind the nightmare ship as it bore down at them, sending bolts streaking outwards from its bow-mounted cannons.

"They can't be that fast," he said.

"They are," said Angel. She yelped as the Ta'Krell scored another direct hit. "Shields are almost gone."

Hrain fought against his rising panic. *Come on, think of something.* He could use telepathy, but he was rusty, and he had no idea if he could even punch through their hull, let alone his own, without giving himself a brain aneurysm.

"The charges," said Angel. "Use the charges."

That was it! He had forgotten about the two interspatial charges in the cargo hold. *I suppose this occasion is as good as any.*

Interspatial charges had been outlawed after the third Maurian-Talurian war. Still, the Navy had equipped their secret ship with a pair of them.

Hrain keyed in the command to arm one of the charges.

"No, use both," said Angel, her voice desperate.

He hesitated for a moment. *Interspatial charges are hard to come by. I'll probably never find another one.* Then, Angel screamed as a plasma bolt tore through her shields and sizzled into her aft armor.

"Ok, we'll drop both," he said. "But we need to get closer. Set up a power fluctuation in the sublight repulsion coils. Let's bait them."

"This better work," said Angel, as she turned off the engine regulators.

Hrain eased back the throttle with a trembling hand. The nose of the ugly ship filled the rear camera display, flashing with green fire as it rained blast after blast down upon Angel. He lowered his mental defenses ever so slightly, until he could sense something. The Ta'Krell were hungry for information, and they wanted him alive.

"Primary shields are down," said Angel. "Raising emergency screens."

"No," said Hrain. "Leave them down."

The plasma barrage stopped. The Ta'Krell ship was within ten thousand kilomarks, and it was slowing.

He took a deep breath and tried to force the panic out of his mind. "Yes, come and get us."

He opened the payload doors and routed the payload bay camera to a side display. The two bloated bombs crept out on mechanical arms, stopping just past the lip of the doors. Their black bodies reflected dully in the light of Angel's belly.

"They're energizing a tractor beam," said Angel. "If they catch us with that, we're done."

Hrain flipped the release lever. The magnetic clamps reversed, and the bombs were repelled away. They seemed to hang for a moment, traveling parallel with Angel. Then, Hrain reset the engines and went to full throttle.

The sensor board lit up as the Ta'Krell tractor beam lanced out. "They missed!" said Angel.

"Raise emergency shields," said Hrain. "All power to aft emitters."

The Ta'Krell ship slammed into the spatial charges. A white flash tore through space, and Angel shook so violently that Hrain's shoulder popped as he was thrown against the restraints.

On the tactical screen, the huge ship was awash in a field of swirling white light and black pools of spatial distortions. It was intact…mostly. The forward third of the ship had been blown off, exposing flickering internal decks. Debris that normally would have expanded outward in all directions was being sucked in a thick stream towards a point just below the Ta'Krell vessel.

The enemy resumed firing.

"How can they still be there?" he said, checking his displays. The ship was generating a massive hyperspace field that was counteracting the singularity created by the spatial charges. Plasma bolts ripped into Angel's ablative coating and klaxons screamed as the Ta'Krell launched more missiles, two of which made it past the singularity.

"Angel, jump to hyperspace, any heading," he said, as another blast shook them. "Angel, can you hear me? Angel!"

Something stabbed into his mind. His vision blurred, and strange colors played across his eyes. He was drowning. Sparks flew, but he barely felt them as they singed his fur.

A voice, not his own, boomed in his mind.

Son of Ramas. Where did you come from?

He hadn't spoken to with mindspeak since his days at the orphanage.

I won't tell you.

You will. Where!

He imagined Pogue's wall—the mental recreation of the stone wall that had surrounded the orphanage. It had always seemed so solid and impenetrable. *You can't get me in here.*

Outside, thunder boomed. The wall shook. Mortar cracked, and bits of rock crumbled from the top, but it held.

His body was forced against the back of his seat. Angel was talking to him, but he didn't understand her words. The darkness enveloped him, and he felt nothing more.

Chapter 11

Flames flew from the Scorpion's exhaust. Morgan tightened his grip on the steering wheel, his arms tense. Tendons bulged in his neck. He pushed the gas pedal harder, but it was already buried in the floor.

He risked a glance over his shoulder. The blue POD was inches from his door, floating on a pillow of light. *Man, she's fast.* He grit his teeth. She'd never be able to stay with him through this corner.

The turbo hissed as he upshifted. The Scorpion's computer beeped out a warning as they shot past a holographic speed limit marker. The POD dropped back a few inches.

The road ahead veered off to the left. *One more second...brakes!*

The blood drained from Morgan's face as brake pedal descended without any resistance and clunked into the floorboard. He downshifted and pulled the emergency brake, jerking the wheel in a last-ditch effort. It was no use; he was going way too fast to make the turn.

He watched in slow motion as he skidded off the road. The restraining field flared into full power.

"Ahh!" he screamed, as he tore through the guardrail.

He opened his eyes, gasping. Warm beams of golden sunlight streamed into the room. He kicked off the sheets and lurched to his feet.

"Just a dream," he said, heart thudding. When was the last time he'd had a nightmare?

After regaining his breath, he threw on blue jeans and a faded T-shirt. He dug out his leather boots from under a pile of dirty clothes.

As he sat at the desk lacing his boots, he noticed the two tickets to the space show on Starlight Station. He picked them up. Each said:

'Admit One: ISF Lunar Show'.
'Starlight Station Observation Ring'
'Saturday July 13th, 2250'.

He turned a ticket over. Printed on the back, along with the ticket's identification chip, was the message:

'Firefly Demo: Ride Group B. For more information, visit DN:ISF.lunarshow50.civnet1'

He had dropped Liz off last night without so much as mentioning Captain Batson's visit, let alone the tickets. He had been too tired to look up anything and had gone straight to bed after dinner with his parents.

He pressed the ticket against the screen of his desk computer. It loaded the datanet address, and a view of Starlight Station filled the screen. The curve of the earth was partially visible against the backdrop of space.

He flipped through the historical information. He knew most of it already. The station had started out as a joint venture between China and Russia, and had been absorbed by the ISF after the end of the third cold war. On the screen, dozens of ISF and civilian ships circled the station's three massive rings, along with vessels from independent Earth navies. There was a Commonwealth cruiser docked at one of the pylons extending from the core between the top two rings. According to the website, it was a real-time feed.

Morgan scanned the links, paying little attention to 'History of the ISF' and 'Space Force School of Engineering'. His hand hovered for a moment over 'StarFighter School', but then he saw what he had come for. Halfway down the page was a button labeled 'Firefly Program'. He pushed it.

'Error: This page requires the use of a holographic emitter.'

"Stupid thing," he muttered, wishing he had retinal projectors built into his eyeballs like everyone else. He switched off the terminal and got up, heading for the door. Captain Batson's words echoed in his head. *We're showcasing the new Firefly fighters, and we'll be giving a few rides.* He wondered if Liz would be interested in something like that. *Would she even want to go with me?*

He stepped out of his bedroom and into the hallway. He could hear faint snoring through his parents' closed door. *Good, they're sleeping in.* He began tiptoeing towards the main part of the house, grateful for the plush carpeting.

The living room was empty. The ceiling illuminated as he entered, displaying the unobstructed view of the early morning sky. He waved the brightness level down to its lowest setting, then sat down at the computer terminal and scanned the ticket. The ceiling darkened, becoming a star field. Starlight Station materialized in the middle of the room. Holographic ships flew around in graceful loops, passing through the sofa and the arm-chair.

It took a moment for Morgan to find the button linking to the Firefly information page, because all of the links were arranged in a three-dimensional pattern. He poked it.

"Sweet," he said, as the ship coalesced from random photons in front of him. He had seen many fighters before, ISF and otherwise, but nothing compared to this. The ISF's mainstay fighter, the ZX-07, was an aggressive ship with sharp lines and a gray hull. *A clunker, compared to this.* He reached out and spun the model of the little ship.

The Firefly's matte black hull was smooth and graceful. The bow was a pointed ellipse that thickened to hold the cockpit. It flowed into the main body of the ship, which resembled an upside-down garden spade. The hull morphed into two swept wings at the rear of the canopy, each with a cylindrical engine nacelle. Lines marked recessed flaps and fins for atmospheric maneuvering. The aft edges of the wings melded seamlessly into a large central engine at the rear. If not for the gun emplacements, he would have thought it a race craft.

He skimmed through the specs. *Hybrid fusion drive, rocket boosters, ablative armor, gyroscope stabilization, dual-mode repulsors skin. What would it be like to fly this thing?*

"Morgan?"

He turned. His mom was staring at him, sleepy-eyed and pajama-clad. She looked from the floating station to the Firefly, and back to Morgan.

"It's that Captain Buffoon isn't it? He's got you thinking of joining the space force."

Morgan stood. "I'm not joining anything. And his name's Batson, not Buffoon."

"I don't care what his name is. Why are you looking at this stuff?"

"It's none of your business."

"It is," she snapped. "Whatever notion he put in your head, you can drop it right now."

Morgan clenched his fist. *Why does she have to be so controlling?* He shot her a dark look, took a breath, and tried to calm down. "Actually, it's got nothing to do with joining the space force." He pointed at the Firefly, which his mother was regarding with distaste. "The Captain told me about this new fighter they'll be showcasing at Starlight Station on Saturday. It's called the Firefly." He paused. "There's a space show. Batson gave me some tickets. I wasn't going to go, until I realized that Liz might, maybe, be interested in going."

Her scowl softened. "The girl from yesterday?"

"Yeah. She likes cars, so I thought she might like ships too."

"I see." His mom came into the room and put a hand on his shoulder, her brow knitted together as she tossed the thought around. "I knew there was something going on between you two."

Morgan shrugged. "Yeah, she's really cool. And, well…" he trailed off.

"Well what?"

"Well, she's pretty cute too." He felt himself blushing and looked away.

"So you noticed that, huh? Well, I'm glad you have an appreciation for the other half of the human race! I was beginning to think you didn't care about finding someone."

He winced and looked down. *Of course I care! It's just that all the girls at school think I'm weird, or stupid. Amie Han said I was the most boring kid she'd ever met.*

"Hey, I didn't mean to get you all riled up," she said, hugging him. "I just want you to be happy. You know you can tell me anything."

He nodded. "I know. It's just that girls aren't into vanilla guys."

"That is not true, and don't use that silly word. Morgan, look at me. You are my special boy and I love you. You are handsome, smart, and kind. There is nothing that technology can add that will make you any better than you already are. Someday a lucky young lady will realize that."

"I guess." He paused. "Liz didn't seem to mind. She said different was good. That's why I thought she might, you know, want to hang out."

"Ha! See, what did I just tell you?"

"Do you think she could mean it?"

"I don't know why else she would say it." She indicated the space fighter, which was still hovering over their heads. "Did you ask her to go with you yet?"

"No."

"Then what are you waiting for?"

He gaped at her.

"I know what you're thinking," she said, regarding the Firefly. "And yes I changed my mind. You can go. Just promise me you'll come back down to Earth for your second date." She caught him up in a bear-hug, nearly squeezing the air out of him.

"I promise," he gasped. "Come on mom, let go before I need an ambulance!"

Chapter 12

Being back on the bridge of his ship was the best medicine Mog could have hoped for. It anchored him, offering purpose in a shattered existence. As such, he was justly piqued when the ship's doctor ordered him to his quarters, citing the post-discharge care regimen.

Kalesh var sai. Too bad Saran wasn't sent to the dark place by the Ta'Krell.

Of course that was exaggerated sentiment. Mog had often butted heads with the old surgeon, but Saran was a valued crewmember and, if not a friend, a steady acquaintance. This was just a proper continuation of their relationship. In a way, being sent to bed was a relief.

Mog stripped off his uniform and threw it in the corner for the steward to collect in the morning. He showered, ate the simple meal of stew and bread that the cook had laid out for him, then rolled into bed.

"Lights off." He darkened his bedside window, pulled the blanket over him, and closed his eyes.

In old stories, many seafaring captains could find no rest on land. After a lifetime spent plying Mauria's rolling seas, dry land became alien to them. So it was for Mog, although it wasn't the stillness of space that calmed him. It was the support of hard deck plates against his footpads, the tug of artificial gravity, and the subsonic hum of the interstellar drive.

The *Narma Kull* was an old ship, built a half century ago near the end of the last Talurian war. She lacked amenities of modern naval vessels—things like painted walls, synthetic forests, and acoustic damping of the space frame. She had been built to end a war, and these things had been far from the minds of the designers when they drafted the blueprints for the mighty Vinitavi.

When Mog had assumed command nine years ago, he had been taken aback by the unapologetic simplicity and undiluted power the old ship exuded. She made the three-year-old Navy corvette on which he'd cut his teeth seem like a luxury liner, and he'd had a hard time adjusting. Now the throb of her reactors soothed him like his father's cooing had when he'd been a pouchling. *Narma Kull.* It was an old name, from a tongue mostly forgotten in the Empire, but not completely unknown to the clans of Ganjon. *Dire Wolf.*

He was just sinking into oblivion when the door chimed.

He waited, wondering if this was another hallucination of Isamal's syndrome. He still wasn't free of them, although he was getting better at recognizing them for what they were.

The chime sounded again. *No, not a hallucination.* He grunted and called for lights. The steward had laid out a new robe, this one embroidered with the insignia of the Naval Command Office. Mog looked around briefly for his old night robe and, not finding it, threw the gaudy thing on.

"Enter," he growled.

The doors parted, revealing the ship's young helmswoman. Meela hesitated in the corridor. "Commander?"

Mog wasn't sure if that was a greeting or a request to enter. "Boardman," he said. "What can I do for you?"

Meela's eyes darted uncertainly from side to side. "I was wondering—I know you just got back, but I wanted to know if I could talk to you. About what happened."

Meela was the youngest member of his bridge crew, assigned shortly before the start of the Ta'Krell conflict. She was a great pilot, but he knew little else about her. He'd always regretted that he'd never had the time to get to know her like the others. *War has a way of doing that.*

He tipped an ear. "Come in." He gestured at the small circular table where he took his meals.

She bowed and sat down. Mog closed the doors. "Tea?"

She bowed again without meeting his eyes. "Please."

Mog ordered up two mugs of hot Talurian tea with extra spice. He sat down across from Meela. *She's won't look at me. Why is that?*

"Sir," she said, as she picked at her claws. "How does one do it?"

"Do what?"

"How do you go on? How do you live after everyone you've ever loved is gone. Your mother, your father, your sisters…your lover." She met Mog's eyes then, and hers were full to overflowing. "Did you lose anyone, Commander?"

Mog felt his lips pulling back in a snarl and had to fight for composure. If he'd know this was what she'd meant to talk about, he wasn't sure if he would have let her in. "Of course I lost people. We all did."

"Then how do you do it? How did you walk back onto the bridge like nothing happened?"

Like nothing happened? The room swayed, and suddenly he was in the foothills beneath the mountains. The Ganjon forest burned. His mother was screaming for his brother. *Nam, run! Get away from here! Get to the ocean!* But Nam couldn't run fast enough. They were bombing the coast from orbit…streaks of fire and flame ripped through the air into the cliffs beyond, and the earth split apart. *No escape.*

Mog started at the door chime. It was the steward with their tea. He excused himself to let the man in. By the time the steward left, the imagery had faded from his mind, leaving only the faint smell of burning wood. *No, no that's the tea.*

He took a sip of the tea, which was much too hot and burned his tongue. He winced, then took another sip. "I lost my only brother," he said quietly. "And my parents. They were old, but still lived in our ancestral home in the mountains. I suspect I also lost many more than that. Old friends…to tell you the truth, I haven't yet tallied my loss. I've only had my mind back in order for a short while, and to keep it that way I focus on the task at hand."

Meela bowed her head. "I've tried that. But I'm a combat pilot trapped on a ship in space dock. Sir, I don't know how to weld hull plates or solder circuits. When I'm on duty, I sit there waiting for someone to give me some mundane task to do. I've calibrated the helm console a hundred times. Do you know what I do while the computer is running its diagnostics?"

Mog tipped an ear.

"I pray to Ramas for the souls of my family. I pray that I'll get a message from Vurl, but I know in my hearts that he's gone. He wasn't even on Mauria, but the merchant ship he served on hasn't been heard from in months."

"I'm sorry."

"Me too." Meela pushed her tea away. "I'm sorry sir, I shouldn't have bothered you with this."

As she stood to leave, Mog reached out and put a hand on her shoulder. "It's no bother. Please stay."

She hesitated. "Are you sure?"

"Yes."

She sat back down, wiping at her eyes. *She's too young to have to go through this, barely older than Nam.* Mog looked out the window at Sledgim. *Why couldn't this planet have died instead of Mauria?*

Meela was watching him uncertainly. He cleared his throat. "My parents were old when they had me. The doctors said they were too old, and that it was a bad idea to try. But they had met late in life, and had both always dreamed of a family. So, they tried anyway. When I was born, my mother was nearly seventy years old. And when Nam came, she was seventy-five.

"There were complications with my brother. One of his hearts had a hole in it at birth, and they almost lost him then. The surgeons gave him a new heart, but it was never the same. He always was slow to develop. If you were ever to look through the old family image files, you would see that my clan has always been large of stature. But not Nam. He was always so small…he could fit in dad's pouch until he was six years old.

"At first, when he came, I didn't pay him much attention. But then as the years went on and my parents had to spend more and more time with him, I grew to resent him. For ten years I hated my little brother, and I made sure he knew it. Yet, for some reason, he still loved me, still looked up to me."

Meela shifted in her seat. Steam wafted from her forgotten tea. After a long moment, Mog pointed at it. "That should be nearing the perfect temperature right about now."

Her ears twitched. "Sir, why are you telling me this?"

"Because Talurian tea is no good cold."

"No, I meant—"

"I know what you meant." He closed his eyes. *I will not cry.* "I'm telling you because I've never told anyone, and if I don't do it now I never will. Now, where was I?"

"Your brother loved you."

"Yes, yes he did. I still remember the day when I told them all of my decision to join the Navy. My parents begged me not to go, but Nam said nothing. I thought at the time he must be glad to finally be rid of me. It wasn't until my father's stroke five years later that I learned differently. I went home, for the first time in two years. Nam was there, and we had this long talk.

"I won't bore you with the details, but suffice it to say that he was proud. He didn't want me back there, because he knew I could do things out here that he could never do." Mog waved a claw around. "He was selfless, my brother. Mother was too old to care for our father, so Nam left the university where he was studying to be an architect. He stayed at home with my parents. He was there in Ganjon right until the end.

"He never blamed me for not returning. In his letters, he always seemed so proud that his older brother was a boardman in the Navy. It was strange, Meela, but in absence I grew closer to my brother than I'd ever been when we were children. A year ago, there was this family reunion that Nam organized. Father was ailing, and Nam somehow convinced even the most distant members of the Old Salt River clan to come back to Mauria."

"It must have been something special," said Meela.

Mog looked away. "I don't know. I...I made an excuse. I didn't go. We were on a mission—this was just before you joined our crew. It was the mission where our old helmsman deserted. When that happened, I remember wondering if we were still fit to carry it out. Kah is a decent helmsman in a pinch, but that mission required some fancy flying."

"Kah is no ace," offered Meela.

"No," said Mog. "The universe had given me an out, yet I refused it. I ordered the crew to press on. Kah got the job done well enough, although we took a lot of damage. Looking back, I so wish I'd aborted and turned us towards Mauria. I missed my chance, Meela. You see, I never saw Nam or my parents again."

Meela said nothing. She'd stopped looking at him some time ago to hide her face in her hands. He listened to her ragged breathing for a moment, then stood and went to his desk, withdrawing a folded note from one of the drawers. It was strange to hold paper—why he'd printed it he couldn't say.

"Here," he said, handing it to Meela. "I want you to read that."

She took it without looking at him. "What is it?"

"The last thing Nam ever said to me. A hyperspace letter."

She unfolded it and began to read. When she was done, she folded it neatly and handed it to Mog. "He wanted to help too."

Mog slipped the note into his robe's pocket. "You asked how I carry on like nothing has happened. Well, I carry on, and I may look like I've got it together on the outside, but on the inside I burn."

"Why don't you end it then?" said Meela. "Like Laleg did?"

"Do you want to end it?"

Meela gazed out the window. "Sometimes, when I'm walking back to my quarters, I take the long way around. I go past airlock two, and I think about how easy it would be to just slip inside and close the door."

"Don't."

Meela turned back to him, her eyes razors. "Why not?"

Mog reached out and took her hand. With his other, he patted the note in his pocket. "All I know is that my brother would be here on this ship if he could, trying to help. That's what he did." He indicated the planet. "On that dreary rock, and perhaps lost in the black, running and afraid and alone, are people just like Nam. People like…what did you say your mate's name was?"

"Vurl."

"People like Vurl. If they're alive, we're the only hope they have at life. If they're dead…we're the only ones who can avenge them."

Meela sniffed. "How do you avenge an entire empire? How far would you go?"

"I don't know. It might not even be possible for a long time."

"But if—when—it is possible, will you do what it takes to avenge them all?"

Mog looked down at the bleak rock whose mines had fueled the Maurian war fleets for a millennia. They had resources. They had shipyards. And, so far, they were hidden. How long would it take? How long could he wait? Maybe the Ta'Krell would never come. Maybe they thought they had silenced the Maurians once and for all. In that case…*Out of the silent planet comes death…death to the Ta'Krell.*

"Would you do it?" said Meela. Her eyes bore into his soul. "If you could find the planet where these monsters came from, would you avenge your brother?"

In his mind, Nam screamed as he burned. Mog's answer was hardly a whisper. "Yes."

Chapter 13

At breakfast on Monday, the question Morgan feared had been ripening within his mother finally burst out of her like a zit. "So, have you called that girl yet?"

It was too bad Morgan couldn't grow a beard like his dad. On occasions like this one, they were useful for hiding blooming cheeks. "Come on mom, it's only been a day!"

"It's a fair point," said his father from the other side of the table.

Helen shot her husband a look, and he quickly went back to pushing his eggs around on his plate.

Morgan stared down at his bacon. *That's the reason. If I called right now it would be obvious that I'm desperate. Got to play it cool.*

It wasn't until Tuesday morning when he realized he'd been kidding himself. He pointed his toothbrush at the mirror. "You're a coward." He spat, straightened his hair, and went back to his bedroom, snatching his phone from the nightstand. *What do I say?*

Now that he'd come this far, he realized he hadn't thought about the actual asking. He couldn't just call her and say any old thing. That was a surefire way to screw it up. He needed a script.

It was a good thing the research lab had loads of hiding spaces. He spent much of the morning between crates at the loading dock, slowly indexing pallets while recording and re-recording sentences into his phone. He played the latest version to himself, then promptly deleted it. *The trick is to sound excited and disinterested at the same time. That last one was way too eager.*

Later that day, when he went back to the house for lunch, his mother showcased her multi-tasking ability by grilling salmon and her son at the same time. "Morgan, stop making excuses and call her already. People make plans! If you don't call her now someone else will."

Morgan grimaced, wishing he'd taken a working lunch back at the lab building with the scientists. "I know, I know, I'll call her tonight," he yelled back towards the kitchen. *I will. I really will.* He set his jaw, but beneath the dining room table his knees were trembling.

"If you want, I can give you a few pointers," said his dad from across the table. "I've got some good one-liners from back in the day. Worked pretty well on your mother."

"Ick," said Morgan. "No thanks, I've got this."

"Suit yourself."

At work on Wednesday, Morgan was a zombie. He disliked coffee, especially the stuff served at the lab's autocafé since it gave him indigestion, but today he welcomed the bitter brew. He was on his third cup by nine o'clock as he did his rounds, inspecting the hydroponic samples. It wasn't a necessary task, since the growth indices could easily be recorded by the lab's computer, but summer jobs often demanded such work, if only to keep teenaged interns out of everyone's hair. Today, Morgan didn't mind at all.

He'd slept terribly. His mind had run amok all night, imagining the horrible and demeaning ways a guy could get rejected. With respect to Liz, it boiled down to four scenarios. He'd imagined them all as stick-figure cartoons, because for some reason that was a little less painful.

In scenario one, a dopey stick boy calls a pretty stick girl with the intent of asking her out. She answers (gasp!). Stick boy then proceeds to choke up as she repeatedly says 'hello', until finally he disconnects. Sometimes, this one ends with the phone being thrown across the room.

In scenario two, the boy calls the girl but the girl is not there. Immensely relieved, the boy hangs up the phone, glad that no stick friendships will be ruined this day.

In scenario three, the boy calls the girl and she answers (gasp!). Somehow, he actually gets the words out of his mouth. Cue awkward silence (or, in a few of the scenarios, muffled giggling). The girl, being nice, lets him down gently with one of a variety of excuses. Friends-zone is preserved, but boy still feels like he's been eviscerated. He hangs up the phone and morphs into a stick-figure dog, which then slouches off with his tail between his legs.

The final scenario was the worst, and it was the one that had kept Morgan up until four in the morning. It was still stuck in his head now, as he walked towards bay six to sample the fertilizer mix. In this one, the boy actually gets sensible words out of his mouth when the girl answers. The girl seems surprised. She pauses, saying nothing. The boy asks if she is still there, his heart in his throat. She answers. "Yes, I'll go with you." The boy jumps for joy and sprains his stick ankle when he trips over his own bulbous balloon feet.

There was a sudden crash as Morgan walked right into a cart containing the latest formulation of low-gravity wheatgrass. The whole thing went over with a bang. A woman in a lab coat came running, saw the mess, and made a concerted effort not to laugh.

"Here, let me help you with that," she said. Her name was Zeb. She was an old family friend that had been employed at the lab since before Morgan was born.

"I got it," Morgan snapped.

Zeb's eyes were glowing. *Probably texting the other workers about how much of a buffoon I am. She better not be recording.* Morgan picked the cart up off the floor and started rounding up the samples. Zeb was subvocalizing something.

"You can say it out loud," said Morgan with a sigh. "I'm a klutz, I know."

Zeb looked horrified. "It's not that at all. It's just, you mother's on the line. She wants to know why you aren't answering your phone."

Morgan glowered at the scientist. "Tell her I left it in my car."

Zeb nodded, appearing a touch puzzled. "Ah. She wants me to ask you something."

"What's that?"

"Have you called her yet?"

Morgan threw his hands up in the air and stalked off towards the other side of the lab.

Later that night, it was the dread of further questioning along with the strange bravery that comes with sleep deprivation that finally drove Morgan to pick up the phone. He retreated to his room to do it, mindful of his mother's gaze as she watched him climb the stairs. For one gloriously terrifying moment, he thought the whole thing was impossible since Liz had never given him her number.

Of course that wasn't a problem. When Liz had driven the Scorpion, the car's computer had recognized her as the driver and automatically linked with her bioware. It was a simple matter to pull her number out of the Scorpion's memory banks.

It was a much harder matter to actually dial it. He paced the floor of his room, palms sweaty, heart pounding. He'd rehearsed this a hundred times, but could never have imagined it would be so difficult. He started to laugh.

A snippet of something his father's father had told him once came to him. *People fear what they don't know. They fear the darkness. They fear the foreigner. But a fish doesn't fear the water, just like you don't fear the desert heat. Today, I'm going to make you a fish.*

"I've just got to jump in and do it," he muttered. He pressed send and held his breath.

She answered instantly, throwing him off. "Hi Morgan!" *Of course the phone went off inside her whippin skull. At least s*he sounds happy.

"Hi. Uh, what's up?"

"Not much." His phone vibrated in his hand. *She wants to send video?* He hadn't thought of that. He reached out a trembling finger, hesitated, then pushed accept. Liz's face filled the screen. She grinned and waved. Instead of deploying a camera, she was in her room looking into a mirror. It was a common technique used by some people when they were in their own homes. The video feed he was getting was a mirror image of her, as recorded by her own eyes.

She was just as beautiful as he'd remembered. He opened his mouth, but no words came out.

She laughed. "Hold your phone so I can see your face, silly! All I can see is your forehead."

Morgan looked at the lens of his phone's camera and realized it was pointing too high. He angled it down.

"That's better. Man, you look beat. Hard day?"

He nodded. "Yeah, I spent ten hours working for my parents."

"Cool."

They stared at each other. "So," she said. She was twining a lock of golden hair around her finger. "It's nice to hear from you…"

"Yeah." *Just spit it out!* He tried to swallow, but his throat was too dry. The phone flashed a warning that the anti-shake compensation was having a hard time stabilizing his outbound video feed. He sat down on the bed. "Liz, I have something I've been meaning to ask you." He pulled the space show tickets out of his pocket.

"What's that?"

"I…" he looked down at the tickets, gulped, and then the words were there, the words he'd been playing over and over in his mind like a broken record. Before he knew it they'd already exited his mouth.

Liz didn't seem to miss a beat. "Of course I'll go."

"Really?"

She laughed. "Are you kidding? It sounds awesome."

Morgan collapsed on the bed, the phone tumbling from his hand. "Yes," he mouthed silently, pumping a fist in the air. "Yes yes yes!"

"Hey, where'd you go?" she said.

He scooped the phone back up. "Sorry," he said, his voice as cool as he could make it. "I dropped you."

She made a face. "You are a weird one, Morgan Greenfield. But that's cool with me."

Chapter 14

Mog leaned back in his chair and massaged his eyes. Scraping together a fighting force from the remnants of the Navy had not been easy for Ruba. Personalities were the biggest problem, with tempers running high as survivors from various ships were thrown together into new crews. Some ships were scrapped instead of salvaged, often over the protests of their commanders, and the parts sent off to patch up more space-worthy craft.

There was lots of work still to do, and the King had simply tossed Mog into the middle of it. Mog thanked the stars that Ryal and Kremp had already seen to the refitting of the *Narma Kull*, leaving him free to see to the Navy's needs. In order to help him keep up with all the infernal forms, Kremp had installed a wrap-around workstation on the command platform. Now Mog could balance the fleet's resource allocation requests, repair priorities, and officer assignments from the center seat. The workstation also had basic helm and tactical controls, should his officers become incapacitated.

He took a sip of Talurian tea and scrolled through the latest roster reports. In addition to the gross loss of tonnage, there was a scarcity of senior commanders and experienced crew. They had all been called to defend Mauria once the Ta'Krell had broken through the Maurian lines, and most had perished in the fight for the planet.

This wasn't to say all was lost. A few veterans had retired to Sledgim, which Mog refused to call Mauria Prime despite the King's insistence. Many of these veterans had answered the call and come back to the service. Also, there were the deep space explorers that had been away during the war and were only now slowly returning, plus the lucky handful of battle-scarred warriors who had somehow escaped destruction.

He recalled one of the early battles, when the *Narma Kull* took fire from the Ta'Krell for the first time in defense of a colony world.

Meela, plot a retreat course, there's nothing we can do.

His words echoed in his ears, and for a moment he could smell the fear that had permeated the bridge and hear the dismay in his own voice as he gave that order. That colony had burned, just like Mauria would.

The flashbacks weren't as bad now, and he knew them for what they were. Still, the fetor of scorched fur and blood seemed to linger, haunting him.

He sipped his tea.

A tremor coursed through the ship. Mog looked around at the bridge crew, most of them newly assigned from Sledgim's naval college. Almost all were cadets, some with less than a year of schooling under their claws. As before, the youngsters tensed up at the noise, the fur on their necks prickling, ears swiveling in every direction.

It was the *Narma Kull's* third stint in the graving docks, and the repairs and upgrades were coming along smoothly. The shipyard's teams were pulling double shifts to get the cruiser back in fighting trim. One would think the cadets would be used to it by now, but the bangs and clangs on the hull still had them on edge. Most had never been in space before. Before being conscripted, they had grown up as miners, ignorant of the Empire's existence. Such was life on Sledgim.

Mog drained his tea and looked back at the manning reports. He would give anything to have his old crew back, and not just for performance reasons. With so many dead, the *Narma Kull* didn't feel like home anymore.

Laleg, where are you my friend?

He waved a claw, summoning the new yeoman for more tea.

Ryal walked up to the command platform after the yeoman had left with Mog's mug. "The station master says that's the last of them. They're all done. Now all we've got to do is wire them up."

"Good," said Mog. "Our cadets are jumpy enough without the ship shaking all the time."

"Well, they're as eager as the rest of us to kill some Ta'Krell. They'll learn what it's like soon enough."

"That's what I'm afraid of." The last thing he needed was a bunch of bloodthirsty, untrained kids. They might ignore his orders in the heat of battle, or—just as likely—freeze up when the carnage started.

"So," said Ryal, after a pause. You won't mind if I help Kremp wire up the new heavy guns, will you? I've been itching to check them out."

Mog bowed his head. "Not much to do up here except calibrate consoles and fill out reports. Yeah, you're relieved. Go do whatever you want with the PPCs."

Ryal looked delighted. He turned to leave, but stopped, eyeing Mog. "Are you alright?"

Mog licked his lips. His mouth was dry. He looked around for the yeoman, but he hadn't returned to the bridge yet. He growled softly. "I'm tired, Ryal. I'm tired of running numbers. No matter how I look at it, there is just no way to defend this system from the invaders. It'll take decades for the new shipyards to be built, and the ones we've still got can't produce ships like the *Narma Kull*. It won't be enough for when the Ta'Krell come. We're going to need help."

Ryal tipped an ear. "I agree with you. The Talurians are the only ones, though. They might be cold-blooded bastards, but they're a class-one technological civilization. There's no other species like them in a thousand light-years, with the possible exception of the Wetu, but they don't ever leave their sulfuric planet. The question is, will the Talurians help us, after all we did to them? And even if they can help, how in Ramas' holy name do we get them here without tipping off the Ta'Krell?"

"I don't know," said Mog. "But the King intends to find a way."

"And how's he going to do that?"

"I have no idea. Ruba doesn't let me in on all of his plans, but he did requisition a fast courier ship for personal use two days ago."

Ryal's ears perked up. "You think he's going to go after them himself? He's the one that ordered the destruction of that border world of theirs. What was it called? Was full of farms and stuff…"

"Pasture."

"That's the one. They'll skin him and hang his coat up at the palace gates."

A chirping sound from the upper level ended their conversation. It was a communications alert. A few seconds went by, and when the noise didn't diminish Mog turned around. The new communications officer, a short tan-furred male with a black nose and dark eyes, was staring at his controls with an expression of frantic embarrassment. He was middle-aged, not a cadet. Mog didn't recall the man's name, although he was sure he'd known it at some point when he was pulling in the *Narma Kull's* replacements.

"Boardman," said Ryal. "Silence that buzzer before I get a headache."

"Sorry," said the comm officer. "I'm not familiar with these controls. They're more complicated than those on the cargo freighters."

"What's your name?" said Ryal.

"It's Ja'tar," said the officer. He finally managed to silence the alert, but Mog knew the man's troubles weren't over.

"Well Ja'tar," said Ryal, staring up at the man. "I suggest you start memorizing that control layout. You'll need to know where everything is by feel. Muscle memory, got it?"

"Sure, sure."

"That's yes sir," growled Ryal.

"Right, sorry," said Ja'tar. "We didn't keep it that formal in His Majesty's Shipping Service. And, sir, the person on the other end of the line shouldn't be kept waiting."

"Why's that?" said Ryal.

"It's a transmission from the planet. It's, well, His Majesty."

"Well, why didn't you say that in the first place?" said Ryal. "Put him on. Quickly, Ja'tar, quickly."

After a moment, Ja'tar found the button he was looking for. The viewscreen flicked on, and the King's concerned face filled the front of the bridge.

Mog stood. "Greetings Ruba," he said. All around, the crew snapped to attention and bowed. Mog remained upright.

Ruba cleared his throat. "Having trouble with your receiver?"

Mog cast a sideways glance at Ryal. Behind them on the upper level, Ja'tar was probably dying of embarrassment. Mog saw no need to make things worse for the boardman.

"We've been a little busy up here," he said.

"I see," said the King. "Well, I am afraid we are all about to get a lot busier. I just received a secret report that three unidentified vessels are approaching the system. I'm forwarding the data to you. Our long range sensors are having trouble identifying the ships from within Mauria Prime's hyperspace bubble, especially since the ships are generating interference to mask their signatures."

Mog forced back rising apprehension. *We're not ready.*

"When will they be here?" he said.

"It is difficult to tell, but our best estimates put them at our defensive perimeter within eighteen hours. I dislike hasty conclusions, but my intuition tells me these vessels are an advance scout belonging to the Ta'Krell."

The bridge fell into morbid silence. Mog swallowed hard, trying to project an air of confidence. Somewhere in the depths of his mind, a planet burst into flames.

"I beg your pardon, sir," said Meela. "Is there any way to know for sure?"

"Not without launching an active scanner probe outside of the system, where it could be detected in normal space," said Ryal. "That would be a dead giveaway that we're here."

When the King spoke, his voice was almost inaudible. "We cannot take any chances. We will evacuate."

Whispers sprang up from every corner of the bridge. On the upper level, where the officers were farthest away from the viewscreen's audio pickups, the comments were the most heated.

"Running is for cowards," hissed a junior boardman. "I'd rather die."

"Where would we go?" asked another.

"Don't worry," whispered Nali. "Commander Mog would never agree to run."

Mog's insides grew cold. "When will we know for sure if these ships are Ta'Krell?"

"Not until they enter the system," said the King.

Mog kept his face as impassive as possible. Stay, fight, and most likely die. Run, hide, and maybe live.

He didn't have to look around to know that all eyes were trained on him. He couldn't stall any longer. He knew what his duty demanded of him, and as much as he hated to say it, Ruba's analysis of the situation was correct. They should hedge their bets, so that no matter what, the remnant of Mauria had a chance at survival.

"You're right," said Mog. "We should send the civilians out of the system."

The whispers became shouts.

"Only three ships?" said a cadet. "Surely we can defend against that."

"What, are you numb?" said another cadet. "Have you watched the battle footage? Any one of their cruisers is a match for us."

"Early on, sure," said another. "Now we know their tactics, and we've got PPC cannons. We can kill them, can't we Mog?"

Mog looked around. The cadets were young, filled with fire but lacking experience. They had been in classrooms when Mauria fell, not on the front lines. They had no idea what they were facing.

He allowed them to argue for a moment before slamming his clawed foot into the deck. The resulting clang silenced the voices, but tension hung in the air.

"Just one Ta'Krell dreadnaught would be enough to destroy half of our fleet," he said. "If there are three, then we don't stand a chance. We can't avenge the homeworld if we're all dead."

He looked around, waiting for someone to contradict him. Ryal glared at him, but said nothing. The new cadets avoided meeting his glare.

"I am glad we agree," said Ruba. "But I see that this decision weighs heavily on your crew."

"Damn right it does," muttered Ryal.

"My crew obeys my word," said Mog.

Ruba bowed his head. "If our transports start filling now, they should be able to get away before the Ta'Krell arrive. It will be the Navy's job to make sure they escape. Mog, you will take the four most powerful warships and escort the transports to the edge of the system, to a point where they can use their hyperdrives with minimal risk from Sledgim's gravitational influence. Chart up a hyperspace course for Taluria. You will leave as soon as those transports are full. I will take the rest of our ships and stay behind. We will hold off the enemy for as long as possible and destroy them if we can. We will ram them if we have to. The Ta'Krell will not be allowed to follow."

"Bad idea," whispered Ryal in Mog's ear. "What if those are only frigates or scouts? If we keep the fleet together, we can destroy them. Splitting our forces could mean losing the entire system."

"And if they're not just frigates?" said Mog under his breath.

"We could get the Talurians to help. Pay them anything they want."

"Subcommander Ryal," said Ruba. "We have been trying to contact the Talurians since this whole thing started. The Ta'Krell are jamming the hyperspace relays between here and Taluria. There is no way to get a message out, and even if we could convince them, there is simply not enough time."

"How did he hear that?" said Ryal.

Mog waved a hand at Ryal, silencing him. "We will do as the King commands," said Mog.

"Thank you, Fleet Commander," said Ruba. "Begin making the necessary preparations. May Ramas' face shine upon you."

As soon as the viewscreen was off, the bridge erupted with shouting. Mog needed some time to compose his thoughts. As they argued, he descended the command platform. He stood before the blank viewscreen, his back towards the crew. After a minute, he whirled around with a roar, drowning out all other voices.

"I understand your anger," he said, as the clamor subsided. "I feel it too. If there was an alternative, I would take it. But Ruba's right. We could lose everyone if we stay here. We have to save the race." He paused, teeth bared. "What I am about to say does not leave this ship's hull."

"We're going to stay and fight, aren't we?" said Nali. "We'll have our revenge!"

Mog locked eyes with Ryal, who was watching him intently. "I agree with Ruba about the evacuation. The *Narma Kull* will escort the civilians out of the system. However, once we clear the asteroid belt, we'll send the convoy on its way without an escort. Our warships will power down and wait. If the approaching ships are a Ta'Krell force that our combined fleet can take, then we turn back around and fight. If they are an overwhelming force, then we follow the escorts and don't look back."

"We should fight no matter what," said one of the new cadets.

There were grumblings of agreement and dissent. Ryal cleared his throat, and the bridge quieted. "It's a fair plan," he said. "We won't be abandoning the King to certain doom, and we can still catch up to the convoy if there's nothing we can do here."

"It makes sense," said Meela.

"Yes," said Nali. "Thank you sir."

"Don't thank me yet," said Mog. "For all we know, those are three dreadnaughts and we'll have a front row seat to Sledgim's annihilation."

"Or they could be something else entirely," said Meela. "Not Ta'Krell."

Mog tipped an ear. "Perhaps." But, he doubted it. Why would they be running with stealth systems engaged if they weren't hostile?

"That's enough conjecture," said Ryal. "Attend to your stations."

Mog caught Ryal's eye and thanked him with a nod. He strode back up to the command platform and slumped down in his chair. He hated waiting. It would be good to have something else to do.

"Get Nali's new assistant up here," he said to Ryal. "We'll need him to run some tests on the new targeting sensors. I'm going to go find Kremp and help him get those fancy new guns wired."

"I thought I was going to wire the cannons," said Ryal.

Mog grinned. "Ok, we'll both go wire them together."

Chapter 15

Morgan kicked a dislocated chunk of pavement. It skittered along the edge of the road before plunking into a storm drain. He had parked near the entrance of Liz's road, his car pointing away from the neighborhood to facilitate a quick escape if needed.

Liz was still grounded for racing without her father's permission. The plan was for her to sneak out on the pretense of getting the mail. By the time her father realized she hadn't come back in, it would be too late.

Morgan checked his watch. It was almost nine o'clock. *What's taking her so long?* He wiped his sweaty brow and pulled out his phone. How had he ever worked up the nerve to call her? *I can't believe she said yes! Don't screw this up!*

He put his phone back in his pocket.

A minute later, Liz opened the door and came down the driveway. *It's actually happening!*

She was looking down at her feet, but she had the trace of a playful bounce in her step. Morgan leaned against the car door, one leg crossed over the other, trying to look casual while observing her out of the corner of his eye. She was dressed in blue jeans and a faded orange tee-shirt. She had ditched the ponytail, and her hair fell about her shoulders, radiant in the morning light.

Close your gaping mouth, quick!

"Hey," she said, walking up to him. She gestured at the car. "I see you didn't wash it."

The Scorpion was still covered in dirt and dust. He had forgotten all about that. "I didn't get a chance."

"Good, it looks better this way. So, we going or what?" She looked nervously back over her shoulder at her house.

He nodded. "Yeah. Here you go." He scampered around the Scorpion and opened the passenger door.

Liz giggled. "You don't need to do that, it's not like we're on a date."

"Huh?"

She flashed him a look. "Come on, let's go before my dad misses me." She pulled her door closed.

Morgan kicked the Scorpion's tire. "Idiot," he cursed through clenched teeth. He got in the car, his mind replaying her words over and over as they drove off.

It's not a date. You fool!

He'd allowed himself to be caught up in a childish fantasy. Now it all made sense. The laws of the universe had returned to normal. *She's not your girlfriend.* They were just two kids hanging out. She might as well be Greg, his childhood friend that had moved away.

But she wasn't Greg. If this wasn't a date, what was it? *Can you just be friends with a girl?*

"It's so strange that everyone used to drive cars like these," said Liz, as they turned east onto Route 86. She was peering down at the floor, which was currently set to transparent. She watched as the tires rolled over cracks in the road.

"What's hard to believe is that people stopped driving them," said Morgan. "Especially for off-road racing; you need one of these if you're going to race on dirt."

"But what about drag racing? You'd never beat a floater in a drag race."

"Drag racing isn't real racing."

"You're just afraid you'd lose."

"No I'm not."

She smirked at him.

"Fine," he said. "You want to drag race? How about you borrow your dad's POD and we have a go at it."

"You're on," she said.

Somehow, Morgan managed a smile. *At least she's a friend. You can be happy with that, can't you?*

Ground traffic was light, since it was Saturday and they were still twenty miles out from the sprawl. Their conversation shifted to driving in the desert, the moral implications of ignoring speed limits when there wasn't anyone around to see you speeding, and the best places to eat this side of Tucson. Now that the pressure was off, conversation came easy.

It was almost nine thirty when they pulled into the bus terminal. He had no trouble finding a vacant spot next to the single boarding platform. The dilapidated shuttle bus, known to the locals as the Hopper, was hovering alongside the platform with its doors open. The ancient LED screen above the doors read "Next Stop: Tucson."

The message might as well have been painted on the bus's side, as Tucson was the only place one could go to via the Hopper nowadays. It was essentially a puddle jumper that let you skip over the sprawling suburbs and get straight to the heart of the old city, saving an hour or more of driving. Once at the air and space hub, you could go to anywhere in the Commonwealth.

"We've gotta move," said Liz, throwing open her door. "Mac takes off at nine thirty."

Morgan killed the engine. He grabbed his backpack, which his mom had packed with snacks for two, and got out. Liz was already climbing up to the platform, weaving her way through a tightly packed group of camera toting tourists that was coming down the stairs. Morgan followed.

Blairsford was a common landing spot for the few tourists seeking to visit what was left of Saguaro National Park, which wasn't much after the Protected Lands Act of 2100 had been repealed in the name of affordable suburban housing. It was easier to get to the park from here than to try to land in Tucson and charter transportation out of the congested city.

The Hopper had seen better days. The deck was crooked, and sagged even more to one side when they boarded. In front of him, Liz waved her hand across Mac's sensor array, and something chirped in

117

acknowledgement. Mac was the robot who functioned as the interface between the Hopper's computer and the human passengers.

Morgan pulled out his phone. "What's up Mac," he said, waving his phone. The slit in the metal man's face lit up with a green flash.

"Hello Morgan Greenfield," it said. "It has been four months, twelve days, and six point seven hours since you last boarded."

"If you say so," said Morgan, looking around. "Sorry that nobody's given you a tune-up since then."

"This unit is not in need of repair."

Morgan pocketed his phone. "Whatever you say." He turned and followed Liz down the aisle.

"Enjoy your ride," said Mac.

The bus was less than half full, and they found seats easily enough. Morgan looked around. *Zombies everywhere.* With few exceptions, the other passengers were all staring off into space, their eyes aglow as they did their online shopping, played games, and who knows what else.

The doors clanged shut, and the bottom of the bus seemed to drop out from under them as the repulsors cycled from park to drive.

"I hate this thing," said Liz. "My dad and I made a few trips back and forth on it when we were looking for houses in Blairsford."

"It is pretty sketchy," agreed Morgan. *Weird, she never mentions her mom. Mr. Lutstone said something bad happened. I wonder if her parents got divorced.*

It wasn't the sort of thing he felt comfortable asking her. He opened his backpack and pulled out a granola bar. "Want anything?"

She shook her head. "I ate a big breakfast. I might grab a snack in Tucson."

A deep humming reverberated up through the Hopper as the stabilizer wings extended. A moment later, the seat pressed into his back and the bus shot upward. Then, with a slight lurch, the repulsors disengaged and the thrust pods fired.

As they tore through the sky towards Tucson's space port, with the city spread out far below them, a silly thought came to Morgan. Just what would his parents do if he didn't return? What if he found a job on the station? He could hide away up there, leaving Greenfield Grain and that humdrum future far below. He could even take Captain Batson up on his offer, assuming he could transfer the money for flight school admission from his account before his parents figured out what was going on.

You'll never do it, whispered the voice in his head. Mom would cry for days, and dad would look like a kicked puppy. They were counting on him to take over the business. Maybe the space force had part-time positions. He could run Greenfield Grain by day and intercept Martian pirates by night. He imagined the ruckus it would cause, landing a Firefly behind his parents' house at 5 AM.

"What's gotten into you?" said Liz.

Morgan jumped. He realized he'd been chuckling. "Nothing," he said.

Liz eyed him suspiciously. "You are loving this, aren't you?"

"What?"

"Don't try to deny it. You're trying to pass this off like it's nothing." She deepened her voice, "Hey I was thinking, instead of racing on Saturday maybe I'd go up to Starlight to see this space show thing they've got going on. I've got two tickets, and I figure I might as well use them. You know, it might be interesting, if you had nothing going on."

"Did I really say it that way?"

She tapped her ear. "I've got the whole thing recorded. You made it sound like you were going to the grocery store." Her face lit up. "Drop the act already. We're going to space!"

A few passengers turned to look at them. Morgan blushed. "Ok, you got me. It is pretty cool."

"Say it with some conviction," said Liz. "Space here we come!"

"Here we come!" He smiled. It felt good, whatever this was. *So what if it's not a date.*

Chapter 16

Since the last watch, two Navy bulk transports had launched, carrying forty thousand people into orbit. The first ship held Sledgim's elite, primarily individuals from the southern continent. These people were a rarity on Sledgim: geologists, physicists, chemists, doctors, engineers, philosophers, and theologians. Handpicked by the King and his chief advisor mar-Drakmara, these lucky ones had been allowed to take their families and closest friends.

The second transport contained a broader sampling of the general population, including the surviving refugees from Mauria, Sledgim's historic families, some merchants, and any remaining relatives of Navy officers and crewmen. Leader Paryah had elected to stay below. Mog had reviewed this last group and had found that Kremp and a number of the crewmen had relatives on that transport. The rest of the *Narma Kull's* crew had lost their families when Mauria burned.

He remembered the last thing his little brother had sent him. A simple communiqué, just after the war had started.

Mog, it's been ages. When are you coming home to visit? You don't have to answer. I know with the war on, it'll be a while.

That's why I'm writing this. I'm joining the Navy. Our parents hate it, but they don't understand. We must win this fight! Besides, I can't let you get all the glory. Do you have room for one more on that ship of yours?

The word is the aliens call themselves the Ta'Krell. That's got to be some sort of joke, right? Anyway, you probably can't tell me what's going on, but it would be great to hear from you.

Love you always,

-Nam

Mog had dug that letter out and read it over and over, until the words were engrained in his mind. *Why didn't I respond? I was too busy. We were on deployment. Excuses, lame excuses.*

He wiped his eyes and pushed the thoughts away. He didn't have time to dwell on his own sorrows when there were still six half-empty transports on the planet's surface. The unidentified ships were seven hours away. There were riots in the streets as Sledgim's miners—who had only just learned of the Empire's existence and their potentially imminent eradication at the hands of storybook demons—stormed the spaceports. The Navy maintained a tenuous guard around the transports, admitting individuals based on a hastily-devised lottery system. Mog wondered how much longer they'd be able to keep the crowds from overrunning the checkpoints. The word had spread. If the three approaching ships were Ta'Krell heavy cruisers, then the majority of Sledgim's three hundred thousand inhabitants were doomed.

Tension was high on the bridge of the *Narma Kull* as the officers worked to coordinate the dozens of hodgepodge craft that had scrambled through the skies and into space. Leader Paryah's government had collapsed soon after Ruba's arrival on the surface, so the vessels coming up were just as likely to be hijacked and full of armed miners as they were to be crewed by the remnants of Paryah's forces. Anything with a working rocket engine had been launched. Some of these ships were relics dating back to the discovery of Sledgim, and had been squirreled away beneath the ice for centuries. System failures were common, and a few had already gone crashing back down to the ground. Many of those that attained escape velocity were dangerously overloaded with confused, angry people who knew nothing about being in space.

In short, Mog's commanders had their hands full, and often had to execute emergency trajectory shifts when panicking civilian pilots risked orbital collisions in search of protection beneath the battle-scarred Navy warships.

There still wasn't confirmation that the incoming sensor targets were Ta'Krell, but no one on the *Narma Kull* or in Ruba's improvised command office doubted it.

After helping Ryal and Kremp run a few superconducting power conduits, Mog had retired to his cabin at the end of the shift. He had returned to the bridge early and relieved Subcommander Uir, the night watch's shift leader. Now, he paced back and forth across the upper level. The crew was attending to their work as best they could, but they were on edge. Ruba would soon give the order for the convoy to leave. If the three approaching ships were Ta'Krell dreadnaughts or heavy cruisers, then the defense fleet would be obliterated and the Maurian population would be all but wiped out.

"Another transport's coming up," said Ja'tar. "We'll be able to see them in ten seconds."

On the viewscreen, a gray pinprick rose through the planet's atmosphere. A minute later, the transport's twinkling windows were visible.

"They're joining our formation," said Ja'tar. The transport, easily two hundred times the size of the *Narma Kull*, slid across the viewscreen.

The *Narma Kull*, being the most powerful vessel in the evacuation fleet, was at the rear of the formation. The three transports, represented by detailed miniatures on the command platform's displays, were at the front, each guarded by a heavy tri-hulled Makura-class frigate. The various other transports, supply ships, and indigenous vessels had no dedicated military escort. These ships were covered by a roving watch of fighters—five squadrons with ten ships each.

Mog pulled up a tactical analysis, but found the details difficult to sort through. The command platform's consoles were not optimized for displaying detailed information. He spent a moment pulling up the vessel registries of all the civilian craft that had converged on Sledgim since the fall of Mauria. The presence of these ships had been troubling him for some time, since it meant that Sledgim's top-secret location was no longer as secret as the Navy would like it to be.

He swiveled around to face the upper level workstations at the back of the bridge. "Nali, do any of the civilian ships have tactical capabilities?"

Nali tapped the sensor controls, and a top-down holographic plot appeared.

"Most of them are unshielded, with only cutting lasers or other tooling apparatus. But, I've identified heavy weapons signatures and shield generators on a few of the craft." She adjusted the controls, and four bulky vessels were highlighted and expanded in three-dimensions. "These all have above a class three armament. According to their registries, three of them are deep space explorers and the fourth is an asteroid miner. Sir, I doubt their captains have the permits for the amount of weaponry I'm detecting. Not that that matters anymore."

"For once I'm glad people don't play by the rules," said Mog. "Send a message to their captains. Order them to offload anybody they don't need to the other transports and to take up defensive positions. They'll be helping us today."

"Right," said Nali. "I also had an idea about those bulk transports. They don't have any guns, so it should be safe for the smaller unshielded ships to fly in close to their hulls. The transports can extend their shields around everybody."

Mog tipped an ear at her. "And keep the little guys alive a bit longer. Good. Pass that along too."

The transpod doors opened and Kremp strode onto the bridge. His gray fur was matted and his uniform torn at the shoulder. "Commander, we're done with the power cabling. I energized one of the guns and took a few readings at the coils. They're incredible! To think, the engineers on this rock had developed these little gems, yet we've never seen them in the fleet."

"Naval Research has lots of projects that were deemed too expensive for peace time," said Mog. "This war came on too fast. At least we have the weapons now. Let's hope it's not too late."

"They'll work, sir," said Kremp. "I've been going over the design with the physicists who created the projectors. It's cutting edge particle manipulation. I've been saying all along that annular beam compression combined with the right capacitors would triple the charge intensity and maintain power flow. Well, now we've got them, and we might finally have something that'll hurt the Ta'Krell."

"Here's to that," said Nali. "Too bad we don't have the time to put a dozen of them on every ship. Then we might actually have a chance."

"When can we test them?" said Mog.

"Soon," said Kremp. "Hopefully, in a few more hours. We still aren't done reinforcing the hull."

"Alright," grumbled Mog. He had hoped they could run a test this minute. Blowing up asteroids was always good stress relief. "Let me know as soon as they are operational."

"Yes sir," said Kremp. He shuffled excitedly from one foot to the other. "Also sir, the report on the guns isn't the only reason why I came up here. I've got something else to show you."

Mog raised an ear.

Despite the fact that Kremp was older than the rest of them by nearly fifty years, his face glowed with boyish enthusiasm. "On a hunch, I've had the computer working on something all night. The results just came in. I think we can win this fight!"

"Well, go on then," said Mog with a slight growl.

"According to my calculations, there are actually twenty ships coming at us."

"Twenty?" Mog gaped at the engineer. How could the man think this was good news? "I thought there were only three ships."

Kremp plowed on, oblivious to Mog's bared fangs. "Yes, well, there are actually twenty, flying in three separate hyperspace layers in a tight formation. But the thing is, they're a recon fleet. Little guys, Mog! Except for one of them, the ships don't have enough mass to be much larger than frigates. I don't know what they're planning, but if they attack us directly we'd be pretty evenly matched in terms of gross tonnage."

"I thought they were scrambling our sensors?" said Mog.

"That's true, but I got around that." Kremp sat down at one of the science stations at the port side of the bridge. Mog rose and joined him.

"My program filters out hyperspace distortion around spatial anomalies, so that you can scan them better. I adapted it from a routine the early explorers used when they first mapped Sledgim's solar system. Hyperspace distortions do the same thing to our sensors as the Ta'Krell's jamming technology seems to do. They don't usually use jammers, but we got a taste of it early in the war during the battle of Rotan IV, when they got the drop on us."

"I remember that," said Mog. "We thought Screll refugee transports were coming towards us, fleeing their boarder war with the Talurians. But the vessel's signatures had been altered. They were Ta'Krell."

"Yes, yes," said Kremp. "I've been looking at those records, and I realized the similarities in how our sensor beamforming is thrown off. It's hyperspace distortion."

"So you're saying that the Ta'Krell's jammers work by distorting emissions in hyperspace?" said Mog.

"Yes. It only works for ships in hyperspace, not normal space. The Ta'Krell are jamming our sensors by phasing their emissions through a moving hyperspace reference frame that exists parallel to the one they are traveling in. They've probably got some sort of tiny probe ship just ahead of each of their three groups, generating the distortion. I just needed to compensate our sensor timing signals and phase-correct for that extra reference frame during post-processing. The code tweaks were easy. The math was a bit tedious, but I had help from the computer, and from a bottle of Albersen's. That draught always helps one smooth over the rough edges."

125

"Of course," said Mog. *My head's spinning already.*

"Anyway," said Kremp. "Watch this."

An image of the solar system popped up on the screen. There was a cluster of three fuzzy blobs at the outermost edge.

"This is our current sensor data," said Kremp, pointing at the screen. "Watch as I change the beamforming."

He keyed in a few obscure commands, and the fuzzy blobs began to resolve into more definite shapes. Soon, there were nineteen small blips and one larger one, grouped in three distinct clusters.

"Twenty ships," said Mog. "But perhaps only one with enough shield capacity to withstand a blast from our new guns."

"Exactly," said Kremp. "We've never been able to overload the shields on one of their big cruisers, but we have burned through the shields of their smaller craft. With the PPCs…"

Mog clapped the engineer on the back. "If this is right, then they can't crush us like they did at Mauria. What do you suppose they're doing?"

"I'm not done yet," said Kremp. He made a few more adjustments to the program. A moment later, a collection of dashed lines sprang out from the blips on the screen. "These lines represent the hyperspace vectors each sensor contact is taking. They're breaking formation."

"And making a new one," said Mog. He tapped the screen, the threads of an updated defense coming together in his mind. "It's a sphere. They're surrounding the system."

"It looks like a net," said Ja'Tar. They're trying to wrap us up. We should probably get out of here before they cast it, right?"

"That doesn't make any sense," said Meela. "They'd never be able to keep us here with only twenty ships. We could slip through their perimeter."

"I agree," said Nali. "They're going to close in and attack from all sides. It'll be rough, but we can take them. We fight!"

"That doesn't fit," said Mog. "Don't you see? In every fight so far, the Ta'Krell have held the advantage. It's how they do things. If they were planning a direct assault with only twenty ships, they'd be converging into a tight formation, not diverging. No, they're up to something. But what? Trying to bottle us up with only twenty ships is more likely to fail than a direct assault. It's like trying to capture baitfish with a whaling net. The holes are too big."

"So, what are they doing?" said Ja'tar.

"I don't know," said Mog. "They aren't stupid. They must have something we don't know about. Still, against twenty small craft we may be able to save everyone if we hurry. Get me Ruba on the comm."

It took a few minutes for Ja'tar to establish the priority connection to the planet's surface, since Sledgim's communications network had never been designed to coordinate with so many orbiting transceivers, and was full saturated. When the King's face appeared, he seemed older than ever. He was in his private quarters—a luxuriously furnished room that had until recently belonged to Sledgim's leader— and the dim lighting suggested he had been sleeping.

"What is it, Commander?" said the King.

"We have news about those three ships approaching the system." *Good news*, Mog thought. *Who would have thought we'd ever have such a thing again.*

"News? How do you have news?"

"My engineer filtered out the noise. No time to explain. They've got nineteen small craft and one large one, in three groups. They're going to surround us. We'll send the processed data."

He pointed at Kremp, who ran up to the second level to help Ja'tar. Ruba looked down at his display, which cast a yellow glow over his face. When he looked back up, his gaze might as well have skewered Mog to the aft bulkhead.

"Why do you think this is better?" asked the King.

"I...did I say it was better?" Mog thought back and realized that he hadn't got to that part yet. Someday, he would have to ask the King how he read people so well. He cleared his throat and pressed on. "Well, we are thinking it might be better. There are more *smaller* ships. They probably aren't powerful enough to withstand a direct blast from the *Narma Kull.* We can take them out one by one. We'll gang up on the big one and take it down together."

Ruba looked up from his display and studied Mog's face. His expression softened. "You believe your engineer implicitly."

Mog realized it was not a question.

"If your analysis is correct, then we might have a chance. This does not fit the Ta'Krell's methods. Mog, this is an advance patrol. They'll have reinforcements on the way."

"That makes sense," said Mog. "We need to send our civilians out before those reinforcements arrive. It will also make the Ta'Krell more confident if they see us running. We can loop our military escort back around and blast a hole in their ranks. On the initial departure, we'll hide our escort ships in the shadow of the bulk transports, so that the approaching Ta'Krell don't even know we've got a second fleet until it's too late. We can break off and hide in the asteroid belt. Then, when the time is right, we spring the trap."

"I see you've thought this through," said Ruba. "The *Narma Kull* will lead the covert escort force, which will then become the hammer. The rest of our warships will set up a defensive perimeter around Mauria Prime. They shall become the anvil for you to smash the Ta'Krell against."

The transpod doors swooshed open and Ryal stepped onto the bridge. He was covered in grime and he looked like he hadn't slept. "We've got those fancy PPC orbital defense guns tied into the fire control system," he said. "But it's a bit of a hack job. Kremp, there you are! Did you already tell them about the guns?" He paused when he saw the King on the viewscreen. "Ah, hello Your Majesty. What did I miss?"

"Oh, nothing important," said Ruba. "Only that you're getting your wish. Yes Subcommander, the *Narma Kull* will have her revenge."

Chapter 17

They left the arrival platform and merged into the sea of people. The concourse resounded with hundreds of voices, mixed together with overlapping advertisements and the distant roar of engines. A little kid was screaming his head off, begging his mother to let him download some new game. Robotic vendors hawked cheap bioware to unsuspecting tourists, air transports whooshed by overhead, and luggage moved this way and that, sometimes trailing at the heels of their owners but more often following pre-programmed routes towards the terminal buildings.

"It's always a mad house," said Morgan, as he dodged a particularly aggressive carry-on bag. He stumbled over a homeless man who was sitting down next to one of the arrival platforms. The man's back was propped up against the base of the platform. 'Anything Helps' was scrawled across his cardboard sign.

"Sorry," said Morgan.

The man didn't seem to notice. He stared vacantly off and scratched at something behind his ear. It was a loaded data port. Lights flashed as the sim card fed stimulant data into his brain. *I wonder where he is? I suppose anything's better than this place.* Morgan pulled out his phone and transferred twenty credits to the man's data port.

"Ah, thanks," said the man, opening his eyes and seeing Morgan for the first time. "God bless."

"Don't mention it," said Morgan.

"Come on," said Liz, pointing at the shuttle port at the other end of the complex. It was a separate construct from the airport terminals, with an attached shuttle launch pad on the far side. "We need to go there."

Fifteen minutes later, they stepped onto the enormous escalator that ran the pedestrian traffic up from the outside concourse to the shuttle port.

"Look," said Liz, pointing up at one of the two square landing pads above them. "One's taking off." The shuttle was rising into the sky on repulsors. When it was about twenty feet up, the turbines spooled up and it began its diagonal ascent. "So it'll fly like an airplane until it gets towards the upper atmosphere, and then use a rocket to get the rest of the way up?"

"Yeah," said Morgan. "Haven't you ridden one before?"

She shook her head. "I've never been to space before."

She must be joking. Morgan had been seven years old when he had first seen Earth from orbit. "So that's why you're so excited," he said.

She grinned.

The escalator passed through the arch leading inside the shuttle port and dumped them out in a wide lobby. They followed the crowd towards the ticket counter. Morgan walked up to a vacant station and scanned the space show tickets through the computer terminal, which hummed for a minute before uploading two boarding passes to his phone.

"Enjoy your trip to Starlight Station," it said. "Gate one is boarding, so you should hurry."

"Thanks," said Morgan.

"Can I get my pass?" said Liz.

"Sure," said Morgan. He handed her his phone, which she studied for a moment. "Just press the transfer button on the side," he said. "It should recognize your NFC."

"I know how it works," she said. "I've used one before." She pressed the button and held the phone against her left palm. Morgan's phone beeped, indicating the data transfer was complete. Tiny lights coursed across Liz's eyes, then winked out.

She handed Morgan back his phone. "Got a ticket to the moon," she said. "Be rising high above the earth so soon, and the tears I cry might turn to rain that gently falls upon your window, but you'll never know."

"What was that?" said Morgan.

"Just an old song." She sniffed. "I always wanted to go to space, but my mom never took me with her on her trips. Her work wouldn't pay for it, and my dad thought it was a waste of money."

"That's too bad," said Morgan. He hesitated. *Should I ask her about her mom?* He decided to risk it. "Does your mom go up a lot?"

She shook her head. "Not anymore."

"Why not?"

A shadow seemed to fall across her face, and she looked away. "Come on, we need to get going or we'll miss this one, and it's a four hour wait until the next shuttle."

Morgan didn't press the topic. As they hurried to the gate, he scrolled through the boarding pass data. It indicated a fulfilled cost of three-thousand Commonwealth credits. He whistled. *This sure isn't cheap. Of course the ISF probably didn't pay face value, but still…*

The security barrier was the usual hassle, but they made it past the scanners and the faceless droid guards without incident. When they reached the gate, boarding was nearly complete. Morgan scanned his phone, and Liz pressed her palm against the boarding scanner.

When they stepped up from the umbilical tunnel to the shuttle's airlock, they found the ship almost full. The shuttle had about two hundred seats organized in six columns, three on each side with a center aisle between. Their seats were next to each other, about halfway back on the port side.

"Excuse us," said Liz, to the large red-haired man sitting in the aisle seat.

"Of course," said the man. He struggled to his feet and squeezed out so they could sit down. Morgan offered Liz the window seat. He sat down in the middle after stowing his backpack in the overhead. The businessman straightened his suit and sat down next to them.

"There's a lot of airplanes down there," said Liz, looking out the window. The shuttle's elevated launch pad offered a good view of the adjacent airport. "I've flown from here a couple times, but never saw how many planes there are."

"Yeah, it's a busy hub," said Morgan.

Liz turned from the window and started saying something, but froze. Morgan followed her gaze. A guy with greasy black hair was strolling down the aisle, wearing black jeans and a black leather jacket.

"You've got to be kidding me," whispered Liz. "Not again. He *is* following me!"

"He's seen us," said Morgan out of the corner of his mouth.

Two seconds later, Victor was leaning against the side of the aisle seat, oblivious to the businessman's obvious annoyance.

"What's up," he said. "You kids on a date or something?"

Liz laughed. "Why would that matter to you?"

Victor mumbled something that Morgan didn't catch and seemed to lose some of his swagger. He cleared his throat. "Look, I just wanted to say I'm sorry about what happened."

"Oh?" said Liz. "Then maybe you'd consider telling my insurance company that the whole thing was—"

Victor held up his mechanical hand. "Not just about the crash, but about all of it, before. You're right, it was all my fault. I just wanted you to know."

Morgan looked from Liz to Victor and back to Liz. *What is he going on about?*

Liz's mouth was hanging open. When she finally spoke, her voice was shaking. "You came all the way here just to tell me that?"

Victor shook his head. "I'm checking out the space show. I honestly didn't know Captain Batson was handing out this many tickets." He glared at Morgan. "I thought the ISF wanted skilled pilots."

"Stuff it," said Morgan

Victor's face hardened. "Tsk tsk Elizabeth, and to think you said *I* was a pig. You should put a leash on this one."

The businessman in the aisle seat put up an arm. "That's enough," he hissed. "Either you two settle down or I'm calling the flight attendants over here."

"Sorry," said Victor to the businessman. He looked at Liz and flinched. "See, I can't help myself. I am a screw-up. But I am sorry, for real."

"I don't believe you," said Liz. "We are not cool, and I'm not taking you back if that's what you want."

"I didn't say that," grumbled Victor. "I just said—"

"Hey buddy, can I get by?" said a man behind Victor. "They're launching any minute."

"Yeah I'm going," said Victor. He straightened. "See you on Starlight." He glared at Morgan, then went aft to take a seat.

Morgan looked at his hands. *They dated! For how long? Why didn't she tell me?* He bit his lip. *Of course she didn't tell you. Why should she? She's not your girlfriend. Get that through your head.*

A low humming filled the compartment.

"May I have your attention please," said a voice over the intercom.

The flight attendants started their routine while the voice on the speakers narrated. He glanced at Liz. "So, you guys were…"

"Yeah," she said. "We broke up a few months ago. I didn't expect to see him again, but then he turned up at the race. Ugh, I can't believe this." Her expression soured. "I'm sorry Morgan, I didn't want to drag you into this."

He shrugged. "It's alright, you're not the one being the creepy stalker." He considered offering to beat Victor up if he tried anything, but decided that sounded a bit too macho. "Is there anything I can do?" he said at last.

"I don't know. Let's just forget about him and try to have fun. Alright?"

"Sure."

Morgan fastened his seatbelt as the flight attendants mimed their safety demo. A small part of him hoped Victor would try something. *Maybe he is sincere. He followed Liz to the race, sure, but then he got tickets from Batson just like us. It's just a coincidence he booked this same flight to Starlight.* Morgan craned his neck, but he couldn't see where Victor had gone. *I'll have to keep an eye on him the whole time we're on the station.*

"Thank you for flying with Commonwealth Spaceways," concluded the announcement.

The humming intensified as the shuttle lifted off the pad on its repulsors. The jet turbines spooled up, propelling them higher. Liz was gripping the armrest, eyes sparkling, her face glued to the window. Tucson spread out beneath them, a gray patch on the desert.

The landing gear retracted with a mechanical whine, and the shuttle shot upward. They rose until the spaceport was a dot and the city a mere patch beneath them.

"Hi folks, this is your pilot," said a woman's voice over the intercom. She had a faint southern drawl. "We're going to light her off nice and easy, then ramp up for a two-gee burn. You all just sit tight and enjoy the ride."

Morgan looked down at Liz's hand and wished he could hold it. *Maybe, when the engines fire, if I time it right.* Heart pounding, he nudged his hand closer.

The rocket fired, and he was pushed backwards in his seat as they shot through the thinning atmosphere.

"Sweet!" said Liz over the roar.

"Yeah," said Morgan, gripping his armrests. "Yeah!" He looked down at his hand. It was not holding hers. *I am a total wussie.*

Soon they would be in orbit of Earth, their pilot plotting a trajectory to cross to a higher orbit and align with Starlight station. It felt like a tipping point. There were so many possible outcomes, and it all hinged on what would happen over the next few hours. Could he work up the courage to change his future?

Single or not? Come back home or not?

He couldn't believe that he was seriously entertaining Batson's offer, but if things didn't work out with Liz then why not? Being a fighter pilot would be much more exciting than working at Greenfield Grain.

Don't throw your future away.

He scowled. The voice in his head was his mother's, and he was sick of her telling him what to do.

Chapter 18

I will always love you, Hrain. Goodbye.

Hrain opened his eyes. "Angel?" He shoved the blankets aside and sat up, his aching muscles throbbing. It was pitch black. He felt a wall next to the bed on one side.

"Lights. Lowest setting."

An orange glow filled the room. He looked around the vast space. The walls were dull gray and featureless, except for a few shelves and a massive door. He noted the low stone stomach chairs, where a creature that walks on four legs might rest on its belly.

"Thank Ramas I'm alive," he said.

This was a Talurian military quarters. Hrain slumped backwards against a pile of pillows—provided for his benefit since the great lizards didn't do anything soft. Not only was he alive, but he had been rescued.

He looked down at his bare, gray-furred chest, noting the shaved patches where regeneration bandages had been applied. So, he had needed some doctoring up. *What about Angel?* He got up, wincing as he put weight on his left leg.

"Computer, where am I?"

"Crew quarters sixteen alpha, deck forty-seven," responded the machine. It spoke in Maurian, but it had a scratchy voice.

"Deck forty-seven? Deck forty-seven of what?"

"Orbital Station Dominance, Taluria III."

"Home," he mumbled.

The station Dominance (the name being only a rough translation into Maurian of the facility's actual name) was the primary defensive installation orbiting Taluria, and had been his home for almost eight years.

He limped towards the door, grasped the awkward handle, and threw it open. He was in a wide, brightly lit corridor. He squinted in the harsh light, which was made to imitate the Talurian sun. There were no windows this deep inside the space station. Metal ribs lined both sides of the corridor.

"Azhark mn-razha ra vharmsta."

Hrain turned. A relatively small Talurian was standing in the corridor. The creature, a male as evidenced by his tail barbs, was about nine marks long, although four of that was his tail. He was wearing the purple plate armor of a junior officer, and he look annoyed. He stared at Hrain through small black eyes. The slit nostrils at the tip of his snout were twitching.

"I don't have my translator," said Hrain, pointing at his bare ears.

The Talurian's nostrils flared, and he gestured at the doorway.

"Oh," said Hrain, hobbling back into the room. On a shelf were an earpiece and a change of clothes, probably taken from his quarters on Angel. He threw the shirt on, deciding to not bother changing his leggings. He scooped up the translator earpiece and flicked on the power.

"Sorry about that," he said.

The Talurian started talking. For a few seconds, all Hrain heard was unintelligible rasping. Then, the earpiece translated the message using reassembled sounds from the Talurian's actual voice.

"I am Vharmsta, the quartermaster's assistant. The Intendant is expecting you."

"I'm doing well, thanks," growled Hrain. "Where's my ship?"

Vharmsta's beady eyes narrowed into slits, barely visible behind the armored scales on his forehead. His thin tongue flicked out, indicating displeasure.

"Intendant first, ship later," said Vharmsta. He jerked his snout, indicating the passageway behind him. "This way."

It wasn't worth fighting. He wasn't an engineer, and could do nothing for Angel. If he was here, then the Talurians had her as well. *The Mekmek are experts at fixing damaged ships. Don't worry, she'll be alright.*

Vharmsta turned and headed back down the corridor on his four scaly legs. Hrain followed as quickly as he could, wishing he had a pair of earplugs to mute the sound of the creature's claws against the deck. He pitied the Talurian. Having no way to retract one's claws must be insufferable.

The elevator at the end of the hallway could have held a hundred Maurians at once, if they were ever allowed on the station. Hrain was careful to avoid stepping on his guide's barbed tail as he entered. He had in the past stepped on a male Talurian's tale. He shuddered. The pain of those tail barbs was something one never forgot.

"Deck two," hissed Vharmsta. The doors closed and a dull humming filled the elevator.

"I see you guys haven't taken my advice and hired a decorator," said Hrain. "It would make this place much livelier. You might even get some tourists. Wouldn't that be fun?"

Vharmsta's tail twitched. As much as Hrain loved antagonizing the great lizards, it was probably best to save the small talk for Ezek. He at least had the scrapings of a personality.

"Deck two achieved," chirped the earpiece, a moment after the computer rasped something unintelligible.

The doors opened. Hrain wondered if the computer had actually meant to say 'deck two achieved', or if something had been lost in translation.

"This way," said Vharmsta.

"I know how to get there," said Hrain.

A viewing ring ran around the perimeter of deck two, one level below station command and control. Located in the spherical top of the station, the massive oval viewports offered a three-hundred and sixty degree view. Depending on where you stood, you could see the orbital shipyards, the smaller trading station, and the planet below.

The section they were on faced the planet. Taluria was an arid world. It looked like a featureless tan sphere, except for small green and white patches at the poles. One of Taluria's two moons was partially illuminated, a gibbous green and blue object that was the reason the Talurians had made it to space in the first place.

138

Hrain looked around the deck. Most of the people were Talurian, although there were a few groups of Mekmek present. Except for those on break, the Mekmek were at work cleaning the deck and tinkering about in open access panels. He felt their contentment and pride as they worked. There was also a tinge of superiority from two of them as they watched a pair of overweight Talurian guards lumber past. Hrain had always found it odd that none of the Mekmek on the station seemed to resent their lot in life.

The Mekmek were small primates from Taluria's forest moon. Having developed space flight first, they had reached Taluria and helped liberate the lizards from their desert world, only to subsequently be conquered and subjugated.

The station's Mekmek wore simple brown skins that covered their hairless bodies. They averted their eyes as Hrain and Vharmsta walked past. A few were sitting down at rectangular tables, sipping steaming beverages and conversing quietly. The grimfaced Talurian aide ignored the small primates, but Hrain offered them a slight bow, which they returned.

"You know, you guys don't have enough fun up here," said Hrain. "You need to learn how to relax."

"This is a military installation," said Vharmsta. "We don't relax."

And that good sir, thought Hrain, *is why I live on my ship.*

After a three minute walk around the perimeter, they came to Ezek's office. The nearby officers were giving the room a wide berth, going out of their way to walk closer to the station's central core.

"I take it Ezek is in a bad mood," said Hrain.

Vharmsta said nothing as they approached the office door. Ezek's back was visible through the tinted window. The huge ten-mark Talurian was straddling his chair, facing the outer windows looking down at the planet.

"This is as far as I go," said Vharmsta.

"Why's that?" Hrain scrutinized his guide's face, but he couldn't get anything from the reptilian's stare. He got even less from Vharmsta's mind—it was only on rare occasions that he picked up an emotion from a Talurian.

Vharmsta retreated back the way he had come. Hrain eyed the back of Ezek's head through the window, wondering what was troubling his friend.

He extended a foreclaw and tapped on the glass.

Ezek's cracking voice came through a hidden speaker. "Enter."

The door swung inward on a silent mechanism. Hrain went in. "Hello Ezek."

The commander of Dominance Station stood and turned to face Hrian. His golden armor was polished to a mirror shine and flared in reflected light, but his facial scales sagged, appearing only loosely attached to the baggy flesh beneath.

He flicked his tongue out. "Hrain, you need a bath, I can taste you from here."

Hrain snorted.

"Sit down," said Ezek.

Hrain glanced at the belly chairs and wondered how he would go about sitting on one. The contoured stone was meant to fit a lizard's stomach, with concave cutouts to allow the legs and tail to dangle freely.

"I'll stand," he said.

Ezek's nostrils flared. "Whatever."

"Where's Angel? Where'd you find us?"

"First, you answer my questions," said Ezek. "You were supposed to bag me one of those ships. What happened?"

Hrain tensed, but bowed his head and spoke slowly, as respectfully as he could manage. "I will tell you everything you want to know. But first, please, just tell me if the *Angel's Fury* is intact."

Ezek waved a clawed foot. "Mostly."

Thank Ramas. Hrain cleared his throat. "How much damage—"

Ezek roared. "I will get to that. Now, you talk."

Hrain didn't need to be able to read Ezek's mind to know he had pushed it too far. He fingered his whiskers and regarded the big lizard. "We did our—that is, I did my best. I approached in stealth mode and hit them with everything…knocked out their power, sent them spinning. But they recovered and attacked." He proceeded to fill in the details.

Ezek's tongue flicked out twice. "This is not good, Hrain. Did anything follow you?"

"I have no clue. Angel flew out on autopilot."

Ezek regarded him for a moment, his beady eyes giving away nothing. "We may have gotten lucky. Your ship arrived here unpursued. Perhaps their warship was overcome by those charges. If they didn't get a message out, then we might still be safe."

"Yes," said Hrain. *He sounds like he's trying to convince himself.* He and Ezek looked at each other for a moment. *He's scared. As well he should be.* "You said Angel was mostly intact. How bad?"

Ezek shuffled over to his desk and retrieved a pad, then handed it to Hrain. "This is the report that Fleetmaster Uzhrul filed after looking over your ship."

Hrain scrolled through the report on the pad, his insides growing cold the more he read. He forced himself to slow down and read every word.

"As you can see," said Ezek, "Almost every system on your little ship was damaged. Some hull segments yielded and will need to be replaced."

"The computer," said Hrain slowly, as he reached the final lines of the report. "Angel's computer was damaged? How are they fixing it?"

Ezek hissed and cocked his head, staring at Hrain with one beady eye and then the other. "I have no idea. Your ship is in our most advanced repair yard. Uzhrul's Mekmeks are doing what they can. Thankfully your ship is small, but its complexity means it will still take time."

Hrain bowed his head. It didn't need to be said that such priority repairs did not come cheap. Ezek was probably pushing out the repair schedules of Talurian vessels to fix Angel. *But the computer…if they replace her memory banks, what will happen to her?*

141

"Thanks," he said. He didn't know what else to say.

Ezek hissed. "This is a miserable failure, Hrain. We have barely more to go on than we did before."

Hrain bristled. "Failure? You weren't there. Now we know just how powerful they are." *And that Drakmara's brethren are also telepathic.* He kept that last one to himself. He'd never told Ezek anything about his past. Now that the prophecy was coming true, he probably should. *But he'll never believe it.* "They came here to destroy Mauria," he said at last.

"How do you know that? Don't tell me it's one of your silly dreams."

"A hunch," said Hrain. "And, well, yeah. It's one of my silly dreams."

Ezek snorted. "As soon as your ship is repaired, you're to go to Mauria and investigate."

"Gladly," said Hrain. *But not until I see Sledgim.* "Now, where is she?"

The lizard looked confused. "Where is who?"

"My ship. Angel."

"Ah," said Ezek. He typed something into his computer. "I've given you temporary access to the repair yard. Go to bay nine. The Mekmek repair leader is expecting you."

Hrain turned to go. There was no more need for talk. The Talurians never said goodbye to anyone they expected to see again. Hrain had adopted that peculiarity easily enough. He was halfway out the door when Ezek surprised him.

"Goodbye Hrain."

Hrain paused in the doorway. *He thinks I'll never return from Mauria.* His fur bristled. *He may be right.*

He didn't want to think about it. He stepped out of Ezek's office without a word.

He'd have to pull the latest hyperspace charts since he hadn't been to Mauria in some time. The best routes had probably shifted over the years. As to Sledgim, well, there was only one way to get there. Few knew the way, and certainly no Talurians. Hrain had memorized the coordinates.

A planet burned in his mind. *Nail, here I come. Please, please still be there.*

Chapter 19

The sky was thinning to black. Liz strained against the thrust to get a better view, pressing her cheek against the window.

"First time, huh?" said the businessman, shouting over the rocket engine.

She nodded without turning. "Look at all the stars!"

"Attention," said a flight attendant over the intercom. "Please prepare for momentary weightlessness as we enter our staging orbit. This is your final reminder to stow any loose items. Note the sick bags stored in the seat pouch in front of you."

"Are you ready for the best part?" said Morgan.

"You mean freefall?" said Liz. "Yeah, I can't wait."

Morgan had experienced weightlessness many times before, usually when he accompanied his parents on business trips to Starlight Station or the Moon. Like any kid, he'd also ridden zero-gravity roller coasters. He asked Liz if she'd ever done the same.

"No," she said, "but my mom took me on a weightless plane ride for my ninth birthday. It was amazing, but it only lasted for a few minutes."

The intercom clicked on. "Attention: we're cutting the main engine in three, two, one…"

The abrupt disappearance of the low-frequency rumbling was almost as jarring as the absence of force. Morgan squeezed his armrests as the pressure from the seat disappeared. His stomach rolled, and he clamped his mouth shut.

"Sweet," said Liz. She let her arms hang out in front of her. "It's just like I remember. Too bad we can't take these harnesses off and fly around the cabin."

"You wouldn't get very far," said the businessman. "There are sensors around each row of seats that will kick on a force field if something gets too close. You know, to keep things from going ballistic."

Morgan pulled out his phone and placed it in front of his face. "Check this out," he said. He flipped it over quickly while simultaneously pulling his hand away, leaving it spinning about its axis. It drifted slowly towards Liz.

A pair of flight attendants floated past like aerial acrobats, one facing port and the other starboard. The one closest grabbed a handhold in the ceiling and hung horizontally, frowning at Morgan.

"Sir, I have to ask you to put that thing in your pocket."

Morgan scowled and snatched the phone out of the air.

"Thanks," said the flight attendant. He kicked off and went sailing towards the front of the shuttle.

"That looks like so much fun," said Liz, watching the flight attendant. "It's too bad they make people stay in their seats."

"They used to let people move around," said the businessman. "But there were too many lawsuits. Now the only way out of your seat is for a bathroom break."

"And with regards to that, you're better off just holding it," said Morgan. "The flight attendants escort you the whole way, and that robot suction tube takes no prisoners."

The business man chuckled. "No prisoners indeed."

Liz made a face. "Uh, gross."

"If you want, we can visit the core of the space station when we get there," said Morgan. "There are padded recreation rooms where you can fly around. Some have obstacle courses."

"Have you done that?"

"Once with my dad, while Mom was meeting with clients. It was a lot of fun, but I couldn't control myself. I ended up crashing into this other kid and nearly knocked him out."

The sound of vomiting came from somewhere up front, and a translucent energy field flared up around a row of seats. Due to the high seatbacks, it was impossible to see the actual parties involved, but from the anguished cries it was obvious what had happened. Yellow slurry rose above the center seat's headrest before splattering into the restraining field, coating it with puke.

Morgan laughed despite his uneasy stomach. "They missed the bag. I hope they all brought a change of clothes."

"That's disgusting," said Liz. Her face was pale. Her hair floated around her in a golden halo.

"Yeah, they'll be stuck that way for a while. Imagine being the people in that row." Someone in the same vicinity made a tormented choking noise. "Look out, we might get a chain reaction."

"Stop talking about it," said Liz. "Urbp!" Her cheeks puffed out, and she held her hand to her mouth, her eyes wide. "Yerk!" she said, jerking her head towards Morgan.

Morgan squawked and held up his hands.

She smiled. "Just kidding."

He lowered his arms and glared at her. "Not funny."

"Sure it was. You should have seen your face." She looked out the window at Earth. "It's gorgeous down there. The oceans are so blue."

Morgan craned his neck to look past her. A century ago, only a select few got to see this view. How many people had died without ever viewing Earth from above? Now he was three hundred miles above it with the most beautiful girl he'd ever met. *But she dated Victor.* It was hard picturing them together—Liz as beautiful and kind, Victor uncouth and slimy. *Why would she date such a loser?*

The intercom came on. "Alright everyone, get ready for acceleration. This will be just a short burn to push us towards a higher orbit. Thrusting in ten, nine, eight…"

Liz pressed herself back in the seat. "Thanks for taking me up here."

"You're welcome."

"I mean it, Morgan. This is so—"

The rocket fired, and their bodies had weight again. Blood racing through his veins, Morgan inched his arm outward across the shared armrest until he felt the faintest pressure of her arm next to his. He dared not try for more.

"Thanks for coming with me," he whispered, his words safely lost in the clamor of the ship's acceleration. "You…are awesome." He closed his eyes and let the numbing power of the rocket wash over him.

* * *

After a few hours of drifting through space, the pilot sounded the acceleration warning. They would be using the rocket engines to bring the shuttle into a circularized orbit that closely matched that of Starlight Station. Flight attendants prepared the cabin, and the rockets flared to life. It was a jarring transition after the peaceful glide.

"Where is it?" said Liz, after the maneuver was complete.

"It's coming up from behind," said Morgan. "It will take a bit for it to catch up to us."

"Oh."

"Don't worry, it won't be much longer. The boring part is almost over." He closed his eyes to enjoy the last few moments of freefall.

"Boring?" She laughed. "I've been watching sunrises for hours, and you call that boring?"

Morgan smiled. "Glad you like the window." She had been glued to it the entire time.

The intercom clicked on. "Attention passengers, we'll be docking with Starlight Station in about five minutes. We're going to rotate the ship to give you all a better view. If you look to starboard, you'll see your destination approaching just slightly below us."

Unlike the main engine burn, the thruster adjustments didn't vibrate the hull strongly enough to carry noise into the cabin. Morgan didn't realize the ship was moving until Liz pointed out her window at the Earth below them.

"Everything's spinning," she said.

Most of the passengers didn't seem too interested, but a few people seated across the aisle, probably those who didn't get to space often, were looking out their windows. Morgan leaned forward to see past the businessman at the opposite side, but the windows were too small for him to see anything out of.

The intercom clicked on again. "For anyone using our in-flight data connection, we're passing our external camera feed to channel one. That'll get you a better view."

"Sweet," said Liz. Morgan turned, and saw her eyes flicking rapidly from side to side. She touched her palm, blinked twice, and then grinned as her eyes sparkled with photonic overlays.

Morgan pulled out his phone and opened the data connection to the shuttle's computer. It took him a moment to find the video stream from channel one.

Each of the three modular rings that contained the majority of the station's habitable volume connected to the central core with three radial spokes. Umbilical tunnels spanned longitudinally between the ring gaps, allowing people to travel directly from the central ring to either of the end rings. Docking clamps on the outer surface of each ring offered berths for freighters, cruise liners, and ISF patrol vessels. Small puddle jumpers and shuttles stood out like freckles on the station's white hull plating.

The pilot came back on the intercom. "Alright listen up. We're going to synchronize our rotation with the station, so hold on. This gets a little weird, but it'll be over in a few minutes."

Reaction thrusters fired, and the station slid out of view of the camera. The slow sideways acceleration was soon accompanied by a slight downward pull as the thrusters established circular motion.

" Ugh, now I am going to be sick," said Liz.

"Oh yeah gravity!" whooped someone from the front of the ship. "Come on go faster, I've gotta pee."

People laughed. Morgan held onto the armrests as the reaction force changed.

"Prepare for repulsor synchronization," said the pilot.

A deep vibration filled the compartment as the shuttle engaged its repulsors. Gravity appeared. There was a slight clang from the ceiling and then the repulsors powered down.

"And we're docked," said the pilot. "I'm turning the mic over to the flight crew. Y'all take care now."

"Thank you ma'am," said a flight attendant. "Attention passengers, we have successfully docked with the central ring of Starlight Station. The local time is twenty-one thirty-six universal coordinated. Your harnesses are unlocked. Please retrieve all luggage from the overhead bins and exit the shuttle from either the port or starboard umbilical connections. Thank you for flying with Commonwealth Spaceways."

"Finally," said the businessman. He unclipped his harness. Morgan and Liz did the same.

Morgan retrieved his backpack and they followed the line of people out of the shuttle. After stopping at the station's bathrooms, they took an elevator up one level from the landing pad to deck one of the central ring. As was common on most rotating stations, the annular decks were numbered from the outside in.

From the excited conversations, nearly everyone from the shuttle seemed destined for the space show, which was taking place on the observation ring at the forward end of the station. Morgan and Liz followed the crowd.

"Are you two going to the space show?" said the businessman.

"Yeah," said Liz. "You?"

"Yes, but for work I'm afraid. I'm Jonathan Kerrigan by the way. I should have introduced myself earlier."

Liz shook his hand. "We should have too. I'm Liz and that's Morgan."

"Hi," said Morgan. On sudden impulse, he looked back over his shoulder. The deck was clogged with people visiting the shops on either side of the central walkway, but Victor was taller than most and easy to spot. He was a few paces behind them. He locked eyes with Morgan and mouthed something that Morgan couldn't figure out. *What does he want?*

Morgan turned back around. Victor's laser stare bored into the back of his head. Liz was oblivious. *She probably doesn't want to be reminded about him.* Morgan grit his teeth, hoping Victor would buzz off somewhere and not follow them around the entire time. *What if he doesn't? What are you going to do about it?*

"It's like a huge mall," said Liz, as they passed a McDonald's. "Except we're walking on the inside of a monstrous spinning drum."

"Uh-huh," said Morgan.

"Check out the view!" Liz pointed down at the large windows set into the floor between the walkways leading to the shops. The stars outside weren't twinkling, since there was no atmosphere. The sun was sliding into view in one of the windows, which automatically darkened to prevent people from going blind. The earth dominated the view on the opposite side.

"It's like we're in a galactic cement mixer," said Liz.

Morgan looked back over his shoulder. Victor was still there, about fifty feet back, and he was watching them. "Uh-huh."

They dodged a bunch of school kids who weren't watching where they were going. Despite being owned by a military organization, Starlight Station had shops, bars, and casinos on the central ring. These were huge tourist attractions. In addition to the service fees collected at trading hubs on the aft ring, the tourism income paid the salaries of many of the station's personnel. When coming in for shore leave, the multinational crews of the ISF peacekeeping fleet often set up booths selling coins, clothing, and trinkets bearing their ship's crest and serial number.

"This place is just huge," said Liz over the noise of the holoarcade they were passing. From the other side of the walkway, the smell of deep fried goodness wafted towards them from the food court. "It's got everything. Hey, look over there."

Little kids were seated around a booth, their eyes alight and their faces set in frantic determination. Above their heads, miniature fighter drones rocketed past, zipping through holographic hoops. The track seemed to run the entire circumference of the ring. Display screens tracked the position of each remote control fighter as the children piloted them around and around, their hands grasped around joysticks. Occasionally, one of the kids would reach out and press a button in mid-air, although there were no buttons being projected. After a moment, Morgan realized they must be seeing a graphical user interface through their retinal implants.

"Hey," cried one of the girls. "Not fair!"

There was a screeching noise behind them. Morgan turned to see two of the little ships locked together in a shoving match. The girl screamed when one of the ships spun and fell from the sky. Morgan ducked as the tiny vessel tumbled towards his head. It fizzled out of existence about a foot from his face. *Of course it's just a projection.*

"Pretty good graphics with these new games," said Mr. Kerrigan. "And good sound too."

Morgan straightened up. "Yeah," he said sheepishly.

"Still, it can't be as good as the real thing," said Mr. Kerrigan. Did you know that twenty civilians are getting to ride in the new fighters? They've never done that before."

"What do you mean?" said Morgan. "I thought they were giving everyone rides."

Mr. Kerrigan raised an eyebrow. "You mean everyone at the show?" He chuckled. "That would take forever. No, they've got the simulators set up for that. They sold some special tickets to a bunch of rich folks, plus gave a few to some VIP's. I saw Senator Newman earlier with a red ticket."

"Red ticket?" said Liz. She pulled hers out of her pocket.

"Yeah," said Mr. Kerrigan. "Red tickets are for the VIPs. General admissions are blue tickets."

"But look at this," said Liz, holding out her ticket.

Mr. Kerrigan looked down and stopped walking. A man behind them almost bumped into him.

"How did you get that?" said Mr. Kerrigan in a hushed voice.

"A recruiter gave them to us," said Morgan. "An ISF captain." He pulled out his own ticket. He'd had no idea it was so special.

"Someone just gave you red passes?" Mr. Kerrigan had a pained expression on his face.

"Yeah," said Morgan. "Are you sure they're VIP tickets?"

"Quiet," said Mr. Kerrigan.

A family paused to gawk. The little kids had funny pointed ears, and the lettering on the dad's shirt said 'I'd rather be flying the Enterprise'. The shirt made no sense to Morgan, but then again he didn't pay much attention to popular culture.

"You should put those away before you get jumped by fanatics," said Mr. Kerrigan.

They pocketed their tickets.

They had arrived at one of the bridge points along the central ring. There were six bridge points around the perimeter of each ring, located sixty degrees apart. These were the points that connected the rings to each other. Most of the traffic was heading towards the bridge labeled 'Forward'.

"The space show's that way," said Morgan, pointing. "Shall we go?"

"Aren't we already?" said Liz, skipping ahead. "Come on!"

"After you," said Morgan, as he and Mr. Kerrigan followed. He turned and looked around. Victor was nowhere in sight. *Just where's our chaperone got to?*

"Did you tell her about the bridges?" asked Mr. Kerrigan in a low voice.

"No," said Morgan. He slowed, until Liz was a few paces ahead of them. "I can't wait to see what she does."

Each space bridge was a great tube that spanned the fifty-meter longitudinal gap between the stations' rings. Except for a four-foot wide walkway and a few stiffeners, it was almost entirely composed of concave structurally reinforced windows. Morgan had spent hours in the space bridges between rings. They were his favorite places to go whenever he got the chance to visit Starlight Station.

This bridge was lined with people on both sides. Liz was rushing straight ahead and didn't seem to notice the view. It wasn't until she walked past a gap in the human plaque clinging to the edges of the tunnel that she finally paused, turned, and stared.

"I'll leave you two at it then," said Mr. Kerrigan. "I've got to get to work. Red tickets, phew! I'm jealous. Maybe I'll see you flying around out there. Once again, it was nice to meet you."

"Take care," said Morgan.

Liz didn't notice as Mr. Kerrigan waved goodbye at her. She stepped to the side and put her hands against the pressure glass. Morgan joined her.

The view was dizzying. The station's core hung above them, massive, glowing like a pearl from countless spotlights. Yet, it was a mere splinter against the galaxy. In front of them, a thin band of Earth still glowed, the atmosphere alight with the last few golden rays as the sun dropped below the horizon. Below them, land and ocean alike were engulfed in shadow, almost invisible. Here and there, lightning flashed between cloudbanks.

"Oh my God," said Liz.

"Crazy view, huh?" said Morgan, his eyes adjusting to the darkness. They would soon be entirely in Earth's shadow.

Liz's eyes flashed as she looked something up. She pointed at a glowing yellow and white patch of land that was rising in front of them as the station rotated. "Look, there's China. I never thought the city lights could be so beautiful."

"Yeah."

They stood in silence, angling their heads to track the sunset. As their eyes adjusted, the Milky Way took on an unearthly glow. The blanket of stars enveloped them, wrapping them up with the colors of space.

Chapter 20

It was nearly eleven o'clock at night, station time, when they stepped out on the observation ring. To Morgan's relief, Victor was nowhere to be found.

They strolled around with the crowd, nodding and smiling at the uniformed men, women, and robots manning the exhibit booths. Every aspect of the ISF was represented.

They passed space marines in exoarmor, admired a salvaged deck gun from an ancient warship, and tried on various augmented reality graphical overlay programs. Morgan had to use a visor for this. The sudden appearance of thermal gradient vision, sound source localization, plus annotated tags on everything, from the model and serial number of the waiter pouring coffee to the bearing of the nearest ISF starship was overwhelming.

He handed the visor back to the booth's attendant with disgust. "Can't see a thing with all that stuff cluttering the view."

"I thought it was fine," said Liz. "Not much more than what I normally get, minus the space ship bearings. It must be tied to the station's sensor grid."

Morgan stared at her. "You have thermal vision?"

"Well, no," she said. "Not exactly. But I can take spot measurements. I went with the light amplification lenses instead, since I like driving at night. My car has thermal scanners that I can link to if I want a heat map overlay."

"Wow," said Morgan. "I didn't know retinal projectors had so many options." He waited for Liz to speak. She had never asked him why he didn't have any bioware, and he wasn't sure how to bring it up. *If she's ever going to ask, it'll be now.*

"You aren't missing much," she said. "Sometimes I shut it all off and enjoy my base senses. That's nice too, and it's all you need. After all, people have been getting by for thousands of years just fine without all these silly upgrades."

Morgan nodded. *Is she just saying that for my sake, or does she mean it?*

At the engineering tables, cadets demonstrated self-sealing millimeter-thin pressure suits, super-conducting composite heat sinks, and micro-repulsors. Morgan wandered over to a young man who was jacked into a computer simulation. His closed eyelids twitched as he piloted an atmospheric attack ship. The sensor feed from the ship was projected above the booth. The man grunted, and the small oval-shaped ship deployed flaps, cutting sharply to the left. Vapor trails condensed off its wings as it raced towards a speck on the horizon.

There was a furious exchange of green and blue laser fire as the man engaged the enemy drone. Morgan watched, fascinated, as the enemy drone darted up into the cloud cover. The man's ship followed, bursting into the upper atmosphere.

"Got you!" said the man, firing lasers. His target banked and disappeared into the glare of the sun.

"Crap," said the man, trying to follow.

There was a pulse of blue light, and the man's ship exploded. 'Game Over', flashed across the holographic display.

"That's three times!" said the man, opening his eyes and grunting as he extracted the neural probe from his data port. "This thing's impossible."

A cadet took the neural probe from the man. "Anyone else want a turn?"

"What is it?" said Morgan.

"A chance to fly the X-09 against a drone interceptor. Want to try?"

"I would, but I don't have a data port."

"Ah," said the cadet. "That's too bad, you're missing out."

Morgan shrugged.

"What about you?" said the cadet, turning to Liz.

She shook her head. "I only have an L2 interface."

The cadet whistled. "Geez, you two need to get with it."

"So why didn't you go all the way and get an L1 port?" said Morgan as they walked away.

"Well, cost for one thing. I'm not a gamer so I don't need the fastest connection. Besides, most ports aren't grown organically, like my L2 transceivers, lenses, and tympanic membranes. L1 ports are just metal sockets they stick into your skull. I think they look ugly. Plus, they itch."

"Ah," said Morgan. They paused as some younger teens pushed their way through the crowd. Morgan had actually thought people got data ports as a fashion statement as much as for the utility—most kids at school had ones with pulsing lights around the periphery. "I don't know anything about this stuff, as you probably noticed."

Liz turned to him and smiled. "Yeah. You're a bit old-fashioned. But that's cool."

"Actually," he said, "I'm allergic. They grafted an L4 implant into my arm for school, but my body rejected it." He slipped his watch off and showed her the banded white scar underneath. "The graft died, and they had to neutralize the implant before I lost blood flow to my hand."

"Geez," said Liz. "That must have hurt."

Morgan shrugged. "I don't remember it much. I was only six."

"Did you ever try getting something else?"

"No. They ran some tests and said it would just happen again." *This is the part where she'll say 'I'm sorry'. They always do.*

"You're lucky."

"Don't be—what?" he stuttered.

"You're lucky. You can't waste your money or your time on bioware. You won't get sucked in. Instead, you can go out and just live."

"I guess so," he said, unsure of what she was referring to. *Sucked into what?*

They resumed walking, skipping past the exhibits on ISF history. "I can look any of this stuff up on the internet," said Liz. "I could have downloaded any of the thousands of archived feeds from tourists who upload recordings of amazing adventures. If I had L1 circuitry, I could feed all five senses of other people right into my brain. But that's cheating. When I told you I'd never been to space before, I meant it—in person, or otherwise."

Morgan had never thought of that prospect. "I guess I didn't realize people did that," he said.

"All the time," she scoffed. "You can climb Mount Everest safely from your armchair, and bounce around on the moon while sitting on the toilet. Bioware augmentation is awesome, but it also makes people lazy. For some people, especially those with data ports, it destroys your life."

"You mean sim-stim addiction?" said Morgan.

She nodded, then pointed at a booth demonstrating the evolution of EVA suits. A few young men in blue cadet's uniforms were passing space helmets around to curious onlookers. Another cadet poured coffee from a thermal carafe. "I keep forgetting it's night here," she said. "Those cadets look asleep on their feet."

"They're probably getting credit for their classes," said Morgan. She obviously wanted to change the subject. "Want to go find those Fireflies?"

"Sure. I saw a table on space ship design, and the officers from the command school, but not the fighters. I'll pull up the map." Her eyes flashed. "Ah, no wonder. All the fighter demonstrations are taking place on the hangar deck."

"Oh, I guess that makes sense." The hangar deck was one deck above them, set slightly towards the center of the station.

"Elevators are over there," said Liz. "Come on."

* * *

The hangar deck was packed with civilians, station security, and ISF officers. The ISF had gone all out and turned the deck into a museum of historic air and space craft. Fighter planes dating all the way back to the twentieth century were on display. At the various stations, holographic presentations told stories of the craft and the brave men and women who had flown them. The area around the elevator showcased early twenty-first century fighter jets. A MiG-31 was positioned right across from them. Morgan went over to check it out.

"Is it me, or are things lighter here?" said Liz.

Morgan looked up from the MiG's plaque. "Yeah, less gravity."

Liz looked puzzled for a moment, but then her face lit up. "Ah, right. We're one level closer to the station's inner core, so there's less centripetal force."

"You mean centrifugal."

Liz frowned. "No, I mean centripetal. You know, F equals mass times velocity-squared over radius."

Morgan nodded, although he hadn't remembered the actual variables. "Right, except it's called centrifugal force."

"No it's not!"

Morgan pulled out his phone to look it up, but it was frozen midway through trying to pair to the station's data relays. He scowled and rebooted it. It was almost two years old, and he kept forgetting how glitchy it was. "Eh, doesn't matter anyway," he mumbled.

As they strolled between aircraft, Morgan scanned the faces of the crowd. As far as he could tell, Victor wasn't here. *Where did you sneak off to?*

The exhibits soon gave way to primitive space craft from the early days of lunar colonization. Directed audio blared at them as they passed the nearest booth.

"The new ion engines allowed for the construction of colony ships capable of faster travel to the Moon and to Mars. However, problems arose when the nations of Earth turned their focus inward. Colonial uprisings and piracy grew unchecked. After the Martian succession wars and the third cold war on Earth, an organization was needed to ensure peace and cooperation both at home and abroad. Today, the ISF is what makes planetary and interplanetary relationships possible. Formed in 2179 from the combined navies of the Commonwealth, Russia, China, and …"

"Hey, I see something up ahead," said Liz. "There's a huge crowd. Come on."

She led the way around a cluster of booths and past a stage where a holographic space battle was taking place. They passed more modern fighter craft as they walked.

As they came closer, Morgan became aware of a video feed being projected in the air overhead. It was what appeared to be point-of-view camera footage from a fast moving ship. Starlight station was in the background, illuminated on one side by the sun, which was out of frame. A small craft darted into the field of view, its fusion trail momentarily blinding the camera. It was a Firefly fighter!

"Is that going on outside, live?" he said.

"Don't know, but check those out," said Liz, pointing.

They had emerged at the inner wall of a semicircle of people, who had stopped to admire the main attraction. There they were, right in front of him: four polished Firefly starfighters. The ships were surrounded by a perimeter of green-uniformed security guards. Signs indicated that this was a display-only, no touching exhibit.

The sculpted fuselage of each ship was an elongated oval that flattened out at the edges, vaguely resembling the shape of a garden trowel. The noses of the ships towered over the crowd.

To the right of the Fireflies was a row of the older ZX class fighters. These ships, with their harsh angles and stubby wings, paled in comparison.

"The Fireflies look like blackbirds," said Liz, her eyes alight.

"What?" said Morgan.

"You know, the SR-71 reconnaissance aircraft. One of the most beautiful airplanes ever built. We passed by one when we first came down here."

Morgan pulled out his phone and looked it up. "Ah yeah, I see the resemblance."

The crowed murmured excitedly. Morgan looked up at the holographic projection as a second Firefly entered the view of the camera ship. It flipped on its side and fired thrusters, executing a roll over the first ship.

Morgan nudged the man next to him. "Is that live footage?"

"Yeah," said the man. "There's a demo flight looping around the station right now. They're taking a bunch of rich guys out every hour." His face fell. "Man I wish I had the money, but at least they're letting us connect to the feed. It's on channel two."

"Where did they launch from?" said Morgan.

The man pointed past the Fireflies on display. "A couple hundred meters farther along. They've got the partition bulkhead down on each side of the active bay, but there's pressure glass you can look through. I watched them take off, it was whippin."

"Let's go check it out," said Liz.

They came to a pressure bulkhead that extended across the deck. People were pressed up against it in a dense pack. Liz stood on tip-toes next to him, trying to get a glimpse through one of the large rectangular windows in the bulkhead.

"I love this low gravity," she said, jumping and landing lightly back down. "There's a VIP lane about twenty feet to the right. Red ticket holders. Let's do this."

Morgan followed her through the crowd. *We're actually going to do this!* "Excuse me, sorry," he said. It was like being in the pit at a rock concert. He glanced up and saw that the fighters were on final approach.

A massive door set into the edge of the station's ring was parting, revealing hard vacuum beyond. Four gray dots were rapidly approaching. Blue-white fire flashed as the ships fired their engines in reverse-thrust configuration.

"Jack 'Jumpin' Jones," sniggered Liz. "What a silly name."

"What the hell are you talking about?" said Morgan.

"Oh, sorry," said Liz. She tapped her ear. "There's an announcer giving a background on each fighter pilot. I just tuned into the channel."

The crowd cheered as the three Fireflies switched to repulsors. They floated to a graceful stand-still in the middle of the bay and touched down on shock-absorbing struts.

The holographic view switched to a different part of the bay. Four other Fireflies were taking off. In each ship, an elated passenger waved at the crowd. The ships rode out on a shimmering cushion of energy, hanging a moment just outside before rocketing down towards Earth. Soon, all that was visible was the fierce glow of their engines.

"Switch to channel two," said a woman with glowing eyes next to Morgan. "The POV cam is awesome!"

Morgan snickered to himself as hundreds of people stared off into space, slack-jawed with faint streaks of blue-green light dancing in their eyes. *Zombies everywhere.*

"Come on," said Liz, turning away from the bulkhead window. "Now's our chance."

They slipped between a few preoccupied onlookers and came to a roped-off area next to the pressure bulkhead. A short ISF officer with close-cropped black hair stood by the airlock, surveying the crowd. Morgan recognized him just as the man turned to address Liz.

"Captain Batson?" said Liz.

Batson's expression went from military deadpan to friendly recognition. "Liz, Morgan," he said, extending his hand. "It's good to see you."

The captain was dressed in a crisp blue uniform, accented in places with dark gray trim. Four gold bars were embroidered on each one of his shoulders.

"You too," said Morgan. Batson's grip was just as firm as he remembered. "About those Fireflies."

"What about them?"

Morgan pulled out his ticket. "You never said these were special tickets. I thought everyone could fly in them."

Batson regarded the ticket for a moment, then smiled. "I must have forgotten to mention it."

Before Morgan could respond, a light above the airlock door switched from red to green. There was a loud clunk as the door slid into the bulkhead.

"Good timing," said Batson.

An ISF officer stuck her head through the door. She saluted Batson. "Sir, flight group one is back on deck and ready for another run." She looked at Morgan and Liz. "Just two riders?"

"There's the one already inside," said Batson. "Tell Ricky he can take a break, he's been at it all day. Andy, Yin, and Jack can run these kids out."

"Yes sir," said the officer.

Batson looked at Liz and Morgan. "You're up."

"Sweet, thanks!" said Liz. She prodded Morgan.

"Uh, great," said Morgan. "And thanks."

Batson motioned them through the door. "Follow Lieutenant Kirkwood, she'll direct you to your craft."

"Hey, they're just kids, why do they get to go?" shouted a man from the other side of the VIP barrier. "I'll buy those tickets. What do you want for them?"

"Not for sale!" shouted Liz.

"Come on baby, name your price," yelled another man.

"Stuff it," said Liz, and she slipped through the airlock into the hangar bay.

Someone made a catcall. Morgan grimaced as he followed Liz into the bay. The air was fresh and cold, as if it had just been pumped in.

"This way please," said Lieutenant Kirkwood.

She set off across the deck at brisk pace towards the four fighters that had just landed. The fighters had their canopies raised, and the pilots' heads were visible in the front seat of each craft. They were wearing helmets with energized shades that obscured their faces.

The previous riders—three middle-aged men and a young woman—were walking back towards the bulkhead airlock on wobbly legs. "Have fun, kids," said one of the men as they crossed paths. "Hope you didn't have too much for dinner."

"Alright" said Lieutenant Kirkwood, pointing at the nearest two Fireflies. "You, mister, over there. You, miss, over there."

Liz cleared her throat. "What, no safety training? No suits? We just get in?"

"That's right," said Lieutenant Kirkwood. "Climb on up and sit in the seat behind the pilot. The Fireflies have pressurized, field-reinforced cockpits, so you don't need a suit. Just sit back and hold on."

Morgan turned to Liz. "Well, this is it then."

"Yes." She turned towards her ship, paused, then doubled back. Before he knew what was happening, she hugged him. "Thanks for today," she said. "It's the best day I've had in a long time."

"You're welcome," he said, as she let go. She twirled around and bounded off towards her ship. Morgan stood as if welded to the deck, watching her go, his whole body tingling. *Wow.*

He turned slowly and walked to his fighter in a daze. He climbed up the short ladder and up onto the front of the left wing. *This is bananas, I'm actually going to fly in this thing!*

The pilot greeted him as he finagled himself into the rear seat. "What's up kid?" He was young, probably mid-twenties. He wore a green uniform, and was looking over his shoulder at Morgan with an amused grin. He had his visor up, revealing tufts of sandy hair at his temples and brown eyes.

"Not much," said Morgan.

"Not much?" His voice was incredulous, and he whistled as he cycled the glass canopy closed. "You should have seen your face when that chick hugged you. And you get to sit your butt in a Firefly-class starfighter, and you say 'not much'? You must be tripping."

"I must be," said Morgan. "It's been a different sort of day."

"A master of understatement, I see," said the pilot. "What's your name?"

"Morgan."

"Nice to meet you. I'm Jack. No time for chit-chat. You're my last rider tonight and our shift's almost up. You'd better strap in."

"Strap in?" Morgan looked around and found a five-point harness attached to his seat. That was odd. "I thought these things had restraining fields?"

"Sure they do, and we'd be using them if we were authorized to pull over 5 g's. For now I'd rather save the power. Besides, never trust your life to electronics if you can do the same job with something mechanical."

Morgan fumbled with the harness, pulling each side over his shoulders and joining them with the straps across his hips. The harness tensioned itself automatically when the last clip was latched in the buckle.

"Alright, let's fly," said Jack. His hands moved in a blur over the controls. The cockpit lighting switched off, leaving them in the dim glow from the holographic displays. The repulsors hummed, and the ship lifted off the deck. Outside, the flight crew had retreated to a small enclosure in the center of the bay that functioned like a control tower.

Jack adjusted a virtual display screen. "Copy that Yin, I'll tell him. Hey Morgan, someone wants to say hi."

"What?" said Morgan. He had no idea what Jack was talking about.

Jack tapped his helmet. "Intership comm comes through here, private channel. Look to the right." He pointed out the window.

Liz was waving at them from the other fighter. Morgan waved back.

"You and her together?" said Jack.

"Uh…yeah," said Morgan. "Uh, that is we came here together. We're not technically together, together."

"Ok then," said Jack. "Not an item but hopeful, huh? Come on, you can tell me, my mic's off."

Morgan reddened but said nothing. *Yeah right, like I'm going to tell you.*

"And what about the other guy? Is he with you guys too?"

Morgan looked to the left as the third Firefly came alongside them. The pilot saluted, and Jack returned the gesture. The passenger of the other fighter was mouthing something at them.

Morgan stared. *He did it again! First the race track, then the shuttle ride, and now this. He is a stalker! But at least he can't bother us from the back seat of that ship.*

Victor waved at Morgan, then gave him the finger.

"Friend of yours?" said Jack.

Morgan shook his head. "Definitely not."

The pilot shrugged. "Whatever, I'm staying out of it. So, what do you want?"

"What?"

"What do you want for a ride? Intense, gut-wrenching, or please save me I'm gonna die?"

Morgan glanced over at Victor. *There are cameras everywhere. They'll record what we do.* "Do whatever that idiot's pilot is going to do, but twice as fast," said Morgan, tapping the glass canopy in the direction of Victor's fighter. "Assuming you can."

"Can and will," said Jack. He tapped a control on the side of his helmet, energizing the heads-up display within the semi-transparent visor, which he flipped down. "Andy's a good pilot, but he learned from me."

Morgan took a deep breath. He reached out to grip the steering wheel, but of course there wasn't one. The co-pilot control bezels were dark. He put his hands in his lap and waited, biting his lip. *Don't worry, it'll be just like racing…except for the hard vacuum outside and the rocket boosters under my butt.* He wished there was a steering wheel. *I'm a fish out of water.*

Chapter 21

Hrain peered out the duraglass window that overlooked docking bay nine. The *Angel's Fury* rested on the deck, her charcoal hull casting a shadow over two Mekmeks that were welding something on the ship's belly. A third Mekmek was tinkering with one of the landing struts.

He swallowed the last morsel of the snack he'd grabbed on the way down to the hangar bay, wishing he had something to drink. *Ick, Talurian fire crab is disgusting.* Even Angel's synthesized food rations were better than Dominance Station's cuisine. Still, he felt his strength returning.

He took the service lift down to the hangar bay. As he limped towards Angel, he noticed that portions of the hull had a motley, patchwork appearance. *They tore us both up pretty good, huh girl?*

Angel's plating had been repaired with metal of a slightly lighter shade than her dark hull. A fourth technician was closing up an access panel on the starboard hyperdrive pod. She noticed him and smiled. It was a strange expression: a peculiar uplifting of the lips that only the Mekmek did.

"So," she said, her wiry tail twitching, "I finally get to meet our resident Maurian. I've heard lots about you. Ezek must like you if he pulled my crew from fixing Sub-Intendant Zroth's flagship."

Hrain flattened his ears and bowed. "Hrain, at your service."

The Mekmek flicked her tail from side to side. "I'm Mel, the work leader. Your ship is amazing. I've never seen anything like it, and I've seen a lot of ships."

Hrain straightened up. "She is amazing, and honestly I've been worried sick about her. Will she fly?"

"She, huh?" said the Mekmek with a smirk. "You military types are all the same, in love with your hardware. Yes, *she'll* fly well enough, but it'll be a few more days. It would have been months, but Ezek sent your ship to the fabrication bay before it came here. It spent two days under the care

166

of the station's repair drones. They reformed half of the hull and auxiliary systems. We're just doing final calibration and testing. Come, I'll show you all that we've fixed so far."

"That dirty lizard," muttered Hrain. Ezek had been trying to get the *Angel's Fury* into Dominance's automated shipyard since Hrain had first arrived at the station. *Now Ezek's engineers have scans of every square millimark. They can study every system, maybe even reverse-engineer her and make a copy.* Sudden dread filled him. *Did they discover Angel's secret?*

"Mel, how is the computer?"

"It mostly works," she said. "We had to replace some memory modules and one of the secondary controllers with Talurian parts. The computer scientists made a custom translation board to help things talk, but a few obscure processes still refuse to start. We're running diagnostics on those. Want to see?"

"In a little while," said Hrain. "Right now I just need a moment for myself. I've missed her, you know."

"Ah yes," said Mel. She made a strange tittering noise. "I understand. By all means, take your time." She stepped aside.

Hrain walked up the boarding ramp that ran up into Angel's hold. He made a quick survey of the lower deck, then ascended the stairway and ran down the short corridor to the cockpit. Most things were functional, but there were a few unfinished repairs here and there.

"Angel, how've you been?" he said.

"Command unrecognized."

His hearts sank. "Angel, it's me."

"Command unrecognized." Her voice was cold and lifeless.

He plopped down in the command chair and closed his eyes. He wanted to roar, but Mel and her crew would surely hear. *I made it home, but she didn't.* It was silly, he supposed, mourning a computer. *But Angel is more than that. Maybe she's still in there somewhere.*

"There's no time," he spat. He needed to get to Sledgim.

He wondered if the orphanage was still there. *I could rescue the others.* There had been a lot of children, and he had been friends with many of them. Pogue had taught him many things about telepathy—the Art of Ramas, as he'd called it. And then there was Ram, and of course Nail. Thinking of her made him sick. *Will she remember me? Will she forgive me? Is she even alive?*

A planet had burned in his dreams, and his dreams had a way of coming true. Lots of things were coming true. Drakmara and Father had been right.

He hung his head and wondered—and not for the first time— if things would be different if he had joined Father and set out to fight the Ta'Krell ten years ago, instead of running away to Taluria. Would it have helped? Would Angel still be with him? Would a planet have burned?

"Angel," he whispered, patting the dash. "I don't know if I can do this without help. If you're in there, I'm going to find you. I'm going to find them all."

He hesitated for a moment. Going to Sledgim wasn't part of his deal with Ezek, but then again, no Talurian knew that the Maurian Empire actually contained eight planets. Some might suspect it, but none had ever found it. The existence of Sledgim might be the Empire's closest guarded secret.

Taking someone else there, someone who wasn't a Maurian, was a crime punishable by a gruesome death. *But, they want to kill me anyway. And I need Angel.* He flipped on the external intercom. "Mel, can you come up here for a minute? I just got word from Ezek. You've got new orders."

Chapter 22

A blue glow from the atmospheric force field washed over the cockpit as the Firefly exited the bay. Jack switched off the repulsors and they glided towards Earth. Anticipation filled the silent cockpit to bursting.

I wish we were flying these things ourselves, thought Morgan. *Then, I could show Victor what's what.*

Out in front, Liz's Firefly shone with reflected light from the sun. *Does she know Victor's in the third ship?*

Before Morgan could ponder that any longer, Jack lit the rocket engines. Morgan was thrown against the seatback as they shot past Liz's Firefly. The next instant, the Earth dropped from view as Jack pitched the nose up.

He cut the engines and flipped the ship around to look the way they had come. Earth spread out below them, glowing in brilliant greens and blues. The sudden absence of acceleration, combined with the strange view of a dwindling Starlight Station, was extremely unnerving. Morgan settled back down in the seat. His hands, tingling and bloodless, were locked around the harness straps.

Jack pitched the ship down and rolled one-hundred and eighty degrees. Then he flipped back the other way, cycling them between weightless freefall and rotational acceleration. The heavenly bodies cascaded all about in wild arcs. "Just confirming my thruster sensitivity settings," he said happily.

Stars…Station…Earth…Sun…Stars…Station…Stars…Earth…

Morgan closed his eyes. No, that was worse, he was going to throw up! He opened them again.

Jack stopped the mad maneuvers. "How you doing back there?"

"I'm…good," said Morgan. He had just noticed the Moon—it was brightly lit and seemed to hover just above the Earth's atmosphere. It was strange that it seemed no bigger than it did when viewed from the ground. He looked up at the stars and felt small.

"Good," said Jack. "Now, get ready for the real thing."

Morgan redoubled his grip on the harness as Jack shoved the throttle forward. He just managed to catch a glimpse of another starfighter coming alongside them when he was thrown backwards. They were heading straight at Starlight Station.

"This is FF-01 to Starlight, coming in for a close flyby," said Jack. There was a short pause. "Copy. Adjusting point five degrees."

Starlight Station was rushing at them. Morgan could see the end of the central core and the tri-spoke attachment to the ring they had exited from. For a terrible moment, he thought Jack was going to drive straight into the hangar bay at full speed.

"Ahh!" he screamed, as Jack flipped the Firefly over. The station obscured all else from view.

Something changed—there was a new noise and a sudden shove as the Firefly jumped vertically upwards. Morgan's stomach rolled. The rockets cut out and he was weightless again.

He opened his eyes.

They were skimming across the station's white hull, hovering mere inches above it! The deep bass note of the repulsors throbbed as Jack began a spiraling corkscrew course around the station, opposite of the station's spin.

"Look out!" said Morgan, as Jack aimed them right at a docked freighter.

Jack only laughed. "Pew Pew Pew!" he shouted, shoving the flight stick to the side and pirouetting around the freighter. He kept the fighter's bow in perfect alignment as they passed the unsuspecting vessel. "Pew Pew Pew!"

Morgan's stomach rolled as Jack rocketed up and over a parked shuttle and then came crashing back towards the station.

"What kind of flying is this?" said Morgan between clenched teeth.

"The only kind, kid," said Jack. "This is how you take out a target."

"Are these…" He gasped as the breath was knocked out of him. "Are these push-pull repulsors?"

"Yep," said Jack. "I can stay locked in about a foot or two off of the station's hull, clinging like a tick."

Everything inverted as Jack flipped the Firefly over. Apparently it had repulsor generators on its upper surface as well.

They reached the end of the station, and Jack whipped the nose down. Morgan thought his guts were going to fly out the top of his head as the ship dove over the edge of the ring. Thrusters fired, and the g-forces doubled.

"Crap," said Jack. "Lost my hold."

"What do you mean?" said Morgan.

"We were going too fast to stay with the station without exceeding the five g safety limit. Look."

He changed angle and Morgan saw the receding outline of the station against the backdrop of the Earth.

"It's no problem," said Jack. "We'll catch it again." He pushed the main throttle forward, igniting the rockets. For a while nothing seemed to happen, but then the Firefly's relative velocity reached zero and it began to close on the station once more. Morgan squinted—two black streaks were winding this way and that over the station's white hull. The other fighters! He watched as they approached the edge of the third ring.

The two little ships fired thrusters and dove, sticking to the edge of the ring and then disappearing beneath it.

"Yeah yeah," said Jack into his helmet mic. "I'm coming. And I'm going to catch you."

Starlight Station loomed before them. Morgan ducked involuntarily as Jack skimmed under the station's hull into the gap between the rings and the central core. The other fighters had already traversed the length of the station and had turned around, zigzagging in and out between the spokes.

The gap was internally lit by huge floodlights mounted both on the inner surface of the rings and the outer surface of the station's core. The lights whipped past, leaving streaks in Morgan's vision. He grimaced as Jack darted around one of the spokes and flew straight at the nearest fighter.

"Ahh!" yelled Morgan as the other ship bore down on them. Then, it simply wasn't there. He caught a glimpse of its thruster exhaust as it darted towards the stations' core. Jack had nudged their course in the other direction. Repulsors hummed as they skimmed along beneath the ring.

The other Firefly rose out of nowhere, coming alongside as they rampaged through the gap. Morgan could barely what followed. It was a dance as beautiful as it was deadly. Left, right, up, down—all the directions became a jumbled mess. At some point the third Firefly joined them, interleaving maneuvers as they bounced around inside the station.

One moment they were flying backwards, the next they were back in open space. Jack cut the engines.

"How was that, kid?" asked Jack, as they drifted.

Morgan tried to speak, but all that came out was a petrified squeak. "Ood," he finally managed to gasp. "Ga, good. Real good."

"That's the idea." Jack tapped his helmet. "Yin says that your together, not-together lady friend wants to talk to you."

"Oh yeah?" said Morgan. "Give me a minute." He looked down at his shaking hands and willed them to unclench the harness straps. Finally, they did. "Ok, can you put her on?"

"One second," said Jack. He flipped a switch on the dash, then spoke again. "Local comm received, I read you, Yin. You guys are on the horn."

"Copy," came a woman's voice. "Nice flying, Jumper. I'm coming up on your starboard side."

"Copy," said Jack.

Another Firefly came alongside them, its rockets in reverse-thrust mode. The pilot matched velocity and killed the engines. Liz waved at

Morgan from the back seat. The pilot, who must be Yin, nodded her head and offered a salute, which Jack returned.

"Ok, you can talk and they can hear you," said Yin.

"Morgan, that you?" Liz's voice was slightly compressed by the comm circuit, and she sounded out of breath.

"Yeah," said Morgan, returning her wave. *I hope she can't see how bad I'm shaking.* He mustered all his nerve and forced his voice into a more casual, lower octave. "How was it?"

"It was so, so good!" said Liz. "Craziest ride ever. Did you see Victor out here? He tried to get the drop on us, but Yin wasn't having it. We got a target lock on him and blasted his ship! Simulation weapons only, unfortunately."

"Must have missed it," said Morgan. "I couldn't tell who was who."

"I sent Andy packing alright," said Yin. "Silly boy, trying to play games out here."

"Silly boys," corrected Liz. The sound of laughing overloaded the comm for a moment. "So what's next?"

"How about the *Sagitta*?" said Jack. "We've got the time. I think Andy went over that way, after you sent him packing with his tail between his legs."

"Sure," said Yin. "The *Sagitta's* a beautiful ship."

"She is indeed," said Jack. He clicked off his mic and looked back at Morgan. "Not as beautiful as Yin though, but you didn't hear that from me."

"Feeling a bit of starship envy?" said Yin. "Is that Firefly not good enough for you?"

Jack clicked his mic back on. "You know that's comparing apples and oranges. But the *Sagitta's* been looking great. Her hull's complete. When's the last time you did a fly-by?"

"Not for two weeks," said Yin.

"What do you say then, want to go take a look?"

"Sure," said Yin. "We're game. Your rider up for it?"

"I guess?" said Morgan. "Although I have no idea what you're talking about."

"Only the first in a new class of long range cruisers," said Jack. "She got christened a few weeks ago. Don't you watch the news?"

"Not often."

Jack threw his hands up in the air. "Well she's a treat, take my word for it. A prototype fast cruiser that'll be the envy of Martians and Earthers alike. Newest tech. It'll really put Mars in their place. Most of it is classified, but we can do a fly-by. You'll see."

Jack eased into the throttle, following Yin into a higher orbit. He built up some speed, then cut the engines. Morgan looked all around, but there was no sign of Victor. He highly doubted Victor's absence would be permanent.

Morgan noticed a dark object on the horizon, just above the haze of the Earth's atmosphere. The *Sagitta* was hard to see because its hull was matte gray and reflected little light.

The cruiser had a rectangular I-beam profile similar to that of many ISF capital ships. It was a shape that suggested a high degree of utility and strength. A small bridge tower extended up from the top of the ship near the bow. Towards the aft of the vessel were two smaller rounded enclosures attached to each side of the primary hull.

Jack matched Yin's reverse thrust as they approached. "Weird. There's no sign of Andy's ship. Anything on your scanners, Yin?"

"Negative, Jumper," she replied.

Morgan was just about to comment on how large the *Sagitta* was when there was a brilliant blue flash. He yelped and closed his eyes.

"What the—?" said Jack, as a shrill alarm pierced the cockpit.

Ghost outlines danced in Morgan's vision. He rubbed his eyes, but the phantoms wouldn't go away. Outside, streaks of starlight broke into shattered color, bending around the three ships like rainbows on a soap bubble.

"We've lost all power," said Jack. He flipped a mechanical switch on the dash. "Yin, do you copy?"

Morgan held his breath, listening, but there was no response. "Jack, what's going on?"

"Don't know kid, sit tight. I'm going to reboot everything."

Jack flipped more switches and the displays flickered back, displaying various boot sequence text and vendor logos as the multitude of computers that orchestrated the Firefly's control suite came back up.

There was the faintest jostle, and everything snapped back to the way it should have been. The stars were fixed points of light. The *Sagitta* hung lazily before them, as if nothing had happened. *And there's the other fighter,* thought Morgan, relief gushing through him.

The comm crackled to life. "Hey JJ, you guys alive?" said Yin. The transmission was faint and ridden with static.

"We're fine," said Jack. "But the fusion reactor's dead cold and we're on backups."

"Same here," said Yin.

"Liz, are you there?" Morgan winced at the tinny, frightened sound of his own voice.

"I'm here," she said. "I'm ok. You?"

"Yeah, I'm alright."

Jack slammed a fist into the control board. "I can't restart the reactor. It's like all the power's been sucked out."

"I think someone on the *Sagitta* owes us an explanation," said Yin.

The communications panel began beeping.

"They'd better have something good," said Jack. A moment later, a woman's voice barked through the speakers.

"Captain Stone to Firefly spacecraft. You are in restricted space. Report, now!"

"Lieutenant Jones here. We're fine, but the tank's empty ma'am. We've got civilian riders from the space show on Starlight. They should probably be checked out. Also, if you don't mind me asking, what the hell was that? Over."

There was a pause before Captain Stone spoke. "Careful, Lieutenant. You'll be the one explaining to me why you're here. This is restricted space. As to your question, we were running engine tests. Your ship's power circuits aren't shielded against our drive. Now sit tight, shut up, and wait for our tugs. We're bringing you in. Stone out."

Jack killed the comm circuit. "Alright then, nice to talk to you too."

"What kind of engines put out interference like that?" said Morgan.

Jack didn't answer. The cockpit was dead quiet. Morgan hadn't realized just how silent it could be in space until the power went off. He fought to still his shaky breath.

"Well," he said finally, breaking the silence. "Do you think they'll tell us what really happened?"

Jack snorted. "They'd better tell me. But as for you, I'm guessing you're out of luck."

Chapter 23

Captain Eliza Stone pulled herself into main engineering. Hovering in the entranceway, her eyes flicked left, then right, taking in the circus act that was her engine room.

Crewmembers flew this way and that, shouting commands and arguing with each other. Others clung to the walls, scrolling through event logs and juggling holographic diagrams with puzzled expressions. In the middle of the engine room, the dormant tokamak fusion core was the main attraction. Diagnostic computers were jacked into access ports, interconnected by temporary cabling that snaked every which way in all three dimensions.

It's a spaghetti mess, thought Stone. She cleared her throat. "Where is Roland?" She enunciated each word carefully, and punctuated the question with her mag boots, which made a resounding clang as she slammed them into the deck.

Heads turned, and the clamor died instantly. A junior lieutenant nearest to the entryway met Stone's eyes and promptly fumbled her data tablet, which spiraled away and bounced off a stowage locker. "Up there ma'am," she said, pointing at the upper level.

"As you were," said Stone. Disengaging her boots, she pushed off from the deck with practiced ease and shot diagonally across the compartment, snagging one of the two handholds and pulling herself up to the second level. She adjusted herself to face the towering computer racks. A pair of boots protruded above the back of one of the racks.

Chief Roland was shouting. "This system cannot magically engage itself, and there's no trace of a command call. Either someone threw the manual interconnect, or the blasted AI did it on purpose."

The rest of his words were drowned out by the whine of an electric ratchet. A moment later, a sheet metal access cover flew up from behind one of the computer racks, ricocheted off the ceiling, and came spiraling towards her. She caught it and set it gently down on the deck.

"Jones, go fetch me my TX-57 scan tool would you? I don't trust this thing's built-in diagnostics."

"That is an uneducated statement," replied a sterile synthetic voice. "My onboard diagnostic routines are more sophisticated than those of your scanner."

"Shut it," said Roland.

"Command unrecognized, please elaborate."

"Computer, deactivate AI interface."

There was a series of beeps, then silence.

"That's better," said Roland. "I'll never get used to a ship that talks back at you. I swear, letting a class one AI out of the box was a huge mistake. Damn thing is probably still listening to me. Jones, get me that scan tool."

Crewman Jones, a large man with a ruddy complexion, came bumbling around the computer core. He straightened when he saw Stone.

"As you were, sailor." she said.

"Yes Captain," said Jones, lowering his salute. He turned sideways to glide past her, grabbing onto the railing and somersaulting head-first down towards the lower level.

"That you skipper?" The pair of boots sticking out from behind the computer rack disappeared. A moment later, Roland Hanselman's head popped up.

"Ah, of course it's you," he said, looking displeased. He pushed off from the ceiling and disappeared behind the computer once more. Stone glided between the isles of humming machines until she rounded the one Roland was working on. His large form was hunched over the mess of patch cables and blinking lights.

"Report."

"Sorry Skipper, no time to talk." He probed a circuit, which beeped twice and flashed an error code.

"Make the time," she snapped. She had been calling for a report from the bridge for the last ten minutes and had thus far received only useless speculation from Roland's junior staff.

The engineer glared sideways at her. His beady eyes flicked across her face. He scowled, then turned back to the control panel.

"Don't know what happened," he grunted, as he pressed buttons. "We were running a simulation when the system engaged. The nacelles drew too much power and tripped off the fusion core. We've had a few emissive blasts as the field coils dumped their energy into normal space. I think it's stabilizing. We'll know in a few."

"You think the AI did it?"

He shrugged. "I've got to blame something. Look, I'm working it. I'll get you a real report as soon as I can."

"That's not go—"

"Decker to Captain Stone," chirped the comm.

"Stone here."

"Captain, we're bringing the other two fighters in now. Shall I send security back down to the hangar?"

"Affirmative," she said. "Put the riders in the brig with the other civilian, but have your men hold those pilots." *I am going to smack those idiot flyboys.* "Stone out."

"Civilians?" said Roland. "What are you talking about?"

"We've got some visitors from the station. Some sort of demonstration. One ship is already onboard, and now there's two more. Our engine trouble keeps knocking out their ships."

Roland's brow raised. "How so?"

"Never mind for now," said Stone. "Get the ship stabilized, then meet me in your office. We'll compare notes then."

* * *

179

Four magnetic thruster pods locked onto the Firefly. Gentle acceleration ensued as the pods fired, tugging them along.

"This wasn't what I had in mind," said Jack.

The *Sagitta* loomed before them. Morgan noted the multitude of rail guns, laser turrets, and deflector emitters. It had more guns than any ship he'd ever seen.

"How many weapons does this thing have?"

"More than enough," Jack grumbled.

"I thought you said it was a deep space explorer."

Jack swore under his breath. "I shouldn't have brought you out here. This is no good."

"What?"

"Radio's not working. I've been trying to contact the station. There's loads of interference on all channels. It's coming from the *Sagitta*."

"Why would they jam us?"

"Be quiet, let me think."

Morgan shut his mouth and gripped the harness tighter as he watched Yin's fighter enter a rectangular opening in the side of the *Sagitta*. Two crewmen were visible through the blue haze of the bay's force field. Yin's fighter touched down next to another Firefly. The crewmen helped Liz and Yin out of their fighter. The crewmen oriented them, and then the group pushed off from the hull, aiming towards the inside of the ship.

When they were out of sight, Morgan looked at Earth, which was partially blocking the sun. On the dark side, lights twinkled through thin atmosphere. Somewhere down there were his parents, completely oblivious! He grinned...but then his smile faded as a strange thought struck him. *What if we get stuck up here? Who's going to tell mom and dad what's going on?*

He clenched his fists, wondering what Liz thought of all this. Things hadn't exactly gone as planned. *Is she freaking out? Is she mad at me?*

They passed through the hangar's force field and set down next to Yin's fighter. There was a clunk as magnetic interlocks secured the ship.

There were twelve other Fireflies on the deck, arranged in two rows of six, plus the other ship next to Yin's fighter.

Following Jack's lead, Morgan unclipped his harness.

"Now what do I do?"

"Keep quiet," said Jack. "You're not even supposed to be here. Don't touch anything, don't look at anything, and comply with any orders you are given."

Morgan nodded.

A crewman locked his magnetic boots to the outer hull of the Firefly as the canopy withdrew. Morgan grabbed his backpack from under the seat and pushed off unsteadily. He rose a few feet above the fighter before the crewman grabbed his leg and pulled him back down.

"Get over here," said the man.

"Sorry!" said Morgan. He let go of the hull as the crewman passed him down into the arms of two others. From the pistols on their hips, these must be security forces.

His feet hit the deck, but he found his legs misaligned. He couldn't stand, and the momentum of his body carried his torso over into the floor. Before he could push off, a pair of heavy hands pressed into his back.

"Hey!" he shouted, as a pair of magnetic cuffs clamped around his wrists.

"Whoa there," said Jack, floating down to the deck under his own power. When his feet touched the floor, they stuck. "Take it easy on the kid."

The crewman and the two guards glared at the pilot. "What the blazes were you thinking?" said the crewman. "Bringing a civilian here? Are you jacked in the head?"

Jack laughed. "Well my name's Jack so, er, yeah."

The guards looked at each other, and their frowns deepened. "Answer the question," said the crewman.

"I didn't bring them in here," said Jack slyly, pointing at the hangar. "You did. We were just flying past for a quick look, and something hit us. The next thing we know, we're powerless. What would you say happened?"

"I'm not authorized to speculate on that," said the crewman. He turned to the guards and gestured at the other end of the bay. "Take the civvie to the brig. You, pilot, come with me."

* * *

Stone's dark complexion, already creased with age, seemed doubly furrowed with worry. Her eyes darted left and right, absorbing the scrolling data feed.

The door whooshed open. Stone looked up from the holographic display of *Sagitta's* space frame as Chief Hanselman entered the engineering office. The chief scowled when he noticed her floating behind his desk.

"Captain—"

"I killed the comm circuit in this room," said Stone. "The computer can't hear us." She pointed at Roland's collar. "Come on Roland, I know you have something. What is it?"

Roland fumbled with his collar. A short beep sounded when his personal comm powered down. "A computer glitch. A bug in the AI. I don't know how or why, but it did this. I need to isolate it. If you let me get back to work—"

Stone slammed her palm down on the desk. The motion sent her drifting upward. "One moment. If what you're saying is true, then we are all potentially at the mercy of *Sagitta's* computer."

Roland looked up at her. "Yes."

"God help us. If it gets out…Roland, we have three Fireflies on board from Starlight Station. They're from the space show. The pilots were probably showing off for their civilian riders. The bubble pulse from the engines knocked their fusion cores out of alignment."

"I see."

"Just what am I supposed to tell them? That we lost control of our—of our what, exactly? Those pilots don't have the clearance to know. If they figure it out, if they talk, it will jeopardize everything. And then there's the civilians. We need them off this ship before they're missed."

The engineer nodded.

"Roland, are you sure it's the computer? It was supposed to be a completely restrained AI. Class one yes, but restrained. Lobotomized. No personality. Harmless!"

Roland ran his hands through his thinning hair. "We were running the simulations. The AI was there—it's the only thing capable of modulating the field in real-time. We had to test it. We brought the fusion reactor online in diagnostic mode, engines offline. However, as soon as the reactor hit crit, the computer aligned the engine relays. There was no command logged from the bridge, but I found a trace of one in the secondary system. It came from data cluster 28."

Stone whistled. DC-28 was the top-secret processing rack that contained *Sagitta's* artificial intelligence. Normal helm command inputs would be routed through DC-5.

"The command came from the AI node," said Roland. "I couldn't trace the instruction set due to the encryption on cluster 28. Either way, it all happened by the books, just like Dr. Fowler's theory said it would. The capacitors, the driver coils, the engines…it's a good thing the field wasn't modulated, because who knows where we would have ended up."

"Why wasn't it modulated? I thought the AI's job was to do that."

"Yes, that's right. For the test, I had it tied into a stand-alone simulation network. I don't think it knew it wasn't adjusting the actual field parameters."

"You didn't trust it."

"No."

Stone granted him a small smile. "What do you need?"

"An hour, maybe two. It could still be something else, something I haven't thought of. These systems are all untested. There might be a ghost in the machine or a legitimate bug in the code; perhaps a saboteur. Either way, wiping the computer core would set us back months, maybe years. Everyone's stumped. If only Dr. Fowler hadn't been on the *Starfire*. I bet she'd know what to do."

Stone scowled. She didn't know much about Dr. Fowler, except that the physicist had viewed her work as humanity's only hope at continued survival. If it had been up to Dr. Fowler, the *Starfire's* design would have been public knowledge ten years ago. *But look what we've done. We've made it into a weapon. But we had to! If Mars gets warp drive first, we might as well all start saluting the Martian flag.*

"It doesn't help that Howard's rushing us," said Roland. "Sure we had latency issues, but we could have solved it without needing some illegal AI to do the math for us."

Stone leaned against the desk. "Howard isn't willing to risk the wait. We need this ship now, before the Russians or, God forbid, Mars makes a move. And we can't afford another Starfire situation."

Roland snorted. "The field modulation didn't kill the *Starfire,* it was leakage current through the coil insulation."

"Your theory, Roland, but not NAVSHIP's. Besides, even if I believe you, what was I to do? Disobey Howard? He's the 08 division head."

Roland shrugged.

"Is there anything else that could go wrong? Could this happen again?"

Roland held out his hands and rolled his eyes. "This isn't the *Odyssey*. She's new, finicky."

Stone looked past Roland to the place on his wall where he kept a model of their old ship. She pushed off and glided over to it, tracing it with her finger. *Damn it.*

"Missing the old girl again?"

"Huh?" said Stone. "Oh I suppose so."

184

"The *Odyssey* was a fine ship. It's a shame about the decommissioning."

"They should have turned her into a moored trainer," said Stone. "The cadets need a real ship to practice on."

Roland nodded. "It's funny. I still see bits of her in the *Sagitta*. I don't know what it is. Sometimes, if I stand in the right spot in engineering, the hum of the conduits sounds almost like home."

"I know what you mean," said Stone.

* * *

With his hands bound, Morgan was helpless to resist as the two guards launched themselves down the *Sagitta's* corridors, carrying him between them like a sack of potatoes. The walls, floor, and ceiling were outfitted with nylon webbing, forming strategic handholds for zero-gravity transit. Morgan soon lost all sense of direction as he was guided along. It was all he could do to keep from puking.

They stopped abruptly at a door set into the corridor wall. It opened inward with a slight hiss of differential pressure. The guards shoved Morgan head first into the small anteroom. A woman sat at a simple desk in the center of the space. Behind her was another pressure door.

"Is this the last of them?" she asked.

"Yes," said one of the guards. "Three pilots, three riders."

Three of us, thought Morgan with a sinking feeling. *Bad things come in threes. First the race track, then the shuttle, and now we meet again here.*

The woman rose, gave Morgan a cursory look-over, and gestured at the closed door behind her. "In there with him then. He can stew with his friends until Stone figures out what to do about this, uh, situation."

The guards made quick work of it; one of them maneuvered him across the room while the other opened the cell door.

"Thanks," Morgan grumbled, as one of the guards removed his handcuffs.

185

"Don't mention it," said the man. He pushed Morgan into the cell and swung the door shut behind him.

Carried forward helplessly by his momentum, Morgan traversed through the center of the small room and slammed into the opposite wall next to a small window. He rebounded, tumbled sideways, but managed to grab hold of one of the straps that lined the wall. He pulled, bumped into the wall, and clung there miserably. His stomach rolled. *Oh please don't throw up!*

He felt eyes on him. Slowly, he turned his head, looking from Victor to Liz and then back to Victor. They were floating in opposite corners of the room, not speaking, but glaring at each other. Morgan got the impression that his arrival had interrupted something. *What, exactly?*

"Liz, are you ok?" he asked.

She turned her head, tears pooling in her eyes. "What do you think?"

He bit his lip. *What has he done to you?* As he turned to face Victor, his blood began to boil. "You," he said, pointing. "What are you about, huh? Following us around like this."

Victor snorted. "Me, following you? Yeah right. I got here first, remember?"

"That's not what I mean. I saw you on the station trailing along." He pointed at Liz. "You can't keep your eyes off her. You're some sort of sicko, aren't you?"

Victor laughed. When he spoke his voice was trembling. "Sick? Ha ha, sick! Yeah, I am sick. You have no idea how sick I am." He scratched at the back of his neck. "Tell him, baby. Tell him how sick I am."

Liz was silent.

Victor slammed his fist into the wall. "Tell him!"

Morgan cringed. Victor regarded Liz like a starving wolf, his prosthetic hand clenching and unclenching. *He could probably crush my throat with that hand.* Morgan reached into his pocket and felt for the Scorpion's ignition key. Good, he still had it. He didn't relish the thought of a fight in zero-gravity, but if Victor made even the slightest move towards Liz…

186

"I can admit it now," said Victor, watching Liz. "I do freely admit it. I'm sick. I need help. You were right."

Liz said nothing, but her lip was trembling.

"I need you, Elizabeth. You're all I think about. That's why I'm here. Not just to tell you, but to show you." He turned his head and pushed his hair up and out of the way. The light caught on something metal—a small ring at the base of his skull.

"You came here to show her your data port?" said Morgan.

Victor ignored him. "I hurt you baby, and I'm sorry. I abandoned you. I was a fucking idiot. But today I'm going to fix all that. I'm done with sims."

"You've said that before," said Liz, her voice almost a whisper.

"Yes, yes I have," said Victor, giggling. "And I meant to be, I really did. But you have no idea, Elizabeth. No idea! Luna Seven is so strong, so amazing. I *need* it, you see. Even now, I need it. But no longer!"

"What are you talking about?" said Liz, her voice rising. "What are you doing?"

Victor's mechanical fingers caressed his data port, tracing the outline against the back of his neck. His skin glistened with sweat. He tensed.

"No!" screamed Liz. She pushed off from the wall. Morgan reached out and managed to grab her before she got to Victor. "Morgan," she snapped, pushing away, "let me go!"

Morgan didn't let her go. Together, they watched in horror as Victor's mechanical fingers pried under the flange of the data port. Blood and white fluid spurted out.

"Wraaahhhhgggg!" roared Victor. His hand twisted, then jerked. Six inches of bloody conduit and tattered bio-fibers trailed behind the data port as he ripped it from his neck. He brought his hand around and stared at the crumpled bloody mess, then looked up at Liz. "I did it for you," he gasped.

"No," sobbed Liz, as Victor curled up into a fetal ball and began convulsing. "No, no, no!"

Liz was pounding at Morgan's chest. "Please Morgan, let me go."
Numbly, he obeyed.

She pushed off from the wall and scooped Victor towards her,
covering the wound with her hands. Blood floated in globules, more
coming out all the time from between her fingers.

There was a hiss as the cell door swung open and the jailor poked her
head in. "Medical to the brig, on the double," she said into her
communicator. She cast a quick glance at Morgan. "You! Don't try
anything."

He held up his hands. "I won't."

"Move over," said the woman, coming fully into the room. She had a
pressure bandage in her hand.

"Hurry," pleaded Liz. "Hurry, he's bleeding out."

Morgan watched in a daze as the woman pressed the bandage against
the back of Victor's head. Liz was holding Victor's hands in hers, her eyes
squeezed shut, tears running down her cheeks. He backed away, trying not
to wretch. *All that blood. What happens when someone rips a data port out of their
brain?*

Liz was running her fingers through Victor's hair, whispering
something in his ear. *He made her happy once.* Morgan forced himself to look
at Victor's contorted face and saw not an enemy, but a wretched, tortured
fool.

He looked away. "Please, don't die," he muttered. "For her. Don't die."

* * *

The doors to Roland's office opened and Boyle popped his head in.
"You deaf, chief? I've been calling you on the comm."

"It's off," said Stone. "Why."

Boyle turned, noticed her, and flushed. "Sorry ma'am, I didn't know
you were in here. We've got a problem. The reactor restarted all by itself.

The drive caps are charging and there's nothing I can do; emergency bleed shunts are still fused open from last time."

Roland cursed. "We'll have to dump more energy into the engines. With zero field modulation, we won't go anywhere. That should dissipate it. And check to make sure there aren't any more ships out there."

Stone couldn't believe what she was hearing. "Really? We're going to do this all over again?"

Roland threw his hands in the air. "Yes, damn it. Once it's done, we'll shut the system down entirely and pull into spacedock for a full teardown."

Boyle had been talking into his comm. "The bridge reports there are no ships within range," he said. "The field is set to static mode."

"Ok," said Roland, looking at Stone.

Stone clicked on her own internal comm implant. *This had better work.* "Stone to bridge. Please confirm zero field modulation, and then bring the engines online, full power."

All was quiet for a moment. Then, the room shifted. The ceiling thudded into Stone's back, sending her toppling down and over Roland's desk. Boyle managed to stay on his feet, but only by grabbing hold of the computer terminal in the wall and magnetizing his boots. Roland's head made a dull thud as it struck the frame next to the door.

"Brace, brace, brace!" came the acceleration alarm from the corridor outside the engineering office. "Warning: Acceleration. Brace, brace, brace!"

"Bridge, report," said Stone.

"Lawson here. I don't know what's going down in engineering, but the *Sagitta* just jumped to warp."

Stone glared up at Roland. He was hovering above her with blood spurting from his head. He moaned and clutched his face. "Bridge, disengage all engines."

"I'm sorry," said Lawson. "Helm is not responding. We're exceeding 100C. Something is modulating the warp field."

189

"I'll be right there," said Stone.

Roland had managed to get himself oriented. He was breathing heavily, but seemed to be alright. Stone and Boyle helped him towards the office's door.

"You ok?"

He nodded. "Just a scratch. Sorry, I'm bleeding all over the place."

Stone batted a few drops away from her face. "It happens. Get to main engineering and get us stopped. And have someone rip out the computer core."

"I'm on it," said Boyle.

The three of them exited the engineer's office together and kicked off, shooting down the corridor, Stone in one direction and the two engineers in the other.

Chapter 24

Mog studied the asteroid on the viewscreen, which was dimly illuminated by his ship's navigational lamps. The crater they were hiding in could have swallowed what was left of the Maurian Navy whole, but—per the plan—it had to settle for a paltry appetizer.

The rock walls surrounding the four warships were scarred from ancient impacts. The sight made Mog nervous. The *Narma Kull* was running in low power mode. Without her shields, even a rock the size of his fist could puncture the hull and vent their atmosphere into space.

He took a deep breath, held it for a moment, and let it out in a slow hiss. Five hours had passed since the *Narma Kull* and the three heavy frigates had split off from the evacuation fleet and hidden here. The transports were nearly clear of the system.

I wish we'd had a chance to test those PPCs. It had taken too long to finish the hull bracing around the new guns. Kremp assured him they would work, but a test firing now might give their position away. Not immediately of course—the approaching Ta'Krell couldn't possibly see into the system until they broke through the hyperspace distortion. It was the residual energy signatures he was worried about. *They need to see the exhaust from the transport ships and nothing else. Nothing to suggest we are here.*

He scrolled through his displays, watching the vector plot of the approaching ships. They were almost at the edge of the system, and had spread out as Kremp had predicted.

"The computer has an updated report on the approaching craft," said Nali.

Mog sat up straighter. "Go ahead."

"Energy signatures are correlated with ninety-five percent confidence. They are Ta'Krell."

"I'm so surprised," said Ryal.

Mog bowed his head. For the first time since the start of the war, the announcement didn't sound like a death sentence.

"The tables have turned, haven't they?" said Ryal, stepping up to Mog's command chair.

"I hope so," said Mog.

"I know we're going to win," said Ryal. "You know why? Because I'm sick of losing."

Mog bared his teeth. "Win or die."

"No running," said Ryal, placing his metallic hand on Mog's shoulder.

An alert sounded from Meela's console. "Commander," she said. "The vanguard ships just punched through the system's hyperspace distortion barrier. They're in our reference frame, passing over us in three, two, one...no indication that we've been detected. They'll be surrounding Mauria Prime shortly."

"Sledgim," said Mog. "Call it Sledgim."

He stood and walked to the front of the bridge. The viewscreen towered over him. He imagined the Ta'Krell commanders, their eyes set on the ice world and its ragtag defense fleet. They were counting on an easy victory. They wouldn't see the little ants crawling out of the crater behind them.

He turned to face his crew.

"I don't have to tell you that this is our last stand. It is going to be difficult. Our fleet has never matched theirs, but today we have the element of surprise. We have some new weapons, but more importantly, we have nothing left to lose. So, let today be different. Let today be the day when we send the Ta'Krell straight to the bloody pit!"

He thrust a fist in the air as the crew shouted battle cries—old veterans and new recruits showing like vigor. He lowered his arm, waiting for the commotion to die down.

"Thank you, my friends, for standing with me against the darkness once again. This ship—"

He walked over to the bulkhead and laid a hand on the polished metal.

"This ship is Mauria. You are Mauria. Today we honor a kingdom that was, and fight for what may yet be. The rules are simple. Stay at your posts. Follow my orders. Do Mauria proud. That is all."

"Let's get them!" shouted Ja'Tar.

"To the death!" said Nali.

"Yes," said Meela, her voice quivering. "Tell me when, sir, and I'll fly us right down their throat."

Mog walked over to his helmswoman. "Soon," he said, patting her shoulder. He reached down and pressed the helm station's communication's panel.

"All hands, this is the commander. Battle stations."

* * *

No sooner had the medical team taken Victor from the brig and slammed the door shut than the ship lurched. Morgan was relatively unaffected since he was floating in the middle of the room, but Liz had been clinging to the door, begging the medics to let her accompany Victor to the medical bay.

She shrieked and lost her grip, spiraling backwards into Morgan. He caught her and grabbed hold of the webbing next to the window.

The small speaker set into one of the walls erupted with a shrill klaxon, followed by "Brace, brace, brace! Warning: Acceleration. Brace, brace, brace!"

"Are you alright?" said Morgan, as Liz scrambled to grab hold of the webbing.

She didn't answer. She was staring out the porthole. Morgan tried to see past her, but the window was tiny and her head blocked the view. He swore as the momentum of his floating legs pulled him in the wrong direction. By the time he had himself repositioned, Liz had turned away from the window.

She looked like she'd seen a ghost.

"Liz, what is it?"

"A warp bubble," she said. "That's what this ship does. It makes the warp bubble."

What on Earth is she talking about? Morgan pulled himself back towards the window. What he saw made absolutely no sense.

* * *

"Commander," said Ja'tar. "Mar-Ruba's fleet has engaged the Ta'Krell."

"Acknowledged," said Mog. "Status on our evacuation fleet?"

"They're almost out of the system. The big transports have their shields wrapped around the civilian vessels. No sign of pursuit."

Mog bowed his head. As he had assumed, the Ta'Krell weren't concerned about letting unarmed evacuation transports escape. They were confident that they could destroy Sledgim quickly, before the hyperspace wakes of the transports dissipated.

"How long until we clear the asteroid belt?"

"Thirty seconds," said Meela, adjusting one of her holographic displays. Mog felt the faint tug of acceleration as the thrusters altered their course. There were no asteroids visible on the screen, but the *Narma Kull* was going fast enough that Meela had to program course corrections well in advance of visual contact.

"Alright, we're out," said Meela. "Our escorts are still proceeding out at constant velocity. They'll be clear of the inner belt's orbit in ten seconds."

"The Ta'Krell should be picking up our signatures soon," said Ryal. He stepped forward to peer over Meela's shoulder. "Set in a hyperspace jump. We want to come up right behind them and pinch them between our forces."

This was the most dangerous part. Mog had gone over the parameters for an in-system hyperspace jump a hundred times, and it still made him nervous. If the *Narma Kull* were a civilian ship with a conventional hyperdrive, he would never attempt this, but the Navy had developed a tactical drive that could compensate for close-proximity gravity wells such as planets and asteroids. At least, it could in theory.

"Ja'tar," said Mog. "Signal the three frigates to form up on our flank, thrusters only. Once we're in position, coordinate the tactical jump. The *Narma Kull* will paint the first target. Have them concentrate all weapons on our mark." *Those orbital guns had better work. This is going to be trial by fire.*

"You got it," said Ja'tar, with a slight tremor in his voice. A moment later, he said, "Escorts in battle formation. Meela's helm is linked."

Mog bowed his head, listening to the gentle beeping of the bridge. This might be the last quiet moment of his life.

"Do it," he said. "Full power, maximum shields. Jump!"

There was a deep throb of power, and the view on the forward screen morphed into a kaleidoscope of color.

"Ten seconds to the exit point," said Meela.

Mog held his breath. He couldn't shake the thought that this was all in vain. The Ta'Krell were forming a sphere. Why not a concentrated attack formation? They must have some advantage he hadn't counted on. What was it? The *Narma Kull* had her own surprise. He could only hope that the new PPC cannons were enough to offset whatever the Ta'Krell were planning.

"They've seen us," said Nali. The nearest three ships are adjusting course."

"Good, that will take some pressure off Ruba."

"Dropping out of hyperspace," said Meela.

With a mild tremble, the dancing colors on the viewscreen disappeared. Mog could just see the small dot that was Sledgim on the screen. He exhaled, not realizing he'd been holding his breath. A red bracket marked the presence of the nearest Ta'Krell ship.

"Start a tactical analysis of all ships in the sector," said Mog. "And magnify that ship right there."

The viewscreen zoomed in. When it focused, it showed a light cruiser. Shaped like a fat arrowhead, its annular engine ring emitted a long fusion tail as it burned hard to intercept the *Narma Kull.*

Small as they were, the Ta'Krell light cruisers were still a formidable threat. They were faster than any Maurian ship, and outgunned even the largest capital ships with their hard-mounted forward cannons. However, they were only lightly armed at the beam and stern. It was too bad that the majority of the Maurian fighter craft had been destroyed. Fighters were ideal for attacking the undefended flanks of such craft.

"Should I hail them?" said Ja'tar, with a toothy smirk.

Ryal laughed. "Hail them with fire! Nali, set the PPC cannons to full compression mode and charge the capacitors. Make ready the forward torpedo launchers."

"PPC cannons online," said Nali. "Warhead control confirms torpedo tubes one and two are loaded."

There were two blue flashes, and two more Ta'Krell vessels appeared.

"Looks like we're forcing them to change formation," said Nali. "There's a hole in their sphere."

"They want to deal with us quickly," said Mog. "We're only four ships. They think this will be easy. Ja'tar, tell the frigates to tighten up and get behind us. Our shields are the strongest, so we'll take the initial attack. As soon as the Ta'Krell fire on us, give the frigates the go ahead to break formation and target the lead ship."

"I'm on it."

Ja'Tar's voice was strained. Mog glanced around, noting the numerous new crewmembers. The cadets from Sledgim's naval academy had never seen combat. This was trial by fire indeed.

"Meela, go to full burn," he said.

"Yes sir."

The gentle rumble from the twin fusion engines became a roar, and Mog felt the push of the acceleration despite the inertial suppressors. He glanced down at the recessed restraining belt in the side of his chair, but dismissed the idea of strapping in.

"We're entering weapons range of our heavy guns," said Nali. "Permission to fire?"

Mog glanced over at Ryal. "This one's yours, Subcommander."

Ryal puffed out his chest. "Nali, send them to the dark place."

The lights on the bridge dimmed as the new weapons soaked up the ship's power. Mog didn't dare to blink. Everything hinged on this. A second went by, and then another.

Nothing happened.

"Status?"

"I'm not sure," said Nali. "Something's gone wrong. The capacitors are charged, but the cannons aren't firing."

Mog tapped the control panel next to his chair. "Kremp! Where are my guns?"

"Bolted to the hull," said the engineer.

"They're not working."

"Yes, I can see that. I'm on it. Will keep you posted. Kremp out."

Mog growled. "Nali, we're going to have to do this the hard way. Charge the plasma cannons."

"Without the PPC's," whispered Ryal, "they've got us on range and firepower."

Mog said nothing, lest the dread that had filled him pass into his words.

"We are entering their weapons range," said Nali. "Stand ready."

Almost immediately after she spoke, the nose of the lead Ta'Krell vessel erupted with a blinding volley of transplasma. The Ta'Krell's version of the magnetically jacketed, dimensionally unstable plasma had always been particularly disruptive, causing severe spatial distortions as the plasma burned.

The bridge bucked. Mog gripped the command chair, staring at a wall of green fire that engulfed the bow.

"Forward shields down to sixty percent," said Nali. "There's some damage to the outer armor, but there's no risk of burn through yet."

"Can we fire?" said Mog.

"We're still out of range," said Nali. Another ten seconds."

He swore. Why couldn't the PPCs have worked? He could see lines of disruption starting to form where the shield grids overlapped.

"Forward shields failing," said Nali. "Five seconds to range."

"Bridge to engine room," said Ryal. "Aux power to the forward shields."

The fatigue ripples in the shields faded. *Auxiliary power,* thought Mog. *Can't remember the last time we've had auxiliary power.* The repair crews at Sledgim had worked wonders. A twinkle of hope returned.

"Sir," said Nali, with a delighted snarl. "Plasma cannons locked."

Mog jumped up and pointed at the lead ship. "Fire all!"

Five streams of transplasma bolts struck the lead Ta'Krell ship, soon followed by three more streams from the *Narma Kull's* supporting frigates. The vessel's forward shields burned with blue fire.

"We hit em good!" said Ryal. "They're stumbling!"

The bridge rocked again as the two flanking Ta'Krell vessels lashed out.

"Keep the pressure on that center ship," said Mog. "Meela, fly us straight at them. Nali, ready a torpedo."

"I have a torpedo lock," said Nali.

"Not yet," said Mog. "Wait for them to turn and hit them broadside at closest point of approach. I don't want to lose that torpedo to their anti-missile system."

For an instant, the three Ta'Krell ships occupied the entire width of the viewscreen. The *Narma Kull's* target was in the center, coming straight at them. *Come on, turn!*

Just when Mog was beginning to doubt his strategy, the enemy's resolve broke, and they changed course, diving down. Meela was ready, firing thrusters and tipping the *Narma Kull's* bow down to track the target as the vessels passed each other. Mog suppressed the urge to look up at the ceiling as the other two enemy vessels slipped off screen, raining heavy fire down upon the *Narma Kull's* dorsal shield array.

"CPA in two seconds!" said Meela, as the Ta'Krell ship passed by.

"Nali, secure plasma cannons," said Mog. "Fire torpedo!"

There was a dull thwump as the port torpedo launcher cast out its deadly payload. A second later, a glistening black warhead accelerated into view, propelled by a fiery red stream from its rocket engine. The Ta'Krell ship tried to veer away, but it was too late. The torpedo arced downward and, for a brief moment, became indistinguishable against the enemy's black hull.

The piercing explosion rocked the enemy ship. For a millisecond, the enemy's shield bubble held, but it had been weakened from the Maurian fleet's concentrated fire. A massive ripple coursed through the shields from bow to stern, and they flickered out altogether.

"Fire two!" roared Mog.

There was another thwump, and a second torpedo made a beeline towards the damaged ship's unshielded engine assembly. The impact blew the annular fusion nozzle right off. A second later, the ship was engulfed in a brilliant flash.

"Got em!" screamed Nali.

Cheers erupted on the bridge.

"Bring us about," roared Mog over the din. "Coordinate all fire on the next nearest enemy."

They had done it. They had drawn first blood. He sat back in his command chair and pulled up a damage report.

"Not too bad yet," he muttered.

The stars danced across the viewscreen as the *Narma Kull* turned. One of the tri-hull frigates slipped into view, soon followed by the other two. They were engaged in a heavy firefight with the remaining Ta'Krell ships. Nali magnified the view as Meela pushed the engines hard to close the distance.

Mog eyed their relative speed on his display, willing the numbers to change more rapidly. After what felt like an eternity, sensors indicated that the *Narma Kull* was gaining ground on the other ships.

The closest Maurian frigate was in trouble. Plasma bolts were starting to penetrate its dorsal shields, leaving scorch marks on the hull. Three small objects lanced out from the rear of one of the Ta'Krell cruisers. Mog held his breath as they made their way towards the weakened frigate.

The frigate flipped sideways, and one of torpedoes overshot it. The AMS cannons took down the second warhead. The third, however, went straight through the ship's weakened shields and struck the central engineering section, which shattered in a fiery explosion. The frigate came apart, sending out scattered debris that broke across the *Narma Kull's* bow.

"There goes the *Dunentra*," said Nali.

Mog clenched his fists, his claws digging into his palms. Commander El was an old friend from his academy days. She was deeply religious. Hopefully her faith had given her some peace in her last moments.

Ryal cursed as debris bounced off the *Narma Kull*. "Reload torpedo tubes," he shouted. "Hit those bastards with everything we have."

"Lay in a pursuit course," said Mog. "Keep our nose on them."

He glowered at the viewscreen as the tail end of the offending vessel grew closer. Below the screen, Meela sat bolt upright, muscles knotted. Mog felt a surge of admiration for his young helmswoman. Dogging a vessel one fifth the size and twice as maneuverable without overshooting was no easy task.

The Ta'Krell ship launched two torpedoes, which arced backwards at the *Narma Kull*. If it was an attempt to get Meela to dodge, it didn't work. She stayed true to the course, despite the impressive lurch when the torpedoes exploded in their path, destroyed before they could get in lethal range by Nali's ace marksmanship.

"Fire all," said Mog.

The mechanical melody of the torpedo launchers joined the muted twang of the plasma cannons. Nali had timed it perfectly. The plasma bolts arrived a split second before the warheads, overloading the Ta'Krell's weakened shields and making a hole for the torpedoes, which detonated in the gap between the enemy's hull and engine assembly. It's engine ring blown off, the crippled ship spun sideways. Another volley of blue plasma from one of the Maurian frigates tore into the evil ship.

Mog watched the Ta'Krell light cruise explode, hardly able to believe it. There was only one left! He wondered if Ruba's battle group was faring as well against the spread-out Ta'Krell forces. He didn't have time to check up on it.

"Coming about on the third cruiser," said Meela.

The viewscreen flared as Sledgim's sun came into view, followed by the combatants. The two Maurian frigates had multiple hull breaches. They were trading fire with the remaining Ta'Krell cruiser. The Ta'Krell ship was pinned between the Maurian vessels, and by the looks of things it wouldn't last much longer. Multiple streams of blue bolts tore into its shields, and a constant barrage of torpedoes rocked it mercilessly.

"Sir," said Ja'tar. "The *Eleseum* and *Vorsa Mor* report that the Ta'Krell vessel has been disabled. They are holding their fire."

"Tell them to form up behind us," said Mog.

"Yes sir," said Ja'tar.

The two frigates swooped upwards and slipped off screen.

Mog swiveled around in his chair. He'd been expecting the disabled enemy ship to blow up at any second, as they tended to do if they became too damaged. The fact that it hadn't was very strange. *This could be the opportunity we've needed since the start of the war.* "Nali, what's the status of that ship?"

"They're adrift. I can't scan through their hull, but I don't think there can be much working inside that thing. I think we knocked out their drive. That might be why they haven't self-destructed yet!"

"Sir," said Meela, "if we can board them, we can see who—or what—they really are, if they're Azhra's children or not."

"Does anyone know what a Ta'Krell is supposed to look like?" said Ja'Tar.

"That's what I was thinking," said Mog. *So I can prove they're just as squishy as us.*

"Can it, there's no time," said Ryal. "There's still that one big ship out there, and it's got an unknown configuration. We need to take it out. Let's mop up here before they get that thing restarted, then get to the planet."

Mog scowled. "Agreed. We need to reinforce Ruba's forces in orbit." He paused, contemplating the drifting ship. Even in its disabled state, its presence was offensive. He raised a hand to give the order to fire.

Murderers. They deserve to die.

His hand wavered. It would be so easy.

"Do it," whispered Ryal in his ear.

Mog sighed. "No," he said, lowering his hand. "They're the murderers, not us. There's a better way...Nali, launch a mine and dock it on their hull. Program the warhead to detonate if that ship so much as twitches. If it's still here when we win this fight, we'll come back and capture us some so-called Ta'Krell. Meela, lay in a tactical jump. Get us in the same plane as Sledgim's orbit around the star. Engage!"

Five seconds later, the *Narma Kull* and her two remaining escorts were streaking through hyperspace towards the main battle.

"Commander," said Ja'tar. "Mar-Ruba reports that the planetary defense satellites are almost gone. Our forces are concentrated in the defense of the southern hemisphere, but they'll have to disperse to deal with the Ta'Krell that are entering orbit on the far side of the planet."

"Tell him to hold on, we're almost there," said Mog. "Nali, tell Kremp that we need those projection cannons."

The bridge pitched forward. Mog was dumped out of his chair and only managed to stay on his feet by snagging the command platform railing. A groan sounded from somewhere deep within the ship, and the bridge was plunged into darkness. The red emergency lights flickered on just in time for Mog to see Meela climb back into her seat. Beside him, crumpled over the railing, was one of the new junior boardmen. He must have fallen from the upper deck.

Mog pulled the boardman off the railing and laid him on the deck. He was still breathing, but his eyes were rolled back and his tongue lolled.

"Report," said Ryal.

"This doesn't make any sense," said Meela. "The hyperdrive field destabilized."

"Confirmed," said Ryal from the port auxiliary station. "We're caught in some sort of dimensional web. It's being projected by the large Ta'Krell vessel and reflected between all the light cruisers surrounding the system. There is no way to form a stable hyperspace field in this thing."

"Nazpah," spat Ja'tar. "Mar-Ruba reports all hyperdrives are useless."

On the viewscreen, Sledgim appeared much larger. Explosions like miniature flash bulbs dotted the horizon above the planet.

Mog stiffened. So, this was the Ta'Krell surprise. This small fleet must be an expeditionary force, sent to find and hold any Maurians they encountered at bay until the main fleet could be summoned.

We never had a chance.

"Ryal, where is the enemy command ship?"

"Bearing two-five-seven mark four. I'm putting it on screen, maximum magnification."

The viewscreen flickered, and a ship unlike anything Mog had ever seen appeared in the center. He glanced down at his tactical display. The ship was twice as large as a Ta'Krell dreadnaught. Its hull was white, and countless windows indicated the presence of hundreds of decks. The primary section of the ship was an oval, which tapered to a horizontal fin-like tail. A fusion flame burned white-hot from a central engine assembly at the rear.

"By Ramas' claws," said Ryal. "That's a big ship."

Bright white beams lanced out from the underside of the vessel. His heart sank; the target was the *Elnor Kai,* a sister ship to Mog's own command. The beams pierced right through the *Narma Kai* and severed both starboard wings from the hull. A second volley punched through her heart and came out the other side.

Ryal groaned as the *Narma Kai* exploded.

"Meela," said Mog. "How long will it take us to reach them at sublight?"

"Twenty minutes at maximum burn. If we overdrove the engines…" Her voice trailed off as she watched the cloud of debris expand, fires guttering out in the vacuum.

"Transmission coming in from mar-Ruba." Ja'tar's voice was scarcely a whisper. "They're surrendering."

We've failed. He didn't know what to say. Words were meaningless. There was only one thing left to do.

"The transports?" said Meela. "Are they being pursued?"

Ja'tar checked his console. "That's a neg. The Ta'Krell are holding position around the planet."

"At least some will survive," said Meela.

But for how long? Those were big ships, and it would take hours for their hyperspace wakes to dissipate. They could be easily tracked. Mog rose from his chair and walked over to Ryal.

"We need to take out that ship."

Ryal locked eyes with him. "They'd tear us apart."

"I know." He reached out and placed a hand on his friend's shoulder. "Make the necessary preparations to abandon the *Narma Kull*."

Ryal's eyes went wide. "You're going to ram them?"

Mog bowed his head.

Ryal's expression was flat. He said nothing for a moment, then tipped an ear. "See you on the other side, by Ramas' grace."

Mog didn't bother arguing. Gods or no gods, he welcomed death. *Let's see how many of those Ta'Krell bastards I can take with me.*

Chapter 25

The stars outside the brig's porthole window had taken on strange colors. Some were red, some blue, depending on where you looked. The ones straight out were white, but elongated into thin threads of light. Liz pulled herself closer. "I'm sure of it," she said. "It explains everything. This is why everyone on this ship is so uptight."

Morgan bit his lip. "It's impossible," he muttered.

"Saying that over and over doesn't make you right. We're seeing a warp field distortion. I know it. I've seen it before."

Morgan pulled in his legs and arms, becoming a little floating ball spinning slowly in the air behind Liz. He squeezed himself as tight as he could. "Wake up, wake up, wake up!" *Nope, still floating.*

He scowled. "How could you have seen this before?"

She didn't answer.

"It's impossible. Hawking, Einstein, and all the rest proved you can't travel faster than light."

"You're a blind idiot if you believe that," said Liz.

"Am not."

"Are too. It's staring you right in the face. Where's the Earth, Morgan? Where! Point it out. Show me."

Morgan's frown deepened. He went back to the window. He had already looked out of it at every angle. There was no sign of Earth, or the moon, or any other ISF ship. There were only those weird, distorted stars. *She might be right.* "How then." he snapped. "Tell me, if you're so whippin smart. How is this possible?"

Liz's eyes were shimmering pools. Droplets shot from her fingers as she brushed the tears away. "They said there was a malfunction. The engines blew up, and everyone died. The experiment was a failure."

"What experiment? What are you talking about?"

"My mom was a theoretical physicist at EnGineus. Two years ago, she was the lead researcher on a secret project for the ISF. She wasn't supposed to talk about it, but she told me bits and pieces. She invented something, and the ISF put it on a ship. That ship was called the *Starfire*."

"Ah," said Morgan. "That was the ship that suffered the battery explosion, right?" So that was what had happened to her mom. The *Starfire* incident had been all over the news.

Liz was making an obvious effort to keep it together. "There was nothing wrong with the batteries; that's the cover story. It was really the ship's drive. My mom's company made fusion drives and ion engines. Two days before the accident, my mom brought a holosim home. She was working late on it. I came downstairs for a drink before bed and caught a glimpse of it. That's where I saw this for the first time—the warp bubble."

"How'd you know what it was?"

Liz pointed at her eyes. "The sim came with a few channels of additional data. I downloaded some of it before my mom realized I was there and turned off her computer. She was pissed, and made me swear not to tell anyone. She wasn't supposed to bring her work home, but the project was behind schedule. She was under a lot of pressure. She was worried it wouldn't work, that they hadn't gotten it quite right.

"I already knew the ISF had been rushing them. In the last few months before the launch, my mom was hardly ever home. When she was, she would fight with my dad, and cry herself to sleep. In the morning, she'd be gone before we woke up. Dad wanted her to quit. If only she had listened to him."

"I'm sorry," said Morgan lamely.

Liz sniffed. "We got the call twenty minutes before dinner. An hour after that, some ISF admiral came down Earthside. Howard, I think his name was. He told us some bullshit story; that the new battery system EnGineus designed had overloaded. He said Mom died serving the good of the Commonwealth. He gave my dad some medal and then left. After that, my dad went kind of crazy."

Liz waved her hand around. "But, they did it! It wasn't a battery system my mom invented. The *Starfire* had a warp drive, and even though that one didn't work, the one on the *Sagitta* does. Do you know what this means?"

Morgan thought for a moment. "It means we're really, really far away?"

"Yes! My mom is a hero! People have dreamed of visiting other worlds for centuries. All the overpopulation, the starving, the fighting, it can all be avoided now. We can go out there." She waved at the window. "Where no one has gone before."

Morgan said nothing. This must be an accident too, some engine test gone wrong. What would they think back home, when they went looking for and didn't find the *Sagitta* anywhere? Would the ISF tell the truth? *Probably not. They'll blame drug-running pirates or something.*

"Did you hear that?" said Liz. "The sound changed."

The soothing hum was gone, replaced by a more labored drone. Outside, blue streamers had begun to mix with the star trails. *Well, that doesn't look good.*

Liz pushed off and went back to the door. She began slamming on it with her fist. "I know what's happening," she screamed. "A warp ship! You have a warp ship! My mother was Rachael Fowler. Can you hear me? Doctor Fowler was my mom. Let me out!"

There was no response. Morgan looked up at the small camera. There was no indication that it was on, or if there was anything that recorded audio. Liz turned to face him. "Morgan, we need to get out of here. I think something's wrong. Why would they go to warp with us civilians on board?"

"I have no idea. Maybe Jack and Yin will find out and tell us what's going on."

"I don't want to just sit here though, do you?" said Liz.

Morgan looked around. Except for the door and the window, there was nothing in the tiny room to work with. "I don't think there's much we can do, unless your tech can hack that door."

Liz regarded the pressure door and shook her head. "I already tried it when they took Victor. All the access protocols are encrypted. Do you...do you think he's going to be ok?"

It took Morgan a moment to realize what she was asking. He'd forgotten about Victor. Liz was looking at him with an increasingly worried expression. He wanted to go to her, to pull her close and tell her everything would be ok, but something held him back. "I don't know," he said, and turned away.

* * *

The *Sagitta's* bridge towered above the primary hull, and the wrap-around windows offered an amazing view of the phenomenon outside. The stars directly in front of the ship burned a brilliant blue. At the port and starboard beam, the starlight was white, but the stars themselves were elongated into thin streamers that bent around the ship. The stars to the stern were points of light again, although red in hue.

Stone floated on the edge of her chair, one arm propped under her chin. *It's beautiful.* But everything was wrong. They were traveling much too fast, and the engines refused to disengage. Strange blue energy waves coursed over the shields like lightning.

She considered the point of light that was perfectly centered in the forward window. It was the class-g star known as Chara, and it was getting brighter. *We're flying straight at it a zillion miles an hour...but why?*

She looked around at her bridge crew. They attended their consoles without comment or speculation, set to the task of deciphering the terabytes of information that were pouring in from the *Sagitta's* sensors. So far, no one could offer her any explanation for what was happening beyond conjecture.

"Helm, has there been any change in our course?" Stone said.

"Negative," replied Lawson. "We're still heading towards Chara, and the controls still won't answer."

208

"Distance?"

"Twenty-four light years."

Stone ran her hands through her hair. *Incredible.* Chara was twenty-seven light-years from Earth. They had travelled over three light-years in as many minutes. That was much faster than Dr. Fowler's research had suggested the drive was capable of.

"Anyone else feel that?" asked Lieutenant Carver from her post at the navigation station.

"What?" said Stone.

Carver indicated the deck plating. "There's a shimmy coming up through the hull."

Stone pushed off and extended her legs, locking her magnetic boots to the deck. "Yes, I feel it. Helm?"

Lawson worked his control board. "Gravimetric shear is increasing." He swiveled around, frowning. "These readings don't make any sense."

Outside, the blue energy streamers seemed brighter and more numerous than they had been just a few moments ago. An alert chirped from the helm console. "Warp field potential is building and I can't stop it," said Lawson. The shuddering intensified. "We're accelerating again."

"The intercom crackled to life. "Engineering to bridge."

"Stone here."

Roland's voice was strained . "Skipper, we can't get to the computer core. The AI dropped the emergency bulkheads and locked us out."

"Understood," said Stone. "Do you have a plan B?"

There was a pause. "Yes, but you're not going to like it. We're locked out of the reactor, but I can still route main power into the shield grid. With enough power, I might be able to disrupt the warp field around the ship. It might also tear the ship apart."

"You're right, I don't like it." *But if we don't do it we might fly into a star.* "Do it."

"Acknowledged. You better hold onto something."

Stone flipped on the ship-wide announcing circuit. "This is the captain. All hands prepare for deceleration."

There was a lurch not unlike that of an airplane striking turbulent cross-winds. Stone sat back in her chair and gripped her armrests. The ship shook again, more violently.

"Hull stress increasing," said Decker from the tactical station.

"Helm, any change?" said Stone.

"Negative," said Lawson.

The vibration doubled, then redoubled. It was hard for Stone to stay silent. *Let Roland do his job.* She looked down at her control display and watched as the shield modulation frequency shifted, then shifted again. The ship lurched so sharply that she nearly tumbled from her chair. She energized the restraining field.

"Hull stress is critical," said Decker. "The space frame will yield if we keep this up."

Stone could take it no longer. "Roland!" she barked into the open comm channel.

"I know," he said. "We can't make enough power to cancel this field. I'm taking the reactor offline."

The shuddering stopped. Stone cursed under her breath.

Lawson slammed a fist into the frame of the helm console. "Blast it Captain, we're still accelerating. At this rate, we'll reach Chara in fifteen minutes. Although, we're drifting a bit. I think we're going to just miss the star. Our course now appears to be towards empty space."

"Roland," said Stone. "Find a way to pull a plug on that crazy computer. I don't care how you do it. Kill power to the entire ship if you have to."

There was a lurch. "Our speed just tripled," said Lawson. "We're passing Chara." On the screen, the bright blue dot they had been heading towards stretched for an instant into an infinitely long white streak, then slipped off to the side.

Stone blinked. Something else had changed.

"Where are the stars?" said a crewman.

All around the bridge, the crew gawked out the windows. All starlight was gone. Only the strange coursing blue energy ribbons remained. *We're still moving,* thought Stone. *The engines are still humming along.* "Lawson, where are we?"

"There's nothing on my indicators. I can't get a bearing."

"Impossible. Ensign Carver, full spectrum scan."

"I already did one," said Carver.

Stone activated her chair's servo and swiveled around to regard her science officer. The young woman was engrossed in her displays at the back of the bridge. "And?"

"There's nothing. Except…wait a minute." Carver's face transformed into a horrified stare as she watched her screens. "Oh shit!"

Carver looked up from her controls and locked eyes with Stone as the collision alarm sounded.

* * *

The fighting had stopped. Clouds of debris hung all about Sledgim. Ruba's remaining ships, including the King's own, were powered down and awaiting their fate.

With the preparations to evacuate his ship almost complete, Mog readied himself for his final act.

He paced the length of the bridge, visiting the empty stations one by one. The chairs were still warm, the scent of their recent occupants lingering like ghosts. *Fear. Despair. Insanity.* He could smell death on them.

Ramas, if you're real, if this enemy is really the demons of old, then I'm sorry. Let my crew escape this place. I offer myself for their sake.

He would never see any of them again, that much was certain.

The comm system chirped. He flipped on the channel.

"We're almost ready to go," said Ryal. His voice was deflated. "All escape pods and light craft are full."

"Understood. Launch on my signal. Not a moment before."

Mog returned to his command chair and sat down. *There's nothing more you could have done.* He keyed in the collision course, then lifted the safety protocol from the antimatter reactor and prepared to divert all power to the engines. *Not yet. Can't give it away yet.*

His control panel beeped. He turned to his sensor display, expecting to find that the Ta'Krell had opened fire on the planet. But that wasn't it.

It was a strange power reading—an anomaly was forming in the center of the Ta'Krell flagship. The *Narma Kull* was close now. Mog had been flying her in, bow pointed slightly away from the enemy, with all offensive and defensive systems powered down. He was going slow, announcing a message of surrender on all channels.

So far, they had let him approach. They hadn't fired, but he was still too far away to spring his trap.

"Nazpah."

The Ta'Krell supercruiser loomed before him, victorious. What were they doing? What ungodly weapon could they be unleashing? *Mauria, engulfed in flame.*

"Prepare to launch," said Mog. "Twenty seconds."

"Goodbye," said Ryal.

Mog bowed his head. "Goodbye, my good friend, and good luck. Ten seconds."

The space around the Ta'Krell flagship was bending in and out, distorting the light passing through the area. The ship itself, although still intact, appeared to be flexing along every axis.

A blue-white flash enveloped the Ta'Krell ship. Mog glanced towards Sledgim. The planet was still there. He looked back.

"Mog, do we launch?"

Ryal's voice was light-years away. "Mog? Mog!"

The enemy vessel seemed to be drifting in two directions at once. White-hot gas and flame erupted from the parting line down its middle. Mog stood up, mouth agape.

"Can't wait any longer," said Ryal. "Launching escape pods."

"Hold!" Mog bellowed.

Internal detonations sent pieces of hull flying from both sections of the Ta'Krell ship until there was nothing left but a single wing and a dense, expanding cloud of junk. A dark shape came flying out of the debris field. The screen zoomed in to reveal a rectangular object. It was large, but not nearly as big as the Ta'Krell vessel. The twin pods at the rear of the vessel were glowing red.

"Mog, what's going on up there?" said Ryal.

"Get everyone back up here."

"Commander?"

"Target destroyed. Repeat, target destroyed. Abort the evacuation! All hands, battle stations!"

* * *

It was dead silent in the brig. Morgan released his white-knuckle grip from the webbing on the wall. He and Liz looked at each other.

"We've stopped," said Liz.

And we're still alive, thought Morgan. Only a few seconds ago, the computer had been blaring on about a collision warning. His body ached from all the jolts and bumps. No one had designed the brig for comfort, let alone sudden changes in acceleration. If not for the webbing on the walls, they would have bounced around like balls in a pinball machine.

"There's light out there," said Liz, looking out the window. "Come and see."

Morgan did. Far off, barely visible from the small window, was the sun. But it was strange-looking. The color was off. "That's not our sun, is it?" he said flatly.

"No, it's not," said Liz. "We're in another solar system!"

As distressing as that was, two other things were bothering him even more. For one, where were the stars? And, more importantly…

213

"Hey, what is that?" said Liz, pressing her face next to his. "Down below us."

A huge metal something glistened in the light of the strange sun as it drifted past. Morgan squinted. There were multiple smaller objects surrounding it. *Shrapnel?*

"Did we hit something?" said Liz.

There was a small burst of light as something just out of view exploded. Morgan felt a sinking feeling as he watched glowing embers shoot across his field of view. *This can't be good.*

* * *

The bridge was bathed in yellow light. It had happened so quickly that the aft windows took a moment to energize their tint mechanisms. "Status report," said Stone, shading her eyes.

"We've dropped to sublight!" said Lawson. "There's a local star behind us. It's not the sun. It's not Chara either. I…this is strange—there's no way to get a galactic position. All the other stars are gone."

Stone was staring out the port side windows. "What the f—"

"Confirmed," said Carver. "Something is blocking the extra-solar light. As to this star, it doesn't match anything on record. It's a small G-type main sequence star, 0.89 Sol. There's another object on the scopes, bearing ten degrees to port, thirteen degrees elevation."

Everyone moved to look out the forward window. The planet was blue-gray. Blankets of ice swaddled both hemispheres. *An alien world!* Stone frowned. They had come out of warp awfully close to the planet. *Just the slightest miscalculation and we'd have warped through the freaking thing. But it wasn't a human making those calculations now was it?*

"Captain," said an officer from one of the side stations. "There's a field of objects behind us." The man shook his head and rechecked his readings. "I'm showing multiple metallic signatures. Iron, titanium, aluminum, and many alloys I can't identify. And there's intermittent power surges emanating from the field. It almost looks like debris from a ship."

"Put it on the imager," said Stone.

The forward section of the bridge melted away as the holographic display filled the space. The field of glowing scrap metal was enormous. Twisted shards spiraled away in all directions. Some items were more complex. *Machinery perhaps? Is that from us?* She checked her status display. *No pressure loss. If we were damaged that badly we'd know it.*

"Wide angle," she said.

The holographic imagers reset. An enormous metal blade was drifting lazily away from them, its surface charred and blackened at the edges.

"What is that?" said a crewman from the port auxiliary station.

"Is it from us?" said another.

"Negative," said Lieutenant Commander Decker from the tactical station. "Our hull is intact."

"Helm, move us away from the debris, nice and slow," said Stone. "And scan for energy signatures."

Lawson sounded the acceleration warning. Around the bridge, the few crewmembers who were not strapped into their seats did so. Stone settled into her command chair as the engines fired. Unlike the majority of the decks on the *Sagitta,* which were oriented perpendicular to the ship's axis of thrust, the bridge was oriented parallel, so that the crew could easily look forward in the direction of motion.

"I've got something," said Decker. "Putting it on the viewer."

The image shifted again. Something was moving through the debris, coming slowly towards them. A chill ran through Stone when the object changed directions. *It's moving under its own power.*

"Holy crap," muttered a crewman. Nervous whispers spread across the bridge like wildfire.

"Everyone quiet," snapped Stone. "We need to keep our heads on straight if we want to…to…"

Her words evaporated as the black-hulled, wedge-shaped ship rose above them, blocking out the view of the planet.

"Scan complete," said Decker. "The computer's tagged dozens of contacts. The emissions are strange, they don't match anything in the database. We're optically scoping them now. Most are damaged, and there's lots more debris."

"Full tactical analysis on that one," said Stone, pointing.

"Already done," said Decker. "She's not big, maybe three hundred meters long and fifty meters on the beam at the most. I can't get a read on the internal configuration. Our penetrating scans just bounce back. I'm not detecting any guns or laser banks, but there are hot spots on her hull that don't match any known energy signature. That ring drive at the back reads sort of like a fusion thruster, but there's something else going on with it that the computer can't figure out."

An alien ship, thought Stone. *We warp forty-something light-years and pop out in an inhabited system. What are the chances?* When this was over, assuming they made it out in one piece, she would personally help Roland extract and dissect that blasted AI. "Ensign Carver, hail that vessel."

"What do I say?" said Carver.

"You don't need to say anything," said Stone. "Look up SCP forty-seven in the database and run the program. It'll send the standard greetings in all known languages." *We come in peace. Don't blast us to atoms please!*

"Got it," said Carver. "Transmitting."

The bridge crew held their breath. Stone watched the ship get closer. Her eyes narrowed. Twinkling green stars were coming right at them.

The bridge erupted with panicked shouts as the combat klaxon blared, and the sound of imploding compartments resonated upwards through the ship. "Battle Stations!" said Stone. "All hands to battle stations!"

The lights dimmed, taking on a red hue.

"Hull breach on decks four, five, and six," said the damage control officer operator. "We're venting atmosphere."

"Engines to full power," said Stone. "Get us away from that thing. Are our shields even up?"

"Of course," said Decker. "But their bloody ray guns went right through." His hands flew over the controls. The ship jolted again, but less violently. "There, I switched off the repulsion generators and boosted the spread-spectrum fields. We have partial protection against their weapons, whatever they are."

Stone was slammed into the seatback as the *Sagitta's* engines went to full burn. "Decker," she said, her voice grim. *This can't be happening.* "Do we have a firing solution?"

"Yes ma'am."

She grimaced. The moment every starship captain dreamed of—first contact with an alien species—had come and passed. The moment every captain dreaded was upon her. *We are going to have to fire on them. No, I won't do it. Not yet.* "Fire a warning shot. One shot only, tracer round."

There was a dull thud as the tracer lanced out, phosphors burning brightly as it shot across the alien vessel's bow.

"Carver, are we still broadcasting the universal greetings?"

"Yes ma'am."

"Good. Keep them playing no matter what." *I bet they have no idea what we're saying.* Stone grunted as the acceleration changed directions. The ship lurched again and for an instant everything spun sideways.

"We just lost a fusion engine," said Lawson. "Engaging vectored exhaust attitude compensation."

Screw this. "Stone to engineering. Roland, can we use the warp drive to get out of here?"

"Not yet Skipper," said the engineer. "The nacelles are still too hot from our trip in. I'm working on it. What the bloody hell is going on out there?"

"Oh nothing," said Stone. "Just some pissed-off extra-terrestrials. I could use some better shields."

"Aliens? When were you going to tell me about that?"

217

"Shields, Roland, shields!"

"Right. I'll do what I can."

The holographic display tracked the enemy ship as the two vessels danced around each other. Blast after blast tore into the *Sagitta*. The cutaway schematics on Stone's display showed multiple blinking orange and red zones.

"We can't take much more of this," said Decker.

Agreed, thought Stone. She swiveled around and met Decker's gaze. She nodded slightly. *We both know what needs to be done.*

He nodded back.

"More incoming," shouted one of the sensor technicians.

Three more alien ships were swooping towards them, their pointed bows glowing with green fire. *What a crazy way to die. No one will ever know what happened.* Stone shuddered, and shook it off. *Screw that. Let's see if our guns are as strange to you as yours are to us.* "Decker, all forward batteries. Fire!"

Invisible laser beams lanced out, making instantaneous red hotspots on the alien's hull. A second later came the sharp retort of the main rail guns, the vibration traveling through the ship's structure from six decks below. The rounds were invisible except for a tracer on every fifth shot.

For a moment it looked as if nothing happened. Then, the pointed bow of the alien ship imploded, followed by its engine assembly. Shrapnel, gas, and yellow fire erupted from the other side.

Got you. Stone didn't pause to revel. "Next target. Fire!"

Chapter 26

Both transpods opened and the bridge crew spilled out. Ryal raced up to the command platform.

"What happened to the plan?"

Mog indicated the viewscreen.

Ryal stared. "Is that pile of scrap the Ta'Krell's heavy ship?"

"Yes," said Mog. He manipulated his controls, trying to bring the *Narma Kull* into weapons range while powering up the plasma cannons. It was difficult. He was no helmsman, and the controls of his command chair were simplified.

"Meela, Nali, get to it," he growled.

He need not have bothered; the two women had instantly sized up the situation and had sprinted to their stations. Mog pushed away his controls as Meela's station overrode his.

"By Ramas' claws," said Ryal. "What did you do?"

"I didn't do anything. They did." Mog pointed at the strange black-hulled ship that had materialized from the wreckage. "There was an unknown energy signature, then that ship out there was flying out of the wreckage of the enemy."

Murmurs filled the bridge.

"Are they friendly?" said Ryal.

"The Ta'Krell are shooting at them," said Mog. "So that's a yes as far as I'm concerned."

Both of them watched as round after round of Ta'Krell transplasma ate into the newcomer's shields. The ship's hull was scorched, her shields only partially effective. The new ship fired back a single shot that went wide.

"A miss?" said Ryal.

"Perhaps," said Mog. "But they didn't miss before, when they hit the big one. Nali, time to target?"

"Ten seconds," she said. "But sir, the Ta'Krell have sent reinforcements. Three more light cruisers incoming."

Just then, the little ship veered to port, and its starboard side erupted with what appeared to be projectile sabot rounds. Yellow tracers streaked through space. The broadside volley struck the Ta'Krell vessel head-on. There was no sign of a shield impact, and the Ta'Krell vessel came apart at the seams.

"Bral-vai!" shouted Ryal. "Praise Ramas, they gutted 'em."

"They took a pounding though," said Nali.

Mog knew he had to keep their newfound momentum going. "Ja'tar, send to Ruba and our escorts: the fight is back on. Order all ships to engage."

"Commander," said Ja'tar. "I just got word. The King is not in command. As a term of the surrender, mar-Ruba agreed to be taken prisoner."

Ruba, captured? It can't be.

"Sir," said Nali, "if the King is on one of the enemy vessels, we might end up killing him with our own fire."

"Do we know what ship he's on?" said Meela. "Maybe we could rescue him?"

"Working on that," said Ja'tar. "Right now, all I know is they took his shuttle."

Mog weighed the options. There wasn't much of a choice. What was one man's life against the chance of saving a civilization?

"We're not stopping," he said. "We've been handed a break and we're going to take it. The hyperdrive should work now, right?"

He swiveled around. Kremp gave him an affirmative growl.

"Good."

On the viewscreen, the Ta'Krell reinforcements had the new ship ranged. Appearing as small specs on the screen, they rained fire down on the strange vessel. The newcomer was running, lobbing shot after shot at its pursuers with its aft weapons. Occasionally one of the projectiles would hit, but the Ta'Krell must have realized they were dealing with a slug-thrower. They had reformulated their shields, and the metal rounds were deflected harmlessly away. Mog didn't think the new ship would score any more easy victories.

"Meela, program a micro-jump. Put us between them."

"Ready sir."

"Jump!"

* * *

Stone knew they were done for. The damage control board was red all over, and the three-on-one fight had just become a four-on-one. She stared at the huge four-winged ship that had just…just what exactly? *Popped in,* was the term Carver had used. It had just *popped in* alongside them.

There was only one tactic left, and that was to see if they could outrun their attackers. She doubted it. With the engines damaged as they were, they'd be lucky to hold two g's of acceleration.

The big ship fired a stream of blue energy. Stone braced herself, but the impact never came. Instead, a black-hulled craft the *Sagitta* had been trading blows with exploded. Stone blinked. *What?*

"They're on our side!" screamed Decker. "Captain, they're on our side!"

"Yes," said Stone. "Yes!"

But the *Sagitta* was in no condition to keep fighting. "Helm, get us clear and go to maximum burn. Get some distance between us."

"On it," said Lawson.

I need to buy more time. She activated the intercom. "All Firefly pilots, report to hangar bay one and prepare to launch." She had no idea how the fighter craft would stack up against these enemies, and she could be sending the pilots to their deaths. *I wish I never took this assignment.* She'd had a complete career. She could have retired. But there was always the call of that next mission, the promise of doing something great. *And I have. Even if we all die here, we did something great.*

"Shields are on battery reserves," said Decker. "One more hit and we'll lose them."

"Understood," said Stone. *If the shields go down, then they could finish us with a nuke. We won't even know what hit us.* She adjusted her sensor display. The four-winged ship had the two remaining attackers sufficiently distracted. Perhaps there was still time to ensure some people lived.

She flipped on the general comm circuit. "This is Captain Stone. All non-essential crew report to the lifeboats and launch immediately. I repeat, all non-combat crew members, abandon ship!"

* * *

The door to the brig swung open as Captain Stone's command to abandon ship echoed around the tiny room. Morgan and Liz scrambled through it to the anteroom and stopped.

The woman who had been their jailor was lying on the floor, her head twisted backwards at an unnatural angle. Her sightless eyes stared up at them.

"The acceleration," said Liz weakly.

Morgan nodded. Thankfully they had been on the lower side of the brig when the *Sagitta* had gone to full thrust, and had only fallen a few feet to smash into the floor. He tried to move, but his legs didn't want to respond.

"Victor!" said Liz. "Morgan, we have to get to Victor."

"Ok," he said, still staring at the body. He'd never seen a dead person before. He'd heard they were supposed to look peaceful. They definitely weren't supposed to look like this. *It's like we're in a war.* He recalled the glimpse of the strange ship that had flown past the porthole window, firing blasts of green energy. It too was unlike anything he had ever seen.

Liz pulled at his arm. "Morgan, please."

"Yeah, coming," he said. He put one foot forward, then another. It was a lot of work. The ship was accelerating hard, and the force seemed much more than that of normal gravity. His feet felt like they were twenty-pound dumbbells.

"How do we get to the sickbay?" said Liz, stepping out into the corridor.

Morgan shook his head. "I have no idea. It's not like there's a map, is there?"

"No," said Liz. Her eyes were glowing. "There are access channels but I'm locked out. The ship's computer won't talk to me."

"Make way!" came a cry from down the corridor.

A group of people wearing green uniforms, helmets, and oxygen masks were struggling down the corridor. *Pilots!* One stopped, glaring at Morgan and Liz. "Are you two crazy?" she wheezed, between heaving breaths. "Get off this ship now!"

"What's going on?" said Morgan.

"It doesn't matter. Just get off."

Liz shook her head. "No, we need to get to sickbay. My friend is there, he was hurt."

"Sickbay's been evacuated," said the pilot. "The life boats are probably launching as we speak. We're going out to defend them."

"Gabe, come on, forget them," said another one of the pilots. "That's an order."

"Sorry," said the pilot, turning to follow after her companions. She looked back over her shoulder. "Get off the ship." Then, she ran down the corridor and out of sight.

"How?" said Morgan. "Where are the escape pods?" He felt like an idiot. He should have asked the pilots for directions.

"Victor's already off then," said Liz. She sounded like she was trying to reassure herself. "He'll be alright. We need to get off too. Come on, let's follow those pilots."

Morgan didn't have any better ideas, so he agreed.

They had taken maybe a dozen steps under the grueling acceleration when something tore through the corridor behind them with a sound like a cement mixer crashing through an aluminum shed. Air hurtled past in a whirlwind.

Liz screamed as she was pulled backwards. She slammed into Morgan and they both went down, somersaulting backwards, hands scrabbling for purchase. Morgan yelped as his fingers were nearly ripped from his hand. His fist closed on the freefall webbing. Ahead of him, Liz similarly dangled.

The lights went out.

For a horrifying moment it was pitch black. Primal panic filled Morgan, a fear unlike any he had ever known.

Then, dim emergency lights flickered on.

Morgan looked backwards at the great sucking maw of hard vacuum and felt as if his soul was being torn from his body. His lungs were going to explode. He exhaled, and when he tried to breathe in again there was simply nothing to breathe. He screwed his eyes shut. *I'm going to die, and no one will know what happened.*

The deck quivered. Blood pounded in his ears. And then, he heard the rasping, hacking sound of Liz next to him.

He looked up and felt the faint pressure of air against his face. The vents in the ceiling were forcing air back into the space. He could hear it! He gasped, sucking oxygen into his burning chest. Behind them, not three feet away from the tips of his toes, was the glow of an emergency force field.

Liz sat up. Her hair was a mess, and she was bleeding from multiple scrapes. Morgan looked down at his arms and found them equally torn up.

Liz mumbled something at him.

"What?" he said. The ringing in his ears was making it hard to hear.

"Got to move," she gasped. "Before the power goes out again."

Morgan looked at the faintly glowing force field. "Right. Come on."

* * *

The *Narma Kull* was on the hunt, plasma cannons eating into the enemy ship whenever there was a clear shot. Meela dodged an out-of-control torpedo that Nali had winged with the AMS system, then maneuvered them expertly around a disabled frigate to resume the chase. She hounded the Ta'Krell relentlessly, staying glued to their tail. *She's a good pilot,* thought Mog. *A good fighter. We all are. Survive long enough and I suppose that happens. But are we good enough?*

The Ta'Krell had launched fighters. The *Narma Kull* shuddered as a swarm of them opened fire, peppering her shields, probing for a weakness.

Mog checked his armrest's status display. They had destroyed half of the Ta'Krell light cruisers, and the anti-missile system was racking up dozens of fighter kills. With their hyperdrives back, the Maurian force seemed an even match for the remaining Ta'Krell.

He grimaced as the lead Ta'Krell cruiser shot upwards in front of his ship, pounding the *Narma Kull* at point blank range. It was followed by a volley of blue plasma bolts from a pursuing Maurian frigate. Meela groaned and slammed her controls, sending the *Narma Kull* into a dive to avoid colliding with the frigate.

"Target destroyed." said Nali.

"Good job," said Mog. "Now turn us back towards our new friends and find another target. Keep them off of that ship."

"Yes sir," said Meela.

She flipped them around and burned the engines hard, slowing their negative velocity, until the newcomer's vessel was growing larger again on the viewscreen. It was badly damaged. Although Mog didn't know anything about the people manning that ship, they had earned the right to be called friends.

The new ship fired a volley of projectiles, striking the nearest Ta'Krell cruiser in the side. The kinetic energy of the blast nudged the enemy ship

225

off course, sending it directly in the *Narma Kull's* path. Nali didn't hesitate to send two torpedoes and a volley of transplasma into the Ta'Krell cruiser as it flew past.

There was a brilliant flash that washed out the viewscreen.

"There goes another one," said Ryal.

The newcomers had detonated another warhead. The previous two nuclear explosions had done little against the shielded Ta'Krell warships.

"They scored with that one," said Nali.

"They got a cruiser?" said Mog.

"No, they detonated some sort of shrapnel bomb in the middle of one of the Ta'Krell fighter squadrons. The blast disabled all eight fighters."

"Blowing up fighters isn't going to win this for us," said Mog.

"We just lost another frigate," said Ja'tar. "Sledgim ground command reports enemy fighters have entered the atmosphere. They're bombing the surface installations."

Mog snarled. He wished they still had an operational fighter wing. *Nothing we can do. Just keep fighting.* The *Narma Kull* lurched upward, and the edge of Mog's armrest jabbed into his side.

"Ventral shields buckling," said Nali. "We've got two ships and a wing of fighters attacking our belly."

"Everyone hold on," said Meela.

Mog wasn't sure what felt worse: Meela's roll or the subsequent impact from the Ta'Krell's second volley.

"Sir," said Nali. "Small craft launch detected." She pointed at the screen. "It's them."

Eight sleek gray craft shot out of the strange vessel one by one. Mog swiveled around. "Ja'tar, tell our fleet to check their small targets. They've got friendlies."

"The Ta'Krell fighters are moving to intercept," said Nali. "Hold on, they're launching something else. They look like boarding craft! They're heading towards the alien ship."

"Intercept them at all costs" said Mog. *We can't let the Ta'Krell capture that vessel.*

Chapter 27

Morgan's legs burned from trudging through the high gravity. They had passed two escape pod tubes, but each had been empty. The first time it had happened, he feared the ship was completely abandoned. But then the acceleration alarm had sounded. Someone was still piloting the *Sagitta*.

Whatever was attacking had not given up. The acceleration warning came again. Morgan and Liz stopped running and grabbed the webbing that lined the corridor. The ship spun. Their legs whipped out, then came crashing down as the ship resumed straight-line acceleration. Morgan could only imagine what the maneuver was for. *Dodging some missile maybe. But who's firing?*

The deck lurched, and there was the sound of screeching metal from behind. They whirled—a black spear protruded into the ruined corridor, perhaps four feet in diameter. Smoke billowed from beneath it. "Is that the nose of a ship?" said Morgan.

A panel in the side of the object detached with a hiss, revealing a hole leading inside.

"Come on," said Morgan, tugging at Liz's arm.

She stood rooted to the spot. He followed her gaze, dread filling him as a hulking form squeezed through the opening. Two yellow eyes blinked at them through the haze.

"Move!"

Liz had come to her senses, and her shout broke him free. They ran. Behind came the sound of something scraping, like nails on a chalkboard. *Don't look.*

Morgan tried to move faster, but the gravity was oppressive. It was like wading through molasses. He could feel those eyes boring into him. Any second now the nightmare would catch him.

They rounded a corner and stopped in front of familiar orange doors, the lettering barely visible in the emergency lighting: 'Hangar Bay 1'.

Beyond, the way was blocked by fallen stiffeners and twisted wiring from the deck above.

Liz slammed the doors with her fist. "Hey, open up in there!"

There was no answer.

A bone-scraping noise came from behind them. Goosebumps rose on Morgan's skin. He sniffed. There was something foul in the air, like wet dog. *There must be a way in!*

He spotted a raised glass plate, barely visible in the weak red glow from the emergency lights. It was a handprint scanner. He pressed his moist palm against it.

Red letters flashed across the glass: 'Access Denied'.

"Morgan," hissed Liz. "It's here."

Hair standing on end, he turned. The beast loomed before them, shrouded in darkness. The back of its head pressed against the ceiling. Its eyes were all-consuming fire.

There was a clang and a hiss as the hangar entrance parted, filling the corridor with a shaft of light. "Get down!" roared a voice.

They dropped. The next instant, the corridor rang with the bark of an assault rifle.

"You two, get inside."

A big man stepped into the corridor, shielding them. Tendons bulged in his neck as he fired into the darkness where the alien had vanished. "Wally ain't scared, you hear me? I dare you to show your face, dog!"

A green blast lanced out of the darkness and slammed into the man's chest. He was wearing a shield vest, which flashed white and overloaded. The big man grunted and stumbled backwards, his uniform smoldering.

Liz and Morgan tumbled sideways into the room. The man fired again, and the monster screamed. It was unlike any scream Morgan had ever heard, and it chilled his blood.

Their savior ejected his spent magazine and jumped through the doors. "Computer, seal the hangar." A force field flared up, reinforcing the doors as they closed. "That should hold it." He fed a new clip into his rifle. "I'm Wally Brooks, Hangar Technician First Class. Who the blazes are you?"

They introduced themselves as best they could, considering the ringing in their ears.

"So you're the civilians we picked up earlier? What were you doing out here?"

"It's a long story," said Morgan. "What's attacking us?"

"I have no idea." Wally looked down at his smoldering uniform. It had burned through in places. His brown skin was blistered and oozing beneath. He tore his spent shield generator off his belt and tossed it across the hangar bay. "You saw the thing, what would you say it was?"

Morgan said nothing. He didn't want to think about it.

"There was another one of us," Liz cut in. "His name is Victor. They took him to sickbay. Have you seen him?"

"Afraid not. He probably got off already. A bunch of people did, although I heard the buggers are shooting at the life pods." Liz looked horrified. Wally didn't seem to notice. He indicated the doors, which were starting to glow red behind the force field. "We should get out too."

"You'll help us?" said Morgan.

"Of course. I've been guarding this hangar since our flyboys left. I was hoping the rest would show up, but that won't happen now."

The paint on the door started to bubble, and the force field flickered. "How do we get out?" said Morgan. "All the escape pods were launched."

Wally pointed at the fighters. "How else?"

The fighters they had arrived in were still here, off to the side. Morgan took a step towards them. "Of course! We can escape in those."

"Escape?" said Liz, her face hardening. "No way. We're not going to run. We're going to fight." She pointed at the other row of Fireflies. Four armed ships remained.

"Are you nuts?" said Wally.

"I might be. But Victor's out there in an escape pod and he needs help. Morgan, come on, we're going."

Is Victor all she cares about? It didn't matter. They were out of options, and a starfighter was much better than a life boat. *Assuming I can fly it.* Jack had made it look easy. How hard could it be? "Alright," he said. "I'll try."

Wally grunted. "I don't care what you do once you're out. We're all probably dead meat anyway. Each of you just pick a ship and power it up. There are HUD goggles in a compartment under the dash. Put them on. I'll hold this position while you get in."

"You know how to fly?" said Liz.

"Enough to move the ships around the bay." He turned and headed for a control panel. "Use the goggles, they have a training mode. Now get gone before this bugger shows his ugly face."

They sprinted across the hangar, passing the unarmed ships they had arrived in. Had Jack and Yin escaped with two of the *Sagitta's* fighters? They hadn't been with the pilots that had passed them in the corridor. Morgan desperately hoped so.

The *Sagitta* shook from another blast.

"Quick," said Morgan. "Let's take this one."

Liz shook her head. "Let's take two. Better odds. We can work together, cover each other."

Morgan wanted to tell her no, but her face said she wasn't taking no for an answer. "I don't know," he stammered. "If we just took one, then at least—"

"You can't both fit!" shouted Wally. They turned to look at him. "The *Sagitta's* Fireflies are one-seaters. If you want to fight, you take two birds out. Only way to go out together is if you take one of the unarmed trainers you came in on."

"See!" said Liz.

Morgan gulped. *That settles it then.* "Ok, but Liz, I wanted to say, I never got to tell you—"

She hugged him. "Tell me later when this is over." She had tears in her eyes. "I'm sorry about this whole thing."

Morgan hugged her. *It's me who should be sorry.* "Good luck."

"You too."

He let her go as the hangar entrance door collapsed into the force field. "Go, you idiots!" shouted Wally.

They raced to the nearest ships and hauled themselves up the ladders. In the heavy acceleration, it was almost impossible. Morgan thought he was going to have a heart attack, but somehow managed to lift the ladder out of its socket. It slammed down to the floor with a mighty clang.

He hauled himself across the wing of his ship and onto the fuselage. The canopy slid back when he touched it. He jumped in and fell heavily into the seat. There were dozens of toggles and knobs, along with blank touch-screen control panels and de-energized holographic emitters. *What do I do?*

Below them, Wally was scampering away from a control panel on the port side of the hangar deck. Something in the ceiling moved. Morgan looked up. Two machine guns slid out of recessed ports and turned to aim at the hangar bay entrance. A second later, as the force field winked out, the guns bellowed, sending round after round into the corridor.

Morgan shut the canopy, hoping Batson hadn't been lying when he said you didn't need implants to fly. He spoke on a whim. "Computer, start Firefly."

There was no response. He hadn't expected one. He scanned the cockpit. It would be something obvious. There! A row of red toggle switches. He didn't bother reading the labels, but flipped them all at once. The cockpit lit up like a Christmas tree.

Liz must have found the controls for the running lights, because strong floodlights ignited under her wings.

The comm crackled to life.

"You guys there?" said Wally.

"I hear you," said Morgan.

"Yes!" said Liz.

"Get those goggles on. They're under the dashboard."

It took Morgan a moment to find them. He pulled them over his eyes just as the lights in the hangar went out. The racket from the machine guns died, and for a moment Morgan was weightless. Then, with a lurch, gravity returned, but it was weaker than before.

"Power's failing," said Wally. "Quick, hit the button on the top right of the goggles."

Morgan did so.

"Just look at the controls," said Wally. "The HUD labels stuff. Blink your left eye twice for more info, right eye twice to clear."

Morgan looked down at the control stick and blinked his left eye twice. Tags popped up indicating which triggers did what. *Cool!* He looked ahead at the hangar bay's open space doors. The opening was a dark hole surrounded by the faint glow of the force field emitters. *At least that force field is still working.*

Something was moving below. He squinted into the deep shadows in the corner of the bay. One shadow in particular seemed darker than it should. *We're not alone.*

"Use repulsors to get out of the bay," said Wally. "It's the little lever next to the main throttle."

Morgan quickly found it thanks to the HUD. He pushed it forward. His ship rose on a shimmering blue energy cushion. Liz's ship was already in the air, and Wally's soon joined them. Morgan grasped the control stick, keeping his fingers off the triggers, and gave it an experimental nudge to the side. His ship moved a few inches closer to Liz's fighter. He twisted the stick, and his ship rotated a few degrees. *Ok, this is pretty easy.* He let go of the stick when he had it lined up with the bay opening.

"Nice work," said Wally. "Now, edge the stick forward. Let's get the hell outta here."

Morgan nudged the stick and he began to cruise across the deck. He tried to remember the other things Jack had told him. *Strap in, kid.* He did so as he glanced around the hangar. The figure was gone. *Where is it? What is it doing?*

"Alright," said Wally. "Here we go." He glided out of the bay. Liz followed. Their ships hung for a moment, framed by the force field generators before an infinite backdrop of black nothingness. Then, their repulsors lost their grip on the *Sagitta* and they dropped out of sight, as if they had gone over a waterfall.

Once, long ago, Morgan had nearly wet his pants when riding in the bow of his grandfather's little wooden boat. The ocean had stretched out before them, and all Morgan could think about was what it would be like to topple over the side, to succumb to the cold grip of the Atlantic.

His grandfather's words echoed in his mind. *People fear what they don't know. Today, I'm going to make you a fish.*

"I've done this before," he muttered. "I can do it again." *Out you go, little fish.* Summoning all his nerve, he pushed the stick forward.

Something was wrong. Why was his ship leaning to the left? He looked over.

A shaggy, black-furred monster was perched on the edge of the fuselage, its snout only an inch away from the canopy, its claws leaving thin scratches on the wing. Its breath had fogged the glass. Its pupils narrowed into slits as it opened its mouth, revealing razor-sharp fangs.

Morgan jerked as something touched his mind. *Cold, so cold.* All the memories of his life flew past the alien's demonic eyes, which burned into him.

He saw a Mickey Mouse clock on the nursery wall. A cake with three candles. His mother, smiling down at him, young and radiant.

More.

His childhood friends, Luke and Simon and Greg. They'd moved away years ago, leaving a hole he'd never filled. His old cat Daisy. She'd been dead nine years.

More.

His parents working in the lab. His dad crying at his grandfather's funeral in Maine. The day he drove the Scorpion for the first time. The day he met Liz. It was hot under the Arizona sun, despite his refrigerated racing suit.

Where?

The question was strange. The voice in his head had asked it, yet it wasn't *his* voice.

Where is this place? Where are you from?

"Arizona," he said, his mouth moving automatically.

Where?

Earth hung in his memory as he'd seen it from space. He looked down at Arizona, then up. Everything zoomed out. There was Starlight Station, the Moon, the Sun.

Which star?

He didn't know how to describe it. He gasped in pain as a top-down image of the Milky Way galaxy popped into his head.

Which arm? Which star?

"I don't know!"

The creature roared. **Then Die!**

Morgan screamed, and his head snapped back. Outside the creature raised something to the glass. "Go baby go!" he gasped, slamming the main throttle forward. He was thrown back into the seat as backwash from the rockets lit the hangar bay up like day. Burning gas encircled the fighter as it shot forward. The creature howled, then toppled off the back of the wing.

"Morgan, are you ok?" said Liz, as he streaked out of the *Sagitta* on a plume of fire.

He didn't have the strength to answer. It took all of his effort just to reach forward and drag the throttle back. He slumped against the seat back, breathing heavily.

A shadow fell across him. He looked up.

The ship was huge. Silver-hulled, it was long and slender, with a dish-shaped forward section that melded into four wings in an X-configuration.

Its gun ports flashed. He held up his hands as blue energy leapt towards him.

I'm still here! The alien ship wasn't shooting at him. He looked around. There were other ships out there, more difficult to see. Their hulls were black and barely reflected the light from the distant sun. The silver ship was trading fire with two of the black-hulled vessels. "They're fighting each other!"

"Yes!" said Liz. "That's why we're still alive. There are two sides to this battle."

"Where are you guys?" said Wally.

"I'm behind you," said Liz. "Morgan's above us."

"Ok, found you."

Morgan looked around but he couldn't see either of the other Fireflies. He scanned his controls. There were multiple holographic displays, some with floating dots and circles that might be the other ships. There were too many HUD tags, some overlapping others. None of it made sense to his panicked brain. "I can't see you guys at all. Wally, are there sensors or something? There's so many displays, I don't know what does what!"

"Forget the built-in screens," said Wally. "Hit the button above the left lens on your flight goggles."

Morgan felt for the button, found it, and pressed. He gasped as the solid parts of the Firefly became translucent. He looked down and saw the other Fireflies below him through the faint outline of his thighs. As he looked around, the system tagged all the nearby craft with red and green brackets. There were a lot more ships than he had previously thought.

The silver ship above them was marked with green brackets. *Does that mean the computer thinks it's a friendly?*

A blinking red arrow appeared at the far left of his vision, pointing outwards. He turned and saw a cluster of tiny dots coming at him, bracketed in red. As he stared at them, a virtual screen appeared and zoomed in. The ships were small, wedge-shaped darts. Trails of blue engine exhaust fanned out behind them. *Alien fighters!*

He punched the throttle forward as the fighters fired. A barrage of tiny green pulses shot past his starboard wing. "Help!"

"I see you," said Wally.

"I'm coming," said Liz. "Hold on."

Morgan dodged this way and that as energy bolts whizzed past him. His ship jostled as a bolt grazed his shields. He spun, pointing the bow back towards the *Sagitta,* and went to full throttle. A mix of red and green-bracketed craft surrounded the fleeing Earth ship. Some were too small to see from this distance. Lights twinkled between the ships as they fought.

Two small objects that had been marked in green exploded. *Were those escape pods? Other Fireflies?*

"Jack, Yin, do you copy?" he said, a sinking feeling in his gut.

No response. "Jack! Anyone? This is Morgan Greenfield to any other Fireflies! We need help!"

"The other pilots might be on a secure channel," said Wally. "Or, they're dead."

No, please no. A green bolt slammed into Morgan's ship, sending him spiraling. A restraining field energized, pressing him into the seat as his ship's thrusters fought the spin. He watched a strange gray-white planet whip past in the distance as he gripped the flight stick with shaking hands. The lack of stars made it impossible to tell where he was going.

Then he saw the enemy: three small darts, heading straight at him.

He closed his eyes and pulled up hard as the lead attacker opened fire. After a moment, he dared look. *Still alive!* He'd passed over the enemy. He twisted the flight stick and his fighter spun around. *I'm flying backwards!*

He tapped the stick forward to line up his bow with the enemy formation, which was likewise spinning to face him. "Damn it!" he said, as he overshot. He twisted the stick again, and overshot in the other direction. On the third try, he managed to get one of the enemy ships centered, and he pulled the main trigger. "Take that!"

The alien's shields flared with red light as Morgan's laser beam strafed across it. He fumbled the flight-stick, trying to maintain the laser beam, but the enemy ship struck him with a glancing blow from its strange weapons. He screamed as he went spinning again, losing all sense of where he was. Alerts flashed up all across his vision.

"I see you," said Liz. "Hold on."

He gritted his teeth as he worked to stabilize the ship. "Try one of the thumb triggers! The lasers are useless."

There were two tiny flashes from somewhere above him. "Missiles away!" she yelled.

He craned his neck, following the missiles as they accelerated. He pointed the flight stick in the direction the missiles were heading, and his Firefly straightened out. The enemy formation was executing some maneuver to try and evade the missiles, but it didn't work. They slammed into the side of the lead fighter. Ripples coursed through its shields.

Morgan risked a quick look down at the flight stick. The largest side-trigger was tagged with an image of a miniature warhead, with the label 'SRM x 2'. He pushed it.

Two missiles shot from his fighter and arced towards the enemy, impacting with a fiery explosion. This time its shields overloaded. It spiraled out of control and crashed into its wingman. Both ships came apart, spewing debris and fire.

The third fighter peeled off.

Adrenaline coursed through Morgan's veins. He had scored a kill. *Two kills.* "We got 'em Liz!" he yelled. "Woohoo!"

"Uh, guys," said Liz. "I think I'm in trouble. I…cr…the other shi…hel—"

Static overran her transmission.

"Liz, you there?"

No response. He backed off the throttle and cautiously turned to starboard, until the third fighter came into view. It was chasing Liz! She zigged and zagged, but the enemy dart stayed with her, scoring hit after hit.

"I'm coming," said Morgan, going to full throttle. He tried centering the crosshairs on the dart, but it was moving all over the place and he couldn't keep up. He held the trigger and swept the lasers this way and that, but couldn't tell if he was doing any damage, or even hitting the blasted enemy at all. He gave up on the lasers and launched two missiles, tracking the enemy ship with his eyes.

Liz dove and the alien pursued, firing constantly, its engines burning white-hot. Morgan's first missile smashed into the enemy's stern, sending it off course. The second missile shattered one of the four vertical fins on the back of the dart. Unperturbed, the dart pressed its attack.

They were catching back up to the *Sagitta*. The comm crackled again, but Liz's voice was indistinguishable. Morgan squeezed the main trigger but missed as the dart zipped to starboard.

He started pushing the other triggers. One fired some sort of bow mounted machine gun. *Useless!* The next three triggers did nothing, except to cause the message 'Bank Empty' to flash in his HUD. The last one fired burning metal shrapnel out of the back of his ship. *No idea what that does, but it's not helping.*

He tried the missile trigger again. 'Bank Empty' flashed across his vision. *Where is Wally?*

"Wally, you have to help her. Use your missiles. They're the thumb trigger on the back of the stick."

"I don't even know where I am," said Wally. "Where are you?"

"Heading back towards the *Sagitta*."

The *Sagitta* was growing large again as he followed Liz's frantic flight towards it. As they neared, he could see small black specks sticking out of the *Sagitta's* hull. Alien starships traded fire all around.

Liz had almost reached the *Sagitta*. The glow from the great ship's engines reflected from her hull. She dove, heading under the cruiser, but flew right into the stream of fire from the enemy dart. Morgan cried out as energy bolts punched through her shields, just missing her cockpit. One bolt went through her wing and came out the other side.

239

Her engines flickered out, followed by her running lights.

"Liz? Liz!"

There was no answer.

The dart spun around to face him. Fearful of overshooting, Morgan pulled back on the throttle. He lined the dart up in his cross-hairs and pulled the trigger.

"Come on!" He was almost on top of it. Behind the dart, Liz's ship tumbled, powerless. Morgan squeezed the trigger harder, willing the lasers to punch through the enemy's defenses. *Die!*

The dart didn't die. It fired.

'Shields Failing' flashed in his vision. "Ahhh!" he yelled, punching the throttle forward, heading straight at the enemy.

A thick stream of blue pulses swatted the dart like a mosquito. It exploded just as Morgan's Firefly tore through the space where it had been. Morgan looked up. The great silver ship had saved him. *But what about Liz?*

Her fighter was still drifting towards the *Sagitta*. He adjusted his course and nudged the throttle forward. *If I can just connect to her somehow…*

The black specks on the *Sagitta's* blackened hull detached. Morgan's goggles tagged them with red brackets as they accelerated away from the Earth ship. He stared at one, and the secondary view zoomed in. The front of the ship looked just like the thing that had pierced the corridor. *Those are all boarding craft.*

Five seconds later, the *Sagitta* went up in a brilliant blue-orange explosion.

Morgan paid no attention to the burning debris bouncing off his Firefly. He could only stare at the space where Liz's ship had been. He didn't notice the arrow-shaped cruiser passing by. Green fire splashed over his canopy and port wing. His head slammed into the restraining field, and he knew no more.

Chapter 28

Mog couldn't take his eyes off the screen. The alien ship was gone. In its place was an expanding field of burning debris. "Nazpah," he spat.

At least three of the small craft that the newcomers had launched were still intact. He was eager to take them aboard, but first they had to finish off the Ta'Krell.

"Should I shoot down their boarding craft?" said Nali.

"No," said Mog. On the screen, the last of the Ta'Krell shuttles fled the debris field. If they had taken any of the new arrivals as prisoners, he wasn't willing to sacrifice their lives.

Why did they board it?

As far as Mog knew, no living Maurian had ever seen a Ta'Krell in person. On the rare occasion that the Maurians managed to disable one of the enemy ships, the aliens immediately detonated their drive. Mog suspected they were afraid of being found out. *What if these so-called Ta'Krell demons are really just little pink puff-balls or something?*

Why then had they taken such an interest in the newcomers? Had they shown their faces to the strange aliens before they killed them?

"That cruiser's plotting an escape course," said Nali. She threw the image of the Ta'Krell ship that had retrieved the boarding craft up on the main viewer.

"Let them go."

"Mog," said Ryal. "We need to go."

"I know, I see it," said Mog, looking at his tactical display.

While the *Narma Kull* and her two escorts had been busy trying to save the strange ship, the Ta'Krell had pressed the attack on the other side of Sledgim. He selected an available hyperspace exit point and flicked it over to Meela's console.

"Initiating jump," said Meela.

The viewscreen shifted, and they popped out of hyperspace right next to the orbital shipyard. Meela immediately fired up the engines to stabilize their elliptical trajectory.

Mog flipped through his tactical screens. The Maurians outnumbered the Ta'Krell, and the enemy had changed tactics. Instead of bombing the planet's shielded outposts or engaging the Navy in orbit, they were concentrating their fire on the shipyard.

The shipyard was lightly shielded and relied on its point defense platforms. Most of these platforms had been destroyed, and the yard was taking heavy damage.

"Commander," said one of the new science officers, a boardman named Till. "I've been analyzing the flight path from the alien ship. There are a few small cylinders floating back there, emitting some sort of repeating signal. They might be escape pods."

"Excellent," said Mog, feeling a twinge of hope. It was a strange feeling. "But we can't do anything for them now. Let's finish this fight."

The comm chirped, and Kremp's voice came through the speakers. "Engineering to bridge. Mog, I've figured out what's wrong with the projector cannons. It's a problem with the control system. They were designed for orbital platforms and never intended—"

Mog cut him off. "Kalesh var sai, it's about time! Now fix them!"

"Ten minutes and they'll all be working."

"Not good enough. Forget the aft weapons. Can you get me just the forward battery?"

Mog heard Kremp consult with his staff through the comm. "I might be able to get you the bow ventral projectors in three minutes." The ship shook as a Ta'Krell ship opened fire. "Assuming you can keep us together that long."

"You have a deal," said Mog. He switched off the comm. "Nali, fire at will."

They were still at maximum range. The small Ta'Krell cruisers were pinpricks surrounding the shipyard, their dark hulls barely reflecting the light of Sledgim's sun. He looked at his tactical displays. They still had twelve operational ships. The Ta'Krell only had seven, although that wasn't counting the two enemy fighter wings that were bombing the shipyard.

Ryal was giving orders. "Take us straight at them. Draw them away from the shipyard."

"Got another one," said Nali. "There's only six Ta'Krell left."

"We're not any better," said Ryal. "We just lost another scout ship and one of the armed freighters."

Mog tapped the comm panel. "Kremp, I need those PPCs."

"One minute," said the engineer.

Meela turned the *Narma Kull* to face two Ta'Krell ships that had broken off from the shipyard. Nali was throwing everything she had at the enemy, but the divided fire wasn't doing enough damage.

An alert sounded from the communications console. Ja'tar swore. "The mine's transponder just went dark. That disabled Ta'Krell ship must have got their power back."

"Confirmed," said Nali. "Readings show residual energy from a high-yield explosion at the last known coordinates. It's another kill, at least."

"Nazpah!" said Mog. He slammed his fist into his controls, which made his projected screens fizzle. There would be no unmasking of the Ta'Krell today.

The comm chirped. "That's it," said Kremp. "The number two bow turret should work."

Without waiting for the order, Meela pulled the nose up to optimize the firing angle. Mog got out of his chair and pointed at the screen, his entire body tingling. *Finally, some good news.* "Nali, fire at will!"

There was a throb of power, a deep murmur that Mog had never heard before. A second later, a huge blue beam slammed into a Ta'Krell ship. Its shields held for a second, but then the beam punched through the hull and came out the other side.

"Yes!" shouted Ryal.

"Eat that and die, Ta'Krell swine!" screamed Nali.

"Target the other ship," said Mog.

The result was equally spectacular. The crew roared in delight and astonishment. Mog caught Ryal's eye and flashed him a warrior's grin.

"Sir!" said Nali. "The Ta'Krell are breaking orbit!"

"We did it!" said Ja'tar. "We really did it, we've won!"

The bridge erupted.

"All glory to Ramas!"

"Hooray for Fleet Commander Mog!"

"Glory to Mog and mar-Ruba!"

"Long live the King!"

Mog didn't allow himself so much as a nanosecond. There was work still to do. He bared his teeth. "Helm, jump to previous coordinates." He realized before he finished speaking that Meela was already on it. She'd been hunched over her controls, and no sooner had Mog spoken than the stars swirled and they were in hyperspace.

A second later, they were back in the middle of the system, near the debris field from the alien ship. *She's command officer material,* he thought, as Meela turned around and caught his eye. *I'm glad she stayed with us.* He tipped an ear at her. "Nice flying Meela." He paused, trying to remember what her mate's name had been. By the time he had it, she had turned away. He cleared his throat. "Vurl would be proud of you."

She bowed her head.

Ryal shot Mog a questioning look, but Mog waved him away. He flipped on the ship-wide comm circuit. "This is Mog. Hangar deck, rig the boats for rescue! We've won!"

Chapter 29

The fisherman gazed at the horizon as he guided the skiff through the mouth of the river, past the Camp Ellis breakwater. His face was hidden behind a tangled gray beard. Beneath thick black eyebrows, his eyes glistened with love for the sea.

The boy was squeezing the wooden gunwale. He glanced over the side, blanched, then looked down at his feet.

"I can't believe you've never been on the ocean," said the fisherman.

"I've seen it on a map," said the boy, without looking up. "I've seen pictures."

"Harumpf. When I was your age I loved the water. Surfing, sailing, diving, I did it all." The old man smiled wistfully. "Nowadays I just float."

The boy kicked at the peeling floorboards, dislodging a few soggy splinters. The swells were picking up. He bit his lip.

"Your dad never liked the water either. He never went swimming, other than to dip his feet now and then. He can't tell the difference between a bluefish and a striper. I would say to him, 'son, why don't we go for a ride in the boat,' but he always had something better to do."

The boy was shivering. White spray broke over the bow, showering them with mist. He licked his lips, tasting salt.

"Your dad is afraid of water. Did you know that? Where that fear came from I've no idea. Perhaps a bad childhood experience, or a scary holosim. Whatever caused it doesn't matter. The problem is, in all his life he never confronted his fear. He ran from it, all the way to the desert."

The boy moaned as the boat passed over a larger swell.

The old man didn't seem to notice. "Now, I've nothing against a healthy fear. It tells us to run when there's danger, and sometimes spurs us to fight."

The boy tucked his feet underneath the wooden seat.

"It's only a problem when you let it take control. Do you know what the key to mastering fear is?"

The boy twitched his head side to side.

"Do you?"

"No," murmured the boy.

"It's knowledge. You see, I'm not afraid of the water because I know the water. Your father never took the time to learn." He turned the wheel, pointing the bow at open water. The boy closed his eyes.

"When you get back on dry land, I want you to think about what I've told you. Are you listening?"

"Y…Yes."

"People fear what they don't know. They fear the darkness, they fear the foreigner who doesn't speak their language. But a fish doesn't fear the water, and a bird doesn't fear the sky, just like you don't fear the desert heat. Today, I'm going to make you a fish, so that you don't fear the water."

The boy opened his eyes wide. "You're going to throw me over the side?"

The fisherman laughed. "If that's what it takes."

The boy grasped his life vest and shrank away.

"I'm just kidding."

"Oh." The boy eyed the old man nervously.

"Glad we settled that one. Now listen. This boat was made to float on the water. It's just as at home on the water as you are on dry land. When you're out on the water, the boat keeps you safe. Remember this whenever you go on a boat ride. You will go on more boat rides, right?"

The boy shrugged.

"Make sure you do, because that's the best thing you can do. Each time you go, you get to know the water a little better. The same goes for swimming, scuba diving, and fishing. Start with swimming. Get familiar with how the water feels around you. Go for boat rides, and get familiar with how the water feels below you. Before long, you won't be afraid of it at all. Do you know why?"

"Knowledge?"

"That's it. Now it's time for the real lesson. Look up! Come on, it's ok. Take a look."

The boy looked up towards the bow. They had circled around, and the floating docks were only a hundred feet in front of them. Lobstermen loaded hovercarts with traps. The boy smiled for the first time since he had left the shore.

"You see," said the fisherman, "We didn't sink. The water didn't hurt you. Take that piece of knowledge and put it in your toolbox to use against fear another day. Will you do that for grandpa?"

The boy nodded.

"You're welcome," said the fisherman. He reached down and pulled the boy in close. "Now, out you go, little fish."

"Go where?"

"Back to dry land."

* * *

Am I dead? No. His aching ribs and splitting head were proof enough of that. But where was he? It was warm. Something hard was pressing against his back. He opened his eyes and found himself propped against a plastic crate.

He was in a large square room filled with cargo. The walls, ceiling, and floor were shiny metal. Thick support beams ran up to encircle a large dome light. The light cast a dim yellow glow that was just enough to see by.

Something moaned next to him. He turned. A man was sitting on a barrel a few feet away. His gray uniform was torn and bloody.

Morgan's head snapped up as the image of an exploding fighter came to him. "Liz!" He struggled to his feet and hammered his fists against the crate's lid. "Liz! Liz!" A few people turned to stare, the rest ignored him. *I wasn't good enough to save her.* The red characters on the lid made no sense. His forearms were wrapped in bandages with the same writing, a flowing script of tiny red characters. *An alien language.*

He whirled. There were only humans in the bay.

He began limping around, looking for any familiar face. Everywhere he turned were the blue uniforms of command officers and the gray uniforms of enlisted crewmen. They regarded him wearily. Many were nursing wounds.

Why am I still alive?

He tripped over someone's outstretched leg.

"Hey, watch it, idiot."

Morgan looked down. A group of people were sitting in a semicircle between barrels. They were wearing gray uniforms, except for the closest person, who wore a leather jacket. His black hair was matted with dried blood, and he had a bandage with strange lettering on the back of his neck. His jacket was scuffed, his jeans torn.

"Victor?"

Victor looked up, and his bloodshot eyes widened. "H..h..how?" he stammered.

"We stole some fighters."

"Ah." Victor's eyes were glazed. He stared through Morgan for a moment before speaking. "The medics got us out. The doctors stayed behind to help those that couldn't be moved. When the escape pods were attacked, I thought I was done for. Somehow, they missed ours."

"Who attacked?" said Morgan. "Did you see them? Are we on one of those black ships?"

Victor didn't seem to hear. "Andy's dead. He got out with the others, but their Fireflies were shot down before they could get up to speed."

Morgan swayed. "The pilots are dead?" He sat down next to Victor.

"They're all dead," Victor moaned, scratching at the back of his neck. "All of them! Dead. Dead!"

The crewman on the floor next to Victor began sobbing into her shirt. Another crewman glared at them. "Shut up and stop reliving it."

Victor took no notice. A change came over him, and he grabbed Morgan's shoulder. Morgan tried to pull back, but Victor's metal hand was a vice. "What about Elizabeth?"

Morgan opened his mouth but no words came.

Victor's face was a rictus of horror. "What about Liz?"

"She didn't make it." He looked away. "I'm sorry."

Victor's voice broke. "How? Tell me."

Morgan clenched his fists. "Does it matter? She died like everyone else did. Jack and Captain Stone, Yin, the security guards…they're all gone. And you…" He turned back and pushed a finger into Victor's chest. "Somehow you're still alive. How is that fair? You should have died on that ship, not her. If you'd treated her better, if you hadn't made her crash…if you really cared…"

Morgan trailed off. *Would she still be alive? Would I even have met her?* He knew he didn't mean what he'd said, but it was too late to take it back. Victor shoved Morgan's shoulder so hard that it popped. Morgan fell over and Victor scrambled to get on top of him.

"You have no idea what I've gone through, and don't you ever suggest that I don't care about her!"

"If you cared," gasped Morgan, pushing Victor off with one of his feet, "she never would have left you. But you're just a loser, a pathetic druggie."

Victor tried to stand, but Morgan scrambled, grabbed Victor's leg, and pulled him back down. *Stop it! What would Liz think?* He hesitated, fist raised. Part of him wanted to beat Victor to a pulp. *And just what would that accomplish?*

Before he could do anything else, someone put him in a bear hug and pulled him off Victor. Morgan writhed, but the arms squeezed tighter. He staggered into a crate and twisted around. "Alright, I'm sorry. Let go!"

The man let go. Morgan took in the green uniform, the blond hair, and the sideways grin. "Jack!"

Jack's hair was matted to his forehead. His bloodied uniform was torn at the shoulder, revealing a bandage not unlike those on Morgan's forearms.

"Hey kid," said Jack. They regarded each other for a moment. Then, Jack laughed and pulled Morgan into a hug, pounding on his back. "I've been waiting for you to wake up. I'm glad you made it!"

"So did you! I thought you were dead." Out of the corner of his eye, Morgan saw Victor slouch off behind the crates. "What happened out there?"

Jack's grin vanished. "One minute we were launching, the next some huge ship shredded our formation with energy cannons. By the time the *Sagitta's* computer sent us updated shield parameters, it was too late. My systems were fried and I was adrift. The others..." His voice trailed off. "And then, well, I was captured."

Morgan hung his head. "At least you lived."

"Yes." Jack was quiet for a moment. "I haven't seen your lady friend."

"She's dead. I couldn't save her. She got disabled by one of the aliens, and her fighter exploded when the *Sagitta* went up."

"I'm sorry," said Jack. "When I heard how you two escaped from that monster in the hangar bay, I hoped that maybe she was still out there somewhere."

Morgan searched Jack's face. "How do you know what happened in the hangar?"

Jack whistled, beckoning someone over. "There's someone else who's been waiting to say hi to you."

Morgan turned. Wally was limping over to them. "Hey kid, glad you made it. I was worried you wouldn't wake up."

"Wally!" Morgan staggered as the big man clapped him on the back. "Glad you're here."

Wally grinned. "Me too. I saw what happened to the girl. For what it's worth, I'm sorry."

"Yeah," said Morgan.

They stood in awkward silence for a moment.

"So, what do we do now?" said Morgan.

"We wait for Del Toro," said Jack.

"Who?"

"The boss man," said Wally. "Lieutenant Commander Del Toro. He's the highest ranking officer that's been picked up so far, but he's hurt bad. The Hellcats took him."

"The what?"

"Hellcats are what we're calling the aliens," said Jack. "Nasty things. Half the people in here fainted when they saw them for the first time." He pointed at Morgan's bandaged arms. "You were unconscious when they took you. They've been treating the wounded, doing triage."

The silver ships must have lost. "They're going to kill us all," muttered Morgan, remembering the monster that had climbed onto his fighter and penetrated his mind.

"Or they might not," said Jack. "We don't know what they want. They treated our wounds and gave us water. Let's not jump to conclusions until we learn more."

Morgan's adrenaline was wearing off, and he slumped against a plastic barrel. *We're the first humans to leave the solar system, and we'll be the first to be tortured by space aliens.*

"Guys, did any of the aliens try to get into your head?"

Jack and Wally looked at each other, then they both shook their heads.

Morgan shivered, remembering those evil yellow eyes. "There's something I need to tell you. The one chasing us on the *Sagitta* almost got me. It looked through me, into my head."

"Like, it read your thoughts?" said Jack.

"Yeah. It wanted to know where we came from. It wanted Earth."

After he was done telling them everything, Morgan walked back to where he'd woken up. Liz's green eyes bored into him, her voice calling from far away. *Why did you let me die?*

* * *

Someone was yelling. People were rushing to hide behind the containers. Morgan coaxed his aching body out of the fetal position and maneuvered around the crate.

Someone from the *Sagitta* crew barked an order. "Nobody do anything unless I say so. Alberto, you ready?"

"Yes sir."

A burly man pulled a sharp piece of plastic out of one of his pockets. It was the same shade of dark green as the containers in the bay.

"Shhhh," said a woman. "Here they come."

Morgan peeked over the crate. The doors parted—doors much too large to be meant for humans. Two nightmares stepped into the bay, each holding what looked like an energy pistol. He ducked as the lead hellcat swept its pistol in his direction. Hellcat was a fitting name. If Earth's big cats were given a few million years to evolve, they might look something like this. *Assuming at some point they shacked up with gorillas.*

Both hellcats wore loose-fitting tan vests that left their muscular shoulders and arms exposed. The vests were tucked into leggings that stopped just short of their powerful calves. Their feet were bare. Curving claws protruded from between their stubby toes.

The alien on the right curled up its lip and hissed something at the other, revealing sharp fangs. The other hellcat bobbed its head.

The two aliens parted, allowing a closely-huddled pack of humans into the bay. There were at least a dozen of them, all disheveled and weary. A few wore loose-fitting garments that might have been cobbled together by someone who didn't understand human anatomy. The rest wore ISF uniforms.

"Stand down, everyone," said a short man, as he entered the bay. He had olive skin and dark brown hair. His blue uniform—torn and stained at the shoulder—had three stripes on the collar. "We're ok. They healed us up, and did us no harm."

Chapter 30

The King was missing, half of Sledgim was without power, and there were only ten working ships left in the entire Navy. The fact that the Maurians had not been wiped out was due to what? Mog's brow furrowed. *Chance? Fate?* He flexed his claws. His muscles still ached from gripping the arms of his command chair during the battle. *What does it matter? We won. At the end of the day, we're still here. All that matters is what we do next.*

The watchstander at the hangar entrance was a young cadet, recently assigned from Sledgim. She was pacing back and forth with the same bounce to her step that had infected half the *Narma Kull's* crew. Mog glowered at her as she stopped to salute.

"Commander!" she said, straightening. "What can I do for you?"

"Nothing," said Mog. He indicated the hangar bay. "Kremp's in there?"

"Yes sir."

"Good."

The cadet stiffened, some of her pep evaporating as Mog brushed past her. Inside, Kremp was balancing on the lip of an alien fighter's nose, guiding a wiring harness through the vessel's open cockpit into the hands of a technician.

"How's it coming?"

Kremp looked up. If he was surprised at all by Mog's unannounced visit, he didn't show it. "I'm getting there. We've just fabricated a bunch of connectors that should interface with their system. Once it's hooked up, it shouldn't take long for our computer to make sense of their operating system. I'll page you as soon as that happens."

"Understood," said Mog. "I'll be in the briefing room with Professor Drakmara."

"Professor who?"

"Drakmara. He's one of Ruba's councilors, supposedly a wizard at linguistics. He just came up from the planet."

Kremp looked up from his work. "Are you going to try and talk to them today?"

"I hope so. We've determined they use acoustic signals like us to communicate. The doctor analyzed their vocal organs, so we know what range of sounds they can produce. I'm counting on you to get their computer working. We're assuming it has a linguistics database. We'll use that, combined with the recordings from the cargo bay, to program a translator."

"I see. I'll send the data up as soon as I sort it out."

"Thanks. And Kremp, good job getting that PPC turret working. If you hadn't, we might not be having this conversation."

Kremp's ears perked up. "Just doing my job." Mog turned to leave when the engineer added, "Do you want to know what I've found out about these little ships?"

Mog looked over the four alien fighters that had been recovered. They were small, perhaps half the size of a Maurian fighter, of which no examples were left for a direct comparison.

"I have to meet with Drakmara," said Mog. "I just stopped in to see if you needed anything." Kremp's disappointment was obvious. "Although, perhaps I can spare a few moments."

"Good," said the engineer. "I'll make it quick then." He scampered around the fighter's canopy and walked out onto one of the sweeping wings. He pointed at what looked to be a grid of recessed emitters. "Do you know what these are?"

"Shield emitters?"

"No. Those over there are the shield emitters. At first I thought these were graviton panels, but they actually seem to be some sort of subatomic harmonic exciter. The force profile is similar to our graviton plating, although they can work in reverse."

"Like a bidirectional tractor beam?"

"Sort of, but it isn't graviton based. It's much shorter range, and has a much faster response time. They've got them all over the hull. A lot of the ship's computer processing nodes seem dedicated to making these things work."

"For what purpose?"

The engineer's ears drooped. "I'm not sure. I was hoping you'd have some ideas."

"Maybe," said Mog. "I'll think about it. Right now I'm late, but I'll let you know if I come up with anything."

He turned and exited the bay. Hopefully it wouldn't take long to get translators working. He wanted to meet the aliens as soon as possible. There was a set of naval procedures—more of a book really—for first contact with a new species. He'd read it once as a young cadet, and skimmed it again last night just long enough to decide to dispense with the whole thing. They already knew the aliens' tactical capability, and there wasn't a direct threat to the *Narma Kull* now that the creatures' ship was gone. The rest of the procedures were concerned with deciphering the language, then learning their social and religious customs so as not to offend them.

Thankfully, he had a professional linguist on board for the first part. As to the second, he didn't care if they were cannibals who ate their own parents and worshipped black holes. None of that mattered. All he needed to know was what they would take in exchange for an alliance.

"Hey! Mog!"

He turned. Ja'tar was sprinting down the corridor, his ears standing straight up.

"Ja'tar, what are you doing?"

Ja'tar stopped next to him, panting, fumbling with a tablet.

"Trying to find you. Well I was, but now I've found you. Uh, we got a message. It just came in, disguised as background noise. I've decoded it. It's from mar-Ruba."

Mog snatched the tablet out of Ja'tar's hand and stared at the message. There wasn't much to it. Not including the text that authenticated Ruba's security code, the message only occupied a fifth of the device's screen.

"Strange, isn't it?" said Ja'tar. "Get to the planet of the furless aliens. Seek asylum there. Tell Drakmara that Azhra lives."

"The first part is clear enough," said Mog. It also happened to be exactly what he'd been planning to do.

Ja'tar stepped back. "Well yes. I mean, the second part. What does it mean, Azhra lives? He can't mean *that* Azhra, can he?"

Mog reread the message. He wasn't about to admit to Ja'tar that the Ta'Krell could actually be Lord Azhra's immortal army. *The book of Ramas is a joke. It's all crap. It has to be a hoax.* Yet, everyone was convinced it was true. He swallowed hard. *But why would Ruba say this? What if Nali and the others are right? Am I the one who is crazy not to believe?*

He handed the tablet back to Ja'tar. "I have no idea." Now that he thought about it, the first part bothered him too. How did the King know what the newcomers looked like? Ruba must have seen them. The Ta'Krell must have taken prisoners off of the alien ship. If so, then his entire plan was in danger. He had to find the alien homeworld before the Ta'Krell did.

"Are we going then?" said Ja'tar.

"Of course," said Mog. "We need them, especially the technology they used to get here in the first place. I'm sure they won't object to us bringing them home."

* * *

Morgan made little headway learning about the *Sagitta's* warp drive from his fellow prisoners. They either didn't seem to know anything about it, cited the classified nature of the project, or were simply not interested in talking to him.

Lieutenant Commander Miguel Del Toro was less than helpful. After filling everyone in on his group's experience of being poked and prodded by alien doctors, he had ordered Morgan and Victor to the other side of the bay, citing their lack of a security clearance. As if that mattered, lost as they were halfway across the galaxy. *He just thinks I'm some stupid kid.*

Now the commander sat huddled, talking with the remaining crew. *He can't order me to do anything. I'm not even in the ISF.* Yet here he was, skulking back across the bay with his tail between his legs. What would Liz think of him?

"I'll show them," he muttered under his breath. "I'm not just some civilian. I'm Morgan Greenfield, fighter pilot." *Scared little boy, more like. Look at you, you're trembling.*

He was on his way back to the crate where he'd woken up when a commotion broke out near the entrance. The two guards had grabbed a young woman and were dragging her through the doors into the corridor. The woman, an enlisted crewmember by her gray uniform, had gone boneless. One of the guards scooped her up and threw her over his shoulder. Her mouth was open in a silent scream.

Morgan ran towards the archway. *What are you doing? Do you want to get yourself killed?*

He thought of Liz, and told the voice in his head just where it could go.

A group of prisoners had already flooded the spot, cursing the hellcats. Morgan pushed through and came face to face with the energized barrel of an energy rifle. Four more hellcats had come through the door, forming a perimeter around the two that were dragging the woman away.

His blood burned as he watched the woman disappear behind the archway. His voice joined the others. "I'm gonna kill you. You're all dead!" *Did I say that?* His voice hardly sounded like his own.

The hellcat snarled, its fangs glistening. The human crowd drew back for a moment, then surged forward. *I might be able to get that gun.* To his right, servos whined as a crewman with augmented muscles drew his arm back to swing. The man named Alberto pulled what looked like a makeshift knife out of his pocket. Morgan took a half step forward.

Someone grabbed his arm and yanked, pulling him back into the group of people. *Victor!*

"Stand down, all of you," said Del Toro. He slid into the gap between the aliens and humans, his back to the hellcats. His dark eyes radiated fury. "I said stand down!"

Muttering, the crowd backed off. Behind Del Toro, the hellcats withdrew from the bay. The doors slammed shut and locked.

"You're such an idiot," whispered Victor in Morgan's ear. "If you'd so much as twitched, that thing would have shot you dead."

Morgan turned around. "Why do you care?"

Victor didn't answer.

"Cool it everyone," said Jack, pushing through the crowd. "Enough people have died already. They have guns, we don't."

A man behind Victor raised his voice. "So we're just going to sit here while they take us one by one?"

"Stoddard's right," said a woman. "We need to get Uliana back."

Everyone started yelling.

"I'm sick of sitting here doing nothing."

"That's right!"

"Next time they come in, we ambush them!"

Morgan added his voice to the crowd. He'd already fought the hellcats once. He was still alive, despite everything that had happened. *If we can just get a few of those pulse rifles…*

"Quiet!"

For such a little man, Lieutenant Commander Del Toro's booming voice came as a surprise. "I'm in charge here, and we're not going to do anything. No resistance, until we can learn more about this prison of ours."

"What's there to learn?" said Morgan. "It's a ship, isn't it?" They had all agreed on that, even though no one had seen what it looked like.

Everyone had woken up in the cargo bay without any memory of how they had arrived there. "We're light-years away from Earth, prisoners of some monster aliens, and no one back home can get to us. Or are there other warp ships just waiting in the wings to swoop in and save us?"

Everyone was staring at him. No one said a word, but a few crewmen shook their heads. *Can't stop now.*

"I thought not. We have to save ourselves. We're screwed if we just sit here. I say we take this ship! Next time they come in, we jump them and take their guns."

"Yeah, let's do it!" someone shouted.

"The kid's not afraid, so why are we?" said another.

Jack raised a hand for silence. "Morgan, I like you, but shut up. They'll kill us if we try anything. They've got guns, and they likely outnumber us a hundred to one. Don't be a fool."

Del Toro pointed at Morgan. "You, boy." His pale lips curved into a sneer. "Wally told me you figured out how to fight in a Firefly, and that you actually took down some of those darts."

When Morgan nodded, excited whispers spread throughout the crowd.

Del Toro laughed. "That explains the hero complex then. Well, hero, do you think you'll get lucky again? Look around. Do you see any Fireflies in here? Do you see any crawl spaces, access hatches, or anything other than those doors that we could use to escape?"

"Well, no." They'd already scoured the bay. The ventilation ducts were the only thing that came close, and they were far out of reach overhead.

"Good, you have eyes," said Del Toro. "I was starting to wonder. The only way we are going to get through those armed monsters at the door is with diplomacy. Don't let your five minutes of accidental success go to your head."

Morgan's face flushed. "It wasn't an accident."

Del Toro raised his eyebrows. "Oh really? Let me guess. Your computer got a target lock on one of the hundreds of attacking ships, ships that were already weakened by the fighting that had been going on since before we arrived. I bet that ship wandered right across your bow. It did, didn't it? Or did you masterfully chase it down?"

Morgan was silent.

Del Toro smirked. "You probably wet yourself as you pushed every button on that flight stick, praying that something would happen, and when you hit the missiles something did. But what skill was in that? It was luck! They dragged your unconscious butt out of that ship after you got it handed to you."

Morgan seethed but said nothing. *He's right.*

Victor leaned in and whispered in Morgan's ear. "Did you really kill one of the aliens?"

"I got two. With Liz's help."

"Ah," said Victor. He was silent for a moment. When he spoke, his voice trembled with emotion. "It might have been luck, but at least you were there for her, unlike…"

Morgan was stunned. He waited for Victor to finish, but when no more words came he turned around. Victor was gone.

* * *

"Did you really kill an enemy fighter?"

Morgan looked up at the young black man. He'd been so lost in his own thoughts that he hadn't heard him approach. The man was familiar. He recognized him from Del Toro's group earlier—an officer, probably in his mid-twenties.

"Yeah, I did."

"Cool," said the man. He held out a hand. "I'm Jason Carver. I'd be interested in hearing how you managed to do that. Actually, I'd like to hear how you ended up on the *Sagitta* in the first place, assuming you don't mind telling. Mind if I sit down?"

Morgan shrugged and scooted over, making a space between himself and the crates.

Jason sat. Morgan looked around. People were settling in for the night, dragging crates and barrels around, making rudimentary shelters. *For what? Privacy?* It was funny that people could care about such things in a situation like this.

"You don't have to tell me if you don't want to."

"No, it's ok," said Morgan. He thought back to that day at the track. *It seems so long ago. How to begin?* He cleared his throat. "Back in the desert, in Arizona, this girl pulled up in a blue POD 1000. She was a racer, like me, and she just was looking to have some fun." And so he told his story. It was her story too, and someone had to tell it.

When he got to the part where he and Liz destroyed the alien fighters, he was grinning.

"Sounds like you two made a good team," said Jason.

"I guess we did, for a short while." It was hard to believe he'd only known her for a week. It felt like forever ago when they'd first met. Morgan sighed and leaned back against the crate. He had known this part would come.

"She died, didn't she?" said Jason.

"What?"

"That's why she's not here with you. I'm sorry. You don't have to tell how it happened."

Morgan wanted to thank him, wanted to take the easy way out. But he couldn't. "No, I'll tell you. Just this once." And he did so to the last detail. When he was finished, he was crying.

Jason wiped his eyes. "I lost someone as well. I mean, we were a tight crew and we all are hurting, but this is way, way worse."

"A friend?"

Jason nodded. "Yeah," he said. "My wife, who was my best friend."

"Oh." Morgan sniffed and looked away.

Jason shuddered. "She worked on the bridge. See, everyone in here's lost someone. Now it's up to us to live, so there'll be someone left to remember them."

261

"And to get home," added Morgan. "To tell our stories, so people know what happened." The idea of his parents never learning the truth was insufferable. *I will get back to Blairsford if it's the last thing I do.*

"Blairsford," he mumbled. The word sounded weird, almost comical.

Jason blinked. "What?"

"Blairsford, Arizona," said Morgan. He chuckled. "It's where I'm from. It feels strange to say it in this place. But it also feels good. Try it. Say where you're from."

Jason looked around, grimaced, then spoke. "Groton, Connecticut."

Morgan watched as Jason's face contorted. "See what I mean?"

"It's like those words were never meant to be spoken in this room."

"That's it exactly," said Morgan. "But let's not forget to say them every day."

* * *

Mog pressed the pads of his hands into his ears in an attempt to drown out the noise, but it was no use. Although the terrified alien occupied just half of the examination bed, her shrieks (the doctor had already discovered she was a she) were more painful than any vocalization he had ever heard from a living creature. It didn't help that they were so high pitched. Maurian ears were most sensitive to high frequencies.

The alien's voice wasn't the only distinctive thing about her. As it turned out, the furless ones weren't really furless. Their skin was covered in a hair so fine that it appeared invisible unless you were looking for it.

The top of her head was most puzzling. This confirmed what he had suspected after viewing the video feed from the cargo bay. Each alien had a patch of hair that covered its scalp. On some the hair was short. On others, especially on the females like the one in front of him, it hung down past their shoulders. Saran said the men could grow more hair out of their faces, but for some reason they had shaved it off. As with their skin, the color of the hair varied from individual to individual. Sometimes it was black or brown. On this pale-skinned female, it was the color of beach sand.

The alien stopped shrieking just long enough for Mog to wonder if she had gotten tired. *No, apparently not.* She had paused to inhale half the air volume of the room for her next scream.

For her sake Mog didn't want to shout, but there was no other way to be heard. "Saran! How long is this going to take?"

The old doctor waved a hand scanner over the alien's head. "It would go quicker if she would lie still. I believe I will have to sedate her."

Mog took a step forward to better observe the doctor's work. The alien's eyes widened as he peered down at her. He did his best to put on a soothing expression, but all it seemed to do was make her scream louder and thrash against the straps. There must be something about Maurians that terrified the furless ones, because no member of his crew had been able to calm one of the aliens with body language. Then again, forcing the aliens onto an exam table probably wasn't the ideal way to convey a message of friendship. It was too bad there wasn't enough time for a proper first contact.

When Saran leaned in with a bioinjector, the alien's shrieks vibrated the walls. The muscles in her skinny legs convulsed, but the straps didn't budge. Considering how fragile her body seemed to be, Saran—frail as he was—could have pinned her to the table with one arm.

The alien fell quiet as Saran placed the injector against her neck, but her rolling eyes betrayed her terror. The injector hissed. She lurched and started shrieking again. Would the drug even work? The aliens were so different—of all the races he had seen, these seemed closest to the Mekmek, but even that was a stretch. Saran had assured him that the creatures were warm-blooded mammals and that his sedatives would be effective, but Mog wasn't counting on anything.

"No memory modifier this time, right?" said Mog. He'd decided to dispense with that particular precaution. He doubted the female would glean anything from the sickbay that she could use against them. *And so what if she remembers this? She will soon know that it was all for the best.*

"She'll remember everything," said the doctor.

The alien started to relax, and her screams became less intense. Her eyes closed and her cries subsided into dull moans.

"That's better," said Mog.

The guards withdrew to the anteroom. Saran began passing his scanner over the alien's head, focusing on her ears. The information scrolling across the scanner's display was gibberish to Mog. He watched as the alien's chest rose and fell. If Saran's drug was too powerful and she expired, there would be nothing Mog could say to her comrades that would calm them down. Any chance of an alliance would die right here with her.

"Are you sure she'll be alright?" he said.

Saran grunted and continued scanning.

Suddenly, the alien's eyes opened and locked with Mog's.

"I wish you could understand what I'm saying," he said. "We are not going to hurt you, but we need to learn more about you so that we can talk."

The alien moaned. She had a thin gold string around her neck. Part of it was out of sight beneath the collar of her tunic. Mog hesitated, then slowly reached out, being careful to extend a claw only just as much as needed to hook under the chain.

The alien watched him as he pulled the gold cross up from her chest. "This is pretty," he said, trying to look as non-threatening as possible. He let the little ornament fall back against her breastbone. "Did you make it?"

Of course she couldn't respond. Her eyelids drooped.

"What do you suppose it means?" he said to the doctor. "Some indication of rank? Of seniority?"

"It's just a chunk of impure gold," said Saran. "And I have no idea." He gave the scanner one last wave over the creature's head and then flicked it off.

Mog tapped his claws together. "You're missing the point. I meant, what is its function? Perhaps it's a charm, or a family crest."

"It is not relevant to my examination," said Saran.

Mog growled his displeasure, but the old doctor ignored him. The man had always possessed the social skills of a textbook.

"There," said Saran. "I have uploaded my scans into the database. We should be able to create a pair of aural inserts that will fit her anatomy."

"Good," said Mog.

"Their anatomy is not impressive," said Saran. "They possess only one heart. They have a thin hide, no claws, a weak jaw with weaker teeth, and probably no sense of smell. The spine is interesting though, most flexible, and the brain seems capable enough. Be sure to tell Kremp to include a good amplifier in his design. Their ears are weak compared to ours, though not as bad as their eyes."

"I thought you said they had some sort of implants that helped them?"

"A few of them do," said Saran. "One had a synthetic hand, another artificial lungs. Most have communicators in their ear canals. These were all fairly basic, uninteresting devices. I disabled the communicators to keep them from talking to each other covertly—standard procedure."

"Yes I know. What else?"

"Of slightly more interest were the few that have biomimetic circuitry."

"Biomimetic?"

"Yes, bonded directly with and sustained by the cells of the body."

"For what purpose?"

"Compensating for the inherent weakness of their bodies. Better vision, data storage, enhanced tactile communication."

Mog indicated the alien before them. "But this one doesn't have anything?"

"No. This one doesn't. She did at one point, but the biomimetic cells were rendered inert. I've found evidence of similar work in almost all of them—implants that have been removed, cells that have been neutralized. Only one—a male juvenile—has functional biomimetic circuitry."

"Why would they do that? Why would they augment their bodies with technology and then disable it?"

Saran flattened his ears. "How would I know?"

The comm system beeped, and Ryal's voice came through. "Mog, Drakmara's done reviewing the audio logs from the cargo bay, and Kremp just sent us a load of information from the alien's computer. They had a complete library in there, including actual sound clips from their language. Drakmara says it's going to speed things up quite a bit. You should probably come back up."

Mog's ears began to twitch again. He had already had enough of Drakmara, even though he had only been in the room with the man for a half hour. He'd known him once, long ago, and he hadn't been any better then. Drakmara was an educated lord from an old family, and his ego had filled the briefing room to bursting. It also hadn't helped that the professor had taken Ruba's coded message at face value. Mog glowered, remembering the conviction of Drakmara's words. *Of course Azhra is still alive! Now, he and his brood are back to finish what they started.*

Mog snorted. "It's a bunch of crap."

"What was that?" said Ryal?

"Never mind," grumbled Mog. "I'll be up in a minute."

He turned and beckoned the security guards out from the anteroom. "Take her back to her people, and be careful. They're not going to like the sight of her being drugged. Soon, we'll be able to explain everything to them, but until then, don't drop your guard for an instant."

266

Chapter 31

The days dragged by. Or were they weeks? Morgan couldn't tell. They must have traveled some great distance, since the ship's strange gravity never seemed to relent. The general consensus from the spacefarers was that they were under heavy acceleration, traveling in a straight line, but sometimes there were debates among them.

Morgan wondered about that. Occasionally, as he paced around the bay, the gravity seemed to shift, pulling at him in an almost imperceptibly different direction. It wasn't quite the same feeling as spin gravity. But what was it?

The guards brought them food—some sort of bland paste with chunks that made him gag—and water. A makeshift latrine had been set up in the corner. It had taken some convincing to get the alien's to understand the human need for privacy, and to provide some opaque plastic sheets with witch to wall off the commode. The also hadn't understood the idea of toilet paper.

The bay stank. He stank. Everyone stank.

At least he had Jack, Wally, and Lieutenant Carver to keep him company. Jason Carver had become a fast friend, perhaps on account of their shared loss. The poor man had been only one year away for being eligible to transfer to Starlight Station. He and Addie had planned to start a family.

Victor was another matter. He didn't talk to the crew, and he certainly didn't want to talk to Morgan. Reflecting on the last thing Victor had said to him, Morgan had gone over intent on apologizing for some of the things he'd said, but before he opened his mouth Victor told him to get lost.

"You got her killed," Victor had said. "And I've got nothing more to say to you."

Morgan had watched Victor since. He was jumpy, and didn't talk to anyone except for himself, which he did a lot. Most of it was gibberish—fragments of conversations that he'd once had with Liz, mostly. *Or maybe conversations he thinks he's still having with her.* Victor kept grabbing at the back of his neck where his data port used to be. Morgan didn't know much about data ports, and knew less about withdrawal from sim-stim drugs. He suspected some of Victor's erratic behavior might be due to this, but he wasn't about to go ask him about it.

Morgan's story had spread around the prison camp like wildfire, especially the part where the hellcat had climbed on his fighter and used its mind-powers on him.

"Was it really telepathy?" asked Jason.

Morgan shrugged. He, Jason, and Wally were sitting on the floor in a semi-circle, playing blackjack with the deck of cards that Wally kept in his breast pocket.

"All I know is it was in my head, and it wanted to know everything about Earth."

"Don't make sense," said Wally. "If they can get in your head, then why haven't these ones done it?" He waved in the general direction of the space outside the cargo bay.

That was the question, wasn't it? So far, no one had reported any attempt by the hellcats to get into their minds, not even the people that had been taken from the cargo bay and examined.

The sound of a magnetic seal releasing echoed through the bay. Del Toro stood and walked to the doors. "Everyone stay calm. Let me handle this."

Morgan threw his cards down and stood up with the rest of them, although he stayed to the back of the pack this time.

Three hellcats stepped into the bay. The one on the left had shaggy brown fur and dark eyes. His left arm was normal, but his right was made of metal, and ended in four glistening razor-blade claws. The hellcat on the right was much smaller, perhaps a female. It had golden-brown fur accented with dark brown markings, and yellow eyes. Its fangs glistened in the dim lighting, and it carried an enormous rifle that it panned across the bay.

The alien in the center was the fiercest beast Morgan had ever seen. The largest of the group, its fur was black like midnight. Its claws weren't extended, but their black tips glistening from between stubby fingers. As the huge hellcat swept its gaze over the humans, it became apparent why the alien didn't carry a weapon. The yellow eyes were weapons of their own.

Morgan shuddered under that gaze. Was this the same alien that had climbed aboard his fighter? It couldn't be. Surely that monster had perished in the backwash of the Firefly's engines. Yet, the resemblance was striking.

While the other humans looked apprehensively at the creatures, Del Toro walked right up to the group. The black hellcat towered over him, but the little man showed no fear. *He may be annoying, but blast it, he is a good leader.*

"I am Lieutenant Commander Miguel Del Toro. What do you want with us?"

The lead hellcat's wolf-like ears twitched. Something moved behind the three monsters, and a fourth alien slipped into the bay. It was smaller, and slightly rounder. Its coat was gray. Perhaps this was an elder?

It held out something to the one with the mechanical arm, who took the objects with its normal hand.

"Renk pa, took phollz."

Morgan jumped. He'd been too busy watching the brown alien that when the black one spoke, it caught him off guard.

"What does that mean?" said Del Toro.

The black hellcat's ears swiveled towards Del Toro. "Renk pa, took phollz."

Something flashed. There were things in its ears, devices with blinking lights. The brown hellcat held out something to Del Toro and gestured at his own ears, which also blinked with the strange electronics.

Del Toro frowned. Tentatively, he reached out and plucked the thing from the brown hellcat's hand.

"Earbuds," he said, turning to the humans.

The brown hellcat stepped forward, his hand outstretched. The earbuds were so small that they looked like a collection of lima beans in his hand.

"Jones, Carver, go take some," said Del Toro.

As it turned out, they had brought enough of the devices for everyone. Jack handed Morgan one. He turned it over. It looked like any generic earbud headphone. Some sort of status light pulsed orange then green. He put it in his left ear. The fit wasn't comfortable.

"It's got to be a trap," tittered Victor. "They're going to fry all our brains." But he stepped up like the rest of them and grabbed an earbud. "What do I care anyway? We're all dead one way or the other."

The hellcat spoke again, and the words sounded exactly the same as before. Then, the earbud clicked on with a beep.

"Be good, we friends."

Del Toro whirled. "Did you all hear that?"

"Yeah," said Jack "It's a translator circuit."

"He said to be good, and that we're friends?" Victor laughed "What is this crap? Have you seen his fangs? He'll eat your face off!"

"Someone shut him up," snapped Del Toro, pointing at Victor.

Morgan tried not to laugh. *This shouldn't be funny. Why is this funny?*

"Be good, we friends," the hellcat said again.

"Hellcats aren't our friends," said Alberto.

"Yeah," said another crewman. "Toro, tell these freaks that we're not making any deals with murderers. When Earth finds out what they've done, we're going to kick their furry asses!"

Del Toro made a cut-off gesture with his hand. "Quiet, you idiots." Then, looking alarmed, he held up his hands in a placating manner. "Those behind me are idiots, not you. Please, tell me what do you want?"

"We not are hellcats," said the alien. "We not are murders. We are Maurians. I are Mog."

Del Toro pointed at the four aliens. "Is Maurian the name of your species?"

"Yes," said the big alien. "We are not hellcats. That word mean, strange, derogatory. We are proud, honorable. I are Mog."

"You, the one speaking, your name is Mog?"

"I are Mog," said the alien, pointing at his chest.

"You mean, I *am* Mog," said Del Toro.

The smaller gray alien punched something into a device that looked like a computer tablet.

"I am Mog," said the black alien again. The alien's initial words before sounded exactly the same, but the earbud rendered the translation differently. Morgan bit his lip and stared at the back of Del Toro's head. *Hurry up and ask them why they killed our ship and our friends.*

"What do you want with us?" said Del Toro. "Are we your prisoners?"

The alien's lips curled up at the tips. "We want a alliance. You are protected, here."

Morgan leaned closer to Jason, who was standing next to him. "I don't think these things work right. He says he's a friend and wants an alliance? Yeah right."

"But I am honest, I am a friend," said the hellcat.

Morgan froze. He had whispered. How had the alien heard him?

"Ah, that's a little hard to believe," said Del Toro. "Considering you blew up our ship and killed over three hundred people."

Morgan's pulse quickened, and Jason stiffened next to him.

"We not destroy your ship," said Mog. "The Ta'Krell did destroy your ship. We fight Ta'Krell."

271

"That's not possible." People parted as Morgan stepped to the front of the group, unable to believe what he was hearing. Del Toro waved him off, but he ignored him. "I saw you on our ship. You boarded us, you killed the crew!"

"We did not."

Morgan clenched his fists.

"Easy," said Jason, although he himself looked anything but relaxed.

"But they killed your wife," hissed Morgan.

The hellcat's ears twitched. "You are mistaken. The Ta'Krell boarded your ship. The Ta'Krell are the nemesis. We did not kill the furless ones. When you arrived, you destroyed the Ta'Krell. We saw, and we thought we had an ally. We help."

Maybe Victor was right. This could be a trap. Were they trying to lure the humans into a false sense of security? For what purpose? What would that accomplish? *If they wanted us dead, they would have killed us by now.*

"If you're friends, then make him put down the gun," said Del Toro, pointing at the small tawny-furred creature.

"I think that one might be a she," said Morgan.

"Correct," said the female hellcat. Her voice was softer than Mog's. "I am a she. I am Nali." She bent down and placed her weapon on the floor. "I am the tactical officer on this ship. I am sorry, but I had to be sure you would not attack the commander."

"Him?" said Del Toro, indicating Mog.

"Yes," said Nali.

Del Toro appeared to be thinking this over. Morgan looked around. The crew was tense, but not as tense as before. Were some of them buying it? Surely the ones that had seen the hellcats face to face on the *Sagitta* weren't. Morgan wasn't the only one, he had learned. Stoddard and Alberto had caught glimpses during the *Sagitta's* final moments. Their descriptions corroborated his. Morgan looked at Wally. The technician was glaring at Mog with cold fury.

"What do the Ta'Krell look like?" All eyes turned to Victor. "Come on then, what do they look like?"

"No one knows what they look like," said Nali. The translator sounded funny, as if it was trying to impart a feeling of distress to her words. "They kill without showing their faces."

"There are the holy books—" began the brown hellcat, but Mog cut him off.

"We've never captured one, alive or dead," said Mog. "They are more powerful than us."

"But we've seen them," said Morgan. "They boarded our ship, and guess what? The Ta'Krell look just like you."

The four hellcats exchanged looks. "That is impossible," said Mog. "You must be wrong."

But Morgan knew what he had seen in that corridor and in the hangar bay. There was no denying it. The Maurians had been on the *Sagitta*. "I'm not mistaken. Things that look just like you boarded our ship."

"No, the furless one is wrong, is mistaken." said the hellcat with the mechanical arm.

"We call ourselves humans," said Del Toro.

"Ah, humans," said Mog. "And you are from some place? A planet? A kingdom?"

Don't tell them anything, Morgan thought desperately. *They want to know about Earth so they can destroy it!*

Thankfully no one said anything.

"We are of Mauria," said Nali.

The other hellcats tensed. Del Toro looked from one to the other, then back at Mog. "Mauria is a planet?"

Mog closed his eyes. "Mauria was the homeworld. Billions died. My mother. My father. My brother. The same story, on all seven planets of the Empire, and all the outlying colonies, except for the ice world below us. The Ta'Krell, the name is from a holy book. It means destroyers, killer-of-worlds. We know not their true name, but they have adopted this one to scare us."

"Or, they really are Azhra's demons, come back to finish us off," said Nali.

Mog and Nali exchanged a look that Morgan couldn't decipher.

Del Toro was nodding. "The planet we're orbiting, it's yours?"

"It is called Sledgim. It is our last world."

Nali stepped forward. "They came out of nowhere. In these last few months, we have lost everything. We know nothing about them, only that they want us dead. They incinerated Mauria! The planet below—my homeworld—is the last in the Empire. My mother is there, maybe alive, maybe not alive. The bombardment...."

Her voice trailed off.

"Billions are dead," said Mog.

Morgan stared at Nali as tears began running down her face, wetting her fur. *They cry. Does it mean the same thing for them?* The gray alien was trying to hide it, but he was crying too.

"How do we know you're not trying to trick us?" said Morgan.

"Why would we?" said Mog.

"I don't know. Why didn't you just tell us this in the first place? Why did we just wake up in that room back there with no explanation?"

"Because they didn't know how to tell us," said Del Toro. He tapped his earpiece. "Right? You had to figure out how to talk to us."

"Yes, that's it," said the gray Maurian. His voice was older, more seasoned. "I am Kremp, the master maker. I made the translators. When we rescued you after the battle, no one knew what to do. We had never seen your species before. Our doctor took scans while we healed you, but I needed more details. Of the ear, of the inside spaces. It became needed to take another."

Uliana stepped forward. "When you took me, it was for this purpose? To make a translation device?"

It took Mog a moment to respond. Perhaps the translator was having trouble with her Russian accent. "Yes. It was necessary. Big apologies."

Uliana's hands were trembling, but she held them behind her back where the aliens couldn't see them. "It was you, then," she said, looking right at Mog, her words ringing like cold steel. "You took me. You…" she trailed off. Then, she pulled something out. Morgan couldn't see what it was. "Why did you want my necklace?"

Mog bowed his head. "I was curious. It is…pretty. What is it for?"

"Protection," spat Uliana. "Against demons."

Mog blinked. "Does it work?"

Uliana tucked her necklace away. "That remains to be seen."

"Enough of this," said Del Toro. He turned to look at Morgan. "You, boy, you had the closest encounter. Are these—" Del Toro hesitated, his mouth working as if he didn't like the taste of the words. "Are these…people the same as what was aboard *Sagitta* or not?"

Morgan gulped. All eyes were on him. "They look the same," he said. "But, but I don't know. Now that I hear them talk—look, it was dark, the ship was running on emergency power, and we were panicking. Maybe, maybe I saw something else."

"It looked the same to me," said Wally.

Del Toro regarded the technician, then looked back at Morgan. His lips moved with exacting precision. "I do not want a maybe, mister Greenfield. Are these Maurians the same species as the creature that attacked you? Yes or no."

Morgan racked his brain. A huge, hulking form. Black fur, yellow eyes, pointed ears, and nose like a cat's. It was Mog's face. But, there had been slight differences. And then there was that searing pain in his mind. If he hadn't escaped the hangar deck, that thing would have learned all there was to know about humans by pulling the info right from his brain.

"Can you read minds?" he said, looking at Mog.

"I do not understand," said Mog.

Morgan tapped his forehead. "With your brain, can you see into the brains of others? Steal their thoughts?"

A change came over Mog. His ears twitched, and he licked his lips. "Certainly not."

"Then they aren't the hellcats," said Morgan. "If these Maurians could read minds, they wouldn't be going through all this trouble with translators and with talking."

"That," said Del Toro, "is a good answer. Thank you, Mr. Greenfield." Morgan nodded.

"What, you're going to believe him?" said Victor. "Morgan's clearly mad. He was hallucinating. Telepathy isn't possible."

"Quiet," said Del Toro. "Right now all things must be considered. Look around. Did you think any of this was possible a week ago?"

Victor glared at the officer, but was silent.

"I am sorry about the loss of your craft," said Mog. "We tried to save it, but we were not able."

Morgan remembered the silver four-winged vessel that had been fighting the darts. *Of course.* "This ship!" he sputtered. "Can you show us a picture of this ship?"

Mog cocked his head to the side, then reached into his breast pocket and withdrew a thin rectangular object. A series of excited beeps emanated from the device as he tapped away with his large forefinger.

"Here," said Mog. "Look."

He turned and pointed his device at the blank screen next to the cargo bay door. The control panel came to life. The image that appeared was a wireframe diagram of a graceful looking spaceship. Not blunt-bodied, but flowing. A curving bow, four staggered wings, and big engines at the rear. For the first time since he had woken up in the cargo bay, Morgan grinned.

"The silver ship," he said.

"Yeah," said Wally, jumping up and down. "Yeah, that's the one that helped us out!"

276

"Is this good?" said Mog.

"You bet it is," shouted Jack. "That's the big bird that defended the *Sagitta!*"

"Yeah man," said Wally. "I like that ship! Are we aboard right now?"

Mog bowed his head. "Yes. This is my ship. She is the last of her class. She is called the *Narma Kull.*"

Tears were welling in Morgan's eyes. Despite the unexplained physical similarities, these were not the hellcats. These were the Maurians, and they were friends.

"Will you take us back to Earth?" said Morgan.

"Your homeworld?" said Mog.

"Yes."

"If you show us where, we will do our best to take you there."

The hangar erupted with cheers and cries of relief.

"If," said Mog.

The cheering quieted down somewhat.

"If Earth can help us. We need your weapon, what you used when you split the Ta'Krell command ship in half. This is an Earth weapon, yes?"

Del Toro stiffened. "Weapon? I don't know what you are talking about. Our engines malfunctioned, and we ended up here, in a pocket of space with no stars. I don't even know where here is. As to that ship being split in half, our best guess is that we hit it just as we dropped back into normal space."

"It was their drive!"

Kremp, the engineer, was jumping up and down excitedly. He was speaking to the other Maurians, but the earbuds translated indiscriminately. "I was looking at the data. It makes sense now! It wasn't a hyperdrive. Mog, it was a distortion drive."

"Warp drive," said Del Toro. He glared at Morgan and Victor before continuing. "This ship was a top secret experiment. It failed."

"No," said Mog. "It succeeded. You have developed a weapon of unimaginable power. We must form an alliance to stop the destroyers before they complete their genocide. Will you help us?"

For the first time since the conversation had started, Del Toro looked uneasy. "That might take some work," he said. "I'm not authorized to speak on behalf of the nations of Earth, but the ISF, the military arm of the United Nations, would perhaps be interested in a technological exchange. I…can't promise anything here. However, a good faith gesture on your part would go a long way. Perhaps as we are currently stranded here—"

"Of course," said Mog. "We will go to Earth, and we will speak to your nations and to your military. We will bring you home as a gesture of good faith."

We're going to Earth! He's done it! Morgan had to refrain himself from running to Del Toro and hugging him. *Calm down. It's still not going to be easy. What's going to happen when we all show up and knock on Earth's door? Total anarchy, most likely. Riots in the streets.* "Riots, in Blairsford," he whispered, and giggled.

The Maurians turned to look at him. His stupid translator had amplified everything he'd said.

"Blairsford," he said, catching Jason's eye. The lieutenant smiled and winked at him.

"What is this Blairsford?" said Mog.

Morgan grinned. *Hey mom and dad, I just got an alien to say the name of our town. First time ever!* "It's my home town. It's where I'm from."

The big alien flashed what might be a toothy smile. "Blairsford," he growled.

"Yeah, that's right," said Morgan. *Funny. Now that I've got the big guy saying it, it doesn't sound so strange anymore.*

Chapter 32

After the Maurians left, Del Toro called all of the thirty-six *Sagitta* survivors together. They sat huddled in a circle in the center of the bay. Morgan was tired, and his muscles were shaky in the absence of the adrenaline rush that had come with the encounter with Mog.

To his surprise, Victor had joined them.

"I don't see what the problem is," said Victor. "I mean, assuming for now that these aliens are actually the good guys, and that they're bringing us back to Earth."

"They want our help, that's the problem," mumbled Jack through a mouthful of the disgusting stew that the creatures had brought. "They expect us to help them fight a war."

"But it's their war, not ours," said Victor. "We're not obliged to do anything."

"I don't know about that," said a man Morgan didn't recognize. "Like it or not, we're involved now, and we can't expect them to bring us back to Earth without asking for something in return."

"A military alliance is asking a lot," said Jason.

"Not if the Ta'Krell are heading for Earth too." said Del Toro. "We picked sides the moment we dropped out of warp. If the Ta'Krell got the location of Earth when they boarded our ship, then we're screwed, unless we have help."

They were all quiet for a moment.

"There is one thing I don't get," said Jack. "Why did the *Sagitta* slip back into normal space at the exact spot of the hellcat's command ship?"

They all looked at Ensign Blake. She was the only surviving member of the *Sagitta's* engineering team. She was young, perhaps fresh out of engineering school. Pretty, in a shy sort of way. She was biting at her nails, her face partially hidden by her light brown hair.

"What do you think, Ann?" said Del Toro.

Ensign Blake looked uncomfortable. "I'm no physicist, and I don't claim to understand Dr. Fowler's research. I was assigned to this mission because I worked with Lasky Spaceworks on the Firefly design. I'm not too familiar with the *Sagitta's* engines."

"That's alright," said Del Toro. "You worked with Roland's crew, and you must have overheard something. You're certainly more qualified than the rest of us. Please, share your thoughts."

Blake nodded. "Roland and Boyle thought it had something to do with the hellcat's command ship, and by hellcats I mean the Ta'Krell. We only have a few milliseconds of sensor data to go on, but they seemed to think that the command ship was generating some sort of strange energy wave. It affected the fabric of space somehow. We went really fast. The distance we travelled would normally have taken us months, and that would be with the EnGineus drive working at maximum theoretical output."

"They pulled us across space," said Del Toro.

"Yes," said Blake. "I think so. It was some strange interaction with the EnGineus drive, and for some reason they thought the ship's computer might also be involved. The computer core burned out. At the end, Roland was trying to get the drive working manually, but there was just no way without an AI to modulate the field. Even if *Sagitta* hadn't been destroyed, we would have been stranded."

Something stabbed into his palm. Morgan looked down at his clenched fist and realized it was his own fingernails. *EnGineus.* Liz's mother had died because of her own invention, and now her daughter had died too, thanks to him.

He felt the tears coming, and there was nothing he could do to stop them. He stood, excusing himself, and hastened to the other side of the bay towards the latrine. Once out of sight, he sat down with his back against a stack of barrels, pulled his shirt collar over his face, and sobbed.

* * *

"Commander Mog, are you awake?" The night shift leader's voice blurted from the small comm speaker next to Mog's head.

Mog opened his eyes. "Lights," he said. Groggily, he rolled off of the bed and stood. His quarters were a disaster. He hadn't bothered picking anything up since the last battle.

"Yes Uir, what is it?"

"I thought you'd like to know that our salvage operation has concluded."

Mog perked up. "What have you found?"

"Mostly tiny hull fragments. The biggest piece is what looks to be part of a shuttle bay door, but it's severely damaged. There's no sign of the Ta'Krell ship that we disabled."

"They got away?"

"Looks like they got their engines fixed and ran for it."

"Nazpah. Is Ryal up there?"

"He is."

Of course he is. He never sleeps. "Tell him to get down here. I want to talk to him."

"Yes sir."

Mog stumbled into the small bathroom that adjoined his quarters—a luxury afforded only to himself and Ryal. He splashed cold water on his face. He should be satisfied with their victory. *I wanted that ship!*

What did the Ta'Krell look like? The young human's words had disturbed him greatly. *The Ta'Krell look just like you.*

The door chime sounded. *Ah, Ryal. That was fast.*

He opened the door. "Oh. Kremp?"

Kremp held a data tablet in his hand. "Can I come in?"

Mog bowed his head and stepped aside. The engineer entered, stumbled over the toppled bookshelf, and sat in a chair in the corner. He tossed the tablet on Mog's small desk. "That's my best guess as to what happened. I've added links to all the relevant research papers on distortion drive. There isn't much though. No one's worked on that sort of propulsion for hundreds of years, not since the discovery of the hyperspace layer."

"Thanks," said Mog. "I'll read it in the morning."

Kremp looked disappointed, but didn't press the subject. "Ryal tells me we're leaving for the planet of the furless ones—these humans—first thing tomorrow."

Mog bowed his head. "I think so. I just called him down here to discuss our plans. We'll have to get the High Council on board first."

"I thought as much," said Kremp. "Paryah won't like losing the *Narma Kull*. Sledgim's defenses are weak enough as it is."

"I'm not talking just about the *Narma Kull*."

"Oh?" Kremp's ears perked up.

"I'm talking about all of us. We're all leaving. We'll fill the transports to bursting and leave for Earth."

"Abandon Sledgim?" said Kremp incredulously.

"The Ta'Krell know we're here. We can't fight a full-on assault."

"But, you're talking about nearly three hundred thousand people."

"Yes," said Mog. He'd run the numbers already. They had enough super transports to do it, thanks to the few half-empty ones that had recently arrived from the destroyed colony world of Aso. *Those ships will be packed to bursting.* "We could leave an encrypted beacon in the system, broadcasting where we went on a secure channel to authenticated Maurian vessels, so that people retreating here can set course for Earth."

Kremp looked aghast. "We don't even know where Earth is!"

"Drakmara and Meela are working on that. There were star charts in the computers of their fighter ships."

"The High Council won't like this," said Kremp. "Sledgim has been our most closely-guarded asset."

Mog snarled. "It'll be obliterated when those scouts come back with reinforcements. If the council doesn't like it, then they can go to the dark place. I'm the Supreme Fleet Commander, and this is war. They'll do as I say. Besides, mar-Ruba ordered it himself."

The door chimed. "That will be Ryal," said Mog.

"Do you want me to leave?" said Kremp.

"No." Mog stood to let his first officer in. "Stay. I want to hear your thoughts on my other plan."

"And what is that?"

"Getting these humans invested in our cause. A token of good-faith. Perhaps a demonstration of what we have to offer. Something that we can present to them when we arrive at Earth."

"And by that you mean what, exactly? Ship drives, reactors? Surely not weapons?"

Mog tipped an ear. "I don't know yet. I guess I'm talking about whatever it takes."

* * *

Morgan returned from the tour of the *Narma Kull* in a daze. The ship was huge! The pulse rifles and the personal defense shields in the armory had most impressed Del Toro. Jack couldn't stop talking about the automated fabrication unit, which was printing a squadron of Maurian fighter ships from raw materials excavated from the planet's surface. For Morgan, it had been the gravity plating, especially as applied to all sides of the shower stall. The dirt and grime being sonically massaged and then tractor-beamed off of you made for an exciting bathing experience.

Ensign Blake's verdict was that the Maurians were technologically equivalent to the humans, if you averaged everything out. How had she put it? *They've got better military hardware, materials, and engines, but we've got repulsors, which they seem to have entirely missed somehow.* As to computing technology, the Maurians hadn't suffered an AI revolution, but they seemed wary of it all the same. Mog had hinted at sentient computers, but hadn't told them anything concrete.

"We have a proposition for you," said Mog, as they all filed back into the bay. Someone had pushed all the cargo to one side while they had been gone. Bed rolls and new clothing had been laid out, and brighter light fixtures installed in the ceiling. Maurian workers were installing a pump and partitions for a proper toilet.

"I'm listening," said Del Toro.

"You've seen our ship. We have technology that you lack, and you have technology that we lack. Your fighter craft, for instance. Their shields are weak, and you rely on projectile weapons and feeble light emitters. You have no inertial compensation systems, so you cannot perform hard maneuvers."

"You seem to know a lot about our fighters," said Del Toro.

"We have been studying the three that we recovered from the battlefield. We can upgrade your fighters. Make them like ours. Better than ours even, thanks to your variable force harmonic repulsion technology. We will make those three ships the most advanced starfighters ever produced by either of our races."

"Sounds like a good deal for us," said Del Toro. "Why would you do this?"

"To show Earth's government that we are serious," said Mog. "To ensure we can form an alliance."

"A gift?"

Mog bared his teeth, the gesture equivalent to a nod. "A gift."

"This is acceptable," said Del Toro. "Although I want my engineer and fighter technician to oversee the work."

"I'll help, if I can," said Ann Blake timidly.

"Straight on," said Wally. "As long as I don't have to fly one of those things again. I've had just about enough of that for a lifetime, thank you very much."

"Agreed," said Mog. "Your people will oversee the work."

"And we fly them," said Del Toro. "Not you."

"Naturally" said Mog. "We wouldn't fit in your tiny ships. You should know this will be dangerous. The modifications might not be compatible. Also, I ask that your pilots help defend the *Narma Kull* if the Ta'Krell find us before we reach Earth."

Del Toro pointed at Jack. "Just so you know, we've only got one pilot left. Lieutenant, what do you think?"

Morgan felt a rush of adrenaline. *Only one? No, that's not true.*

Jack grinned. "I'd love to have my ship back. This sounds like fun. I can't say I want to fight those Ta'Krell monsters on my own, but if it helps get us to Earth then I'm your pilot."

"Well then," said Del Toro. "We have one volunteer. I'm afraid that's the best we'll be able to do until you get us home."

Mog looked disappointed. His ears drooped as he surveyed the human survivors. "There are no other pilots among you?"

"No one qualified to fly a Firefly," said Del Toro, answering for them. "I'll not let anyone without the proper flight training or physical conditioning touch one of those ships."

"Aw, come on," said Stoddard. "I'll do it sir. I can fly a shuttle. How different can this be?"

Jack snorted. "A lot."

Stoddard pressed on. "I'd love a chance to strike back, for the *Sagitta*. Please Miguel, give me a chance."

Del Toro shook his head. "I can't risk losing anyone to a hopeless mission. You're not flying, that's an order."

Morgan raised his hand. "But what about me? I can fly one, and I can fight. I've already done it."

Del Toro glared at him. "You, the boy hero? Definitely not."

Morgan caught Victor's eye. Victor raised an eyebrow inquisitively. A flicker of hope crossed his face.

"You can't order me not to," said Morgan. His voice trembled, but he pressed on. "I'm not in the force. You can't order me to do anything." *I can't believe I'm doing this.* He considered Victor for a long moment and wondered what Liz would want him to do. *Ugh*. He pointed at Victor, then at himself. "Commander Mog, Victor and I are racing drivers. It's basically the same thing as pilots. We can fly those ships."

"Yes, we can!" Victor stepped forward, a sly grin on his face. "We do this all the time."

"That's ridiculous," said Del Toro. "You aren't touching those ships. They are ISF property."

Mog looked from Del Toro to Morgan, and then back. "You are saying you won't help us?"

Del Toro frowned. "No, I'm not saying that at all."

"Then let them fly, sir." Jason's voice rang out loud and clear. "This is beyond the ISF. If they want to, let them fly for Earth!"

"For the alliance," said Mog. "We must work together for the good of the galaxy. This will be the first step."

Del Toro straightened his uniform and pressed his clenched fists against his hips.

"I can teach them, Miguel," said Jack. "They are young and fit. I've flown with Morgan and I know he can take it. Victor's flown too. They can handle the g's. After what we've all been through, they're as much seasoned war veterans as the rest of us."

Morgan's heart was racing. *Morgan Greenfield, starfighter pilot. War-ambassador from Earth! Founder of the Alliance. Kid from Arizona. Ha!*

Del Toro faced Mog. "Alright," he said. He looked from Jack to Jason. "Considering the advice from my pilot and from my second in command, I will allow the two boys—that is, the two young men here, to train in the fighter craft. I don't like it, but it seems we have little other choice."

"Good. Thank you, Commander." Mog extended his arm. Del Toro regarded it warily before grasping the alien's hand. He shook it. Instead of letting go, Mog slid his hand up and gripped del Toro's forearm. It was a strange sight: Napoleon looking up at Goliath. The commander tolerated this for a second, then withdrew his hand quickly.

Morgan couldn't help but wonder if Del Toro was using this as a way to get rid of his civilian problem. *I'll show him.*

"Feel free to wander the ship," said Mog. "I need to get back to the bridge. If you need anything—", he pointed at the comm panel, now active on the wall of the cargo bay, "just call."

Mog and his officers left the bay. As soon as the doors slid shut, Morgan's shaking legs collapsed. He sat down hard on the bay floor. Victor came over and offered him a grudging smile.

"Alright you two," said Del Toro. "This is not a game. You have no idea what you just signed up for, no clue how hard it is to learn to fly properly. Yet…as the two most useless people on this ship, it is important that you learn how to do something."

"Useless?" said Victor.

"Quiet! You're in the ISF now, and you'll speak only when I say you can speak. We do this on my terms, understand?"

"Yes sir!" said Victor flamboyantly.

Del Toro scowled, and looked at Morgan.

"Understood, sir," said Morgan with a nod.

"Good. You will listen to Lieutenant Jones and Commander Mog, and do everything they you. If you disobey any order, no matter how silly it may seem to you, you'll answer to me." He glowered at Morgan. "I'm giving you the one chance. Don't mess it up, and don't cross me." With that, Del Toro stormed off.

"Sir yes sir!" said Victor under his breath, with a mock salute. He sat down next to Morgan and punched him in the shoulder, slightly too hard to be considered playful. "Thanks for the help back there. But this doesn't make us cool."

"Yeah," said Morgan. "Don't worry. I still hate your guts."

StarFighter will continue…

Seeker

Hrain sat up to grab a tool from his toolbox and smacked his head against the access hatch. He crawled out of the maintenance compartment and slammed the hatch shut. The stealth systems were still broken, among other things.

"Angel, I wish you were here," he said with a sigh.

"Command unrecognized," said the computer.

He wiped a tear away. *Here you go, crying again. It's not like she was Nail. Get over it.*

He sniffed, and focused on the job at hand. It was a rush job, but both he and Ezek had agreed that each day spent in space dock doubled the risk to the Talurian Empire. Ezek had pressed the Mekmek crew hard to finish the repairs. The guidance computer was misbehaving, half the lights flickered, and the gravity plating in his quarters made him want to vomit.

But they assured him the *Angel's Fury* could fight.

"I fixed the matter reclamation unit," said Mel.

Hrain turned to face her. "I'm here trying to get the stealth grid online, and you are messing with the toilet?"

Mel stuck out her tongue at him. "Trust me, we're better off if it works. You wouldn't like the smell otherwise." She went forward to stare out the cockpit's windows at the swirling colors. "It's so beautiful."

She did this at least once every half-hour. It was as if she'd never been in hyperspace before. Which, as it turned out, she hadn't.

"Thanks for taking me with you," she said, for the hundredth time. "I've only ever dreamed of such a sight."

"You're welcome," grunted Hrain. *Ezek is going to kill me.* He hadn't exactly asked permission, and Mel had been so excited at the chance to come along that she'd taken Hrain at his word when he told her it had been Ezek's idea.

"Now, about the computer," he said. "Have you made any progress?"

Mel moved her head in that peculiar diagonal manner the Mekmek used to say no.

"Not at all?" said Hrain.

"Well, the diagnostics take time," said Mel. "And I'm a mechanical engineer, not a computer programmer. I know the basics, but other than running the scans and letting the damaged sectors re-learn the ship's functions, there's not much I can do."

Hrain slumped. It was the same answer she'd given the last three times he had asked. "Well, keep at it."

On the whole, he had to admit he was glad the little technician had come along. The *Angel's Fury* was in much better shape for it, and it was nice to have someone to talk to. It kept him from thinking about Angel too much.

Nail, however, was another matter. Over the last decade, he'd done the best he could to put her out of his mind, convinced there was nothing he could do for her. He'd probably been right. Flying back to Sledgim would only have ended in his capture, or death.

But now things had changed. A feeling of impending dread had been growing within Hrain for some time—dread not for his own safety, but for what he might find when he arrived at Sledgim.

"I thought we were going to Mauria?" Mel was staring at the navigation panel. Hrain flinched. He'd forgotten to suppress the display—but no matter. The sequence of coordinates was critical, and knowing one or two of the waypoints wasn't enough to chart a course to the hidden world. *Besides, I'm never going to let her go back to Taluria. Unless Sledgim really is gone. Then, what's the point?*

"These coordinates, what are they?" said Mel. She was tapping something into the controls, cross-checking the course. "Where are we?"

Hrain's ears twitched. He could feel her confusion blossoming into suspicion. "Don't worry," he said. "We're just making a stop along the way. There's a hyperspace anomaly coming up. You won't be able to see it on the scanners, but it holds a splinched-off pocket of normal space within it. There's a star and a few planets there."

"I've never heard of such a thing," said Mel.

"It's one of a kind, as far as we know. Hold on, we're close now."

They were nearing the anomaly. Hrain joined Mel at the controls. The eddy they were currently following looped around the anomaly without intersecting it. If they popped out here, they would still be a few hundredths of a light-year away from Sledgim.

"Let's drop out here," he said. "Outside the system, in case there are any nasty surprises waiting at the doorstep." *Or inside.* The bubble around Sledgim trapped all signals within it, effectively masking the Maurian base, but acted like a lens, focusing outside signals into the system. It offered the perfect natural defense. *No doubt they know we're here by now.*

"Can I do it?" said Mel.

Hrian indicated the hyperdrive panel. "Sure. It's that button right there." He hardly needed to read her mind to sense her elation.

"I know which one!" The little primate jabbed at the controls, and the *Angel's Fury* dropped to normal space.

"Energy signature detected," said the computer in flat monotone. "Bearing one-three-seven mark four."

Hrain swore, his guts growing cold. They'd come out too close to the system, and whatever was out there would surely have seen him.

"Intercept course," he said. "Ready all weapons." *If it's a Maurian ship, we run. If it's Ta'Krell, we fight!*

"All systems ready," said the computer. "Prepare for acceleration."

Hrain let the autopilot do the flying as he manned the scanners. Mel looked on with childlike interest. It was the strangest debris field he had ever seen. It wasn't the individual pieces themselves: the junk seemed normal enough, although what it was from was impossible to tell. It was *how* all the crap was spread out that was so odd.

It wasn't the conical or spherical spreading pattern typical of debris from a destroyed vessel. Rather, it was a debris highway, stretching on for hundreds of thousands of marks. The velocity of the debris was also worth noting: all the bits of junk were traveling away from the Sledgim system.

Hrain took the controls as they approached the energy signature.

"Strap in, little one," he said to Mel.

Mel did so, a serious look of determination on her tiny face. "There," she said, pointing at the sensor plot. "It's just through this patch."

Angel's shields flared momentarily as they passed through a cloud of tiny particles and gas. And then, there it was.

"Maximum magnification," said Hrain.

It was a tiny ship, battle-scarred. Perhaps a one-seater.

"Computer, scan for life signs," said Hrain.

"Scanning," said the computer. "One signature confirmed."

Hrain bared his teeth. "Species?"

"The life sign matches no known organic configuration."

Hrain locked onto the little ship and prepared to blast it out of existence. If whoever was onboard was aware of Angel's approach, they made no moves to get out of the way or offer a defense. *Is it a trap?*

The ship didn't look like it was something the Ta'Krell would build. It was much too sleek. As they got closer, the marking on the hull became visible. They were alien alright. One of the wings had been shot off.

"Look," said Mel, pointing at the intact wing. "I think those seams are for adjustable flaps. This ship could be capable of atmospheric flight. See if you can match rotation, I want to see more!"

"That's what I'm doing," said Hrain. "Keep it together."

He fired thrusters, using the fine-tuning knob on the dash to dial in the rotation rate. "Let's have a look, shall we?"

This was the most dangerous part. He fired the ventral thrusters so that the *Angel's Fury* drifted slightly upward, then locked the rotation so the dorsal surfaces of both ships were facing each other. They were so close now that he lost the weapons lock on the tiny ship.

"Coming alongside nice and easy," he said, nudging the main throttle forward and then firing braking thrusters. He craned his neck up. They could see the ship's canopy now. It was transparent. There was an unoccupied seat towards the stern, and in the front…a Mekmek?

No, the creature was too large, and had some strange organ growing out of its head. *No, not an organ. Fur. Lots of golden fur, floating about in zero-gravity.*

The alien didn't move. Its eyes were closed. It had a small mouth with thin red lips, open ever so slightly.

The computer beeped. "Warning: The life sign in the target vessel is diminishing. Suspected cause is oxygen depletion. Spectrographic analysis indicates a build-up of carbon dioxide in the vessel."

"It breathes oxygen?" said Hrain.

Mel was working her controls. "I'd say that's a fair bet. I'm detecting tanks…depleted, but with residual oxygen in the lines."

This is no Ta'Krell.

Hrain closed his eyes and reached out with his mind. Slowly, gently, he found the other. The creature…a she by the color of her thoughts…was afraid and confused, and she lashed out when he brushed her consciousness. He withdrew quickly as the computer voiced another warning.

"Warning: Life sign dropping below detection threshold."

Hrain's hands flew over the controls. *If this is a trap, then we'll find out right about now.* He dropped the shields, then reformed them, extending them out and wrapping them around the target ship.

"Computer, pressurize the interior volume within our shields with ship's atmosphere."

"What are you doing?" said Mel.

Hrain unstrapped from his chair and headed back aft. "Grab your mag boots. We're going to save that girl."

About This Book

The idea for *Sagitta* came to me back in 2005. I was halfway through my second year at the University of Maine in Orono, in a dual degree program of mechanical engineering and literature. I had just finished chain watching Star Trek DS9 with my roommate. One day I went for a long mountain bike ride on the trails behind the school, daydreaming about science fiction.

I had burned through all the Star Trek I had (which is all of it), plus the Star Wars movies, and a whole bunch of paperback books. I'd recently finished reading Ender's Game, and thought it would be cool to have a young protagonist go on a sci-fi adventure in my own crafted universe.

I called my parents that night and told them I wanted to write a book. Of course they were supportive (how they endured my endless blabbing about being an author I have no idea). My brother and I plotted it out over AIM, and I started to write. The act of writing, by the way, is an excellent stress reliever from all those engineering classes. A year later, I had my first draft. My best friend Al still has a copy somewhere in a 3-ring binder.

That book is not this book. Some elements are the same, but at 130,000 words long, draft #1 (titled New Hope, sorry George!) was basically a brick of action without any plot or characterization. Of course I thought it was the greatest thing ever. I submitted it to various publishing houses, waiting anxiously for a response (and writing two unrelated, half-finished novels in the interim). Rejection, I should have known, was guaranteed. It came over a year later and crushed my soul.

I re-wrote the book in 2008 during a week at camp in Ellsworth, Maine, trimming the fat to 100,000 words. Then it went into a drawer while I wrote short stories. *Sagitta* (the name taken from my Raidmax gaming computer case) didn't come out again until 2011. That third edit lasted until 2013, mostly because I spent my free time playing Modern Warfare after work. I also was reading more non-fiction, especially books on writing and publishing. I laughably thought I was a good writer. Then I started dating the woman who would be my future wife. At the age of twenty-four, she had read more books than I ever will in my entire life.

Suffice it to say I learned a lot about how my writing stacked up. By working on short stories, I discovered how to actually plot something out. Joining the online writing website CritiqueCircle.com was an eye-opening experience. There, aspiring writers help each hone their skills. I won't get into the details of my short story failures (and occasional successes), but I recommend this path for all aspiring writers, at least in the beginning. Thanks to all the short story practice, I eventually became a traditionally published author of short fiction.

Sagitta came out again for a fourth edit in 2016 and a final polish / alpha read in 2018. Feedback was generally positive, except for all the typos and a somewhat uninteresting main character. Trimmed to about 85,000 words, the plot was simple, the characters passable, and the action plenty. That version went on to be the official beta read copy. Instead of doing it electronically, I opted to create a paperback on Amazon to be a bit easier on the eyes.

I considered that beta version complete, but it still had typos, inconsistencies, and a few things that just didn't make sense. There were also elements missing. Now that most of the mess had been cleaned up, these lacking bits were easier to see: for example, a proper emotional response by a character to a trying situation. The lead characters in particular still needed some work to make them more interesting. I ended up writing two additional chapters to challenge other aspects of Morgan and Mog, highlighting their weaknesses and helping them to evolve.

The "final" version is what you hold in your hands. I say "final" in quotes because nothing is ever perfected, merely good enough. The temptation to polish the stone is still there, especially in the world of digital publishing where it is so easy to tweak things.

For a first book I am content, and I'm going to do my best to let it stay the way it is and focus on the rest of the series. I'd love to know what you think of *Sagitta*. What worked? What didn't? What would you have liked to see more of? Please leave comments, reviews (good or bad) and suggestions on the Amazon review page or at goodreads.com. Also, I keep a blog about this book and my other writing projects at www.starfightersf.com.

I really appreciate your support.

-Chris

The following people were instrumental in helping me finish this book by reading and re-reading the last few drafts in various forms. Thanks...

Alpha Readers:
(for making Morgan more real and spotting all those typos)

Kirsten Benamati   Mike Litvinov
Nate Benamati   Stephen Sweet

Beta Readers:
(for finding what was lacking)

Curt Alpha   Karl Fortune
Joe Blochberger   Jeff Gateman
Marya Callaghan   Lee Schwartz
Mike Coraizaca   Mike Simms
Travis Fields   Keith Travis

Omega Readers
(for that last read)

Kirsten Benamati   Patrick Long
Allen Daley   Noelle Todd
Mike Long   Brian Staskowski

Want to read more from the StarFighter Universe but can't wait for book two? Then please keep an eye out for my novella *Hrain*, available in 2019 exclusively on Amazon.

Finally, don't forget to leave a review on Amazon (good, bad, or indifferent). Anything helps! Thanks.

Link to Amazon Product Page:
https://www.amzn.com/B07NWCW1LL

Made in the USA
Coppell, TX
13 August 2020

33054069R00177